39
FREE
MAGPIE
THE RAVEN'S
DAUGHTERS
JOYCE GEE
I0746188

Ebook ISBN: 9781763650626

Paperback ISBN: 9781763650633

Hardcover: 9781763650671

# CONTENTS

# A NOTE ON LANGUAGE

This is just to let you know that I'm from Australia.

The English I use is Australian English, which is not the same as American English. In Australia, we like S, not Z. The letter U appears in words where it does not in American. Smelt is the past tense for smell. There are certain words that we use on a regular basis which make Americans blush. I'm sorry. Not really. It's all English in the end.

So, I love you readers from America, but please remember that my spelling is not incorrect, it's simply a different version of English to what you use.

# TRIGGER WARNING

Please only read this if you have triggers, otherwise you may spoil yourself. This book is about fighting back after years of trauma and finding happiness again.

To start, I will tell you what isn't in the book. There is no on page rape, no cheating, no incest, no minors, no pregnancy, and no substance abuse.

However, there are depictions of violence and sex. Off page, the FMC was tortured, raped, forced to witness the torture of others, and others were forced to witness her torture. It is implied the FMC abused alcohol as a coping mechanism. Also off page, it is implied the MMC was abused, including by his mother and sisters. There are instances of cross-species flesh consumption. The FMC physically and magically tortures her enemies. There is a battle. The third MC does things to the FMC and MMC without consent.

Please always put your mental health first.

EIVOR HAVARD

THORNE

THORNE

RHYDWEN

This one is for all those who took the hits while waiting for their chance.

Whatever that chance was.

You are strong. You are brave. You deserve the freedom to burn bright.

If they tell you you're the villain, wear it with pride.

We are all the villains in someone's story.

So sing your song while it all burns down.

*And Kyle, if you're reading this, I'm begging you not to. Please.
You're still my brother-in-law.*

JOYCE GEE

# PROLOGUE

Nose crinkling, Eivor tugged at her left cuff when it caught on the heavy bracelet adorning her wrist. "Aunty Oblivion, is this necessary? Father is expecting me for lessons."

"Stop fussing." Smacking the back of her head, Oblivion huffed. "And what did I tell you about calling me Aunty Oblivion? It's Aunty Liv."

*"Are you being annoying on purpose, young magpie?"*

Slanting a look at the raven hilt of the sword hanging from her aunt's hip, she resisted the urge to roll her eyes at its dark whisper in her mind. "Well, would you at least tell me why you insisted on dragging me all the way here? We're almost at the Talaroonan border, and you know what my parents think of King Oisin."

*"Don't you want to test your powers against his?"*

"That's enough from you, sword. Aunty Liv, can't you silence it?"

Oblivion patted the hilt, a half-smirk twisting her lips. "Or you could work on keeping it from your mind. Are you a mind mage or not, Eivor?"

She crossed her arms, refusing to look at the older woman. The surrounding forest had an unseasonable chill, a faint hint of frost coating a fern nearby. It sent a trickle of fear down her spine, and Eivor straightened, squaring her shoulders. Her parents had taught her to never betray her true emotions, to always be in complete control of herself and the situation. Their concerns were understandable when she knew the devastation her unrestrained power could wreck on the people around her. While she had not inherited the power of a husk maker from her mother, Eivor could not complain about what she had developed—especially the side she trained in secret.

*"He's here."* There was too much joy in the sword's voice. *"And he brought them."*

Hoofbeats echoed through the forest, heralding a further drop in the temperature. Ice crackled over the ground, forming a layer over her bare feet. Arching a brow, Eivor did not lift them to shake it off even though she knew it would set off the condition she suffered when she was cold. The approaching horse drew her attention, tendrils of terror scratching at the wall around her mind. Grasping her power, Eivor reinforced her shields, determined not to let the new arrival break through her defences.

"There you are, Thorne," Oblivion drawled, eyeing the woman seated on the back of the massive black horse. "Have you met Malena's daughter, Eivor?"

Eyes of ice settled on her, so Eivor lifted her chin challengingly. "I'm Princess Eivor Havard of Diwan. It's wonderful to meet one of the dullaghan."

"We have met before, pretty magpie," Thorne replied, dipping her head.

"And she won't remember meeting you this time. Nor will you." An icy voice wrapped around them, bringing with it a sense of impending danger.

Oblivion huffed at the man stepping free of the shadows. "Must you be so dramatic?"

"Must you be so disrespectful to your god? You live because I let you."

"No, I live because you know I'd stab you with your own fucking sword, Gebael. Now, you better do what you need to do before Craven notices his daughter missing this close to the border. Especially when he has Alistair fetching sacrifices from the humans."

Thorne's horse snorted, pawing at the ground with an impatience to match Oblivion's tone. Lips thinning, Eivor could not bring herself to look at the god standing a short distance away. He had walked among the first daoine to be created, choosing the nameless woman who would become his Executioner. After binding her to the sword Oblivion and bestowing the blade's name on her, Death had made his way through the rest to select those who would become his Ravens. Her mother included.

Most of them were gone, lost to the servants of the god of thought, or killed by the god herself during the Sundering. It was because of him that her mother was covered in scars and often woke up screaming in the middle of the night. As far as Eivor was concerned, the gods were the bane of all mortals.

"Eivor!" Oblivion elbowed her sharply, slanting a scolding look at the younger duine. "Mind your manners. I know your mother taught you better."

Lifting her chin to stare at the god, she let the faintest sneer twist her features. "Yes, she did. I am 1000 years old, and I have heeded the lessons those around me have taught. Including a healthy disrespect for the gods."

Grinning with pride, Gebael nodded at her. "Good, I'm glad it's working. Tir needs a powerful queen willing to snub the gods without fear. You will be magnificent one day."

"I am already magnificent," she replied, cocking her head to glance at Thorne while raising her hand. "Why are we here? I'm sure each of us has something better to do."

Tendrils of her power twisted around her fingers, desperate to find something to latch onto. It felt unusually alive in the presence of Death and one of his headless riders. A part of her whispered that whatever gave her the ability to force her will on corpses came from the god and that was why she could command the bodies of the dead.

Closing the small distance between them, Gebael reached out to grasp her hand, and Eivor could not stop the cold seeping through her magic. There was no preventing the pleasured gasp that escaped her lips when his power threaded through her own, sending shivers down her spine.

"Every time," he muttered, casting a hand in Thorne's direction.

She saw the shimmer of power surrounding the dullaghan. When Eivor tried to peer through it, it was as though the world on the other side existed in shades of grey. Thorne did nothing, simply sitting on the back of her horse to watch Death weave threads of ice into the gleaming net of magic stretched over the duine woman.

"Can you see what Annawyn has done?" Oblivion crossed her arms, a brow raised as she studied the princess. "I know she has been meddling."

"It suits her for me to give Eivor the gifts I have. We might avoid each other these days, but between us, we've created a mind mage who can raise the dead.

If our wife knew… it's always better if Shianeni doesn't find out what the rest of us are up to."

Biting her lip, Eivor met the blue eyes of the god that mirrored her own. "What have you done to me? Why are you and Annawyn doing this and then taking my memories of it?"

"She does it because she wanted to find out how much stronger she could make a mind mage who was born and grew into their powers. I do it because one day, you will stop a terrible person from spreading war across Tir. You will change the course of nations by picking up the broken pieces of those hurt by the inevitable war between the gods. By binding you to the Veil, I have made you capable of commanding the deadliest people on Tir. All you need to do is grow into your power and find your rage."

"You bound me to the Veil?"

Gebael grunted, eyeing his work with the critical eye of an artist. "Yes, when you were born. Every time we have one of our meetings, I give you a little more power. I suspect Annawyn does the same. You were born powerful, Eivor, but we have made you exceptional, and it's important to make the increases to your magic look natural."

"People would notice if you were suddenly more powerful than you were the day before. Your father knows how important it is to keep your gifts a secret. And to protect you, we take your memories of what Gebael and Annawyn have done. We don't want you to become a tool for the wrong people to use if they found out the truth." Oblivion moved away from them, approaching the massive horse to rub a hand over its neck.

"Any other person would lose their hand, Executioner," Thorne said, never taking her eyes off Eivor. "Though perhaps the pretty magpie will be an exception."

Swallowing, Eivor imagined running her fingers across the glossy black coat of the horse. It was bigger than any she had ridden over the years, and easily put draft horses to shame. She did not know what rank Thorne held among the dullaghan, but if the rider was there at Death's bidding, she suspected it was likely to be Hunt Leader. There was an air of command around the mesmerising woman that made Eivor want to challenge her.

"Keep looking at Thorne like that, Princess, and you'll find yourself in trouble," Gebael murmured, amusement creeping into his voice.

Her gaze slid back to the god. "You say that like I'd enjoy it."

Lips quirking, he shrugged. "I'm the wrong god to ask. That's more Neriwyn's area of prediction. All I can say is that you and Thorne will not be the death of each other."

Squaring her shoulders, Thorne gripped the reins of her mount as dismay appeared on her face. "I should think not, my lord. I am the Master of the Hunt, not some mere rider to fall for the fluttering lashes of a beautiful duine princess. Certainly not Malena's daughter."

"Careful, my friend, lest you speak your downfall into existence. You're lucky there is no god of fate to tempt. Though Alyah is not so far off being such a god."

Rolling her eyes at them, Oblivion strode back to stand beside Eivor. "Is it done?"

The hand cradling hers tightened its grip before releasing her. Eyeing the mottled white of her frozen fingers, Eivor clenched her jaw briefly and forced her hand into a fist to encourage blood flow. At the back of her mind, a voice pondered if Death was the reason she hated the cold, and if it was his fault she suffered because of it. Those thoughts were brushed aside by the reminder that, if anything, what he did to her would lessen the effects. She chose to imagine that her suffering would be worse without his meddling.

"Yes, that part is done. I'm terribly sorry about this, Eivor, but at least you won't remember. Trust me when I tell you it's better that you don't."

Gebael's hand settled on her cheek, but before Eivor could protest, darkness drew her down into its welcoming depths.

# ONE

Below Eivor's window, the courtyard bustled with life. People hurried along, ignorant of the resentment she felt for their freedom. Obnoxiously coloured dresses fluttered in the breeze as wealthy women made the trek across the cobblestone to the palace entrance. The blandly dressed men paled in comparison, a blend of dark colours adorning them. It was a far cry from the whimsical elegance that had been the norm when her parents had ruled Diwan. She was a far cry from the monarch her parents had been, which further compounded her resentment.

"Your Majesty."

Withdrawing from the barred window, Eivor bit back a snarl when her cuffs clinked against the iron. Eyes dropping to the wide bands encasing her wrists, the deep-seated rage simmering in her heart rose. It longed to tear them off and shove them down the throat of the man who put them there. He held her strings, forcing her to dance like a puppet. One day, she would break free, and he would know how it felt to be blocked from using his magic and controlled. If she decided to let him live long enough.

"What?" Shifting her focus to the maid hovering in the doorway to her bedroom, she saw what was being held up. "No."

Inclining her head to the pink gown, the maid sighed. "Lord Cathair said you must wear this, or he will rescind your access to the library."

Bristling at the threat, Eivor sneered and stalked across the chamber to meet the unconcerned gaze of the woman serving her for the week. "Did he now? What other orders did he tell you to deliver?"

"To be ready for him to escort you to the ball."

"Fine."

Brushing past, Eivor considered defying Cathair's commands. He made a point of demanding she wear ridiculous outfits intended to remind her of who was in control. They lacked elegance; the gaudy colours and designs the least of the humiliations she had endured over her hundred years of captivity. She missed the days when she had been a beacon of fashion alongside her younger sisters. But thinking of her sisters guaranteed a downward spiral in her mood, so she carefully pushed the thought aside.

While the maid set the gown on the bed, Eivor set to work on the laces securing the dark plum dress she had donned that morning. The material slipped from her shoulders, pooling around her feet like a puddle of shimmering silk. Stepping free, wearing only her shift and stays, she left it there for the maid to pick up. Whatever torment Cathair had planned for the ball, Eivor would meet it with grace. It might be an empty title, but she was the queen of Diwan, and the Talaroonan lord would not break her.

A fresh bowl of scented water sat on her washstand. It was tempting to demand a bath, but Eivor did not want to give him a reason to burst in on her naked. Those games had gotten less frequent, which was a slight relief after she realised her mere 3000 years was nothing compared to a man the gods had created, and who had served the worst of them. Eivor vaguely remembered Annawyn, the god who almost destroyed her mother and left her a scarred, traumatised shadow of herself.

"Since I'm wearing that hideous arrangement of fabric masquerading as a ball gown, fetch me the pink diamond set," she said, wiping her skin clean. "At least I'll have something attractive adorning me tonight."

"As you wish."

Studying her reflection, Eivor considered what to do with her hair. "And the Fielyn tiara."

Dropping the cloth onto the stand next to the bowl, she picked up the bottle of black raspberry and acai oil from her dresser. It was a new blend, and one she liked enough to request another bottle when she finished with the first. Uncorking it, Eivor tipped a small amount onto her finger and dabbed it on all the crucial spots. Inhaling deeply, she let the rich scent fill her senses, drawing on the positive response it triggered. Her lack of magic did not change her ability to regulate her emotional state. All the years of training and control remained.

"If you're ready, Majesty." Summoning her attention, the maid placed the jewellery on the dresser before returning to the bed. "You don't want to make Lord Cathair wait."

"Powers no. The bastard is insufferable enough as it is."

Eivor waited patiently for the other woman to bring the dress to her in the middle of the room. It was layers of silk and lace that reminded her of the bright pink variation of pig face growing in the rock garden. Sweeping her gaze down its length, she curled her lip in disgust.

"Every time I look at it, it gets worse."

Pressing her lips together, the maid could not help but agree. "It is rather unsightly. You have dozens of better choices, but Lord Cathair requested this one. You'll have to make the best of it."

"I haven't exactly got another choice unless I want to be reminded of how good he is with a knife. The scars from my last lesson are still healing."

Helping Eivor into the gown, the maid did not comment. Like everyone else in the palace, she knew Cathair did not hesitate to punish the queen if she disobeyed him. Many had witnessed his willingness to rend her flesh from her body. He delivered the punishments in public for the added humiliation. They also served as a warning. If the queen was not safe, no one was. King Oisin of Talaroo set the terms for their continued existence. Compliance was better than a slow death in the mines or being sold as slaves.

Tightening the laces, she murmured, "Tell me if it's too much. I know he cut along your ribs. There's no need to cause you pain as well as humiliation."

"Thank you."

She decided not to wait for Eivor to say something, judging it was tight enough. Waving at the chair in front of the dresser, the maid hurried over to prepare what she needed to finish her task. Hiking her skirts up, Eivor studied the black slippers encasing her feet, debating if they would be sturdy enough for the ball. While she had no intention of staying longer than she was required to, it was always better to be prepared.

"I'll need different shoes."

"Start your hair while I fetch a pair."

Chuckling at the gentle command, Eivor carefully settled on the chair. Her fingers closed around the silver handle of the hairbrush, making her flinch at the dull pain in her knuckles. A residual ache remained from Cathair's decision to dislocate them a few days earlier. The healers had confirmed no lasting damage but left them to heal naturally.

Pushing past the discomfort, she dragged the brush through the black and white hair that matched the colours of her feathers when she was in her animal form. Some days, Eivor wanted to cut the waist-length tresses off and have a maid shave her bald to avoid the reminder of the magpie form she had been denied since Oisin invaded.

Partitioning the strands, she set to braiding them by clusters of colour. A white braid followed a black one, each intended to twist up and around the silver prongs of the tiara sitting on the counter in front of her. It was Eivor's favourite; the design resembling the branches of a tree stripped bare. She often imagined ordering one of the misshapen grevilleas in the gardens to be rendered naked so she could string Cathair from the limbs. Wearing the tiara in his presence was her way of focusing her emotions on what she dreamed of most often.

While Eivor braided her hair, the maid exchanged the slippers for a pair of low-heeled shoes. Pleased they were black, she nodded at the kneeling woman to express her gratitude. She never bothered to learn their names. Cathair did not let anyone remain in her service for more than a week to prevent her from developing friendships. He wanted her kept isolated from people, her power, and everything that made her comfortable. There was a reason Oisin left him in charge of her and Diwan. Only a mind mage knew how to keep another mind mage under control.

Picking up the tiara, the maid positioned it on her head. Eivor kept braiding, leaving those completed to the other woman to work through the twines. She watched in the mirror as they worked together to position her hair. Braided ropes of white and black hung from the tiara, securing the silver and gems in place.

Pins dug into her scalp, a reminder of what it took to maintain the appearance expected of her. Hurrying, they completed the task before the first knock sounded at the door. Quickly securing the jewels around her neck while Eivor changed her earrings, the maid did her best not to look flustered.

"Done. Let's go before Cathair feels a need to knock a second time. It never ends well if I push him to repeat himself," Eivor said, rising to make her way from the chamber.

Darting ahead, the maid opened the door and bowed. She knew better than to speak to Lord Cathair. His mouth curled in annoyed disappointment, dark gaze sweeping over Eivor.

"I see you did as told."

She hesitated before dipping into a curtsy, holding the fluffy skirts wide. "Of course, Master. I wouldn't want to disappoint you, and this is such a lovely gown you've chosen."

"I'm in no mood for your games, Pet." Grabbing her arm, Cathair dragged her close. "Whatever foolish plan you're devising, forget it. Tonight, you are to be on your best behaviour. You will praise his imperial majesty for all the wonderful things he has done for your kingdom. After all, he freed Diwan from the tyrannical rule of your parents."

"As you command." Lowering her gaze, Eivor refused to let him see her rage.

"You will sing for my guests."

Clenching her jaw, she nodded. Singing had once been a source of joy, the one thing she had in common with her sisters. Silaine would play her lute, the three of them joined in harmony to delight the court. Her voice was not as beautiful as her youngest sister's, but Eivor had held her own. Wherever Astoria was, she hoped no one was forcing her to perform. From what she knew of Silaine, no one would dare make her do anything. The gods favoured her while leaving Eivor to suffer her imprisonment alone.

"Yes, Master."

Maintaining his tight grip, Cathair led her out of the room. Guards kept a respectful distance, unwilling to get too close. The majority were Talaroonans, their loyalty to Oisin and the man he left in command of Diwan. Like the servants, those assigned to Eivor changed weekly. Every year, they cycled back to their homeland to prevent anyone from developing an attachment to the Diwanians.

"If you perform perfectly tonight, I'll reinstate access to the rooftop."

The flare of her nose was the only sign his offer affected Eivor. She loved and hated the rooftop in equal measure. It was where she would shift forms to take off and fly with her mother and sister. Even though the ability to transform remained blocked while the cuffs restrained her power, Eivor found peace in lying on top of the tower and dreaming of her old life.

"You say jump, I ask how high."

"If only I believed you." Slanting a look at her, Cathair snorted. "You're predictable, Pet."

She needed access to the roof. If it meant obeying every directive he gave her, she would. It had been months since Eivor had been outside, and she wanted to feel the open air. Being locked inside for too long turned her irritable. The sort of irritability that drove her to make poor judgement calls when dealing with Cathair.

"I promise to behave. You tell me to sing, I'll sing. I'll dance with whoever you direct me to. If you want me to fuck someone..."

"Should that be required, you will."

Before they reached the grand ballroom, Eivor touched a hand to her hair to ensure the tiara remained in place. The rumble of voices reached her ears, and she closed her eyes to focus on the sound. He minimised her exposure to crowds, something she was occasionally thankful for without her power. An aspect that fed her enjoyment of being surrounded by people was missing, the emptiness becoming a weight to drag her down. It was the connection between her magic and those it touched. Without it, she was little better than a human.

The guards attending the door bowed while pages opened it for them. It was the entrance reserved for her family, leading onto a balcony with seats to watch from. A wide staircase curved down onto the main floor, providing access for when they wanted it. Eivor missed leading her sisters down to dance while their parents watched on from above, their presence drawing the court's attention. In those days, people had viewed her with admiration, not pity.

"Sit," Cathair said, shoving her towards the waiting seats. "I will summon you when you're needed to work the crowd. Until then, you stay here."

Resting a hand on the gilded rail, Eivor let the gathering view her before settling onto the central chair. Her presence silenced the court, eyes turning upwards to take in the sight of her garish pink gown and the man descending the stairs like a predator among a herd of prey. Watching him go, Eivor reminded herself to note who he spoke to. There was always a method to his interactions. She knew anyone Cathair conversed with for longer than polite greetings was someone she needed to pay attention to.

"Your Majesty, would you like some wine?"

Waving at the page without taking her eyes from her target, Eivor replied, "Make sure it's an unopened bottle of elderberry wine. I want to see you taste it first."

The scuff of shoes confirmed his departure, leaving Eivor alone with four guards lining the wall at the back of the balcony. If she tried to leave without Cathair permitting it, they would restrain her. Settling back on the padded chair, Eivor watched the dancers and wished she had a book to read. Or a bow to play target practice with the outrageous ornaments decorating people's heads.

"Oh, good grief, that woman looks like an over-decorated cake," she muttered. "At least I'm not the only one in a ridiculous shade of pink."

Noticing Cathair deep in conversation with a man she did not recognise, Eivor leaned forward to study him. Black hair rivalling hers was drawn back on the sides, revealing rounded ears. He lacked the moonlight sheen of magic that illuminated the skin of all daoine, but there was something decidedly not human about him. A black coat hung slightly above his knees, not hiding the tall leather boots and black trousers. It brought a curl of delight to Eivor's lips that bordered on being a smile. She appreciated his choice to wear all black, but she hoped he had a splash of colour somewhere.

As though he sensed her staring, the man tilted his head and lifted his gaze in her direction. It was too far away to see the colour of his eyes, but it intrigued Eivor to see how quick Cathair was to lead him away, waving vaguely at the balcony where she sat. Whatever business he had with the stranger, she would find out if it involved her. Too often, she had played the role of a courtesan at Cathair's command.

Eivor maintained her position and swept her gaze across the dancers, grinding her teeth. The swirl of skirts and coats was a momentary distraction, broken when the page returned with a sealed bottle and a glass. While she observed, he cracked the wax and uncorked the wine, pouring it into the glass. Placing the open bottle on the table near her, he sipped the drink and waited for Eivor to signal her approval. She felt silly for being paranoid, but with Silaine and Astoria elsewhere, her death would place Diwan completely in Oisin's control.

"Give it to me." Extending her hand, Eivor waited for him to place the glass in her grasp. "I'll expect you to sample the food brought before me."

Nodding, he backed away, staying in view. It was common knowledge among the servants that the queen refused to eat or drink anything without watching someone else do so first. Only once in the hundred years since Talaroo invaded had anyone attempted to poison Eivor. Cathair had conveniently blamed rebels. After the executions, they had strung hundreds from the city walls; their bodies left to rot as a warning to anyone who entertained thoughts of freeing Diwan.

A sniff of the wine confirmed it was elderberry. Eivor's observations of the crowd noted Cathair had left the stranger to flit his way through the Diwanian nobles. Sipping her drink, she mulled over the rich flavour flooding her mouth. She liked to change her selection every time, preventing anyone from knowing what she wanted to drink ahead of time. If Oisin wanted her dead, he could do it himself or order Cathair to do it. When her death came, Eivor wanted to look her killer in the eye.

"Your Majesty," a guard said. "Lord Cathair is signalling for you."

Draining her glass, Eivor held it out to the page. "I'll take another glass before performing my part for my puppet master."

Nervously refilling the glass, the page watched the guards. The second glass was emptied quickly, Eivor barely bothering to taste it. She was less interested in the flavour than the effects. Wine made her life slightly more bearable. Many days of her captivity had passed by in a haze of intoxication. Before they blocked her magic, Eivor would never have spent her time drunk. Tapping a nail against the stem of the glass, she considered downing a third rather than wasting the bottle.

"One more."

"Your Majesty, Lord Cathair is waiting for you."

Lips thinning, Eivor stared at the page, extending the glass to him again. "One more."

She noticed his hands shaking as he poured the wine. Once he was done, Eivor rose steadily, keeping the glass close as she ambled to the top of the stairs. Sipping the drink, she carefully made her way down, focusing on Cathair. He stared at her, eyes narrowing at how her lips curled in the barest of smiles when the glass touched them.

"My apologies, Lord Cathair. I didn't want to waste any of this delightful wine," she said, tipping the glass back to drain it. "You should try it."

As she held out her hand with the stem of the glass gripped loosely in her fingers for a page to take, Eivor noticed the strange man watching from the shadows. He leaned against the wall, smirking when their gazes met. Mouth twisting, she shifted towards Cathair and offered him her empty hand. The stranger could wait until she had played whatever part her keeper demanded. She would converse and dance with anyone he directed her to. An urge to glance back at the man in black tugged Eivor's mind, but she dared not make an obvious move.

The opportunity to check if he had moved came when they stopped to speak to an emissary from Samphire. It was easy to look in his direction over the blustering diplomat's shoulder. He had moved, slipping among the chattering courtiers like the mist on a wintry morning. Something in his stare dragged icy claws down her spine, leaving Eivor convinced her heart would stop if he whispered her name.

Her mother's voice murmured in her ear from the depths of memory. She knew what the stranger was, and if Oisin was recruiting them into his armies, it was not good news for anyone who stood in his way.

# TWO

"Thank you for gracing me with a dance, Your Majesty."

Smiling serenely, Eivor hoped the obnoxious man bowing over her hand could not see what she was picturing in her mind. Behind her smile, her teeth clenched at the feel of his spittle on her skin. The press of his lips made her stomach churn in disgust, but she had millennia of experience hiding such reactions.

"It was a pleasure, Lord Jeffery. I hope we can reach an agreement over continued free movement through Samphire," she replied. "It would be ever so unfortunate if our gracious emperor, King Oisin, felt a need to bring your leaders to the yoke."

Registering the threat, Jeffery did not smile. "We have not stood in his way for a hundred years, and that will not change. However, as I mentioned to Lord Cathair, Nirimba has been doing increasing business with the danann nation in the McAlister Range."

Eivor's eyes darkened, and the fury in them drove the diplomat to release her hand. "Well then, I shall encourage Lord Cathair to recommend we do something about it. The danann are dreadful people. They're reprobates with wings who use blood magic to control people."

"Is it true what they say about your sister?" he whispered, glancing about to ensure no one was listening too closely. "That their magic has enslaved her?"

"Much like our mother was before our father freed her."

Tutting, Jeffery shook his head, looking uncomfortable. The lie was sour on her tongue, but Eivor preferred to help perpetuate the story Oisin had spun to cover the truth. Better for people to believe General Redmond of the Rainbow Vale stole Silaine and slaughtered the company escorting her to Talaroo. Eivor wished it was the truth; at least then, she would not have to live with the fact her sisters had abandoned her to suffer.

"Such dreadful business. Forgive me for not knowing what it was like when they were unkillable. I imagine it was terrible fearing death at the hands of people you couldn't strike down. To be utterly defenceless against their attacks. It's a pity your sister did not die along with King Oisin's soldiers when they attacked. A better fate than being enslaved by the danann."

"Indeed." Meeting Jeffery's gaze, Eivor inclined her head. "I am forever thankful for King Oisin's protection. If my parents were still alive, they would have given Diwan to King Tigernach. They would force us to worship the gods."

Catching the flicker of guilt in his expression, she bit back a smile. It was the confirmation Cathair was hoping they would find. Worship of the gods was gaining momentum among the upper classes of Samphire. The gods were despicable, and the prevention of a religious movement was one thing she wholeheartedly agreed with Oisin about. She remembered the old gods, and Eivor did not view the new ones any differently.

"Forgive me, Lord Jeffery, but I must leave you."

He quickly caught her hand to kiss it. "It was a pleasure to dance with you, Queen Eivor. I hope it's not too presumptuous to beg another if the opportunity arises?"

"We shall see. Enjoy your evening."

Settling her gaze on Cathair, Eivor ignored attempts to gain her attention as she sauntered through the crowd. He saw her coming, a wry smile turning one corner of his mouth. Eyes darting, she checked who was standing nearby before slipping her hand through his arm. Leaning on him, she arched a brow in disapproval when a page offered her a full glass of wine. Cringing, the man bowed and backed away.

"You were right," she murmured.

Grunting, he led her away from the crowd to an alcove shrouded by heavy drapes. Yanking them back to reveal two women kissing, the expression on Cathair's face sent them scrambling. Eivor sneered, noting the judgemental looks they gave her. She knew what they thought would happen. Dropping onto the lounge, she draped an arm over the back and watched her keeper pace.

"Are you sure?"

"You might have cut me off from my magic, but you know as well as I do that there is a lot we can learn from body language. I mentioned worship of the gods and he displayed guilt. Add in the fact those fucking feather dusters are gaining influence in Nirimba and the reports you've had from your spies in Sam—"

"My spies?" Cathair slanted a look at her, brows raised. "What do you know of my spies?"

Covering her mouth to fake a yawn, she rolled her eyes. "Come now, Master, you know me better than that. I know nothing of your spies other than they exist. I had my own spies once. Before you invaded my home, killed my parents, and stripped me of everything that mattered to me."

"If you don't watch your words, Pet, you won't see a stone of the rooftop for a year."

"Don't ask me these questions if you don't want me to tell you the truth."

Growling, Cathair stalked over to the lounge, grabbing her chin. "Do not test me tonight. I am not in the mood for your rebellious streak."

Lowering her lashes, Eivor dragged her lip through her teeth. "You know, I'd be far more agreeable and cooperative with you if you gave me back my magic. Wouldn't it be better if I wanted to obey you instead of being coerced?"

"Like I've said every time you've asked, no. You're a devious bitch, just like Malena was. Count yourself lucky you weren't born a husk maker like your sister."

"Ah yes, that old threat. Lucky I'm not so valuable you feel a need to attempt to beget more husk makers."

Digging his fingers into her jaw, he said, "I wonder if you might prove adequate in that regard. Malena was one of the original Ravens. Perhaps we wouldn't be entirely disappointed by you."

"Are you hoping the reestablishment of the Ravens under the leadership of my flighty sister will have ignited something in my blood that would guarantee I produce husk makers?" Meeting his gaze, Eivor felt fingers of dread grasp her spine.

"It's awfully tempting to find out."

"Perhaps you should be more concerned about Samphire than the non-existent fruit of my womb. I don't want those fucking cults gaining threshold in my kingdom."

Smiling slowly, Cathair stroked her throat before righting himself. "I might have a solution that won't require us to sacrifice countless soldiers."

Recalling the stranger in black, she wondered if he was the solution Cathair spoke of. "A clean, bloodless method to be rid of those dreadful fanatics? Do tell me more."

"No. Consider it punishment for your thoughtless comments."

Sighing heavily, Eivor rubbed her face, regretting what she needed to say. "As you wish. Have I played my role adequately enough tonight? You wanted me to pander to that disgusting human, so I did. I got the confirmation you desired. However, if you intend for him to stay awhile, I might be able to coax further information from him. He's rather eager for my attention."

"I'm not surprised, Pet. You are a beautiful duine queen, and he is a mere human. Any attention from you is more than he should hope for in his measly lifetime." There was a slyness in the way he glanced at the closed drapes. "Perhaps we will use that."

"Have the clerics made trouble in other regions? Surely, they would not dare risk their lives to spread the word of the gods in daoine lands... or at least, their version of it."

"They would and they have. Oisin treats them as they deserve."

"With copious amounts of pain resulting in death?"

"Of course. You know how much his majesty enjoys inflicting pain."

Swallowing, Eivor fought back the memories of Oisin torturing her. Remembering the slice of his blade through her flesh was the last thing she wanted to do during a ball. Those memories had the power to turn her into a huddled mess. Avoiding Cathair's knowing smirk, she took several deep breaths and focused on the lilting music. It was a familiar song about a wily fox and the staunch hound who chased her across Tir.

"Do you want me to seek Lord Jeffery again tonight? He requested another dance if the opportunity arose," she said, hoping he would let her leave.

"Yes, that's a good idea. See what else you can learn from him."

Hopes dashed, Eivor slid gracefully from the lounge and smiled sweetly. "As my master commands, so it shall be."

He watched her glide from the alcove, the bright pink gown fluttering around her like petals caught in a breeze. The careful extraction of information from a political opponent when the gods were involved was one task Cathair trusted her to do without concern. Eivor hated their creators, and he did not blame her. It was a sentiment he shared.

Without the heavy drapes separating her from the party, Eivor was confronted with a longing for her power. She missed the rush of energy she would have gotten from feeding on the crowd's emotions. Her fingers itched to dance across bare skin, tugging at stray feelings and drinking them in. Fists clenched, Eivor felt the cold metal encasing her wrists, and the throb of the wards worked into them. Those wards prevented her from reaching into the well of her magic to push the people into a frenzy of indulgence.

Searching the dancers swirling across the floor and the clusters of people lingering on the outskirts of the ballroom, Eivor frowned when she could not see the diplomat. Stalking along the outside, she kept to the shadows and tried to avoid conversing with anyone. It was impossible to prevent the odd discussion. Various courtiers and nobles used the walls to make up for their drunken states.

Wine and food flowed freely; servants adorned in the royal livery carefully weaving through the crowd with trays. One swirled past her with a tray of meat skewers, the neatly cut squares of lamb leaving a delicious scent wafting behind them. She had barely eaten all day, and her stomach was protesting.

Watching a woman select a skewer to rip a chunk off with her teeth, Eivor wondered if it was safe to do the same. Plucking food from the trays intended for general consumption seemed a moderately less hazardous choice than the ones paraded in past her nose for her alone. Unless someone wanted to kill dozens of random people, it was unlikely the food would be poisoned. Or their wine.

She wished rage and anguish did not weigh her heart down. The swirling colours accompanying the fervent movements of the dancers beckoned to her.

Eivor longed for who she had been before Oisin set his sights on her home. That woman had been a lively princess who would have embraced the dance, twirling unstopped until dawn came, and she collapsed with exhaustion. But she was long gone, nothing more than a memory of hopes and dreams banished behind a wall of ice barricading the fires of her fury.

"Tell me, pretty magpie, is your beak as sharp as your gaze?"

The deep rumble of his voice sent shivers down her spine before Eivor registered the cool whisper of his power across her skin. Glancing sideways, she took in the strange man in black, finally answering her curiosity over his eye colour. Mesmerising blue eyes regarded her from beneath a mess of black hair. At some point since she had spotted him last, his hair had unravelled, tumbling over his shoulders like a curtain of glossy silk.

"Sharper. My claws are equally so. I don't recommend testing them; you may not appreciate the results. Though your audacity in addressing me so informally when we haven't been introduced..." Clicking her tongue, Eivor risked it and snatched a glass of wine from a passing page. "I suppose I can excuse one such as you."

Copying her, he retrieved a glass from the same tray and lifted it to his nose. "Blueberry wine, how delightful. If there is one thing you can count on to never change, it's the hedonistic nature of the daoine. You never stop indulging yourselves."

"Do you have a name?"

"I suppose I should give you mine, since I know yours."

Eyes hooded, Eivor stared into the dark liquid sloshing around in the glass. "That would be polite. I'd hate to have you arrested and executed. You're too pretty to behead."

Chuckling, he sipped his drink. "Don't worry, Majesty, the wine won't kill you."

"You sound confident of that fact."

"I might be too pretty to behead, but you're too beautiful to see foaming at the mouth and dead from poison. You know what I am, and I assure you, I sense no threat in the wine."

Eivor's anxiety over drinking the wine faded slightly at his words. "Are you here to kill me? Or are you Cathair's solution to the cults in Samphire?"

"Come now, pretty magpie, your mother taught you better than that."

"Should I expect the echo of hoofbeats outside my door in the wee hours of the morning before a headless figure in black comes to claim my heartbeat?"

His lips twitched, and he stepped closer to murmur, "Perhaps it won't be your heartbeat they come to claim. There are other bounties worth hunting."

Smiling coyly, she sipped the wine, watching as his gaze dropped to her lips. "If I am to be hunted by the greatest predator on Tir, at least pay me the respect of a name to scream."

"If screaming it is what your heart desires, you may call me Thorne."

"A prickly name for a fearsome creature."

"You make insults sound seductive, pretty magpie." Thorne chuckled.

Lifting her chin, she gave him an arched look. "I shall have to try harder."

"Oh, please do."

Captivated by the ice of his eyes, Eivor tightened her grasp on the stem of her glass. They possessed an odd glow, almost unnerving in their intensity. Realising she was staring, she glanced away, feeling her cheeks burn when he chuckled again. Taking another step closer, Thorne leaned in.

"Such a delightful queen of stone you are, Majesty. But no wall is impenetrable."

"Considering you're a dulla—"

Pressing a finger to her lips, Thorne tutted. "Hush. I doubt anyone here recognises me for what I am. Most seem to think I'm a half-blood duine. A blessing, perhaps."

"I'm afraid you'll not find me sympathetic to blessings."

"Does that mean I won't find you secretly leaving offerings to Death, hoping he will strike down your enemies and free you from your chains?" Tracing her lips, he delighted in the flutter of her eyelashes.

When his finger reached the corner of her mouth, Eivor feigned an attempt to bite it. "I don't need a worthless god interfering in my life or my kingdom. Should you be here on orders from such a being, then I'll not so kindly request you get the fuck out of Diwan before I have you beheaded."

"And what would you do if given the means to do exactly what you dream of?"

"I'm not so foolish as to whisper my secrets to someone I just met and who might be working with Lord Cathair."

Dropping his hand from her face, Thorne sought her wrist. "Come with me, pretty magpie. There are secrets I'd like to whisper in your ear away from prying eyes."

Eivor studied him, hesitant to allow him to draw her away. She feared Thorne was a test set by Cathair to discover if she was willing to conspire against him. Adjusting her stance, she gazed at her court and wondered if it would be better for them if she were gone. The touch of a dullaghan was a swift, painless death. All Cathair needed to do was give Thorne her name, and her destruction was guaranteed.

"Fine."

Thorne placed her hand on his arm. "Don't worry, I promise you'll enjoy it."

"You're awfully confident you can please me."

"Please you? Yes, if it's what you wish, I can provide a multitude of pleasures."

Covering her mouth, Eivor snorted. "I'm tempted to challenge you to prove it."

He chuckled, guiding her to a dark corner of the room where no one else lingered. A large tapestry depicting a crowned fox hung there, and Eivor's nose flared at the sight of it. It was her father in his animal form, and it hid a passageway few knew about. Hooking a finger on the edge, Thorne shifted it enough for them to slip behind into the alcove. Heavy drapes decorated the walls, disguising the narrow hall on the other side. A servant had left a single lit lantern dangling from a hook in case someone needed the space.

"Pretty magpie, if you want to challenge me, I'm more than willing to play."

Spinning her around, he pushed her back against the wall. Startled, Eivor attempted to hit him in retaliation, but Thorne caught her wrists. Pinning them above her head with one hand, he used his weight to press her to the stone. Brushing his lips along the edge of her ear, it came as no surprise when she snapped her teeth at him.

"I can get rid of those nasty bracelets if you ask nicely," he murmured in her ear.

Freezing, Eivor stared, wide-eyed with shock. "How?"

"Unravelling the wards is a simple task for the Master of the Hunt. Do you want me to? The choice is entirely yours."

"The moment he discovered them gone, Cathair would kill me. Or keep me docile until a new set was secured. Of course, I suspect you'll report it to him if I say yes, and I'll suffer further punishment. I'm not stupid."

"I might have talked my way into your palace by offering my services to Cathair, but that isn't why I'm here. Also, I wouldn't break your shackles until the opportune moment."

Tilting her head to the side, Eivor arched her brow. "And what moment is that?"

"Why should I tell you? I don't trust you. For all I know, you might be Cathair's content little pet. A pity if you are because I'd rather not kill you."

With his free hand, Thorne stroked her throat. Trapped between him and the stone wall, Eivor was an iron rod. He felt the depths of her rage, the unyielding force desperate to break past the chains restraining her. The deep blue of her eyes drew him in, filling him with the temptation to kiss her. Beneath his hand, her wrists twisted in frustration.

"I am far from being content!" Baring her teeth, Eivor snapped at him, and Thorne quickly pulled back. "This is not what I want! Do you think I want to be locked away in a tower behind bars? If I blink wrong, he cuts off my access to various places. I have not felt my magic in a hundred years! Not since I watched that bastard Oisin behead my parents in front of me while my sisters fled and abandoned me."

"You are not the only one who hates Oisin. When Annawyn was freed, he did not heed her call. He denied the god he'd served from the day they created him. She let him be. Why? None of us knows. But his refusal left him marked."

"He tortured me."

A shadow passed through his gaze, and Eivor thought she heard the clip of hooves echoing from the hidden corridor. Pressing his lips to her forehead, Throne sighed. The thought of her being tortured by Oisin bothered him.

"I'm sorry to hear that. Pretty magpie, I'm here to offer you a chance at vengeance."

"Why should I trust you? For all I know, you're testing me for Cathair."

"What if I promised to hold him down while you gut him?"

Desire stirred at the suggestion, and Eivor imagined him painted in Cathair's blood, watching in approval while she tore the lord apart. Breath hitching, she could not speak when Thorne's lips crashed into hers. They carried a hint of the blueberry wine, and she kissed him hungrily. His power curled around them, a whisper of death and frozen wastes. It sung through her body, feeding the lust pooling between her legs. Eivor wanted Thorne to hike up her skirts and take her where they stood. Whining when he withdrew, she reached for him, desperate to feel more.

"Not tonight, pretty magpie," Thorne murmured, his smile suggesting he knew precisely what she wanted him to do. "We'll finish this another night, and I promise to make you scream my name. Multiple times until you forget any other."

"I'll hold you to your promise, dullaghan."

# THREE

"Here you go, Your Majesty," the guard said, pushing open a narrow door.

Brushing past him, Eivor kept a nonchalant appearance when what she wanted to do was run into the sunlight and open air. Reaching the bars of the cage enclosing the rooftop, she wrapped her hands around them and pressed her head to the warm metal. Eyes closed tight, Eivor held her breath and listened to the door click shut. She was alone at last. In the week since the ball, her days had been filled with politics. Cathair kept her close, using the opportunity to have her play to the diplomatic party from Samphire.

She sank to the floor, the layers of her skirts cushioning her knees. Sunlight warmed her back, but the unrestrained mass of her hair shaded her face enough that Eivor was unconcerned about the glare. Gazing out at the city, she wondered what people were occupying their time with. It was a question she enjoyed imagining the answers to. She pictured the soldiers going about their duties and training, while busy market squares played host to a myriad of wares. Inhaling deeply, Eivor pretended she smelt fresh bread and cooking meat, accompanied by the shouts of vendors.

Rolling her shoulders, she winced at the discomfort. The warmth of her gown had reached the point where it stung the cuts decorating her skin. Cathair had shown his appreciation for Eivor's good behaviour by lavishing her with the attention of his favourite flogger. She did not mind the pain. It was preferable to other ways he could have rewarded her. His comments during the ball lingered on her mind, setting off nightmares of being forced to have his children.

"I'm stronger than this," she whispered to the wind, knowing it would consume her words. "No matter what they do, I will not let anyone break me."

Eivor lifted her gaze to the cloudless sky, remembering the freedom of flying across it. She longed to feel the breeze ruffling her feathers, the give of flesh beneath her claws while hunting with Astoria and their mother. Silaine was the wolf, but they had been the real predators of the family. Death's Raven with her magpie and hawk daughters, a flock of ruthless hunters who did not hesitate to kill. Malena had taught them to show no remorse for those they destroyed because if the gods showed none, neither would they.

A chill ran down her spine in a strange contrast to the warmth of the silk encasing it. It took Eivor a moment to realise what it was, and her eyes widened in surprise. Her heartbeat quickened, but she did not turn around. The dullaghan from the ball had haunted her, the memory of his kiss refusing to fade. Their encounter left her confused. Cathair had made no mention of him or given her reason to suspect he knew what they had discussed.

"Sunbathing would be better if you were naked."

"How did you get here?"

His chuckle made her shiver. "Do I really need to answer?"

"I thought they warded the palace against veil walking."

"Someone tried, and those wards might have worked against someone less powerful than me. It doesn't matter now, they're gone. I've made sure of it."

The smugness of his voice drove Eivor to look over her shoulder. Thorne stood just within sight, all gleaming darkness, and the whispered promise of death. Black hair tumbled over his shoulders, almost blue in the sunlight. Unlike the night of the ball, his clothes were tight-fitting, as though someone had poured them on. She wondered how easy they would be to peel off. A long black coat surrounded him, hanging down to barely a finger-width from the ground. It absorbed the light, and Eivor imagined the robes of his headless form were spun from the same material.

"Like what you see, pretty magpie?"

"Why don't you have any weapons?"

His boots were silent as he crossed to her. Eivor suspected he could make a noise if he wanted. Halting, Thorne watched her eyes follow the line of his body. The unbridled lust in her gaze made him chuckle. It was strange for someone to desire him as much as the kneeling queen did after finding out what he was. Such feelings usually turned into terror once the truth was revealed.

"I don't need weapons."

Eivor's lips parted, tongue darting out to moisten them while she thought of a response. "True. Why bother with a sword when all you need is a finger?"

Laughing, Thorne appreciated her quip. "I believe you'd beg me for both."

"Cockiness is most unbecoming."

"I'll remind you of that." Snagging a lock of her hair in his fingers, he smirked. "I'm sure you'll be coming on my sword and finger soon enough."

"You've yet to give me a reason to believe you're not just empty words."

"And you've yet to give me a reason not to keep you in chains."

Frowning, Eivor embraced the confusion, letting it chase away the desire she felt for Thorne. "What do you mean? Is Cathair being recalled by Oisin and you're my new keeper?"

"And if I am?"

Recoiling from him, she shook her head. "I'd sooner die."

"A pity. If you were my pet, I'd open the doors to your cage and set you free. Of course, it would depend on if I could trust you not to turn on me. I don't want a queen dragged behind me in chains. I want one who is fierce and willing to get bloody by my side."

Looking up at the bars encasing the rooftop, Eivor sighed. Her confusion remained, making her suspect he was deliberately twisting her assumptions. It struck her that leaving a dullaghan in command of Diwan was not something Oisin would do. Cathair had served him for millennia, but it had not been until the new god of life freed Annawyn that the dullaghan had changed their allegiance. That was what her mother had told her, and she had no reason to believe otherwise.

"Why did your people choose to become Unseelie?"

Startled by her question, Thorne arched his brow. "Because Annawyn offered leadership when none of the others would. Gebael abandoned us. The new god of life was an inconsolable child who refused to do anything about the mess she made, and the Executioner had vanished."

"And now?"

"Some flock to the Vale where a new Raven Queen has arisen. Others search for the Executioner. Many have remained in Ellinjaa. Still more have sought the new god of chaos in her city on the cliffs, hoping for a quiet life, pretending to be anything but what they are. Chaos is not so bad, at least. Neither is Choice."

"What about you?"

"Be more specific."

Her mouth felt impossibly dry. "Who do you serve?"

"Myself. Many of us have embraced free will. I refuse to be a mindless servant who waits for a name to be given to me to kill."

"That doesn't tell me why you're here."

Dragging a finger down a bar, Thorne hummed as he contemplated the cage. "I'm here because my... friend is convinced you'll want to be our ally. Since I can veil walk, the task fell to me to discover if you're what we need for our goals."

"And what are your goals?"

"To start with, we're going to kill Oisin. There is someone who wants him dead, and my friend wishes to use it to prove he's worthy. Do you think it's something you'd be interested in?"

"If your friend wants Oisin dead, why not give his name to you?" Refusing to look at Thorne for fear he would see her hope, Eivor stared out at the city. "Nothing can stop you."

"Tell me, pretty magpie, would you be satisfied by whispering Cathair's name in my ear, or would you prefer to carve out his heart yourself?"

Biting her lip, she imagined being pinned beneath Thorne in the throes of passion when Cathair burst into her bedroom. The idea of whispering his name to the dullaghan and watching him transform to kill her prison keeper was enticing. But it was not as pleasurable a dream as the one she held of having him strung up in chains and unable to stop her slicing him apart slowly.

"My hands would be far more satisfying. I want to spend days washing his blood from my body. To know it has dried beneath my nails, and I must work hard to get rid of it."

"Then you understand why my friend hasn't given me Oisin's name."

"I want to kill Oisin as much as I want to kill Cathair."

Thorne stiffened at the bitterness in her voice. "Did he hurt you?"

"He taught me my place in his regime."

Magic whispered across the rooftop, forcing Eivor to look at him. Frost clung to Thorne's coat, shadows twisting around his feet like they wanted to consume him. Her memories offered the one time she had seen a dullaghan in their headless state, and the thought of watching him transform sent a thrill through her. Releasing her hold on the bars, Eivor stretched out a hand to swipe her fingers through the swirling shadows. Feeling nothing, she did not stop her whine of disappointment. Staring up at Thorne's eyes, the glow of his power turned the blue to ice.

"How can you look at me like that?" he murmured. "It's too much."

"I...." She shook her head and dropped her gaze to the shadows at his feet.

"If we take command of this city, will you fight us or join us?"

"You're going to overthrow Cathair and the Talaroonan forces?"

"Yes."

Her palms were sweaty, and Eivor rubbed them on her skirts, using it as a distraction while she went over her options. A grain of doubt remained firmly lodged in her mind that Thorne was a test set by Cathair. It seemed a reasonable concern that saying she would join them would cause either her death or worse forms of torture than she had already endured.

Lifting her gaze back to him, she said, "If you serve Cathair, then I ask for you to kill me now. Because, yes, I would join anyone who liberated my kingdom from Oisin. They would have my eternal gratitude. Even more so if they delivered Cathair alive to my tender care."

He smiled, reaching out to stroke her hair. "I'm glad to hear that, pretty magpie. I'd be sorry to destroy the hunger in your eyes when you look at me."

"And until you prove the truth of your claims, I'll hold you to my request for death."

"Your eagerness for me to kill you is troubling."

"There are fates worse than death. I'd rather you stop my heart than face them."

Nodding in agreement, Thorne gestured at the city. "Stand."

Snorting, Eivor did not move. She directed a haughty look at him, hoping he would think her refusal was out of a desire not to follow orders. It was easier than revealing the growing pain in her back and shoulders from the unhealed cuts littering her skin. Cocking his head, Thorne held a hand out for her to take.

"Don't make me pick you up."

"I'm fine where I am."

His brow furrowed. "What are you hiding?"

"What is your purpose in demanding I stand up?"

"Perhaps I want to stand behind you with your body pressed to the bars while I lift your skirts. There are guards on the other side of the door; do you think you can keep quiet?"

Wriggling his fingers to taunt her, Thorne smiled at the flare of her nose. Eivor was hiding something, and he was determined to find out what before he told her what she needed to know. Grabbing a bar, she refused his help to stand, freeing Thorne to watch her move. The thin line of her mouth and the stiff way she held herself told him everything he needed to know. Snarling, he stepped closer, a hand reaching for the laces holding Eivor's dress closed.

"What do you think you're doing?" Hissing indignantly, she tried to turn to face him.

"Be still," he replied, unlacing her bodice. "I want to see how bad it is."

Head hanging, Eivor held her dress up while he opened it to reveal the white shift and stays beneath. An angry growl accompanied a gentle touch to the back of her shoulders. When his fingers pinched the fabric and pulled it away, she realised it had become stuck to the cuts. Her strangled whine of pain brought his action to a halt.

"He did this to you."

"Yes."

"Why?" Gazing at the blood soaked into the garments, he fought back his rage.

"Cathair doesn't need a reason other than to remind me of my place."

"I can't heal this."

Laughing at the absurdity of a dullaghan sounding upset about a lack of healing magic, Eivor glanced over her shoulder at him. "I wouldn't ask you to. He'd find out."

"Three days."

"What?"

"On the night of the new moon, we'll come when the sky is at its darkest."

Turning back to face the city, she barely dared breathe. Questions flooded her mind, demanding to be asked, but Eivor feared she had forgotten how to speak. Accepting her silence, Thorne carefully repositioned her dress before drawing the laces together. His rage over the sight of her blood remained, and he wanted to fade into the Veil to track down Cathair so he could cut him into pieces. Briefly, he entertained the thought of asking Eivor to offer him the name, but a quick death was not a mercy the duine deserved.

"I'll come for you when we launch the attack and free you from those cuffs. In return, I need you to find out the names of Cathair's guards."

"Are you going to kill them?"

Stroking the exposed skin at the back of her neck, Thorne grunted. "You give me their names, and I'll drag him before you in chains."

Her breath hitched. "Alive?"

"Yes."

"I want to believe you."

"What is stopping you?"

Shifting about to face him, Eivor studied the earnestness of his expression. "I know compared to our lives, a hundred years is a drop in the ocean. But it taught me caution. Until it unfolds, I'll treat your news with the appropriate disbelief. Free me, bring me Cathair in chains, and then I'll trust you."

"Noted. I suppose it is a bit much to ask you to trust me without giving you proof of my worthiness. Though your lack of trust doesn't seem to impede your desire for me."

"I'm duine. I lust after anything I find mildly attractive."

"Mildly? It's more than that," he purred.

"True. I won't deny it. I wanted you the moment I set eyes on you."

"How long did it take you to work out what I am?"

"Longer than it should have," Eivor replied bitterly. "I've met a dullaghan before. A long time ago. It was with my mother in the woods, just the two of us. I was maybe 500."

His jaw clenched briefly, eyes searching out the distant darkness that was the forest. "You wore a sky-blue dress and such a serious expression. But you waited at the edge of the grove in silence as Malena asked you to. I watched from the Veil while she spoke to my brother."

"Why were you there?"

"We were delivering a message. Things between the old gods were worsening, and the Executioner was concerned for Malena's safety... and yours."

"Mine?"

"You might not be a husk maker, but you carry threads of Death's power. I don't think you can command us, but it wouldn't surprise me."

Pursing her lips, Eivor longed to find out if she could. "What if I can? Would you serve me if I commanded you to kneel at my feet? Could I turn you into my pet dullaghan?"

Reaching out to grip a bar beside her head, Thorne leaned in with a smirk. "Prove yourself worthy, and I won't need to be commanded to kneel at your feet."

"Empty words."

"I guess you'll have to prove yourself and find out."

"And if I don't?"

"I won't be the one kneeling."

Smiling, she brought her face closer, and he swallowed at the triumphant sparkle in her eyes. Her fingers ran down the line of buttons on his coat, a teasing touch Thorne knew was intended to make him think of her hands on him. There were thousands of years between them, but she was a duine, and had an advantage.

"Do you know what my power is?" Running her hand back up, Eivor toyed with the top button. "I'm not a husk maker or a healer. I'm an adequate warrior, but nothing like my sister Astoria, the infamous Battle Hawk. So, tell me, Thorne, what is my magic?"

The low purr of her voice pulled him in two directions. "I'm well aware you're a mind mage."

"Indeed."

"You're not a god, pretty magpie. You won't be able to dig your claws into my mind and twist me to your purpose. I'm a dullaghan, the Master of the Hunt, and I am immune to such powers."

Twisting her fingers to gather a handful of his coat, Eivor tugged him closer. "Is that what you believe? Maybe you are. We'll find out when you release my magic. If you release my magic."

"Do you think you're skilled enough to twist me about with words alone?"

"Oh, most certainly." Bringing her lips tantalisingly close to his, she whispered, "When I fucked the envoy from Samphire two nights ago, I pretended it was you."

Thorne growled, unable to resist the jealousy her words stirred. "Did he satisfy you?"

"Powers no, but I know how to make a man believe he gave me the best climax of my life. Will you be able to tell the difference between the truth and the lies?"

"Yes."

"Are you sure?"

The game was affecting him more than Thorne wanted to admit. It stirred memories of other powerful people who had never known how it felt to be denied. Eivor was a queen, and she had grown up knowing she was second only to her parents. Her beauty was the sort bards wrote ballads to praise. He doubted anyone had ever told her no before Oisin invaded.

"You're vicious, pretty magpie," he murmured.

"Do you like it?"

"It's a rare person who doesn't flee when they find out what I am. Yet here you are, lusting after me like no one has touched you in hundreds of years."

Her other hand stroked the line of his jaw. "You don't frighten me. Then again, I've always found fear arousing. Perhaps those threads of Death's power make me want to have you buried between my thighs. Tell me, can you perform in your other form?"

"What?" Startled, he pulled back slightly.

"Your headless form. I'm curious."

"No. Our headless forms possess no gender nor the necessary parts."

Pouting, Eivor shrugged. "A pity."

"Is this all you think about?"

"I've been kept in a cage, isolated from people, and let me tell you, you quickly run out of things to think about. There are only so many hours in the day I can dedicate to dreaming about revenge before my thoughts turn to other pleasurable ideas."

Mouth twisting, Thorne wanted to argue, but he remembered the thousand years of imprisonment in the Veil. "Don't you want to know who will free your city?"

"No, not particularly. It's probably a bad idea to tell me. Cathair is far more skilled than I am at fucking with a person's mind, and I am currently defenceless. Not knowing is safer for me."

"Are you sure that's what you want? I agree with you, but..."

Licking her lips, Eivor chuckled. "I'm sure. If Cathair discovers I'm conspiring with you with his death in mind? Well, those cuts on my back are nothing compared to what he would do to me. There might be nothing left for you to rescue in three days."

"How often does he hurt you?" Thorne regretted asking, knowing it would fuel his desire to kill Cathair before they had taken the city.

"Less often than in the beginning. I've learnt how to play my part to protect my hide. Of course, if they had treated me better when they invaded, we wouldn't be having this conversation. My loyalty could have belonged to Oisin, but he imprisoned me instead."

"What will it take for us to own your loyalty?"

The vicious twist of her lips matched the darkness behind Eivor's eyes. "Restore my magic, bring me Cathair in chains, and hold him down while I carve out his still-beating heart. Then we'll talk about the price of my loyalty."

# FOUR

Eivor could not keep still, restlessness driving her to pace the library with an open book in her hands. Her eyes barely saw the words on the page, and she lost count of how many times she had tried to read them. The constant movement created an ache in her back where the cuts remained unhealed. She suspected it was likely the worst of them had wept blood again, and her new maid would silently gather the stained undergarments while staring at her sadly. Grinding her teeth at the thought, Eivor glanced at the wall of glass overlooking a garden.

Sunset had come and gone, leaving the strange blue of twilight before the last glow of light gave way to the glitter of stars in the sky. It was her favourite time of day. Twilight was perfect for stealing kisses beneath flowering trees or leading a merry chase along the pathways when the shadows seemed to come alive. Before Oisin's invasion, her parents had held parties in the sprawling gardens from late spring until mid-autumn. Servants would string lanterns through tree boughs and hang them from hooks and archways to create shifting light as the court danced the night away.

Taking a step closer to the glass, Eivor frowned when movement in the garden caught her attention. She could see nothing, but a deep instinct told her something was there, and she had not imagined it. A breeze rustled the leaves of the hardenbergia vine surrounding the window. Biting her lip, Eivor considered the strength of the trellis used to secure the plant this far above the ground. The library was three floors up, and if the gardeners could climb it, she suspected others could do the same.

She wished Thorne had not told her what was coming. If he spoke the truth, then there was another invasion to be expected. Snapping her book shut, Eivor spun on her heels and strode over to the table she had occupied for half the day.

Paper was scattered across it, sketches of scenes she had pulled from the depths of her mind. When her compliance especially pleased Cathair, he allowed her the materials she needed to draw. Despite the wounds on her back, Eivor knew he was happy with her willingness to extract information from Lord Jeffery.

Servants had begun lighting the lanterns used to illuminate the library. Watching them from the corner of her eye, Eivor carefully gathered her sketches into a pile. Besides the palace staff and guards, no one had permission to enter the library while she occupied it, not without Cathair's supervision. With darkness descending and her increasing anxiety, Eivor wanted to return to her quarters. Somehow, it felt safer to be in the rooms she had called her own since being old enough to leave the nursery.

Clutching the paper and pencils to her chest, she ignored the watching eyes of the servants and guards. Maintaining a haughty expression, Eivor made her way to the doors and waited for the soldiers to let her out. They kept close, escorting her through the palace along paths the court was forbidden from using. Routes to ensure no one could approach Eivor without Cathair.

Every flutter of movement had Eivor jumping at shadows. The sooner she returned to her chambers, the easier it would be to breathe. She felt like ants were crawling over every part of her body, the bite of anticipation making her fingers twitch. Counting each breath she took, each step closer to her sanctuary, Eivor had never been so thankful the guards could not converse with her.

By the time they reached her door, she was ready to scream. Waiting for them to perform their inspection only made it worse. They were quick, confident that the bars on her windows and constant surveillance would prevent anyone from entering.

Someone had lit the fires in each room, providing an almost stifling warmth. Carrying her work to the window seat, Eivor left it there while she took care of her dress. The twisting it took to undo her laces added to the ache. It felt good to shed the restricting layers of silk, leaving the midnight-blue gown in a pile on the floor for the maid to deal with. She took more care in removing the rest of her garments, aware some of the fabric had stuck where bandaging did not protect the wounds.

"Oh dear, you've bled again, Your Majesty!"

The sound of her current maid's distress startled Eivor into motion. She blinked at the bustling woman, wondering how long she had stood lost in her thoughts, staring at the dull red staining on the inner lining of her stays. Tutting as she moved, the woman plucked the garment from Eivor's hands and shook her head.

"Perhaps you should stay in your chambers tomorrow. Rest will help you heal quicker. I've got the ointment the healer left for you. We can put some on now and leave them exposed until you're ready to sleep."

"Yes, thank you." Chewing her lip, Eivor allowed the maid to lift the shift over her head. "I'm not feeling the best. Could you request something simple for my dinner?"

"Would you like me to fetch the healer?"

"No, that won't be necessary unless you think these cuts look infected. My time of the month is approaching, and I always have problems with nausea and headaches leading up to it."

Understanding dawned on the maid's face, and she nodded. "Of course, ma'am. Is there anything I can fetch you to help? Some ginger tea, perhaps?"

"That would be lovely."

"Is there anything else you'd like me to make sure you have before it arrives? It's better to ensure you have the supplies before you need them."

Eivor nodded. She knew anxiety was the reason behind her churning stomach, but her excuse was near enough to the truth that letting the maid check her supplies would not be remiss. They were difficult to track at the best of times, and when they hit, she would spend the better part of a week curled up in bed, suffering from unbearable cramps and headaches. Part of her wished it would arrive that night so she could avoid disappointment when Thorne's promised liberation of Diwan from Oisin's rule failed to eventuate.

"Thank you for thinking of it. It's an excellent idea. I'd like a bottle of wine for after the tea... rosehip. Hopefully, my stomach will settle, and I can enjoy it with my meal."

"Of course, ma'am."

While the maid gently wiped her down with a washcloth, Eivor wished she felt like enduring the sting of a bath. Until the cuts from Cathair's whip healed, she would make do. Staring at the shrouded window opposite her bed, the queen wondered how dark it was without the moon casting its glow. Her nose twitched at the pungent scent of the ointment, and the maid sneezed, muttering an apology as she began slathering it across her back. It was chilly in contrast to the warm flush from the fires.

Sneezing again, the maid huffed. "I'm sorry. Something in this is irritating my nose."

"I understand. It's not the most pleasant thing."

Despite the smell, the ointment soothed the ache. Eivor knew half of the discomfort was her fault. She held herself stiffly to avoid straining the cuts and causing them to open again. It left her muscles tense.

Once the maid was done, she crossed to the chair in front of her dresser. Making sure she did not rest her back against the smooth timber, Eivor unravelled the coiled braid at the back of her head, releasing her hair. Keeping the thick mass over her shoulder, she split it for ease of brushing.

"Do you need my help?" the maid asked, reappearing from the small room that was Eivor's wardrobe. "I was just fetching a light robe for you."

"No, I'm fine brushing it myself. Leave the robe; I'll put it on once the ointment sets."

Watching in the mirror as the maid placed the pale blue garment on her bed, Eivor dragged the brush through her hair slowly. The task was soothing, helping her calm the anxious racing of her heart. Thoughts drifting to Thorne, she imagined him leaning against a bedpost while he observed her. Barely hearing the maid excuse herself to fetch drinks and arrange for dinner, Eivor embraced her fantasy involving the dullaghan. She was thankful Cathair had mostly left her alone since whipping her, because Thorne rarely left her mind for long.

Eivor hated the distraction he had become almost as much as she craved him. No one had invaded her thoughts like Thorne. In the past, her fantasies had been a combination of memories and desires, blending lovers who pleased her body and those who had delighted her sense of aesthetics. Part of Eivor suspected he dominated her thoughts because she could not command him to her bed. He was a challenge.

Throwing the brush down, she huffed and stood. Frustrated desire blended with anxiety, leaving her restless. Crossing to the window, Eivor drew the drape to the side and pressed her face against the glass. Peering between the bars, she wondered if unknown soldiers were taking out the Talaroonans who controlled the palace.

If they seized the ancient fortress, killed Cathair and captured her, they stood a chance of taking over Diwan. Except Oisin would retaliate, throwing his armies against them, and Eivor had seen the devastation his forces caused. Especially the husk makers he commanded.

As much as she resented Silaine for abandoning her and building a new life with the danann, Eivor was also thankful. Her sister was rebuilding the Ravens, which meant husk makers across Tir were being tracked down. She had overheard Cathair cursing Silaine's endeavours because Oisin had lost some of his precious living weapons. So long as the man who killed her parents was suffering the loss of something he deemed valuable, Eivor could find pleasure in it. Even more when she knew her sister was responsible.

Withdrawing from the window, she crossed to the bed and picked up the robe. Slipping her arms into the sleeves, Eivor drew it closed, using the belt to secure it. Determined to distract herself, she returned to the sitting room and her drawings. There was no point curling up on the window seat when the position would pull the skin on her back. Taking her work to the lounge near the fire, Eivor adjusted the cushions before sitting. Shuffling through the incomplete sketches, she found one of Thorne to work on.

She missed her studio, paints, and the freedom to create large pieces filled with colour. Imagining Thorne's eyes captured on canvas for her enjoyment, Eivor let the scratch of the pencil overtake her senses.

The sketch became the focus of her desire, every line of his body that she had surveyed, and the smug smirk that graced his lips whenever he noticed his effect on her. She tried to convey the intensity of his stare and the perfectly dishevelled way his hair tumbled over his shoulders.

"Oh, he's rather handsome," the maid said wistfully. "Who is he?"

Angry over being interrupted, Eivor glared at the woman. "No one important."

"I brought the ginger tea, and there's a bottle of rosehip wine on the table along with a plate of fresh bread, cold roast beef, and some cheese. The kitchen will send up a bowl of stew in an hour after you've had time to settle your stomach. It's a nice mutton stew. I had a taste while I was there to ensure it was suitable for our queen."

"Why wouldn't it be suitable for me?"

"Well, Majesty, it's intended for the servants, but I figured it was what you needed tonight. A nice hearty stew will fill your belly and help you sleep better."

Surprised by her thoughtfulness, Eivor pressed her lips together. It was the sort of thing her old maids had done back when the same cluster of women had surrounded her every day. Most servants would have brought her a plate of whatever was being served in the great hall, believing anything else was inappropriate for a queen. Asking for simple foods when her stomach was upset rarely resulted in what she wanted, and Eivor had long since given up hoping for anything else.

"Thank you. That's all I need tonight. I will see you in the morning."

Cocking her head, the maid waved at the table. "Don't you wish to see me sample the food?"

"No, I'm sure it's fine."

"Majesty?"

"Good night."

Bowing, she did not hide her concern. "Sweet dreams, Your Majesty."

Waiting until she was alone again, Eivor studied her sketch. Thorne's likeness gazed up from the paper as though it had poured out of her memory. Setting it aside, she struggled to rise from the lounge, her body stiff from the awkward position she had sat in.

Approaching the table, the scent of the tea hit her nose first, the strong blend promising some relief. Her hand trembled as Eivor picked it up, spilling some of the warm liquid over the side of the cup. She did not enjoy the flavour, but she appreciated the properties of ginger.

She felt the shift in temperature first. The brush of power came second, wrapping around her. It was suffocating in its intensity, and Eivor gasped when icy fingers danced over her skin. The robe had slipped, exposing her shoulder and several cuts. Thorne's breath was a chill fog against her neck, driving her to tighten her grasp on the cup. A sliver of fear overtook her queasiness, and Eivor lowered the tea before she broke the delicate porcelain. Thorne dragged a finger along the robe's hem, shifting it away from her other shoulder to reveal her upper back.

"They're not healing," Thorne murmured, and there was a hint of rage in the words.

"You're here." Frowning, she thought there was something odd about Thorne's voice.

"Did you doubt me, pretty magpie?"

Spinning around, Eivor realised what had unsettled her. "It's true! I thought it was a silly thing my mother told me."

Instead of the man she had expected, a raven-haired woman stood wearing the same smug smirk. Eivor knew it was Thorne because the eyes had not changed. If she had not carried the memory of her mother's words, she would have thought she was looking at Thorne's sister. The echo of Malena talking about the unpredictable transformation dullaghan experienced going between forms lingered at the back of her mind.

Waving at herself, Thorne chuckled. "I hope you're not disappointed."

"Not in the slightest. This means you've killed with your power since I saw you last."

"I just finished collecting several heartbeats." Stroking Eivor's collarbone, her smirk did not fade. "Can't you feel it? The touch of death lingering on my skin."

Knowing Thorne referred to the iciness, she swallowed nervously. Desire pooled between her legs, encouraged by the fingers trailing over her throat and down towards her breasts. Eivor tried to calm her breathing, aware of the precarious situation of her robe. It would not take much for the flimsy material to end up on the floor.

"You're here for the names," she whispered.

"And to free you."

Lifting her hands, Eivor stared at the cuffs. Until they were gone, she dared not imagine the rush of her magic through her veins. Thorne wrapped her hands around them, thumbs stroking the thin strip of skin between the edge of the bands and her hands. It was just ticklish enough to make Eivor shiver, and the other woman chuckled. A chill spread along her arms, originating from Thorne's hands.

"Do you think you can trust me, pretty magpie?"

"What choice do I have?"

"I can leave them on. Would you prefer I keep you as my pet?"

Stiffening, Eivor met Thorne's gaze. "No one will ever keep me again."

"Good."

"How do you remove them?"

Shrugging, Thorne released her wrists and looked around the room. The stack of papers and pencils on the lounge drew her attention. Wandering over to them while Eivor quickly picked up her tea to drain it, she saw the sketch on top and inhaled sharply.

"You drew this?"

"I did. Do you like it?"

Thorne traced the lines depicting her masculine form. "No one has ever drawn me before. I'm afraid my opinion is uneducated, but I think you're very talented."

"I haven't been able to get you out of my mind."

"Understandably. However, that's a conversation for after we have control of Diwan. Right now, several thousand goblin soldiers are securing the palace and barracks. My task is to capture Cathair and release you."

"Only several thousand... wait, did you say goblins?" Eyes wide, Eivor gasped in horror. "You've released those blood-thirsty creatures in my city?"

"Yes, I have. Don't worry, Prince Rhydwen and General Vesta have control of their forces. Just as I'm in control of my dullaghan, who are steadily working their way through the palace dealing with those who are unwaveringly loyal to Oisin." Folding the sketch carefully, Thorne slipped it into her coat pocket. "Now, those names."

"Free me first."

"This isn't a negotiation, pretty magpie."

"Oh, I think it is."

Smiling slowly, Thorne took a step and vanished. Whirling around, Eivor swept her gaze across the room in confusion. She did not understand why the other woman had disappeared. An icy hand closed around her throat, pulling her back against Thorne's body. Lips brushed over Eivor's ear, as cold as the fingers keeping her from speaking.

"Do not be mistaken, Eivor Havard. I'm only willing to free you because it suits me. Refuse to give me those names, and you'll find out what happens when someone displeases me. I doubt you'll enjoy it as much as what I'll do when I'm pleased."

Eivor knew Thorne could feel the racing of her heart. The hand at her throat did not slacken, but the other tugged on the belt keeping her robe closed. Falling open, the flimsy material no longer acted as a barrier between Thorne and her naked body.

Stroking Eivor's stomach, she chuckled at the strangled gasp her touch caused. Dancing her fingers downwards, she sought the spot between Eivor's thighs that would betray her. Thorne dragged a finger through the slickness.

"Or maybe you will." Carefully tightening her grasp on Eivor's throat, Thorne pressed a fingertip against her clit. "Give me those names, and I'll come back to finish this."

She managed to nod slightly. Thorne released her hold, and Eivor sucked in a deep breath, relieved and disappointed at the same time. Two of the fingers between her legs slid into her, curling to seek the sensitive spot that had her squirming in the dullaghan's grasp.

"Now, unless you never want me to touch you again, Eivor, give me those names."

Resting her head on Thorne's shoulder, Eivor named the guards surrounding Cathair. Every time the finger on her clit pressed harder, she stumbled over her words and wished the hand on her throat would tighten again. By the time she finished, Eivor felt like she had been buried in snow. A chill permeated the room, Thorne's power whispering around them, eager to find its targets.

"Good girl," Thorne murmured, kissing her cheek, and withdrawing her hand from between the queen's thighs. "I accept the names you offered me."

Aching with need, Eivor pressed her throat against the hand that still covered it. "You agreed Cathair would be mine."

"And he will be. But first, my part of our bargain."

Closing her hands around the cuffs on Eivor's wrists, Thorne felt for the threads of the wards. Whoever had made them knew what they were doing, but the magic used was inconsequential to the Master of the Hunt. Her power latched on, unravelling the binds preventing Eivor from connecting with the magic coursing through her veins. The moment the cuffs split open, Throne stepped back and prepared to surrender to the call of the names whispering in her mind. Denying the pull hurt more the longer she put it off.

"Behave yourself, pretty magpie. I'll be back for you."

Overwhelmed by the rush of her magic, Eivor barely registered the shift overcoming Thorne. Only the brush of frozen fingers across her breasts shocked her out of her rapture enough to see the headless figure turning to leave. Shadows swirled at Thorne's feet, melding into the black robes, providing the barest suggestion of the body holding them up. Eivor knew she should fear the sight of Thorne's other self, but she did not.

Not even when the dullaghan faded through the door to the hallway, and the screams reached Eivor's ears. They were not the only noise she heard. In the distance, horns blasted out, warning everyone in the palace and city of the attack. Yanking her robe into place, she focused on the power thrumming through her. It was unchanged, providing Eivor with the confidence she could still tear apart the minds of anyone who got in her way.

# FIVE

No one had locked the door, and Eivor found a thrill in opening it herself. It was a freedom she had missed. Standing in the hallway, she took in the corpses littering the floor and the few guards who remained alive. She knew the only people Thorne could kill with their powers were those whose names were given, or those who attacked first.

"Your Majesty?" A guard realised she was standing there, his eyes wide with fear. "Get back in your rooms, ma'am. It's not safe. The palace is under attack."

Smiling slowly, Eivor lifted a hand and wriggled her fingers. "Oh, I know."

Her magic latched onto the man's terror, and she moaned in delight. Twisting it back on him, Eivor filled his mind with the image of Thorne gliding towards him. Screaming, he crumpled to the ground, begging the air where he thought the dullaghan stood. It startled the other guards, but before they could figure out what was happening, Eivor dug her claws into their minds. She drew on their fears, weaving them into a tight net the soldiers could not break free from. They were only warriors, and she was a mind mage full of rage.

"That feels too fucking good," Eivor said to them. "I almost forgot how wonderful it is."

They huddled on the floor, unaware of her words. Stepping around the dead bodies, Eivor left the guards where they were. She had no intention of releasing their minds until the palace was secure. Glancing back, she wondered if it would be better to kill them. Their weapons were available for her to take. When she finally returned to her rooms, Eivor doubted there would be much left of their minds to salvage. Dismissing her compassion as unnecessary, she kept walking.

Power thrummed through her, emboldened by the ease at which the guards had succumbed. With the horns blasting outside, the halls were a mess of people rushing to hide from the conflict, or guards hurrying towards it. Most ignored her, and Eivor was glad not to waste time. The few soldiers who realised who she was and tried to stop her were left as a drooling mess in her wake. She did not seek the fighting. All she wanted was to reach the throne room to establish her position.

When Thorne dragged Cathair to her feet, Eivor wanted to be sprawled across the stone seat that had belonged to her father. She felt a rush at the thought of the look on his face when he saw her and realised she was free. Even if he was more skillful than she was, her deep well of rage provided Eivor with more desire for his destruction than he could defend against. There would be no mercy, no negotiation. Cathair would suffer, slowly and painfully, before she granted him death.

Anticipation of the scene she had planned out had Eivor almost skipping down hallways to the monarch's entrance to the throne room. No guards stood at the door, and when she opened it, she was pleased to find the cavernous chamber almost deserted.

A handful of nobles huddled in a group in the corner furthest from the main doors, and their stunned expressions when they saw Eivor brought a smile to her lips. She picked up on their thoughts, the confusion over what it meant that she was there. They were inconsequential in the grand scheme, but the audience they would provide to Cathair's defeat gave them enough value to be left alone.

Circling the stone seat she had inherited upon her father's death, Eivor swallowed back the grief it invoked. Craven Havard had earned his kingdom in the god of war's arenas. He had survived battles and challenges to prove himself worthy of such a reward. Diwan had thrived under his leadership even before he set his gaze on one of the Ravens who served the Executioner.

Eivor knew her mother had come willingly, glad to flee the aftermath of the events that left her riddled with scars. She had barely survived the Sundering and the deaths of her danann mates, and Craven had offered her freedom. Glancing down at her exposed body, Eivor wondered what Malena would say about the lines marring her daughter's skin.

Her hands traced the carvings worked into the throne. Next to it, the one her mother had occupied was no less impressive. When Cathair had trotted her out to play queen in front of a court that knew the truth, he had always put her on the consort's seat. It had been another reminder of who was truly in charge in Diwan. Standing in front of them, Eivor wondered where they had stored the three seats she and her sisters had used. They barely mattered now she was the last one in Diwan, but a small part of her needed to know.

Adjusting her robe, Eivor turned and sat on the throne. Her stomach roiled from the clash of emotions coursing through her. They were not all hers, the cowering nobles in the corner projecting so much fear it surprised her they could whisper at all. It would have been easy to turn their emotions back on them, destroying what sanity they possessed.

Several deep breaths helped her focus, and Eivor slid back on the stone to find a comfortable position. She contemplated slinging a leg over the side, but doubted the cuts on her back would appreciate the twist. Especially when she did not know how long she would have to wait before Thorne found her and dragged Cathair into the chamber.

"Your Majesty?"

Rolling her eyes at the timidness of the man's voice, Eivor replied, "Yes?"

"Do you know what's going on?"

"We're being freed from Oisin."

Several gasps of surprise summoned a delighted smirk to her lips. She doubted they would appreciate finding out who exactly was liberating Diwan. Goblins were hardly popular, but Eivor looked forward to meeting the one Thorne had called Prince Rhydwen. They were a matriarchal species, so she was even more intrigued by the one leading the forces alongside General Vesta. Hers was a name she knew well.

"Who? Have... have the danann come? Everyone knows Princess Silaine is with them," a woman said, her voice making Eivor flinch. "But why now?"

"King Tigernach and his precious flying army have not decided to help us after all these years. No, our allies are most unexpected, but oh so very welcome."

The horns outside fell silent, and with them, the murmured discussion of the nobles. Each person in the throne room knew it meant one side had triumphed. Eivor wondered if her heart would ever stop racing, the thudding beat echoing loudly in her ears. She needed it to stop. Each thump added to the throbbing headache, fuelling her nausea. It was a combination of anxiety, too little food, too much magic, and days of poor sleep. Exhaustion would catch up with her as soon as everything wore off.

"Do you hear that?"

"Is that... hoofbeats?"

Biting her lip, Eivor resisted the urge to lean forward. Instead, she slung her legs over the side of the throne, ignoring the pain in her back. She heard the clang as loudly as they did. It was less a sound and more a sensation sending icy shivers down her spine. There were other dullaghan in the palace, Thorne had said as much, but she knew it was not one of them.

The nobles continued to babble nervously, aware of the increasing drop in temperature. Her skin crawled with the sensation of approaching death, and it was familiar enough to assure Eivor her instincts screamed true. Her nails dug into the stone of the throne, a painful method of keeping herself calm. The hoofbeats bounced off the walls, becoming a deafening echo that had the nobles begging Eivor to join them.

She ignored their pleas, confident she was the safest of all of them in the room. Each beat came closer, power rattling the heavy doors. Stretching her hand out, Eivor wrapped her magic around the handles, yanking them open before they were flung from their hinges. Her palace had endured enough without a dullaghan on the hunt doing more damage.

"Gods save us!"

"We're going to die!"

"Majesty, run!"

Her gaze did not leave the figure shrouded in shadows atop the black horse. No head existed upon their shoulders, but somehow, Eivor's magic sensed a thinning of the Veil between the living and the dead. She knew Thorne was staring back, drinking in the sight of her, almost naked and sprawled across the throne.

The horse moved forward slowly, snorting when the dullaghan stopped it in the middle of the chamber. Lifting a hand, Thorne drew Eivor's focus to the rope in their grasp. Following it down, she saw the body at the other end.

"It seems you held up your end of our agreement," she said, gesturing at Cathair. "I honestly had doubts you would. Half expected you to deliver his head instead."

"And be denied the pleasure of seeing you carve out his heart? Oh no, my pretty magpie, I'm looking forward to watching you bathe in his blood."

Cathair groaned, rolling over. There was rope wrapped around his legs, tied firmly, but his hands were free. Blood soaked his hair, staining his face like someone had taken garish red paint to it. The way he fumbled suggested he suffered from a head injury. Eivor drew pleasure from the sight of his inability to get free. It fed her desire to have him strung up on a wall in chains. Behind her, the group of nobles had fallen silent, terrified by the exchange between the queen and the dullaghan they feared.

"Well, isn't this quite the introduction? I can't say I expected the first time we met to involve you all but naked and seated on a throne. I'm impressed."

"Rhydwen," Thorne said, shifting slightly. "What are you doing here?"

"We've got the city under control. Thought I should make sure the queen is safe."

Snapping her focus to the newcomer, Eivor's nose flared. He stood at the back of the chamber, leaning against the doorway with his arms crossed. She thought he looked human from a distance, and the magic pouring off the goblin was like a warrior's blood lust. Unlike the daoine warriors she was used to, his power had her instincts screaming at her to run. Goblins were predators with no morals who would eat anyone who got in their way.

"As you can see, I'm perfectly safe," she said, giving him a dismissive look.

Her illusions of his resemblance to humans were shattered when he peeled away from the doorway, shadows curling around him. Eivor watched his arms unfold, gleaming claws appearing at the tips of his fingers. She had seen drawings of goblins in books, and her mother had spoken of fighting them in her role as a Raven. Part of the prowess was their ability to blend into a crowd before they attacked.

With each step closer he took, Eivor felt an increasing need to flee. She wanted to look to Thorne for reassurance, but refused to appear weak. Rhydwen stopped next to Cathair and slashed a claw through the rope around his ankles. Grabbing the blood-soaked hair of the Talaroonan lord, he hauled him up, and Eivor watched fresh blood running down the side of his face. Several ladies screamed, drawing Rhydwen's attention. A smile bordering on sinister curled his lips, his eyes tracking the group's movements.

"Leave them alone." Drumming her fingers on the arm of the throne, Eivor maintained a blank expression. "They're of no concern to you."

"What about this one? Can I play with him? He smells tasty, and I'm sure I'll enjoy eating him." Licking Cathair's cheek, Rhydwen gazed at her.

Thorne's horse stamped a hoof impatiently, and the dullaghan patted its neck. "You cannot eat that man, Rhydwen. His death belongs to her."

"Can I eat her?"

"She's more likely to eat you first."

Lowering Cathair, Rhydwen dragged him towards Eivor, stopping a short distance from the throne. "Is that true? Do you have claws hidden in that flimsy strip of fabric?"

Leaning on her arm, Eivor waved at him. "You're being awfully bold around a woman, goblin. Didn't your mother teach you better?"

His eyes narrowed, and he released Cathair with a thud. Groaning, the injured man tried to roll away, but Rhydwen kicked his side viciously. Watching her keeper being treated so harshly had Eivor's heart racing with excitement. Stalking up the dais to the throne, the goblin bared his teeth, exposing the sharp points intended for tearing into flesh. He stood in front of her, leaning down to place his clawed hands on the arms of the throne and prevent any escape attempt.

"You know nothing of my mother, duine."

"Thorne called you prince. To claim such a title, your mother must be Queen Calista. All I know of her is what my mother taught me." Sliding her legs off the arm so she could sit straight, Eivor leaned forward with an arched look. "Do you know what else she taught me? How to rip out a goblin's claws."

Running his tongue across his teeth, Rhydwen smiled. "I smell you, and I never forget a scent. You won't be ripping my claws out anytime soon. Though perhaps my mother will reward me if I deliver you to her. Maybe she'll let me keep you to warm my bed until I'm bored and decide to eat you."

This close to him, Eivor took in his appearance. Hair, the colour of fresh blood, hung around his face where it had escaped a thick braid, framing almost delicate features. Rhydwen's beauty did not surprise her, not when she remembered the stories her mother had told of the breathtaking queen of the goblins. Eyes like emeralds held her gaze, and Eivor dug through the list of her jewellery to recall if she had anything that compared. She wanted to drape the green gems across him to highlight the sparkle of those eyes. Imagining him clad in nothing but gold chains and emeralds while she painted his portrait, Eivor inhaled sharply.

Lifting her chin, she half-smiled. "Your mother certainly chose her mate well to create you. Though I imagine it disappointed her when you were born with a cock."

He could not hide the mixture of shame and anger that crossed his gaze. "My queen mother displays more discretion than any daoine ever could."

"What's that word the humans use? Ah, yes, whore. Is that what you're calling me?"

"You're a duine. The gods made your people to be the fucking entertainment."

Sliding her gaze over his shoulder, Eivor realised Thorne had shifted out of their headless form. The woman who had been in her quarters earlier stood behind Rhydwen, her lips curled into a sneer. Grabbing his hair, Thorne tugged his head back.

"What did I tell you about being rude?"

"Thorne, my love," he murmured. "Not here."

Eivor stared at them, slumping back in her seat. The adoration in Rhydwen's gaze as he stared at Thorne told her everything she needed to know. They were more than allies. It explained why the dullaghan had become involved with whatever vendetta the prince was carrying out for his mother. She knew goblins were possessive, and Eivor decided that despite the attraction she felt for Thorne, any pursuit of it was off-limits. Revenge on Oisin mattered more than pleasure.

"Please take your arguments elsewhere," Eivor said, slipping from the throne. "I need to speak to Cathair before he's dragged to a cell."

Pulling Rhydwen to the side, Thorne watched her slink over to the barely conscious man. "Careful, pretty magpie. He's no longer restrained."

Standing over the man who had tortured her for a hundred years, Eivor felt light. "I don't think he's going anywhere on his own for the moment."

Refusing to kneel to be closer to him, she leaned down and felt the cuts on her back aching. His eyes were shut, and his breathing haggard, but he was not dead yet. Driving her magic into his mind, Eivor forced him to consciousness. Staring at her, Cathair's mouth opened and closed, but no words came out.

"You and I will have so much fun together, Master."

He coughed, a trickle of blood escaping from the corner of his mouth. Annoyed someone had damaged him enough to put her plans at risk, Eivor turned to Thorne and Rhydwen. They watched her blankly, and she caught sight of the cowering group of nobles.

"He needs a healer. I won't be robbed of my vengeance because someone broke him before I could. If he dies by anyone else's hand..."

"Apologies, Your Majesty," Thorne replied, scowling. "He fought me. I could have killed him."

She nodded, aware of how difficult it would have been for the dullaghan. "I'm sorry. Thank you. You're right, you could have killed him, but you didn't. For me."

Squinting, Rhydwen glanced back at the nobles. "What about them?"

"What about them?"

"Are they loyal to you or Oisin?"

Humming, Eivor moved away from Cathair. "That's an excellent question."

Magic swirled around her, threads of influence weaving outwards to seek the huddled group. Their terror provided Eivor with a path into their minds. Wrapping them in her power, she bid them stand straight and face her. She sensed Thorne and Rhydwen at her back and felt the brush of icy fingers over her elbow. Inspecting the line of daoine, the goblin clicked his teeth together, feeding their fear.

"Who do you serve?" Eivor demanded, using her magic to compel them to answer.

All but two declared they served the throne of Diwan. Confident they spoke the truth, she bid them leave and return to their quarters. The two men left behind knew they were doomed, abject terror written into every line of their faces. Cocking her head, Eivor studied Rhydwen and considered the best way to ensure they got along.

"You can have them."

The goblin prince purred in delight. "Are you sure?"

"Yes. Anyone loyal to Oisin is yours. Except for Cathair. He is mine and only mine."

"Done. I accept your terms. Thorne wants to keep you cooperative, and if this ensures that... well, I'm a magnanimous conqueror."

Grinding her teeth, Eivor slanted a look at Thorne. "Conqueror?"

The other woman smiled coldly. "I thought I established who was in command earlier, or have you forgotten already? You're free because it suits me, pretty magpie."

Reminded of Thorne's hand on her throat, Eivor sighed. Slivers of doubt wormed through her mind, suggesting she had traded one master for another without considering the consequences. If she wanted to remain free, she needed to play their game.

"Of course." Bowing her head, she dropped her gaze. "Please have Cathair locked up and attended by a healer. I want as much time with him as possible before carving out his heart."

"Don't worry, I'll still hold him down while you do it."

"I'll let you eat his heart when I'm done," she said to Rhydwen.

Grinning, he stretched his claws towards her. "You're giving me ideas, and I doubt you'd like them. We'll see. Maybe I'll get to do it anyway."

Thorne leaned in closer to Eivor, whispering, "Do you want to know what he's picturing?"

"No, thank you."

"He's imagining me holding you while he eats you with Cathair's blood still on his lips."

"I don't need to be reminded of my situation."

"Good."

She watched Rhydwen shift his attention to the two men. "I should return to my chambers and get dressed. There is much to be done."

"Nothing you need to do right now. Our forces are sorting through people, weeding out the Talaroonans. Stay in your room where you'll be safe. Do not leave for anything. I'd hate for someone to get to you before I do."

Meeting Thorne's gaze, Eivor swallowed nervously. Nodding in acceptance, she turned slowly to walk out of the throne room. She wanted to run, but fear of Rhydwen giving chase kept her from fleeing. Before she slipped through the door, she heard the goblin chuckling.

Hesitating, Eivor made the mistake of looking at the two men she had given to the prince. He stood behind one of them, shredding the clothes keeping his claws from the man's flesh. Catching her stare, he grinned and slowly eviscerated his victim.

Lifting his claws, Rhydwen licked the blood from them. "Rest well, Your Majesty."

Slamming the door shut, Eivor surrendered to her desire to flee. Every shadow leapt at her; the fear more goblins lurked in wait drove her to keep moving. Nowhere felt safe anymore.

# SIX

The bottle of wine sat on the table, taunting her. Eivor wanted to snatch it up and drain the contents, but the prospect of only having one bottle left her thirsting for more. She longed for the blissful haze of intoxication, the giddy state she could reach before sleep claimed her. One bottle was not enough to achieve that. Every so often, she heard thumps from outside her door, suggesting someone was dealing with the corpses. When she returned to her chambers, the men she had left insensate joined the others in death. Their demises had been painful, their bodies bearing the brunt of her rage as she used their weapons on them.

Her stomach ached from hunger, but the food her maid provided earlier remained untouched. As much as Eivor wanted to eat, she suspected anything she consumed would end up on the floor. Since returning, all she had done was pace the rooms in a desperate attempt to calm her racing heart. Anxiety clawed at her, fuelled by the fear that at any moment, Rhydwen or one of his soldiers would burst in to kill her. Or worse. Every shadow made her jump with dread at the expectation someone would step out of them.

Eivor did not know who she feared more. She suspected the dullaghan leader was the more significant threat because, as much as her mind knew Thorne was dangerous, her body disagreed. At least Rhydwen was honest about his desire to kill her. He had made it clear what he wanted to do while Thorne left her twisted in circles. Rubbing her face as she paced, Eivor reminded herself that even if they killed her before dawn, Cathair would not live much longer. The Talaroonan lord was as good as dead.

Thinking about Cathair bound and dragged behind Thorne had her scratching her arms in a frustrated attempt to feel anything other than desire and fear. Her nails left red lines on her skin, pinpricks of blood appearing where she had pressed hard enough. The robe lay in a pile on the floor, discarded during her pacing. Forcing herself to sit on the window seat, Eivor stared at the closed door and wondered if she could barricade it. She had already layered it with protective wards, but she did not know if they would work against goblins.

Her gaze returned to the wine. Eivor regretted not asking the maid for more than one bottle. If she had believed Thorne, she would have. She should have anyway. Being drunk would have helped soothe the disappointment when nothing happened. Part of her knew her increasing dependence on wine to get through her days in captivity was something to be concerned about.

Stumbling to her feet, Eivor crossed to the table and picked it up. Her fingers found the wax seal, breaking it off without thinking. The cork came away easily, and she swigged from the bottle, only to retch at the cloying sweetness. Quickly turning, Eivor spat the wine onto the floor, clinging to the table for support. She flinched when she felt the splatter on her bare feet.

Clenching her eyes shut, she breathed deeply through her nose and wished for something to banish the acidic burn at the back of her throat. Tears Eivor refused to let fall stung her eyes, several escaping her grasp to drip down her face. Their tracks chilled on her skin, the drop in temperature alerting her to the dullaghan's arrival.

"I'd say the sight of your bare arse bent over was a lovely way to be greeted, except I smell the wine and the bile." Thorne approached the table, glancing at the items on it. "Where can I find a jug of water? You need something to drink that isn't wine."

"I don't need your help."

"Did it sound like I was asking for permission? I'll check your bedroom. Perhaps your maid left some near your bed."

"Unlikely," she muttered, straightening up.

"When was the last time you ate?"

"Earlier."

Thorne ground her teeth, a huff of annoyance warning Eivor to be cautious. "That is not the answer I wanted to hear. You're old enough to know better than to neglect yourself."

"My apologies. I'll try harder to force my body to cooperate when it doesn't want to stomach food or drink because I'm too busy fearing for my life."

"If we wanted you dead, pretty magpie, you would be dead."

"Why should I believe you?"

Picking up the bottle of wine, Eivor attempted a second swig. Cautiously swilling a smaller amount around in her mouth before she swallowed, she did not look at Thorne.

Lips thinning, the other woman spun and strode into the next chamber to search for water. She noted the rumpled sheets on the bed and the discarded clothes Eivor had considered wearing. The fire had burnt down to a warm glow, a sign the queen had not bothered to add more wood. Finding a jug of water and a cup on the table next to the bed, Thorne returned to Eivor.

"Drink this," she said, pouring a drink to swap for the bottle of wine. "You need it."

"Don't tell me what I need."

Grabbing Eivor's wrist when she reached for the bottle, Thorne growled. "It's clear someone needs to. Your wounds aren't healing as quickly as they should be. Each time I've seen you, I've noticed the dark circles beneath your eyes, and now I've seen you completely naked, I can count every one of your ribs and the bones in your spine. If I must supervise your every meal, I will. I'll fucking feed you if that's what it takes."

"Why?"

"Because we need you for our plan to destroy Oisin."

Mouth twisting, Eivor rolled her eyes. "Right. What am I, your bait to lure him in?"

"Yes."

"You're not joking, are you?"

"No. You're valuable to Oisin," Thorne said, shrugging as though the information meant nothing to her. "If he had your sisters, he might not care. But he doesn't. He never will. The bastard is collecting husk makers. Ravens. You're the first child of an original Raven. Gebael himself attended your birth."

"So, I'm to dance on your strings now instead of Cathair's? Am I to expect better treatment?"

"If you behave, yes."

"And your goblin prince?" Her eyes narrowed.

"I told you in the throne room, Rhydwen wants to eat you."

Wrenching her wrist from Thorne's grasp, Eivor knew it would bruise. "I doubt I'd be a satisfying meal. At least, according to your description of me."

"Oh, I wouldn't be so sure of that. You might be in a dismal state, but the delicious parts still work. I know for a fact Rhydwen would find a meal."

Eivor frowned, confused by the smug smile Thorne wore. Her emotions were crashing, leaving her too tired to make sense of the mind games. All she wanted was to curl up and let her dreams guide her to a place where she could forget everything. Rubbing her face, Eivor was unsure if sleep would be the escape she hoped for. It was likely nightmares of corpses would plague her mind, accompanied by laughing goblins and Rhydwen slicing her open with his claws to eat her alive while Thorne watched on.

"You're exhausted," Thorne said, gently brushing a lock of white hair from her face. "I should fetch one of those obstinate healers running around."

"Can't have your bait in poor health."

"True. It would be inconvenient if you got sick and died before Rhydwen achieved his goal. Of course, I'm also the sort who likes to take care of the things that belong to me."

"Rhydwen's goal?"

"Yes, that's why we're here. Queen Calista holds some bitterness towards Oisin over his refusal to answer Annawyn's call... and because he's gathering husk makers."

Shaking her head, Eivor hated that so much came back to the daoine born with the ability to draw life out of things. "Why are they so fucking important?"

"Because if you control the husk makers, not only do you have mages with a power that cannot be defended against, but you control the danann. Tigernach and his people will not risk harm to their precious Ravens. They would stand aside and let Oisin win rather than kill their potential mates. War's army, the mighty winged warriors and their blood mages, defeated by the idea of love."

Remembering her mother drawing the energy out of a stag to heal a life-threatening injury Astoria had received, Eivor sucked in a shaky breath.

It had been before Silaine was born, and the hollowed-out husk of the once-mighty animal had fascinated her. A strong wind had scattered the ash-like remains, leaving only the antlers behind. The prospect of facing an army of husk makers was terrifying.

"Queen Calista wants the husk makers so she can go up against Tigernach?"

"Yes. Honestly, any ambitious leader with a grain of sense wants to control husk makers except the dar ann. They want to find them all, pair them off, and live their merry lives high in their mountains. Tigernach knows how powerful husk makers are, but he is also tired of war. Your sister stumbling into their midst gave his people hope for a happy future."

"But the gods?"

"The new gods are all peace, love, happiness, and let's have families while also occasionally dabbling in the lives of mortals. They believe in free will for all."

Her eyes drifted to a painting she had done during the Fog. "Maybe there's something to that. What's wrong with wanting to be happy? To want to be surrounded by the people you love. It's better than being alone and bitter, starting wars, and destroying everything good."

"Nothing. Which is in part why we're here."

"That doesn't make sense."

Thorne chuckled. "Rhydwen is Calista's only son. She loves him but despises him for being male. Something you already suspected. He wants to prove himself worthy by destroying Oisin. Having you is a bonus because Malena and Calista weren't friends."

"Why are you helping him?" She suspected she knew, but wanted to hear it from the dullaghan.

"Because why not? I enjoy his company."

"He's in love with you."

The arched look Thorne gave her was filled with suspicion. "Yes."

"But you're not in love with him?"

"I'm a dullaghan. We're not partial to feeling."

Snorting, Eivor reached for the wine. "Oh, but that's a lie. The gods spun their capacity for emotions into all their people. You're as capable of love as the rest of us. I know dullaghan have mates."

"I've seen the price of emotions. Queen Calista cut off parts of Rhydwen's father and ate them."

She choked on her mouthful of wine. "What?"

"She was less than impressed he had given her a son. The only reason she didn't kill Rhydwen when the gods made us mortal is his potential to provide her with granddaughters. Male or not, he's still her blood."

"If she died, would Rhydwen become king of the goblins?"

"No. He has older sisters. Even if he didn't, they would never accept a king."

"So, Rhydwen put together an army and came to Diwan to free it from Oisin to lure him into a war?" Tapping her finger against the bottle, Eivor wondered why Thorne was so willing to give her information. "And what, you're going to use me to bait him into it, only to give me to the Blood Queen for dinner?"

Thorne plucked the bottle from her grasp and took a swig. "Something like that. I doubt she'll eat you. You're too valuable to kill."

"And Diwan?"

"You're going to sign a treaty with the goblins."

She wanted to grab the bottle from the other woman. "You intend for me to sign over my people to be livestock."

"No! The goblins don't hunt haphazardly anymore. No one does unless they want to draw the attention of the gods. Eating a slain foe is one thing, but making a regular meal of other species?" Thorne gave her a disgusted look. "A quick way to end up dead now that we're all mortal."

"Then why does Queen Calista want Diwan?"

"She doesn't."

"Rhydwen."

"He wants to prove his worth to his mother. I'm sure you can appreciate that."

Scratching her cheek, Eivor was thankful for the conversation. Despite her growing list of questions, she had more information than before the attack. The assurance she was not destined to die yet helped. Staying alive meant she had time to form a plan, not just for revenge against Oisin, but for gaining freedom. Even if she had to flee her home and abandon the throne, Eivor was determined not to remain a captive.

"Wonderful," she murmured, crossing to the lounge. "And I doubt my desire to please my parents comes anywhere near what your prince feels. My life was good before Oisin. I had a happy family, parents who adored me, sisters who respected me, and friends."

"Oisin killed them?"

"Yes. They kept me isolated. A new maid every week, constantly changing guards. The only lovers allowed were ones Cathair selected."

"Like the envoy from Samphire?"

"Indeed. Cathair traded a night with me for a lot of things."

Exchanging the bottle of wine for the untouched cup of water, Thorne joined her on the lounge. She held the drink to Eivor's lips, arching a brow expectantly.

"Drink. I can tell you're dehydrated."

"Perhaps I should die of dehydration just to spite you."

"While I don't doubt you're spiteful enough to do it, I'm disinclined to let you."

Begrudgingly sipping the water, Eivor said, "Right. More value alive."

"Exactly." Encouraging her to keep drinking, Thorne smiled. "Good girl."

"I'm not a child."

"Did I say you were?"

"You praised me like one." Scowling, she turned her face away from the cup.

The dullaghan snorted. "And now you sound as petulant as one. Perhaps I was remiss in my praise."

Her stomach protested the mixture of wine and water with no food. Glancing at the table, Eivor wondered if she could manage some of the bread. Anything was better than nothing, but not if she brought it back up. Catching her look, Thorne hummed thoughtfully and rose to return to the table. Having been left out uncovered for hours, the food was not the best, and she poked the bread in disgust.

"No, this won't do. Don't go anywhere, pretty magpie. I'll be back shortly."

Opening her mouth, Eivor snapped it shut without speaking when Thorne vanished. Sighing, she stretched out on the lounge and studied the ceiling, wondering if she dared ask for paint. It had crossed her mind many times to transform the blank surface into a scene of some sort. Requesting paint from Cathair had been out of the question, but she suspected Thorne would indulge her.

"This is ridiculous," she muttered. "I refuse to let them lock me away."

Thinking about all the things she needed to go over to know what was happening in her kingdom, Eivor massaged the back of her neck. A headache made her skull feel like there was an army trapped inside trying to beat their way out. She wanted to crawl into her bed and see if sleep would finally claim her, but Thorne had instructed her to remain. The prospect of going to bed reminded Eivor of her vomit splattered feet, shifting her thoughts to a warm bath. It was one thing she had not tried during her fretful pacing.

Sliding from her seat, she moved stiffly to the next chamber and into the bathroom. A large tub sat along one wall, connected to pipes that drew from a vast underground reservoir of water. Wards were worked into one set, allowing warm water to fill the bath. The process was slow, but Eivor figured the reward of a soak was worth it. Especially if it helped soothe her headache. Perching on the side while she waited, she watched the door nervously.

She felt it the moment Thorne returned. The drop in temperature alerted her before she heard the whisper of magic. Part of Eivor wanted to ask why it was always so cold when the dullaghan veil walked into a room, but she was afraid of the answer. Hearing her name called, she considered not answering. Biting her lip, Eivor decided it was better to respond and hurried to the doorway to greet Thorne.

"What are you doing?" Thorne stood in the middle of her bedroom. "There's food coming. Warm stew. I couldn't bring it with me. It wouldn't have stayed warm."

Eivor waved over her shoulder. "I thought a bath might help."

"Good idea. You are dirty."

"I'm sorry if my appearance offends you."

"You realise that not only did you vomit on your feet, but you walked through blood. There's blood on your legs, and the cuts on your back have bled."

Looking down at her legs, Eivor saw the blood splatter she had failed to notice. "Oh."

"Oh indeed. Deal with your bath. I'll wait for the stew and bring it to you."

Watching her slink back into the room, Thorne tutted. The first task that drew her focus was rebuilding the fires. Most of the lanterns had burnt out, only a few still clinging to a spluttering flame. There was little point in relighting them when the night was over halfway done. Carefully adding wood to the dying fire in the bedroom, she listened for a knock at the door. Once finished, she held her hands to the warmth in appreciation.

The knock came, a familiar pattern of raps against the wood. Cringing before she opened it, Thorne prepared for the giddy man on the other side. Rhydwen held a tray in his hands; claws retracted to give him an almost human appearance. Peering around the room as he entered, the goblin scowled at the mess on the floor. He had people dealing with the palace staff, so they knew they could continue working. There was no need for them to cease fulfilling their duties because of a leadership change.

"Did you at least ask for a servant to deal with that?"

"No. I was more concerned with feeding the queen," Thorne replied, reaching for the bowl of stew. "But feel free to fetch someone while I deal with this."

Eyes narrowing, Rhydwen sniffed the air obviously and looked at the doorway to the next room. "I smell lavender. Where is our new pretty little pet?"

"You realise she's older than you, Rhyd?"

"So?"

"Why do I bother?" She sighed in frustration. "You're a brat."

"You love it."

"Don't call her a pet. That's what Cathair used, and it won't endear you to her if you behave like him. Be nice, and she's far more likely to cooperate."

Following Thorne, Rhydwen whistled at the sight of Eivor's bed. "I'm sure I can think of a few ways to endear myself. I am a lowly male, and we're only good for two things."

"Stay here," she said, directing a scolding look at him.

Eivor lay in the bath, an arm slung over the side while the other covered her face. The small room stank of lavender, making Thorne's nose twitch.

Hearing a snort behind her, she shot a glare over her shoulder at Rhydwen before carrying the bowl of stew to the queen.

"I have food."

"And company." Opening her eyes, Eivor peered out from between her fingers. "Why are you here, Your Highness? I assure you, I'm behaving like a good little captive."

Rhydwen wandered around the chamber, examining random items. "I'm sure you are. You've had plenty of practice behaving like a good little captive for Cathair. He is still alive, by the way. The healer tended to his injuries, and I ensured we strung him up for you."

"Thank you."

"You can thank me by eating the stew Thorne is fretting over."

"I do not fret," Thorne muttered, perching on the side of the bath.

"Yes, you do. You've been fretting over her since you saw the cuts on her back. What did you do to earn those stripes, Majesty?"

Eivor quietly accepted the spoonful of stew Thorne pushed at her, lowering her gaze. "They were a reward for good behaviour."

"Really?" Drawing the word out, Rhydwen joined them and stared at her.

"My willingness to do what I was told pleased Cathair, so he rewarded me with an incentive to continue behaving suitably. If you examine me closer, you'll see the remnants of what happened when I did not meet expectations."

Baring his teeth, the prince clenched his hands. "We might be cruel in battle and to those who require torturing, but..."

"But what? You draw the line at whipping a woman for following orders?"

"Yes."

"I've been a prisoner of war for the last hundred years, Your Highness. I'm under no illusion of what that entails." Accepting more stew, Eivor felt uncomfortable with the strange situation and with Thorne and Rhydwen watching her.

"Well, you don't have to worry about us doing that."

Stirring the bowl's contents while Eivor chewed a piece of meat, Thorne shook her head. "We don't want to hurt you, Eivor."

"But you want to use me," she replied after swallowing her food.

"Yes, but there's no reason you can't work with us. You're a means to an end in the war against Oisin. Afterwards? Now, that's a different game."

Grinning, Rhydwen rested his hands on the side of the bath and leaned down. "It could be a fun game. There's no reason we have to be enemies."

She met his gaze, tempted to delve into his mind. "I thought you wanted to eat me."

"I do. You smelt delicious earlier, despite the stench of fear. Though Thorne has that effect, so it really wasn't a surprise to smell you on her."

Realising what he was talking about, Eivor cursed herself for not catching on sooner. She had jumped to conclusions based on the reputation of the goblins. Watching the emotions flicker over her face, Rhydwen laughed.

"Now that's precious. You thought I wanted to eat your flesh."

"It was a reasonable assumption," she muttered crankily.

"True."

"Rhyd, please stop distracting Eivor. This isn't a comfortable spot to sit, and I'd like to get her to bed before dawn," Thorne said, shoving another spoonful into Eivor's mouth.

Straightening, he grinned. "Excellent idea. I'll see to preparing her bed."

Before he left the room, Thorne met his gaze. "Alone, Rhydwen."

"That's no fun."

"She needs rest."

Eyes darting between them, Eivor realised she did not know what she was dealing with, and a part of her was excited by the prospect.

# SEVEN

"Your Majesty, it's time to get up."

Batting away the hands shaking her shoulder, Eivor grumbled. She wanted to stay buried beneath the piles of blankets. The lingering effects of a headache remained; jagged claws anchored in her mind, deterring her from uncovering her face. It was light outside, and the thought of exposing her eyes to it added to the pain threatening to bloom into something worse.

"Please shut the drapes," she mumbled. "My head hurts."

The maid left her alone, hurrying to the window to draw the heavy fabric over it. "You stay right there, my queen. I shall fetch a healer."

"No, please, don't go to the healers. Lord Cathair forbids them from tending to me without his permission. Asking them to come will get me in trouble."

"Don't you remember what happened?"

Lifting her head, Eivor peered out from beneath the blanket. "I..."

"The invasion. Lord Cathair is imprisoned and awaiting your judgement."

She shot upright, a pillow tumbling to the ground. Memories rushed through her mind, driving Eivor to lift her hands to check for the cuffs. Seeing them gone confirmed the truth of everything she remembered. Reaching for her magic, she groaned with relief. It flooded her veins, a welcome sensation after so many years without the connection. Unfortunately, it did not banish her headache, and Eivor pressed her fingertips to her temples. She wanted the pain to ease so she could think clearly enough to make sense of things.

"It was yesterday?"

"Last night, Majesty. The sun rose a few hours ago, but I thought it best to let you sleep. Everyone is nervous about what to expect with the gob—Prince Rhydwen in charge. You need to be seen."

Groaning, Eivor muttered, "I need something for this headache."

"I'll send for a healer."

"Thank you."

"There is water next to the bed. I was instructed to make sure you drank."

Screwing her face up, Eivor peered at the waiting drink and knew who had left it. Her memories remained muddled, but she recalled Thorne pushing her to eat and drink. One of the last things she remembered was being fed stew in the bath while Rhydwen looked on. After that, Eivor was uncertain about what happened. Including how she got to bed. Snatching the cup from the table, she made a point of drinking it while the maid observed.

"Excellent, Majesty. I'll send for a healer and food."

"Have you been instructed to make sure I eat?"

The maid smiled faintly. "How did you know?"

Grinding her teeth, Eivor latched onto her frustration. It was something to hold close as an anchor in the swirl of confusion. Despite what Thorne had told her, she had doubts. She needed to know where she stood and how much freedom her new captors would allow. Diwan had begrudgingly accepted Cathair's leadership because he was a duine. Rhydwen was a goblin, and where her people had not protested the Talaroonans, they would likely resist him.

Burying back under the blankets, Eivor heard the maid chuckle. Footsteps confirmed her departure, leaving the queen free to drift in silence. With the tendrils of pain planted firmly in her mind, she wanted to avoid thinking as much as possible. Silence had never been something her thoughts could achieve. As a youth mastering her magic, Eivor struggled to find a calm centre for her focus. It took longer than most youths to discover her quiet, but she located what she needed in the end. Found it deep within the darkness.

Focused on her power, Eivor let her mind slip down into it. After years of separation, she needed to familiarise herself with the connections. She knew what she had done to the guards was a dangerous act born of anger and could have easily harmed her. Before she tried to wield her magic in such a manner again, Eivor wanted to be confident she had control of it and not the other way around. When she lost control, no one was safe.

"Your Majesty, I have a healer."

Grumbling, Eivor tugged the blanket away from her face. "Wonderful. Give me something for this headache, please."

"I have orders to examine you, Queen Eivor."

She did not recognise the voice, but the accent reminded her of the red-haired prince. It told her the woman was a goblin, and the orders likely came from Rhydwen. Or Thorne. Probably both. Keeping her eyes shut to stave off the throbbing pain behind them, Eivor waved vaguely in the healer's direction.

"Fine, do what you must."

"Are you happy to remain where you are?"

"I'd prefer it, to be honest. This headache started last night, and I'm afraid I'll empty what little contents I have in my stomach."

Huffing, the healer approached the bed and pulled back the blankets covering Eivor. She stared at the scars decorating the other woman, shooting a look at the one who had fetched her. Arms clasped behind her back, the maid nodded once in confirmation. They might not have been in the city for long, but her prince had warned her of what had been done to the queen. Knowing there were wounds on Eivor's back, the healer gently encouraged her to roll over so she could inspect them.

"How dare a man do this to you," she muttered angrily, tracing the welts. "This is an insult to the sanctity of life."

"Not everyone shares the beliefs of your people, healer," Eivor replied.

Magic danced across the cuts, pouring out of the goblin's fingers to knit flesh together. "They should. As the givers of life, we are superior."

The ache in her back faded, taking away some of the pain in her head. "You did not need to heal those. They were mending on their own."

"Prince Rhydwen asked me to tend to you. He said they cut off your magic for years, which explains the slow healing and the scarring. The daoine are only as strong as their connection to their magic. Without it, you slowly wither away."

"You know a lot about my people?"

"A long time ago, my duties included serving the arenas."

Curiosity ate at Eivor. "Did you ever heal my father?"

Stroking her fingers over a collection of scars, the healer sighed. "Aye, a few times. Craven was a bold fighter, willing to take risks when others were not. The gods favoured him."

"Should I fear your prince?"

"No. Though feeling your magic, I suspect he should fear you."

It felt like being bathed in sunlight. The healer's magic worked through her, repairing what damage it could. Not all the scars from Cathair's treatment could be smoothed over, but she did her best. Queen Calista had given her orders to keep Eivor healthy. Judging by her state, it would take time and effort to restore her physical health.

She did not know if Rhydwen was aware of his mother's plans. Glancing at the maid, the healer inclined her head at the door, indicating the other woman should go. Uncomfortable leaving her queen alone with a goblin, even if she was a healer, the maid hesitated, but a second look had her hurrying out.

"Roll onto your back."

Eivor grumbled, unwilling to move. "Must I?"

"Yes."

"Why?"

"Because I told you to." Rolling her eyes, the healer encouraged Eivor to move. "I'm here to help you, Queen Eivor. Hopefully, what I'm about to tell you will assure you that you can trust me to want what is best for your health."

Flopping over, Eivor peered at the healer in fascination. "Colour me curious."

Inspecting the scars on the front of her body, the healer clicked her tongue in frustration. "I hear they have the bastard who did this in chains."

"Waiting for me to deliver my justice."

"Please tell me you intend to make it painful."

"And slow."

"Good. My queen selected me personally to come with her son to liberate Diwan from Oisin's control. She knows his ways, so we expected you to need help to recover."

"For what purpose?"

Her fingers dug into Eivor's stomach, magic seeking the scar tissue she could heal. "Rhydwen is her child, but Queen Calista has little use for a son. She is, however, curious to find out if goblins can inherit certain powers. To that end, she is willing to give you her only son, your freedom, and your kingdom if you give her grandchildren."

Spluttering, Eivor lifted herself onto her elbows to stare at the healer in shock. "What?"

"There's nothing wrong with your hearing, so I know I don't need to repeat myself."

"And if I refuse?"

"Then you'll find out what the prison cells look like beneath the Spire."

"So, my choice of cages?"

Perching on the side of the bed, she studied Eivor. "I think you're misjudging who is in a cage. If you reject Rhydwen, she may decide he has no use. We are mortal now."

"Am I supposed to care what happens to him?"

"No, but he is pretty to look at. It would be a shame to kill him."

Laughing at the comment, Eivor agreed. "Yes, he is rather pretty. Does your queen think I'm so easily swayed as to fall into lust over some good looks?"

"You don't have to marry the man. Just use him to sire some of your children. He's a good man, despite everything, and he would be a wonderful father."

Her amusement faded at the seriousness of the healer's expression. Rubbing her face, Eivor did not know how to respond. It felt like a trap that would only lead to another cage with no chance of escape. Refusing Calista was a guaranteed return to imprisonment, but the thought of accepting the terms offered for her freedom left her feeling sick. She knew of arrangements like what was being proposed. Oisin had attempted to secure Silaine through one, but their parents had denied him and set into motion the downfall of Diwan.

"How do I know this isn't a trick?"

"I have letters and documents for you from my queen. You need to read them before you decide what path to tread. Queen Calista is nothing if not thorough. She wants this, and she will negotiate reasonable terms to get it."

"Does he know?"

Bringing her hands to Eivor's head, the healer shrugged. "No idea. And as I suspected, your headache is a combination of neglect, stress, and your body adjusting to the return of your magic. You'll need to take things slowly while you recover. The first step is ensuring you eat regularly. With your magic restrained, you failed to recognise your body's needs, but that didn't stop your power from consuming energy."

"I suppose it didn't help that I drank many of my days away."

"Depression does that. You sought a way to cope, and I imagine it suited Cathair to have you half-drunk most of the time." Withdrawing her hands, the healer smiled. "Now, how do you feel?"

The pounding in her head had lessened, leaving a gnawing in her stomach that demanded to be fed. It was an appetite for food that Eivor had not felt in a long time. She knew the maid had planned on summoning breakfast for her, but not if it had arrived.

"I'm hungry. I'd also really like to sit in the gardens."

"The hunger is to be expected. Why the gardens?"

"I haven't left the palace in a hundred years. Occasionally, I was allowed out on a rooftop. I want to smell the flowers, touch the grass, and hear the rustle of leaves in the breeze."

Rising, the healer nodded in understanding. "The first thing I did when we were freed from our imprisonment in the Veil was jump in a puddle."

"You haven't told me your name."

"Jola. Now, I will sort out some medicines for you to help replenish what your body has lost. Get out of bed and clean yourself up. I'll send in the maid."

"And then what?" Eivor said.

Arching a brow, Jola snorted. "How would I know? I'm just a healer. I'd start with going over the papers from Queen Calista. At least you'll know where you stand before you attempt to make sense of ruling your kingdom."

Left alone to drag herself out of bed, Eivor felt like someone had dropped her off a balcony. While her body ached less, she realised the reality of what came next was something she was ill-prepared for. Her parents had raised her in the leadership of a Diwan that no longer existed. The isolation Eivor had endured left her with no idea of the kingdom's state. She did not know how the harvests had been or what was going on with trade.

"Feeling better, Your Majesty?"

"Yes," she replied, knowing it was a lie. "I need to look in command today."

Tutting, the maid waved her towards the dresser. "Don't worry, I know what you need. Perhaps you should start on that bramble resembling hair."

"Excuse me?"

"Look in the mirror."

Standing in front of a mirror, Eivor's eyes widened at the sight of her hair. Instead of her normal sleek appearance, knots had turned it into a mess sticking out in every direction. It added to her questions about how she ended up in bed when the last thing she remembered was being in the bath. Swiping a hand across her face, Eivor kept moving into the bathroom to deal with more pressing needs. When she returned, the maid had finished laying out a dress, and she admired the choice before crossing to the dresser.

"May I ask what you did to create this mess?"

"I mustn't have brushed it after my bath." Flinching when the maid put the brush to the tangled mess, Eivor dug her nails into her knees as a distraction. "Between the headache and the tiredness, I don't recall going to bed. It was a stressful night."

Nodding sadly, she did her best not to hurt the queen. "I left you and soon found myself rounded up by goblins along with others and ushered into chambers. It didn't matter what I said about needing to get back to you, they wouldn't release us."

"I'm glad they didn't harm you."

"They only attacked Talaroonan soldiers. Nobles were gathered and locked away to be dealt with. The rest of us were questioned and released back to our duties. By then, you were asleep with a dullaghan watching over you."

"Thorne was with me?"

"Sitting where you are. She told me to make you drink water and eat when you woke, then left me to look after you."

Lips thinning, Eivor tried to remember what happened. "I suppose she wanted to make sure their newly captive queen didn't do something stupid."

"I'm sure that's it." Smiling faintly, the maid caught her gaze in the mirror.

Falling silent, she mulled over the situation while having her hair brushed until it was a tame mass of black and white. Weaving it into a simple braid, the maid left strands loose to hand on each side of Eivor's face. Satisfied with her efforts, she instructed the queen to stand so she could dress her. By the time it was done, Eivor was pleased with her appearance.

"You must be starving, Majesty."

"I am."

Ushering her through to the next chamber, the maid was pleased to see the food she requested was on the table. Fussing at the other end of the table, Jola sorted through a collection of pouches. She looked up, brows creasing at the sight of them.

"Oh good, you tamed the hair."

Snorting, the maid returned to the bedroom to tidy up while Eivor approached the table. Before she selected an item to eat, Jola shoved a mug into her hand and pointed at the slices of bread. She sniffed the cup and screwed up her face at the bitter scent.

"What is it?"

"Good for you. Before you drink it, have a slice of bread. You need something plain in your stomach or you'll throw up."

Accepting the advice, Eivor selected a piece and nibbled the corner. It had a hint of warmth from the oven. Bursts of flavour informed her it was not as plain as it appeared, herbs lending it a taste that needed no improvement. Taking care not to eat too quickly, she sipped at the drink Jola had prepared.

Medicines were not her interest, but the blend resembled something Eivor remembered her mother making. Closing her eyes, she let the memories swam her mind of her mother mixing herbs while telling stories of distant places she had visited as a Raven. They were a comfort.

"Can't say I've seen someone look like they're enjoying my mixtures," Jola said, cocking her head curiously. "Or is it something else?"

"My mother."

"Ah, yes, Malena. She was outstanding."

"You knew her?"

"I did. We weren't enemies, no matter what you might have heard. Perception is strange, and sometimes a fearsome reputation is more story than fact."

Finishing her bread and the drink, Eivor frowned. "What do you mean?"

"Everyone thinks of the Executioner and the Ravens as... I'm not sure how to describe it. In truth, they simply followed orders. If someone upset the gods, they delivered punishment. That was what Death created them to do. The dragons and their riders were created for much the same purpose."

"I saw my mother's scars. The reward for her service."

"The only people who took pleasure in what happened were Oisin, Cathair, and their ilk. For the rest of us, what Annawyn did to Oblivion, the Ravens, and their danann mates was a reminder of what happens when you displease the gods."

"Why does your queen want to destroy Oisin?"

"Because when we were released, and Annawyn demanded subservience, he refused the call. Calista's second daughter was sent to deal with him, and she paid the price of his defiance. Annawyn all but destroyed her mind. Her suffering was ended peacefully when the god of life made us mortal."

Inhaling sharply, Eivor understood Calista's desire for revenge. "Why didn't Annawyn kill Oisin?"

"Despite his defiance, she had a soft spot for him. That, and she was too busy plotting her destruction of Tir to spite the memory of Shianeni. Punishing Maribel was an immediate reaction, but my queen blames Oisin. Rightly or wrongly, here we are."

"Oisin killed my parents in front of me. He tortured and raped me. I would gladly deliver him to Queen Calista for the chance to join her in making him pay."

Placing a bundle of papers in front of Eivor, Jola sighed. "Sit, start reading those, and I'll bring you a plate of food. This isn't what I would have requested from the kitchen, but I'll just be thankful if you eat."

"I'm a little old for a nursemaid."

"No, you're not."

Grabbing the bundle, Eivor did not argue with the healer and wandered over to the lounge. Noticing her sketches still on the low table, she realised someone had spread them out to examine them. Making herself comfortable, she untied the silk ribbon holding the different folded documents together and broke the seal. Calista had numbered them, the elegant script making her smile. Unfolding the first letter, Eivor prepared for whatever it held. Her eyes followed the lines of writing that explained what the goblin queen wanted and why.

Lifting her gaze from the page, she stared at Jola. "I wasn't expecting this."

"I'm not privy to her words."

"This is all very strange."

"Yes, I imagine it is."

Waving the letter around, Eivor wished her father was there to discuss it with her. "How is it that the hardest part to understand is that she has provided me with multiple copies of her proposed treaty so I can have my advisers look over them and keep them on record? Where's the trap?"

"Why does there have to be a trap?" Jola placed a plate of food on the lounge next to her. "It could simply be an opportunity for you to take advantage of."

"I would argue we're not entering this negotiation on equal terms."

"True."

"But what do I have to lose by agreeing? Queen Calista is offering me everything, and all I must do is keep her son as a lover and have his children. I mean, that's it. I'll have my throne, freedom for my people, an ally that strikes fear into most without lifting a claw... and I'll get my revenge."

Jola noticed the maid watching from the doorway and nodded. "Or you could look at it as an opportunity for new beginnings. Rhydwen isn't a terrible man."

"No, I'm sure his mother has made him awfully keen to please."

"Eat. You can't think clearly on an empty stomach and with a body demanding more fuel than you provide. Besides, you don't need to decide today. Her majesty would much rather you consider your options. It gives you time to get to know Rhydwen. Torture might be the preferable choice once you've had a conversation or two with him."

Selecting a piece of fruit, Eivor chuckled. "Does conversation matter? He's only got one purpose here, and I don't need him to talk to do it."

Snickering, the maid could not resist saying, "You could keep him gagged."

"Tempting."

The entire situation seemed increasingly odd, leaving Eivor questioning if she had finally broken down under the pressure of captivity. She did not know if she hoped she had. Finishing her fruit, she reached for another piece and bit into it while her thoughts chased in circles. Jola returned to the table to fuss over her pouches of herbs while the maid quietly tidied around the chamber.

"I don't think I'm going to mention this to Prince Rhydwen," she said.

"Why?"

"Because if he doesn't know, I'll get to see a version of him that isn't trying to win me over. If I tell him, he'll go out of his way to preserve his life."

Humming thoughtfully, Jola nodded. "This is true."

Eivor smiled slowly, staring at the unlit fire. "Besides, it could be fun. Let him think he has the power here, only to put him in his place when I get bored with the game."

"Queen Calista would approve."

"Though if he knows..."

"It's not like other places don't make arrangements like this." Jola glanced at her.

Licking her fingers to chase the juice dripping along them, Eivor shrugged. "I always knew my parents would have a say over my choice if I had children. My first concern is the possessive nature of goblins."

"You're worried if you accept the prince, he won't like you having other lovers?" Jola's mouth twisted in understanding. "He's a man, Your Majesty. It's not his decision, it's yours. Let him be jealous. It'll make him keener to please you."

Leaning back on the lounge, Eivor bit into a strawberry and waved it at the healer. "You know, I think I like that approach. I'm going to look forward to learning more about goblin culture."

# EIGHT

Walking around the table, Eivor recalled the last time she had set foot in the chamber. It had been the final emergency council session in the hours before Oisin invaded. Her father had dominated the meeting, issuing orders to the commanders of their army. They had not known how doomed their defence was. Husk makers had cut through their front lines, taking out integral sections and allowing the Talaroonan forces to break through. Those memories tormented her dreams, the screams of their soldiers as husk makers sucked their life energy out of them.

Eivor stood behind the chair where her father had once sat. She knew Cathair had taken it as his own, and she wanted to burn the memory of him from the wood. Watching her from the side, Jola was a silent presence. They were waiting for Cathair's advisers to be delivered to the chamber. Until they arrived, Eivor used the time to face the memories. It had only been a hundred years, but it felt like longer since she had sat by her father's side, learning the art of ruling.

"It's strange to think how much time I spent in this room," she said. "Listening, learning, arguing, making plans... and now I'm forced to admit I'll never hear my father speak again. I'm alone, and somehow, I need to live up to his legacy."

"How old were you when he first brought you in here?"

Humming, Eivor stroked the heavy chair. "I don't remember."

"Do you think he brought you here from the beginning?"

"Maybe. It's possible. I miss him."

Jola approached the table, leaning on the back of a chair. "So long as you remember him, he's here with you. What happened is not your fault."

"I know."

"Do you?"

"Are you trying to get into my mind, healer?"

"Helping you is my duty, Majesty. You know as well as I do, the mind and body are inseparable. If the mind is ill, the body will soon follow. You are allowed to feel whatever you need to feel about what you went through."

Staring at her from the end of the table, Eivor frowned and wondered if she should sit. The conversation was too much to face when she knew people could arrive at any point. She did not know how many of her father's advisers remained. It was another pressure to contemplate alongside her lack of awareness of the state of affairs in Diwan. If she focused on the kingdom, Eivor hoped it would help everything else settle into place. Including what she would do about her decision.

"I don't know what Cathair has done to my kingdom. I assume Diwan is still relatively prosperous, because why would they waste it? My father taught me to rule, except I've never done it without him. He certainly didn't teach me to take back control after being invaded."

"You're 3000 years old, Eivor." Jola smiled knowingly and inclined her head at the door. "And you're a powerful mind mage. Make these people obey."

"Even the ones from Talaroo who answer to Oisin?"

"Make them kneel. They should grovel for your mercy."

Making an appreciative sound, Eivor swept her gaze across the table. "Why do I have the feeling you're going to be a bad influence on me?"

"Because I'm encouraging you to embrace your power and position?"

"When you put it that way."

"There is no other way to put it." Jola gave her an arched look that left no room for argument.

Slipping into the chair, she placed her hands on the table like she had seen her father do countless times. For a moment, Eivor thought she felt him standing beside her. It was impossible. His spirit was not bound to his bones, there was no reaching out to him across the Veil. Oisin had burnt the bodies of her parents while she watched, helpless to do anything. The last thing her father had said to her was to be strong.

"You're right, Jola."

"Of course I am. I know what I'm talking about."

Flicking her hand at the seat next to her, Eivor inclined her head. "I could use your help to navigate through interactions with your fellows."

"Well, the important thing to remember is while Prince Rhydwen is... I hesitate to say, in charge, but I suppose he is. Anyway, the point is the officers in charge of our forces are all women. Once you earn their respect, they'll follow you happily."

"They don't respect the prince?"

"No, most certainly not. He is simply a figurehead. They have their orders from the queen, including indulging her son. General Vesta is the actual leader."

Drumming her fingers on the table, Eivor felt sympathy for Rhydwen. She had spent the last hundred years being a figurehead. Cathair and Oisin had turned her into a puppet queen, but Rhydwen did not even have that. If she accepted the terms of Queen Calista's treaty, he would become her puppet instead. Biting her lip, Eivor imagined commanding the arrogant red-haired prince to kneel at her feet while knowing she was the one with all the power and he had to please her.

"What is the best way to win their respect?"

"Show them you're in control and are someone to fear despite everything."

Hearing the doors opening, Eivor smiled at Jola. "I believe I can do that."

Returning the smile, she moved to stand behind the queen. "I'm confident you can."

The first person to enter the chamber was a goblin soldier, her eyes narrowing at the sight of Eivor and Jola. Another led in an unfamiliar duine man. When he saw Eivor, his lips curled in a sneer, and the look in his eyes told her he was one of Cathair's advisers. Arching a brow, she beckoned him close and watched the scorn.

"Where is Lord Cathair?"

"Did I ask you to speak?" Eivor did not move. "Bring him here."

Smirking at her tone, the second soldier pushed the man forward. "Go on then, kneel before your queen and beg for your pathetic life."

"When King Oisin hears—"

Lips curling, Eivor crooked a finger, and her power wrapped around him. "Oh, we're counting on the bastard hearing. Now, come here and beg."

Unable to resist the tendrils of magic clawing at his mind, the man stumbled free of the soldier's grasp and dropped to his knees next to Eivor's chair. Gazing at him in contempt, Jola waited to see what the queen would do. She knew the two women on the other side of the room planned to spread the word of what they witnessed.

"Are you from Talaroo?" Eivor did not look at him and studied the soldiers instead.

"Yes."

"Why are you loyal to Oisin?"

"Because he is my king. I have served him for millennia."

She tutted in disappointment. "That's unfortunate. What did Cathair have you doing here?"

"I helped keep the Diwanian nobles under control."

"Anything else? Anything useful to the running of my kingdom?"

"I tracked down and removed dissidents from the court."

Wondering how many of her people had died because of the kneeling man, Eivor decided he needed to be used to make a point. Slowly shifting her gaze to him, she thought of the bodies Cathair and Oisin had strung up on the walls to ensure compliance. He had been part of that.

"Well, thank you for telling me how little value you have." Smiling at the two women, Eivor nodded. "He's all yours, but I want him to suffer before he dies."

"You don't want to do it yourself?" The first woman looked curious.

"Actually…"

Shuffling through her memories, Eivor searched for one that suited her intentions. Images of Oisin and Cathair torturing her filled her mind, but she latched onto the agony of the experience. It was easy to feed it into his mind, keeping the moment looped in his thoughts. He felt everything she had, every cut, burn, and the bite of their whips. The sound of his first scream was music to her ears, and Eivor closed her eyes, smiling contentedly. Recalling her pain was unpleasant, but worth it to make him suffer.

Coming forward to haul him up, the soldier grinned. "What did you do?"

"He thinks he's being tortured by the two men he's loyal to."

"How long will it last?"

"Until I stop it, or he dies. Enjoy. If his screams get too much, cut out his tongue." Glancing at Jola, Eivor shrugged. "That wouldn't take away from their pleasure, would it? I'd hate to ruin a meal."

The healer eyed the man in distaste. "Considering what they'll do to him will make him scream, it won't be an issue. They're always tastier when they scream themselves hoarse."

"Excellent. I'm sure there will be more of them. Bring in the next."

The two soldiers exchanged delighted grins before dragging the screaming man out. Eivor watched them go, lips curled in a tiny smile. She did not need Jola to say anything to know she was pleased with what had happened. Once the door fell shut, Eivor leaned forward, resting her elbows on the table with her hands laced beneath her chin.

"Well, did I make a good impression?"

"Did you use the memories of your suffering on that man?"

"Yes."

Jola grunted, eyes narrowing. "Are you—"

"I'm fine."

"You'll need to talk to someone about what you went through."

Her lips thinned. "What I need is to take control of my kingdom and punish those who took everything good from my life. I don't need to talk. I know what happened to me."

"As you wish. The next adviser is coming."

It did not surprise Eivor when the next duine escorted in by a pair of goblins was another man she did not recognise. There was a mix of terror and resentment in his eyes when she signalled for him to be brought close. From the eager expressions of his guards, they knew what she had done to the last one. Eagerness became excitement when Eivor delivered him into their hands, screaming in terror at the memories buffeting his mind. He was not the only one to be dragged from the council chambers without the ability to stand.

With each Talaroonan loyalist brought before Eivor, Jola grew increasingly concerned. She knew what the queen was doing, even if no one else did. Her power sensed Eivor's waning energy, adding to her concerns. She would exhaust herself if no one stepped in to stop her. Jola wanted to, but the only reason she did not stop the queen was the admiration in the eyes of the goblins bringing their prisoners in to face her justice.

"What's going on?"

The doors burst open, drawing their attention to the woman storming in. Thorne looked at Eivor before shifting her gaze to the kneeling duine and two goblins standing to the side. She scowled, moving closer to put a hand on the shoulder of one.

"Give me his name."

"Don't you dare!" Eivor snarled at the dullaghan. "You have no business here."

Smiling coldly, Thorne tightened her grasp on the goblin. "Give me his name."

Ice filled her veins, and the goblin gave Eivor an apologetic look. She knew what Throne was capable of, and she did not fancy dying. Leaning in, she told the dullaghan the name of her prisoner. The moment the hand on her shoulder released her, she scrambled away, followed by her companion. Jola quickly grabbed Eivor to stop her from leaping out of her seat to confront Thorne.

"Jola, take the other two and get out. Queen Eivor and I need to talk."

"I'm not sure that's a good idea," Jola replied.

"I wasn't asking. Get out."

Sighing, she nodded and signalled for the two soldiers to leave. Squeezing Eivor's shoulder, Jola followed them. She would stand on the other side of the door and keep anyone from disturbing whatever unfolded within. Her concern was not for Eivor's life, but for the emotional damage she had inflicted on herself while dealing with each prisoner.

"You have no right to interfere with my handling of those vile men." Slamming her fist on the table, Eivor glared at Thorne. "I'm taking back control of my kingdom."

"There are other ways, Eivor Havard."

"Sure, but this is making me feel better."

Closing her eyes, Thorne embraced the ice of the Veil. "I accept the name given to me."

Breath catching, Eivor watched the dullaghan transform into the headless figure shrouded in black. Stretching their hand out, Thorne pressed their palm against the back of the pleading duine. He gasped once before collapsing. Heart pounding in her chest, Eivor stared and wondered how long Thorne would remain in that form.

"You're done for the day, Eivor."

"I'm done when I say I am!"

Gliding over to her, the headless rider grabbed the chair and moved it. Scrambling away before they could catch her, Eivor drew on her power to protect herself. Doing her best to keep the table between them, she tried to make sense of the strange threads of magic surrounding Thorne. They were the same thinning of the Veil she had sensed the night before, but Eivor did not know if she could influence them. Or if she dared use the side of her power she had always kept secret.

"You don't want to play this game," Thorne said, standing on the other side of the table. "Unless you're hoping for a repeat of last night."

Reminded of the icy hand on her throat, Eivor shivered. "I'm not sure I'm safe, so forgive me for wanting to keep my distance from you."

"You realise how pointless that is?"

"How did I end up in bed?"

Thorne crossed their arms. "I put you there when you fell asleep in the bath."

"Did you..."

"Did I what?"

Glancing away, she felt ridiculous for broaching the subject. "Do anything to me."

"You were asleep."

"So?"

"Cathair?" Unfolding their arms to grip the back of a chair, Thorne remained in headless form, and the temperature dropped further. "Did he do things to you when you slept?"

"Why are you here?"

"Eivor."

Waving at Thorne dismissively, she started for the door. "If you're going to disrupt my work, I may as well take a break and go for a walk."

"You need to eat and rest. Ask Jola if you don't believe me."

"And as I told Jola, I don't need a nursemaid."

Frustrated by her attitude, Thorne reached out with their power and stepped through the Veil. It was easier to use the distorted space to close in on Eivor than chase her around the chamber. They returned to the land of the living and grabbed her arm, yanking the queen away from the door before she could open it.

Yelping, Eivor swung a fist at where Thorne's head should have been. Connecting with nothing, she felt an icy fire spreading down her arm and through her body when her hand passed through the weave of magic.

"You silly girl."

Clutching her hand to her body, Eivor whimpered, "Please stop it."

Scooping the queen into their arms, Thorne kicked the door to signal for Jola. The healer pushed it open and growled at the sight of Eivor. Ignoring her, the dullaghan walked through and waited for the crowd of goblins and prisoners to move.

"What did you do to her?" Jola demanded, getting in Thorne's way.

"I didn't do anything to the queen. She tried to punch me in the face."

A surprised murmur spread through the goblins. Pinching the bridge of her nose, Jola was thankful for Thorne's admission. They would respect Eivor's attempt to harm a dullaghan with her bare fist, even if it could have cost her life. Hurrying after Thorne, the healer was concerned it still might. She did not know what to make of the information her magic was giving her about Eivor's state. People did not touch the space where a dullaghan's head was not. But if the pained whimpers escaping Eivor's lips were anything to go by, punching Thorne was a decision she regretted.

"How do I help her?"

Thorne kept walking. "You don't."

"She can't die."

"Don't you have better things to do?"

"Queen Eivor is my responsibility!" Jola wanted to make the dullaghan stop but understood the urgency in their stride. "Will this maim her permanently?"

"She has a connection to Death's power, so the likeliness is this will do nothing to her other than cause a great deal of pain."

Clenching her jaw, Eivor wanted to scream. It felt like her entire arm had frozen while the ice continued to spread through the rest of her body. Her attempts to move her fingers increased the agony, and her magic did nothing to soften the pain.

"Please make it stop," she whispered.

"I will as soon as we're in your quarters."

Goblin guards lurked in the hallway outside Eivor's chambers. They opened the door to admit the group without asking questions. Hurrying to where she had left her bag of medicines, Jola frowned when Thorne continued through to the next room.

"I'll be right there!" she called out.

"Leave! You're not needed."

Laying Eivor down on her bed, Thorne stepped back and released their hold on their headless state. Entering the chamber in time to see it, Jola huffed.

"I'm not leaving until I'm sure she's fine."

"Are you arguing with me?" Cocking his head, Thorne rolled Eivor over and reached for the laces on the back of her dress. "Go away and make sure no one disturbs us."

"You can't be serious!"

"Now, Jola."

Her claws appeared, and she snarled. "If you hurt her!"

He gave up, ripping the bodice open to drag it off her arms for a clear view of her bluish skin. Against her better judgement, Jola left them alone. She did not want to, but Thorne was a dullaghan, and she had no power to stop his kind. Struggling to get away, Eivor cried in pain when he grabbed her numb hand and pinned it above her head before reaching for the other one.

"Stop fighting it, Eivor Havard," Thorne murmured. "The more you fight, the more it will hurt. Trust your magic to know what to do."

"I can't."

Feeling the chill of her skin, he tightened his grasp on her hands. "Breath in and focus on my hands. Let go of your magic."

She wanted to do what he told her, but panic gripped her mind. The cold was everywhere, leaving Eivor uncertain she would ever feel warm again. If it did not stop her heart. She wondered if this was a slower version of how dullaghan killed their victims. Inhaling deeply, it seemed as though her lungs had filled with shards of ice. Struggling to turn her focus to the hand holding her wrists together, Eivor realised she felt a press of lips on her neck. They moved, caressing her throat before capturing her mouth to draw the breath from her lungs.

"The cold is my power." Thorne caressed her side with his free hand before returning his lips to hers. "Give it back to me, pretty magpie. Let it return to where it belongs."

Darkness crept at the edge of her vision, threatening to drag Eivor down. Responding to her fear, her magic slid through the encroaching coldness and found the familiar threads. They clung to her fingers, sticky tendrils of power that Thorne reached for, his hand entwined in hers. It felt like her lungs were burning with a desperate need for air, but Eivor kept kissing him. He was above her, around her, and the only thing that still made sense in the chaos of her mind. Drowning in his ice was almost peaceful.

"Good girl," he murmured against her lips.

"Please."

Slipping his free hand beneath the ruined dress, Thorne stroked her cunt. "You need to eat and sit beside a fire wrapped in blankets."

"No," she whimpered.

"Yes. Show me how good you can be, and maybe I'll reward you tonight."

Leaving her laid out on the bed, Thorne stood and straightened his coat. Chest heaving, Eivor realised she still felt cold, even if it was no longer burning through her. There was a lingering numbness to the hand that had passed through the space where Thorne's head had not been. Flexing her fingers, she flinched.

"I don't understand what happened."

"When we're in our headless form, our heads are on the other side of the Veil. It is what allows us to track our victims and stop their hearts. You put your hand into that space."

Rolling onto her side, Eivor stared at him. "Would it have killed me?"

"It should have killed you the moment you touched it. I told you, you've got threads of Death's power through your magic. Count yourself lucky."

"How did you know how to save me?"

Mouth twisting, Thorne held her gaze. "I didn't."

"So, I could have died?"

"Yes."

"Note to self, don't do that again."

"I'll let Jola know she can examine you. Remember what I told you to do?"

Eivor rolled her eyes and struggled to sit up. "I don't take orders from you."

Burying a hand in her hair, Thorne smirked. "Protest if it makes you feel better, but I know the thought of me telling you how good you've been gives you pleasure."

"It does not."

"As I said, protest. You want to hear me say those words in your ear."

His fingers dug into her scalp and Eivor did not dare fight it. Tilting her head back, Thorne leaned down, brushing his lips over her cheek on his way to her ear. Biting her lip, she swallowed a whimper at the chill left behind by his touch.

"Behave yourself, and I'll show you what good girls get as a reward."

# NINE

"Well, I guess I should be relieved." Slumping onto the table when she heard the door click shut, Eivor groaned. "My kingdom is not in complete disarray."

"Drink," Jola murmured, sliding a mug of something sweet-smelling across the table.

"Must I?"

"It'll help stop that headache at the back of your skull."

Massaging her neck, Eivor could not argue with pain relief. "I can think of other things to help take care of it. A pair of firm hands and some lavender oil…"

"You're having dinner with Prince Rhydwen. Perhaps you can ask him to lend his muscular hands after your meal. If he's no good at the task, we'll find someone to teach him."

"I'm still unsure if I should talk to him about Queen Calista's treaty. His mother is giving him to me to keep as a concubine, so I suppose I should mention something. Then again, the games I could play if he's unaware."

Selecting a seat at the table, Jola studied Eivor thoughtfully. She understood the desire to find control wherever possible, but she doubted toying with Rhydwen would provide the queen with as much satisfaction as she hoped. In the three days since they liberated Diwan from Talaroo and imprisoned Cathair, Jola had watched her claw her way into command.

It was admirable. Many of the goblin officers admitted their appreciation of her firm stance on dealing with Talaroonan loyalists and a willingness to work with them. Eivor had dined with them every day, dividing them into smaller groups to allow for a better opportunity to get to know them. She was a politician; she knew how to win support.

"Would you like my advice?"

"About what?"

"The prince. I've known him all his life. I was the queen's personal healer during her pregnancies with each of her children. Be honest with him. Rhydwen has been the subject of games since birth, and as a result, he doesn't trust easily. Except for one person."

Curious, Eivor took a sip of the pain relief. "I assume you mean Thorne."

"Yes. Thorne has always been honest with Rhydwen. If you want to make the best of your alliance, then having him resent you for playing games with his life is probably not the way to start. You've been through enough torment without inflicting it on each other. Wouldn't you rather have peace in your life?"

"I grew up watching my parents working as a team to rule Diwan. When it was just family, my father was a different man. They trusted each other to alleviate the strain of leadership and be safe to let down their guard. I understand your point about not inflicting torment on each other. But my parents chose each other. Their relationship was not the result of a treaty."

"No, it wasn't. But you're mistaken about one thing. Craven approached Malena with an offer to build something together after the Sundering. It was an alliance, much like what Queen Calista has proposed. I'm suggesting you approach Rhydwen like your father approached your mother. That is, with a plan."

Humming, she drained the last of the drink Jola had given her. "He's in love with Thorne. How cooperative do you think he will be?"

"He's also in love with being alive. Be honest with Rhydwen; make him your partner in this treaty instead of your pawn. It'll make your life easier."

"We're going after Oisin together."

"Yes. Do you want to fight a war out there and in bed?"

"No."

Jola tapped the table pointedly. "Well then, take my advice. Tell him the truth and negotiate where you stand. You're going to have to bed him for the treaty, so why not make it fair from the onset? Be a team, just like your parents were."

"Thank you for the advice. You're right; I don't want to fight everyone. When the day was over, my parents could wrap their arms around each other and breathe. They could relax and let the mask fall. I want freedom, and since Rhydwen is the price of keeping both my life and my liberty..."

"I'll arrange for his favourite wine to accompany dinner. You can ply him with alcohol, the information about the treaty, and then ask him to give you a massage."

Snorting, Eivor said, "Prince Rhydwen, here's some meat, some wine, your mother is giving you to me as part of a treaty and oh, do you mind giving me a massage?"

"Exactly."

"What is his favourite wine?"

"Raspberry."

Eivor rose from her seat, smiling in delight. "A fine choice. I hope we have some in the cellars. Did you also request for our meal be some of his favourite foods?"

"I requested a nutritious meal you'll both enjoy," Jola replied, standing to stretch before she followed Eivor. "I'm glad your appetite has returned. It's a sign your body and magic are working in unity again. You'll start putting on weight soon."

A pair of goblin guards waited outside the chamber doors to accompany Eivor. She looked forward to selecting her protection, but they needed to prove which soldiers were loyal to Diwan. Oisin and Cathair had killed most of the Diwanian army during the invasion, leaving only those who surrendered. Of those, they had removed most from duty or sent them to distant parts of Talaroo. Until they could sort out a new army for Diwan, the only protection they had was the goblins.

"I'm glad you insisted I finish up for the day. Some time to myself before dinner would be nice." Eivor did not hurry on her way to her chambers. "Maybe I'll read a book."

"Rhydwen enjoys reading."

"I'm sure he does. From what you've told me, it sounds as though Queen Calista treated him like a decorative pet. What use is he to me? Besides the obvious..."

"He might not have any power or influence in his mother's court, but that doesn't mean he hasn't learnt a lot. Rhydwen is a warrior, educated in strategy, and knows how to sweet talk a crowd like his life depends on it. Sometimes it has."

"Fair enough. It means he's a fast learner and an adaptable one."

The doors to her chambers had a second set of guards, who smiled in greeting when they arrived. None of them accompanied Eivor and Jola inside, confident the queen was safe. Their sense of smell was enough to confirm the rooms were empty. Any whiff of something out of place would set off a search. Inhaling deeply when the door clicked, Jola grunted.

"The servants have been in here recently."

"I envy your ability to smell things."

Jola gave her an arched look from the small table where she kept a few medicines to use on the queen. "Your youngest sister becomes a wolf. Does she have the usual sense of smell in her natural form?"

"Silaine possesses a heightened sense. I used to dismiss it, but I see the usefulness now." Checking on her stack of sketches, Eivor noticed a box beside them.

"What about you?"

"Sharper vision. Useful in court, admittedly. I notice things others might not."

"What have you got there?"

Lifting the lid of the box, she smiled in delight. A dozen small glass pots of coloured powder sat inside, carefully capped to protect the contents. It had been years since she had seen their like, and her fingers itched to work on a drawing good enough to lend splashes of colour to. Humming in approval, she lifted a pot to examine the vibrant red powder that reminded her of Rhydwen's hair.

Joining her, Jola sniffed the box, concerned it was a threat to the queen. Spotting a folded scrap of paper, the healer plucked it out from between tubs and opened it to read the familiar, neat script carrying a message for Eivor.

"It is from the prince. He looks forward to dinner with you."

Blinking in surprise, Eivor realised she had believed them a gift from Thorne. "Oh."

"You don't sound pleased."

"Oh, no, I am. It's a perfect gift, but I didn't expect it to be from him."

Jola knew who she had thought sent it and sighed. Tucking the note back into the box, she patted Eivor's shoulder and headed to the next room. The maid had left a simple but elegant dress on the end of the bed. It was not quite what she suspected Eivor wanted to wear. One thing Jola had noticed after the first day was that the queen liked dark colours and slightly revealing outfits. She took pleasure from the hint of temptation and having people view her as an object of desire. For a mind mage, it was one of the easiest ways to slip into a person's thoughts. Desire lowered defences, allowing Eivor a better grasp over them.

"Do you need help to get out of that dress?" she called to the queen. "I won't stay long. You wanted some quiet time to relax before dinner."

Placing the lid back on the box, Eivor wandered through to her bedroom. "Please."

Fingers moved with ease to loosen the laces holding the gown tight around Eivor's body. While Jola released her from the encasing of silk, she studied the outfit laid out for her. The layers of pale green were not suitable for a private dinner with a prospective lover. Going over her choices, Eivor looked forward to arranging for a tailor to update her wardrobe. Cathair had dictated her clothing, allowing no input from her about what she wanted. It would feel good to have control over that part of her life again.

Shedding the dress like a second skin, Eivor stepped out of the puddle of fabric to stride into the small room with rails of dresses hanging from padded hooks intended to display them suitably. Her fingers caressed fabrics, rubbing embroidery thoughtfully as she regarded her choices. She wanted to present herself attractively to Rhydwen, but she struggled without knowledge of what they considered appealing in the goblin court.

"What does the prince like?"

Appearing in the doorway, Jola was thankful for the window casting light into the smaller space. "What do you mean?"

"Goblins and daoine have different tastes. I don't know what to wear to appeal to him."

"I see." Pinching the fabric of a hideous cream gown, Jola cringed. "Not that."

"Oh gosh no... unless..."

Tapping her chin, Eivor studied the dress Cathair had supplied for a ball. It was another unfashionable creation of silk and linen with puffed out sleeves and far too many layers. She wanted to shred all the outfits like it, and the idea had her lips curling slyly.

"It is rather unappealing and should be destroyed."

"Majesty, what are you thinking?"

"That sometimes being dressed outrageously can have benefits."

Chuckling, Jola nodded as she realised the direction Eivor's thoughts had headed. "An interesting approach, considering you plan to discuss the treaty."

"Exactly. I know he's in love with Thorne, so I'm fighting an uphill battle to win his affections. Not that I need him to be in love with me, but friendship would be lovely."

"Friendship is the most important basis for a lasting relationship."

Inhaling sharply, Eivor brushed aside thoughts of the friends she had lost to Oisin's invasion. "Indeed. Passion only gets you so far."

"And trust."

"I'll tell him the truth."

"Before or after you offer to let him shred that dress from your body with his claws?"

"Telling Rhydwen after the fact would be playing a game."

"Indeed."

Leaving her alone in the room, Jola fetched the dress left by the maid. Eivor was busy pulling the cream creation from its hooks when she returned. The rustle of fabric was noticeable in the quiet, and screwing up her face, she hung the unwanted gown on an empty spot. It was not the first time Jola had surveyed the wardrobe, but this time she considered them from the perspective of what Rhydwen would like. She knew Eivor's plan would work. It would appeal to the goblin's possessive streak. Especially once the prince knew she was the key to his freedom.

"I'll ask around to see if anyone brought court worthy outfits with them. We can collaborate with your tailor to provide designs. Perhaps we can mix court fashions. You're the queen; you should set the trends, not follow them."

"What is Queen Calista like?" Carrying the gown out, Eivor dumped it on her bed. "Does she care about such things? Am I still being the vain princess?"

"My queen is the most beautiful of us, and she likes to ensure everyone knows it."

"Where did the prince get his hair from?"

"Her, and his eyes. The man chosen to father him was tall, broad shouldered and had cheekbones that could cut glass. He was a highly coveted courtesan, and it was no surprise when Calista selected him for her own. Rhydwen might have disappointed her by being born male, but his beauty made up for some of it."

Eivor could not imagine having her worth measured by her looks. Glancing at the mirror, she knew people considered her striking, but next to Rhydwen, her beauty paled. She wondered what their children might look like. Stripping out of her undergarments, Eivor decided she would wear nothing but the gown for her dinner with Rhydwen. There was no point wasting a perfectly good shift and stays if he took her up on her proposal. Pressing a finger to her lips, she went through her collection of jewels and knew what else she needed to wear.

"Thank you, Jola. That should be everything."

"I'll set out what I'd like you to drink before dinner and in the morning. It's the same things you've been taking, including your contraceptive, so don't worry that I'm sneaking in anything."

Laughing, Eivor waved her off and headed back into her wardrobe. "I'll see you tomorrow. Don't forget the wine."

Seeking the drawers of jewellery, she went through them until she found what she was looking for. It was a choker of emeralds set in gold, each gem reminding her of Rhydwen's eyes. Next to it sat the matching bracelets and earrings, and Eivor hoped the prince would appreciate her efforts. Stroking the smooth stones, she imagined being draped over the lounge in the sitting room wearing nothing but the emeralds while he used his tongue to convince her that saying yes to the treaty would not be disappointing.

Eivor gathered her selection, leaving the bracelets behind, and returned to the larger room. She took her time to clean away any traces of dirt before dabbing a small amount of the black raspberry and acai oil on her skin. With the sensitivity of the goblin's nose, she did not want to use too much. Pulling the dress on was a frustrating task, but there was no need to lace it up tightly. It was there simply as an undesired wrapping to entice Rhydwen. The jewellery was far more critical, and she took care to secure them. Releasing her hair from the coiled bun restraining it, Eivor brushed it out and left it hanging over her shoulders.

She did not know how long it would be before Rhydwen arrived. Going through to the sitting room, Eivor located the book she was reading. Settling on the window seat, she gazed out at the darkening sky while her fingers stroked the jewels adorning her throat. It was easy to slip into a vague state in which time lacked meaning, and all she was aware of was the mottled colours of the sunset. Captivity had taught her many ways to pass the days without noticing the dragging hours. Resting her head against the wall, Eivor cradled the book in her lap and memorised every shade and shape of the skyline.

"I knocked," Rhydwen said, startling her out of her daze. "It didn't look like you were napping, but I suppose it's possible the daoine sleep with their eyes open."

Regarding him across the room, Eivor drank in the sight of his red hair drawn back in braids at the sides and curled around under the remaining tresses. A forest green tunic accompanied tight black trousers and a wide belt.

Rhydwen cocked his head, lips curling in dismay as he watched her slip from the seat. The cream gown was not the sleek elegance he had expected to find her in. He tracked Eivor's movements to the table where her sketches and the box of coloured powders sat. When she withdrew several sheets of paper and approached, Rhydwen caught a whiff of a delicious scent lingering on her skin.

"You smell lovely, Majesty."

"Thank you. I'd like you to read those."

Recognising the writing as his mother's, he stiffened and accepted the papers. "What is this? Why do you have letters from Queen Calista?"

"They'll explain everything. Before we continue, you should know what she wants."

Striding over to the lounge, Rhydwen dropped onto it and read through the letter on top. His lips twisted in anger, eyes flicking between the page and the woman watching from a distance. The words did not surprise him, not really. Before they left the Spire, Calista had hinted that his future depended on securing Eivor. He had wrongfully assumed she wanted the Raven's daughter as a prisoner. It had not occurred to him that his mother would offer him as part of a bargain.

"So, my mother wants me to fill you with children."

"Yes. Considering I'm still working on a council of advisers, I haven't given the treaty to anyone else. However, Jola is aware of it, and so are the top commanders of your army. We can't destroy it and pretend it doesn't exist." Shrugging, Eivor stroked the emerald choker on her neck. "Either we agree, or our lives are probably forfeit."

"Does Thorne know?"

"You tell me. Where is your beloved dullaghan? I haven't seen them since..." Recalling the incident that nearly killed her, Eivor squared her shoulders. "If Thorne knows but hasn't told you, then they're working with your mother."

Rhydwen's gaze settled on the jewels her fingers kept dancing over. "It seems like you've made up your mind. Though your dress leaves much to be desired."

"Perhaps its only function is to entice you to tear it from my body."

"You deliberately picked something to wear for that purpose?"

Smiling slyly, Eivor glanced at the doorway to her bedroom. "And if I did?"

"What makes you so sure I'll agree to this? Why should I exchange one entitled queen pulling my strings for another?"

"Because it keeps you alive. Here, in my court, you'd have freedom. I know how it feels to be caged and forced to dance on strings for survival. Your mother wants what she wants, but it's up to us to decide everything else about it."

Placing the papers on the table, he rose and crossed to where she stood. The slight flare of her nose told Rhydwen his proximity set her instincts on edge.

Even the sweet scent of Eivor's perfume did not mask the change in her smell accompanying the emotions coursing through her.

Stroking her cheek, he lifted her chin with his knuckles and watched the flutter of her lashes. He had planned to torment Eivor and toy with the reluctant desire she felt for him. Part of him resented the way she was offering herself so quickly, but Rhydwen appreciated her skipping the games.

"You could have kept this information from me," he murmured.

"Don't be fooled, I thought about it. I'm aware the power is in my hands, and I doubt your mother would care if you didn't agree to the treaty. As others have reminded me, I'm a queen, and I can take what I want."

"But you're asking me to come to your bed willingly."

"Yes... but not just that. If this is the situation we find ourselves in, let's forget the games. I don't want to watch my back in private with the people I invite to my bed."

Surprised, his eyes widened. "You're offering me your trust."

"In return for yours."

"King?"

"Consort."

He sniffed her neck, inhaling the mixture of raspberry, acai, and excitement. "Did Jola tell you my favourite fruit?"

"She did, but I've been using this oil for a while now. Do you like it?"

"It almost makes up for this hideous outfit you're wearing. Of course, I didn't miss the pretty baubles adorning your neck and ears. A rather obvious hint now I know what you're offering. Did you think I'd appreciate it?"

"Don't you?" Tilting her head back to expose her throat, Eivor hoped he would not take it as an invitation to kill her instead.

"I came here planning to play games with you."

"Who said you couldn't? So long as we know it's a game. When I selected what to wear, I imagined being spread out on the lounge wearing nothing but these jewels while you show me what that pretty mouth is good for."

Dragging a nail over her throat until it reached the choker, Rhydwen purred. "Did you now? Did you also imagine me slicing through this hideous gown with my claws?"

"Yes," she replied, feeling her skin prickle from the sharpness of his nail.

"What do you want from me, Eivor?"

"I want you to agree to be my consort and the person I can trust to be by my side. In return, I offer you the same."

Licking her cheek, he slipped his hand down to the dip in the gown that displayed the swell of her breasts. "You want us to trust each other?"

"What have we got to lose?"

"Our lives."

"I'm not asking for love, Rhydwen." She frowned, worried he would turn her down. "I'm asking for a partnership."

"No one has ever offered me equality."

She ran a hand through the silky thickness of his hair before cupping the back of his head. "Equality and power. We could be good together. All you need to do is say yes."

# TEN

His lips were softer than Eivor expected, and the prick of his claws through the gown's fabric was as unrelenting as his kiss. If Rhydwen had not broken the skin of her hip, she suspected it was only because of the layers of silk between his hand and her body. A claw hooked the hem at her breasts, a lingering promise for the fate awaiting the dress. He had not spoken a word in response to her offer of power and equality. Instead, Rhydwen had claimed her mouth and stolen all the replies she had prepared.

Pulling back, he smirked at the dazed way Eivor stared at him. "I like this look on you, Songbird. All flustered because I kissed you."

"Songbird?" Eivor forced the word out, despite how her brain wanted nothing more than to resume kissing the smug man holding her upright.

"I've heard stories about your singing. Perhaps after dinner, you can grant me the pleasure of hearing your voice." Releasing his hold on her, Rhydwen glanced at the door. "Speaking of dinner. I wonder what delights they're going to present us with."

Rubbing her face, Eivor attempted to bring her thoughts back on track. A knock had Rhydwen striding to the door to greet the servants. Keeping out of the way, the pair watched the platters be placed on the table, covers removed to expose the foods prepared for their enjoyment. Several bottles of wine were arranged to the side. While that happened, a pair of servants quickly lit the lanterns in the chamber and checked on the fires in both rooms. Breathing deeply, Eivor inhaled the mouth-watering scents and hoped Rhydwen could not hear the hungry grumble of her stomach. All but two of the servants departed, the ones staying situating themselves to the side of the room.

Eivor gestured at them. "We don't need your services for dinner."

"As you wish, Your Majesty."

Bowing, they quickly left. Rhydwen chuckled, moving to the table to inspect the meal. While he did, Eivor selected a bottle of wine and uncorked it. Her nose detected hints of raspberry, confirming Jola had done as planned and requested the prince's favourite. Pouring two glasses, she returned the bottle to its spot before picking up the drinks to approach Rhydwen. Grinning, he accepted the one she offered, passing it beneath his nose to inhale the sweet scent.

"You're spoiling me."

"Lucky for you, I love raspberry wine." Smiling, she sipped her drink. "Those strips of beef look almost perfectly cooked."

His brows rose in surprise. "They're not too rare for you?"

"Not at all. I've never hesitated to eat my kills while in my magpie form."

"I can't imagine insects are all that filling. Crunchy, though."

Laughing, Eivor reached for a small piece of toast laden with a tomato and herb mix and drizzled with oil. "I prefer rabbits to insects. Astoria and I would have competitions to see which of us was the trickier hunter. She always believed a hawk was superior."

"But you prefer the slow, careful hunt."

"My middle sister is many things, but patient is not one of them."

Placing his glass on the table, Rhydwen snagged a strip of meat with the tip of a claw. "How much do you know about her whereabouts? Did Cathair keep you informed?"

"Only about Silaine, and only because she is with the danann. I'm in the dark when it comes to Astoria. Do you know where she is?"

While he tore the strip in half with his teeth, Eivor finished eating her selection. Plucking some meat from the platter, she surprised him by doing the same. Rhydwen watched, doubting she was performing for his sake. There was a comfortable savagery to her approach he found alluring.

"She's taken up with the young god of air. Dawn, she's called. The daughter of Life and War. They say your sister is her favourite lover and a pirate who fights to free enslaved people being transported across the oceans."

"I heard the gods have been breeding. Just what we need, more of them."

"My mother has questioned if it's not better for there to be more gods. Perhaps the more there are, the less powerful they become. They may be fracturing their power to create others," he said, reaching for another piece of meat.

Humming thoughtfully, Eivor contemplated the prospect. "That's an interesting way to look at it. I don't know if Oisin and Cathair destroyed my mother's journals. She had a room dedicated to her observations. I read a lot of them."

"You know what Annawyn did to the original Ravens?"

"Of course."

"My mother told me the story. She didn't like what happened because, as much as she hates the Executioner, it was a terrifying insight into what could happen to any of them. If Annawyn was willing to torture and kill Death and War's favourites, then what else was she willing to do?"

"Your mother served Annawyn."

He nodded. "She did. They even made me... serve Annawyn. But by the end, it was out of fear. Her vendetta against Oisin is because of what happened to my sister."

"Jola told me."

"I'll never forget it. Annawyn made all of us watch, and we couldn't stop it."

Reaching out, Eivor cupped his cheek gently. "I'm sorry for what happened to your sister. I can't imagine how it felt to watch it happen."

"For the sake of trust, I'll admit I still have nightmares of it."

"There's nothing wrong with that. It's perfectly normal to have nightmares of traumatic events in our lives. Restraining our emotions doesn't help us heal."

"What are your nightmares of?" Covering her hand, Rhydwen caught the flicker of grief in her eyes. "I suppose it's obvious. They tortured you for years."

"Oisin and Cathair tortured and killed my best friend in front of me. I still hear the echoes of his screams and my promises to do anything they wanted if only they spared him."

Rhydwen imagined how he would feel if someone did that to Thorne. "You loved him?"

"He was the light of my life."

"I don't know how I would cope if that happened to Thorne."

Lips thinning, Eivor withdrew her hand and reached for another piece of food. "You don't cope. It never leaves you. All you can do is plan your revenge."

"You haven't been to see Cathair yet."

There was a softness to his tone that surprised Eivor. She knew the question was inevitable, and part of her was thankful he had asked it. Biting into the ball of goat cheese and herbs with its coating of breadcrumbs, she delayed answering. Respecting her silence, Rhydwen sampled a selection of roasted root vegetables. The empty plates and utensils suggested they were supposed to sit to eat, but it felt more comfortable to graze.

Watching him use a fork to skewer a potato, Eivor murmured, "I'm not ready."

"It's only been a few days. In the meantime, he's strung up, and we're keeping him alive. Mostly isolated. Though perhaps his guards get a little... pokey."

"Pokey?"

"Clawey?" He cocked his head, the barest hint of amusement glittering in his eyes.

"Good grief, stop."

"They tickle him with their talons?"

Unable to hold back a giggle when he wriggled his claws at her, she covered her mouth. Grinning, Rhydwen bit into his potato and groaned at the crisp, seasoned skin. He tasted rosemary and salt and something he could not place. The cooks knew what they were doing.

"I'm sorry for being so rude to you when we met."

"Don't be, Majesty. It was hardly an ideal introduction. However, I appreciated your quick wit. I hope it's a sign we won't bore each other."

Noticing his claws had retracted, Eivor licked her fingers clean of food. "I'm sure we'll find mutual interests outside of revenge on Oisin."

"And our children."

A noticeable shift of her shoulder told Rhydwen his reply unsettled the queen. He wondered if it was the thought of having children in general or specifically with him. Sighing, Eivor selected something else to eat.

"I'm sorry for that as well."

Slanting a look towards the bedroom door, Rhydwen said, "I always knew my mother would use me like this. Like my father, I'm a desired male in the court, and it was always my fate."

"Exactly. This isn't what you'd choose for yourself, and I'm sorry the right has been taken from you. But I meant what I said earlier. I want this to be a partnership."

"You're hardly being given a choice either, Eivor. But we could always decide we'd rather die. Or be tortured. My mother would probably send me to a pleasure house where I'll be forced to serve whoever paid for it. Some days I question how sane she is."

Eivor blinked, taking in the sadness in his eyes. "You love your mother."

"She's my mother."

"I..." Shaking her head, she dismissed what she was going to say. "How about we agree to raise our children the way my parents raised me?"

"And when my mother comes to claim them?" he murmured. "What then?"

"We have a few years before it's a problem. I don't know how the change in our lifespan has affected the maturing process of my kind. Typically, daoine youths didn't come into their full power until around 300."

"Are you suggesting we quietly come up with a plan to defy my mother?"

Shrugging, Eivor returned to the strips of meat and bit into one, allowing a trickle of juices to trail from the corner of her mouth. "Just because we accept the treaty now doesn't mean we have to abide by it in the long run. Why can't we plan? We have years to prepare."

Rhydwen approached, leaning in to lick the trail of red from her chin. "I find the thought of you intending to defy my mother from the onset rather exciting. No one I know would ever be so cocky. Except for Thorne, but Mother fears them."

"How exciting?"

"You tell me."

Grabbing her wrist, Rhydwen brought her hand to his crotch. Stroking the bulge of his cock through the fabric, Eivor smiled, dragging her bottom lip through her teeth. His lips hovered over her skin, taunting her with their closeness. It was difficult to decide if she wanted the prince to kiss her or hunt down any last traces of meat juices. The tickle of his breath was warm, and Eivor felt desire pooling between her legs.

"I find your excitement impressive," she murmured, pressing her hand firmer to his erection. "You'll have to show me how well you can use it."

His lips brushed over her cheek. "Dinner is going cold."

The randomness of his comment had her scoffing. "What?"

"The food, Majesty. We should finish our meal before the outstanding efforts of your skilled cooks go to waste. Though I'm sure some of it is still delicious cold."

Stepping back, Rhydwen enjoyed the crimson flush of her cheeks. Amusement chased away the confusion in her expression, the twitch of Eivor's lips suggesting she was not angry. He liked the assurance. A goblin woman would not have appreciated it. Games with them were different, and Rhydwen was eager to explore what Eivor would let him get away with.

"You're right; we should eat some more before moving on to sweeter things." Shifting her focus, Eivor plucked a crumbed cheese ball from the table. "Tell me about your interests, Prince Rhydwen. What do you like to do?"

Watching her lips caress the food as she bit into it, he cleared his throat. "Interests?"

"Yes, those. For example, I enjoy drawing, painting, and the occasional attempt at sculpting. Hunting on foot, horseback, and by the wing. Before my imprisonment, I was adequate at fighting. I don't mind wrapping my hand around a sword hilt."

"I'm sure you're a master at handling swords."

"Do you handle swords often, Your Highness?"

"I have experience. My training encompassed many weapons and methods."

Dipping her gaze, Eivor took another bite of her food. "Surprising when you have efficient weapons at hand. All you need to do is flex your fingers, and…"

"And?"

"You'd have your prey at your mercy."

The mischief in her eyes when she lifted them to his had Rhydwen appreciating his decision to play. Selecting another roasted vegetable, he was glad for the moment of silence while they ate. His mother had always warned him the daoine were dangerous. Her claims that they oozed attraction seemed a joke to his isolated mind. Now he understood why Calista had said what she did.

Since arriving in Diwan, Rhydwen had watched the gleaming people wear seduction and magic like a layer of clothing. They flirted and teased as easily as they breathed. More than once, he had discovered groups of them too impatient to make it back to a chamber before they took their pleasure.

"As to my interests, I've got many. I enjoy reading, chess, fighting, and astronomy. Hunting, of course. A mutual one we'll have time to share."

"I look forward to it."

"Dancing."

She smirked. "I'm sure you're an excellent dancer."

"Unfortunately, much to my mother's disappointment, I'm not musically inclined, but I write decent poetry."

"Please, do keep listing your accomplishments."

Hesitating while he assessed if she was joking, Rhydwen decided her pleased smile was genuine. "I'm well-versed in battle strategies, though I've had little opportunity to practice my knowledge. There are also the usual things expected of a male of higher rank."

"What?"

"It's not important here, away from the goblin court."

"Oh, but you have my interest. What are the usual things expected of a man like you?"

"I can decorate, sew, embroider, and design. We need to know everything about fashion to ensure we're pleasing to the women allowed to see us."

Aghast, Eivor stared at him. "Do you enjoy those things?"

"I find embroidery to be quite relaxing. Thorne carries a kerchief I made with a rather lovely pattern. I'm a prince, not a grunt."

"But you can fight?"

"Yes, they expected me to learn and to train daily. Would you like to see why?"

Before Eivor could answer, Rhydwen tugged his tunic free of the belt and pulled it over his head. She stared at his broad chest, the light of the fire dappling shadows across his muscles. Making a noise of appreciation, she stepped closer to pluck the shirt from his fingertips. It fluttered to the ground, discarded as

Eivor ran her hand over his shoulder and down the front of him. Her fingers toyed with the buckle of his belt, and Rhydwen arched a brow, eyes darting to the table.

"I must insist you continue to train daily. Preferably where I can see you shirtless," she murmured, bringing her hand up to run her fingers through the smattering of red curls. "I bet you're considered one of the most beautiful men among your people."

"Perhaps. I suppose all that matters now is if you find me beautiful."

"When I first saw you in the throne room, I wanted to paint you naked, draped in gold and jewels. I still do. To say I find you beautiful doesn't do you justice."

Rhydwen's breath caught at the admiration in her gaze. "You mean that?"

"Every word."

"If we didn't have this arrangement foisted on us?"

"The treaty doesn't influence my attraction to you. I also harbour a great deal of desire for Thorne, but when I realised the two of you were involved, I was willing to ignore it out of respect. My mother always told me goblins are possessive."

"We are. Knowing what your animal form is, I researched magpies before we arrived. Are you as territorial as the actual bird?" Trailing a finger across her chest, Rhydwen partially shifted it into a claw. "I read magpies mate for life. Which seems the antithesis to daoine nature."

"I can be very territorial over things I consider mine. Is that a problem?"

"On the contrary, I look forward to seeing what happens."

Snagging the tip of his claw on a fold of cream silk, Rhydwen arched a brow. Her lips parted as she contemplated how to respond. The scent of her arousal reached his nose as he dragged his claw downwards, tearing the fabric easily. Remembering the fantasy she had admitted to, he released his other claws and brought them to Eivor's hip. They sliced through the gown, but Rhydwen was careful not to cut her skin. Stepping forwards, he backed her towards the lounge, halting before her legs hit it.

"You can say no," Eivor whispered. "We both can."

"Do you want to?"

"Not in the slightest."

"Good."

Her nose flared when he resumed his efforts to shred the dress slowly. It felt as satisfying as she hoped, and Eivor inhaled sharply every time the tip of a claw scratched her skin. Clenching her thighs together, she wanted to tell Rhydwen to hurry, but the smug curl of his mouth kept her silent. When his hands sought the bodice holding the silk to her body, she bit her lip to keep from groaning in excitement. By the time the gown littered the floor as scraps of fabric, Eivor was tired of waiting.

"I hope you didn't like that dress."

"Cathair chose it."

Chuckling, Rhydwen gently nudged her onto the lounge. Laying back, Eivor did not resist when his hands wrapped around her ankles to pull her to the end. Dropping to his knees, he spread her legs, lifting one over a shoulder while pushing the other to the side. He leaned in, pressing his nose to her mound to inhale deeply.

Propping herself up on her elbows, Eivor stared at his crimson hair between her legs, wanting to run her hands through it. It was agony waiting for Rhydwen to make a move, so she wriggled impatiently, hoping it would be enough encouragement for him to do something.

Stroking the back of her thigh with a claw, Rhydwen gazed at Eivor when she squirmed. It was clear she enjoyed the brush of his claws, so he repeated the action before lowering his mouth to her entrance. She tasted as sweet as she smelt, and his tongue lapped up her arousal. A hand grabbed his hair, fingers twisting through the strands to urge him on. There was no dig of talons, just the weight of her grasp as his lips sought her clit. Dancing his fingers along her side, he gently scratched the tips over her skin, feeling her buck into his mouth as a response.

"Oh, fuck."

Rhydwen chuckled at her breathy moan, and she whimpered at the sensation. It left him determined to make her orgasm with just his mouth and the brush of his claws across her skin. With his other hand, Rhydwen continued to trail the tips of his claws over her body. Each time they found a sensitive spot, she squirmed and gasped, encouraging him to repeat the action. Eyeing the creamy expanse of her skin, he brought his hands to her breasts. Fingers seeking Eivor's nipples, he pinched them between the tips of his claws.

Her reaction was immediate, hand tightening in his hair as she moaned. Carefully twisting, Rhydwen did not pinch tighter for fear of piercing her. There was no need; the desperate squirm of her body and flood of arousal told him how much Eivor was enjoying it. He kept going, coaxing her closer to her peak, and the whimpered pleas were music to his ears. Releasing her nipples, Rhydwen trailed his claws down her stomach and legs, slipping an arm around to hold her still so she could not shift from his mouth.

Eivor felt the coil of her orgasm building, each stroke of his tongue and fingers edging it closer to unravelling. She had not expected the tease of Rhydwen's claws to send desire coursing through her, but each tantalising scratch left her wanting to beg for more. Tightening her grasp on his hair, Eivor attempted to buck into his mouth. Claws dug into her hip and breast, the sharp prick of them enough to send her over the edge. Whimpering, she arched her back, feeling his tongue lap up her arousal.

"Rhydwen," she mumbled, squirming with sensitivity. "Powers, fuck, please."

Lifting his head to grin at her, Rhydwen licked his lips. "Was that a please continue?"

"I..."

"As you wish."

She let out a strangled gasp when he slid two fingers into her. Spreading them, Rhydwen allowed the tips of his claws to come out. Eivor tightened around the invading digits, the tantalising risk enough to coax her towards a second orgasm. Adding a third finger, he pressed his thumb to her clit. Using the tip of his claw on the bundle of nerves was something he would never have dared with one of his kind.

Turning his head while his fingers gently stroked the sensitive spot inside her, Rhydwen bit Eivor's thigh hard enough to leave a mark. Repeating it on the other side, he dotted his bites across both her legs until he felt her muscles spasm. Her hand in his hair tightened to pull him away, and he let her.

Withdrawing his fingers, Rhydwen trailed them over her stomach. He wanted to smell the lingering traces of her enjoyment. Eivor stared at him, barely able to move but unable to resist the shivers of tortured pleasure each touch sent racing through her. She wanted to be annoyed by the smug smile he wore, except she could not blame Rhydwen for being pleased with himself for his efforts.

It was too much work to keep her head up, and Eivor dropped it down on the lounge, letting her eyes shut while she waited for her heart to stop racing. With the way he continued to touch her, she doubted it would.

"Well, Songbird, did that measure up to your fantasy?"

"Surpassed it."

Chuckling, he licked one of the bite marks on her thigh, eliciting a moan. "Is it the pain or the threat of danger that you enjoy so much?"

"A little of both." Untangling her fingers from his hair, Eivor let her hand fall.

"I look forward to exploring that."

"Your control is incredible."

"It's expected. Though I would never have dared do what I did to a goblin woman."

Struggling to prop herself up on her elbows, Eivor stared at him. "You'd never used your claws inside a woman before?"

"Not like that. I wouldn't have hurt you."

"An interesting choice for our first exercise in trust."

"And I'll gladly do it again. Now, don't move. I'll fetch us a drink and something to eat. You'll need your energy for later."

Groaning, Eivor wished she had something to throw at him.

# ELEVEN

Hands on her knees while she struggled to breathe and laugh, Eivor blinked furiously to dislodge the tears clinging to her eyes. A short distance away, Rhydwen sounded like he was in a similar situation, laughter broken by the occasional choking cough. No one else was in the area except a handful of guards tasked with ensuring their leisure time was undisturbed. Walls of tall greenery hid them away, the grassy pathways littered with the lilly pilly fruits they had been lobbing at each other.

"We need to work on your aim," Rhydwen said between heaving breaths. "I wouldn't trust you to protect me right now."

"Speak for yourself!"

She snagged one of the small red fruits from the ground and threw it half-heartedly at him. Darting out of the way, Rhydwen waved dismissively and staggered to a bench. The stone was cool, sunlight blocked by the maze of bushes surrounding the area.

Catching sight of a guard staring at him in disgust, he wanted to shrink back and apologise for his unbecoming behaviour, but Eivor straightened and beamed at him, and Rhydwen remembered it did not matter what the guards thought. If they said anything about it, he would politely remind them it had been the queen's idea. He was obeying the request of the woman his mother had given him to.

"Thank you." Drifting over to a lilly pilly laden with fruit, Eivor plucked a dark purple one from a branch to pop into her mouth. "I needed this after the morning we had."

"You mean you didn't enjoy putting together the first few advisers for your new council? I thought the justiciar would die from outrage when he saw the proposed treaty."

"So did I. Not to mention all the 'what would your beloved parents say?' he kept throwing around. Honestly, my father would tell me to make the best of the hand I've been dealt."

Watching the sway of her hips as she approached him, Rhydwen smirked. "And are you making the best of the hand you have?"

"Well, if my aching muscles are anything to go by..."

Standing in front of him, Eivor put her hands on his shoulders and smiled. Grabbing her hips, Rhydwen leaned forward to kiss the taut silk covering her stomach. The scent of their morning activities had faded, but enough remained to make him purr. He had enjoyed every moment of waking her up slowly before making her scream his name in pleasure.

It had been two days since Eivor had given him the letters and documents from his mother. Two days in which Rhydwen had taken every opportunity to discover if her offer was a trick. Part of him still screamed not to trust the Diwanian queen, but it was being drowned out by the desire to sink into her gleaming blue eyes and radiant smile.

Eivor stroked his cheek, magic alerting her to the circling battle of his thoughts. She understood it, her mind often breaking out warnings that throwing herself into any relationship was a mistake. But captivity had kept her treading water in the pit of her emotions for a hundred years, and now she could swim for shore. All she had to do was grasp Rhydwen's hand to pull him with her. They had both been prisoners, and this was their opportunity to break free. Together, they were stronger. Together, they could keep themselves from being dragged beneath the waves.

"When you said you wanted to see the gardens, I wasn't sure what to expect," he murmured, resting his cheek on her stomach. "I should have known you were the sort to engage in vicious fruit battles."

"You started it."

"Did not."

"So, you didn't throw one at my nose?"

He chuckled sheepishly. "Well, maybe my aim isn't that good either. Your mouth was open, and I thought I'd be helpful. But the result was better than expected."

"It was certainly a lot of fun." Running her hand through his loose hair, Eivor realised she felt relaxed. "You've never just played a game for fun, have you?"

"No."

"We used to do this at least once a week. A picnic in a grove, and then games. It was family only, a time for just us."

"I can't imagine that, but if it was anything like this…"

Pressing her lips together, Eivor felt his grasp on her tighten. "Another promise for me to make. Rhydwen, I know this is a lot, but our eyes are open going in."

"We're two consenting adults aware of what impact our decisions will have."

Opening her mouth to reply, Eivor's throat froze. An icy chill ran down their spines, prompting Rhydwen to pull away from her. They stared at Thorne standing a short distance away, arms crossed as he regarded the two of them embracing. His power stole the warmth from the sun while a stony expression banished the remaining good feelings from their game.

"I see I wasn't missed," he said, regarding their closeness with displeasure.

Rhydwen swallowed nervously, removing his hands from Eivor's hips. "You're back. How was my mother? Well, I hope. Was she pleased with the news?"

"It thrilled Queen Calista as much as you'd expect. She asked if I had any letters for her from you, pretty magpie. When I told her I didn't, she seemed keen to know if Jola was looking after you. Would you like to tell me what's going on?"

Inhaling sharply, Eivor knew the suspicion in his voice confirmed Rhydwen's belief that the dullaghan did not know what the goblin queen wanted. Sharing a look, they silently argued over who should tell him. Thorne cleared his throat impatiently.

"Jola gave me letters and a treaty from Queen Calista," Eivor replied. "My freedom and return to the throne of Diwan are conditional on agreeing to her terms."

"Are they?"

"I have no reason to believe her threats aren't real. I can't say I'm particularly keen on becoming her prisoner in the Spire."

"And I like not being dead." Shrugging, Rhydwen felt a need to point out his life was at risk. "Or being sent to the pleasure houses."

Eyes shifting from one to the other, Thorne's impatience faded into fury. "She wants you to marry, or you both die?"

Shaking her hand, Eivor sighed. "Marriage is unnecessary. She wants Rhydwen to father some of my children. I'm to take him as my concubine."

"And neither of you thought there might be a third choice?"

"Not one that gives us what we want."

Hating himself for feeling nervous about Thorne's reaction, Rhydwen said, "Eivor told me the truth. She showed me the letters. We agreed to the terms together. I know you're angry with us, but Eivor is offering me something no one else ever has."

"And that is?" Thorne stared at him blankly.

"Equality. The freedom to make my own decisions. A partnership. We go into this knowing what the price of failure is." His eyes darted to the nearest guard, aware they could hear the conversation. "Trust me, Thorne. We know what we're doing."

Eyebrows raised, Eivor followed his glance and scratched her neck. "You can't be angry with Rhydwen for agreeing to this. Be angry with the Blood Queen for asking it."

"I'm angry with him for not waiting until I returned to discuss our options."

Thorne's reply had Rhydwen jumping to his feet. "I beg your pardon?"

"You will be."

"I am not your pet, Thorne."

Putting a hand on his chest, Eivor frowned in concern. "Rhydwen, the bushes have ears and eyes. This is an argument to be had in private."

"You can modify their memories."

"I'd rather not. That is a breach of trust."

Cocking his head, Thorne studied them. "Interesting. I didn't expect that. Perhaps you're already a positive influence on him, pretty magpie."

Eyes narrowing with suspicion, Rhydwen covered Eivor's hand on his chest. Lacing his fingers through hers, he lifted them to his lips to kiss the inside of her wrist. She kept her power close, unsure she wanted to glimpse what was going through his mind. There was little point in trying to gain insight into Thorne; the wall of ice surrounding his thoughts was unscalable. Offering Rhydwen a faint smile, she inclined her head to the pathway. Eivor held back a sigh of relief when he nodded.

"It's getting late, Songbird. I'm surprised Jola hasn't come searching for us," Rhydwen said, clasping her hand. "The servants will deliver dinner soon."

"A civil discussion over dinner sounds like a good idea," she muttered.

Leading her towards the arch cut into the wall of lilly pilly trees, Rhydwen growled when Thorne took Eivor's other hand. Nose flaring along with her anxiety, her eyes darted back and forth between them. The tension was a palatable force rolling off each man, accompanied by swirls of power that made her want to flee.

If they did not stop their posturing, Eivor suspected she would need some of Jola's potent headache medicine. She could cope with hundreds of people in one place, their emotions never affecting her, but something about the two men was wearing her shields down.

Eivor clenched her eyes shut, face screwing up in discomfort. "Restrain yourselves, or I'll be in no fit state for a conversation."

Concerned, Rhydwen halted them. "What's wrong, Eivor?"

"You're giving me a headache. I wasn't taught to keep out goblin or dullaghan powers, and your spat is wearing me thin."

Keeping their distance, the guards pretended not to be listening in. Aware every word was being observed, Rhydwen dipped his head to Thorne in acknowledgement. As annoyed as he was, he did not wish to cause Eivor pain. Picking up the pace, he led the queen through the garden towards the palace, with Thorne trailing behind, doing their best to restrain their powers and emotions as they went.

Courtiers strolling through the gardens watched them go, whispers chasing their footsteps. The newly selected advisers had spread the news of the treaty with his mother, and Rhydwen was thankful he could not hear every word.

"They're talking about us," Eivor muttered.

"Nothing spreads as fast as court gossip."

Grunting, Thorne recalled the position he had found them in on his return. "If you've been frolicking around the palace like you were in the garden, what else do you expect?"

"We haven't been. Apart from a council meeting today, that's the first time we've appeared together." Huffing, Eivor felt stupid for having dismissed the chatter of servants. "There's no such thing as privacy in a place like this. I should be used to it."

"Dare I ask what you've been doing while I was away?"

"Is it any of your business?"

"Yes, it is. However, that explanation can wait until we're alone."

Dread curled around her spine. Squeezing Rhydwen's hand, the warmth of his skin spread to hers. In contrast, the hand Thorne clung to was chilled, and she suspected her fingers had taken on the mottled paleness that came when her body got too cold. She hated winter for that reason. If she let Thorne continue to hold her with his power behaving the way it was, her hand would soon reach that numb state she detested. Biting her tongue, Eivor chose not to mention it. It was a weakness she preferred to keep quiet. When cooler weather approached, she would deal with letting Rhydwen and Jola know, but until then, she would have to find a way around it when the dullaghan was present.

Looming above them, the palace seemed as cold as her hand felt. The sun was low in the sky, warning of the oncoming night. Soon enough, they would find midsummer upon them, the longest day of the year one for celebration. Eivor looked forward to the traditional festivities and dancing around bonfires until dawn broke above the horizon. Glancing at Rhydwen, she wondered if goblins celebrated midsummer.

People bustled about the hallways, but they stopped whatever they were doing to observe the queen with her escort. Eivor sensed the disgust coming from several of them. She wanted to stop, tear into their minds, find out the reason for their disapproval, and deal with it. But she did not. Those people could wait until she had finished combing through the higher levels of the court. Freeing Diwan from Oisin's control was what she needed to focus her powers on, not lashing out in frustration at insignificant courtiers.

When they reached her quarters, Jola was waiting inside. Her eyes widened at the sight of Thorne looming behind Eivor. Rhydwen released her hand, striding over to the lounge to throw himself dramatically onto it. Tugging at the firm grasp holding her in place, Eivor scowled at the dullaghan when he refused to let go. Clearing her throat, Jola shuffled through the papers she was reading and inclined her head at the open door into the bedroom. It was a signal none of them missed, but Thorne did not move or release Eivor from his hold. She bared her teeth, anger twisting through her magic.

"Go on, pretty magpie, show me those claws," he murmured. "Because I'm not letting you go until you make me."

"Are you jealous Rhydwen happily came to my bed without waiting for your permission or that he had me first? You were quick to boast, but it was empty words."

"I'm angry neither of you stopped to think the consequences through!"

"You mean the ones where we get to live?"

Rhydwen growled from the lounge. "If you hurt her, Thorne, you'll get to find out how my claws feel in your throat."

"Death blessed you at birth, you stupid woman. Your relationship will draw the attention of the gods! The daughter of a Raven and the son of the Blood Queen. If you don't want the gods in your life, don't do things that'll interest them."

"What do you mean, blessed by Death when I was born?" Eivor's anger faded into confusion. "Mother never mentioned that."

"After I delivered the news of our successful liberation of Diwan from Cathair and Oisin to Queen Calista, I went looking for answers. You should have died instantly that day, but you didn't. I knew Gebael was present for your birth, but not that he blessed you."

Jola scoffed. "The god of death didn't hand out blessings. He ended them."

Turning icy eyes to her, Thorne shook his head. "I spoke to my brother, who serves Aiden, and Rain told me when Eivor was born, Gebael blessed her. His words were 'to always walk with the Veil', and I do not know what it means. Except it's why she didn't die when she touched me."

"Walk with the Veil?" Rhydwen sat up. "You're 3000 years old, Songbird. You'd have discovered by now if veil walking was a power of yours."

"I don't think that's what it meant."

Pinching the bridge of her nose, Eivor muttered, "You said Death's power was stronger in me. Perhaps I'm just harder to kill?"

"Whatever it means, we'll find out," Jola said coldly.

"I also found out the gods kept your youngest sister from returning to Diwan to try freeing you. They ordered the danann not to help." Glancing between the two royals, Thorne scowled. "We need to be careful. The gods are powerful; they know things."

Eivor felt winded by his comment about Silaine. "Silaine was going to return for me?"

"She would have joined you in captivity."

"But she wanted to come back?"

"That's what I was told. I didn't ask too many questions for fear of drawing attention. Those fucking humans are everywhere in Ellinjaa these days. The ones who served the new god of death when he was a mortal man."

"Don't like humans?" Sniggering, Rhydwen hoped the light-hearted comment would help Eivor find a focus through her shock.

"Humans are fine. It's simply an insult to loyal servants of Death that they've been given so much. Especially the man bearing Eclipse."

Hearing mention of a sword her mother had spoken of in bedtime stories, Eivor gasped. "There's a human out there with Death's sword?"

"Yes."

"I wonder what my mother would have said about that."

Thorne stepped back as though she had slapped him, letting go of her wrist. "Eivor, they knew what was going to happen here. Death knew they would kill Malena. They left you here to suffer under Cathair's control."

"Yes, I've worked that out. They left me here as a prisoner but saved Silaine. It's always been about my darling little sister. The precious husk maker."

"Husk makers are a powerful force, even without the bonds to their danann counterparts. They say the god of life had the ability as a mortal mage and used it to slaughter hundreds in battle on her own. People fear them."

"Don't speak to me of what people think about husk makers!" Snarling, Eivor raised a fist at Thorne. "My mother was one of the first. I know more about them than most."

He smiled slowly, stepping closer to her. "Then what are you going to do about Oisin and his collection of them? Are you going to sit here in your palace, playing games with Rhydwen, or are you going to crush him?"

Indignant, Rhydwen said, "We weren't playing games."

Shushing him, Jola knew it was not relevant what they had been doing. What mattered was keeping Eivor on task. The goblin army could not face Oisin's forces alone. They needed the Diwanian queen to muster support. She could convince others to join their cause when Queen Calista could not.

"Thorne is right, Eivor. You must focus on Oisin. By now, he'll know Diwan is no longer in his control, and he'll want to recapture you and the kingdom." Jola glanced at the door in concern. "You know what your mother wants you to do, Rhydwen."

"In other words, remember my priorities," he grumbled.

Eivor studied Thorne, mouth twisted. "Is the attention of the gods the only reason you're concerned about Rhydwen and I agreeing to the treaty?"

"It's currently the main one. The rest doesn't matter for the moment." Touching her cheek, the dullaghan smirked. "And maybe I am jealous."

"You'll have to get used to it. I'm not giving up my life or my kingdom because you believe you have a sole claim to Rhydwen."

"Pretty magpie, I have a claim on you as well. I'm no mere dullaghan to strike out without the blessing of my gods and command my kind as I please. Your name and his belong to me. No other dullaghan can accept them now I own them."

Snorting, she shook her head. "You don't own me."

"Don't I?"

His power wrapped icy hands around her spine, urging Eivor to close the space between them. Sucking a breath through grit teeth, she drew her magic inwards to push away the influence. Aware something was going on between them, Rhydwen scrambled from his spot on the lounge. Thorne glanced at him with a chuckle and extended a hand for the prince to take. Watching the confusion flicker across his face before he slid his fingers through the older man's, Eivor understood the implications of what Thorne had said.

"How is this possible?" she whispered.

Lips curling, Thorne shrugged. "I didn't know it would work when I tried. But it did. I've known Rhydwen was my mate since the moment I first saw him, and I claimed his name that day to protect my sanity and his life. You, however, my pretty magpie. I claimed you because I wanted to."

Betrayal was written into the lines of Rhydwen's face. "Why didn't you tell me?"

"There was no need."

"I disagree!"

"Jola, I don't recommend telling anyone about this." Looking at her, Thorne saw the calculation on the healer's face. "What I did will protect them."

"Considering there are dullaghan out there taking names for payment, it wouldn't be so farfetched to suggest Oisin might try killing Eivor," she said.

"Exactly. Now he cannot."

Sliding an arm around Rhydwen's waist, Eivor cupped his cheek. "I understand."

"Did you make me love you, Thorne?" Rhydwen demanded angrily.

"No. I can command your body, not your heart."

The admission took some steam out of Rhydwen's anger, but Eivor did not remove her hand. She felt the deep-seated hurt he was experiencing. It was a pain she wanted to take the edge off for him. Pressing her thumb to his lips, the queen sighed.

"We can't change what Thorne has done to us, my prince, but we can believe it was done with our best interests in mind. Think hard on what that means for our future."

He frowned before realising what she was referring to. "You're right, Song-bird. I apologise for my reaction, Thorne. You know how brash I can be when upset."

"Jola, I suggest you leave us for the night. I'm sure whatever it is can wait for the morning. The three of us need to talk."

Nodding, the healer headed to the door, opening it to reveal a servant with their hand ready to knock. Shifting out of the way, Jola let them in with their delivery, nose twitching at the scent of food. All the fires and lanterns were lit, a task she had seen to while waiting for Eivor to return. She sighed and slipped from the chamber with a last look at the tense trio.

Whatever they did to each other would not be her problem until morning. The servants followed soon after Jola left, knowing the queen and prince pre-ferred to dine without help. Even if they were not aware, the hostility in the room drove them to go.

"Shall we sit and eat while we argue?" Eivor inclined her head at the table.

"Before you ask, I cannot release your names."

Sneering at Thorne, Rhydwen grumbled, "So, we're just bound to your whim with no say in the matter. You should have told me!"

Closing her eyes, Eivor let go of Rhydwen. "Please, let's eat. I'm hungry, my head hurts, and I'd like for us to pretend to be polite. There will be no shouting, no fighting, just three people having dinner together while discussing a complicated situation."

"As you wish, Songbird."

Thorne nodded once. "I'm sure we can manage that, pretty magpie."

"Good, because if you don't, I'll ensure you'll regret it."

# TWELVE

His room was quiet, bereft of warmth without Eivor's presence. It felt strange to have returned to it to sleep, leaving the queen behind. A few days was all it had taken for the beautiful duine to dig her claws into his heart, but Rhydwen knew he had tossed it at her feet the moment he saw her sprawled across her throne wearing nothing but a light robe, the scent of her blood and arousal drawing him in. He had not wanted to leave her after dinner, especially not after Thorne's revelations.

A sliver of moonlight pierced the room, competing with the single lantern hanging on a hook beside the door. Shadows danced across the walls, soundless whispers calling to his underdeveloped magic. All goblins could wield shadows, but beyond shadow walking, they did not bother to teach most males. In the years since Thorne had stalked into his life, he had turned his focus to learning under the patient gaze of the dullaghan. Rhydwen had needed to be careful while they remained in the Spire. Now he was in Diwan, all but the property of Queen Eivor Havard, and if there was one thing he felt certain of, it was that she would encourage him to use it just like Thorne did.

Compared to Eivor's quarters, his room was small. Simple. A sitting room gave way to a bedroom with a small window looking out across the sprawling forest bordering the palace grounds. There was a tiny bathroom through another doorway, barely big enough for what it held. Unlike the wardrobe housing dozens of outfits for Eivor to choose from, Rhydwen had a wooden cupboard tucked into a corner for his meagre belongings. Back in the Spire, he had been provided with a selection as lavish as Eivor's when his mother was pleased with him. When she was unhappy, he was lucky to get a scrap of fabric.

Rhydwen stretched out his magic, pulling the shadows around him. It was easy to slip through them, appearing in the bedroom in front of the cupboard. There was no lantern in his bedroom, but goblins had an advantage in the dark. Peeling off his coat, he yanked open a door to hang it from a hook. His brows formed a deep furrow as he took in the fresh additions to the clothes on his shelves. They had not been there the last time he looked, making the prince wonder who was responsible. He doubted it was Eivor who had commanded new garments to be added to his small pile of possessions. Brushing his hand over the fabric of a shirt, he smiled.

He resented how excited he was by something as simple as new clothes. Most of his life had been lived at the mercy of his cruel mother. Anything he had was because she had allowed him to have it. He knew she had loyalists watching his every move, preparing reports to send back to her. Thorne was on his side. Rhydwen had no doubt he could count on the dullaghan. The real question was if he could count on Eivor. She was the key to his future, and even if his mother had given him to the duine queen, he wanted Eivor to be his safe place. Just like she had offered the first night after telling him about the treaty.

Flicking the door to the cupboard shut, Rhydwen stepped back to undress. Thoughts filled with the memory of Eivor's hands, he wondered if he should slip back to her quarters. He did not want to spend the night alone, deprived of the press of her body against his. Before coming to Diwan, it had always been Thorne who held him tight through the nightmares. It was always Thorne who kept him in one piece. Now he knew the truth about why the Master of the Hunt had initiated their relationship, Rhydwen could not help but wonder.

Everything he thought he felt for and knew about Thorne was in question. Despite his assurances the bond could not make him feel things for the dullaghan, Rhydwen could not help but doubt. He doubted, and he regretted it. Thorne did not deserve his doubt when, for a hundred and fifty-odd years, the dullaghan had done nothing but support and protect him as best he could within the viper's nest of Calista's court. Very few people dared interfere with someone claimed by a dullaghan, let alone the most powerful one in existence. It struck him that while he doubted the origin of his feelings, he had the freedom to do so when Thorne had no choice. What the Master of the Hunt felt for him was involuntary.

"Fuck!"

Slamming his fist against the door of the cupboard, Rhydwen did not flinch at the pain radiating along the bones of his hand. Guilt twisted through him, deep and painful, the agony of betrayal leaving a million cuts in his skin. He was wrong to doubt Thorne, and he owed it to his beloved headless rider to hear what he had to say. All of it. Every concern, every truth, anything Thorne needed to tell him to clear the air between them.

Ice filled the room, the familiar drop in temperature warning him before the shadows split away to welcome the dullaghan. "What's wrong, Rhyd?"

He welcomed the slide of arms around him and rested his head against the cupboard. Thorne did not turn him or move him away, simply pressed their bodies together while the prince fought back tears. The seep of cold was a relief, a reminder that he was always safe in the dullaghan's embrace. Squeezing his eyes shut, Rhydwen felt the sticky trickle of teardrops escaping his control.

"Tell me what you need, my sweet prince," Thorne murmured, nuzzling the side of his neck. "I'm sorry for everything I've done wrong recently. You're right to be angry with me for not telling you the truth years ago... for letting you believe I didn't love you."

"But do you?"

"Love you? Yes. Since the moment I saw you. If I could have killed that bitch your mother had given you to, I would have. When the gods made us mortal, I thought about hunting down every single person she had given you to. But that would have made problems for us. The last thing I wanted was for you to end up like your nephew. What Calista did to Tristan was... Maybe I should have stolen you away."

Cracking his eyes open, Rhydwen frowned at the memory of his eldest sister's son. "Why didn't you? I would have gone anywhere with you."

"Because I knew our path would lead us here. Before the imprisonment, Alyah told me I needed to bend the knee to Annawyn. I was the one Shianeni used to put the other gods to sleep in their tombs before she banished all immortals to the Veil. Do you remember when I was called away to the city of

Milla to help the new gods of chaos and paths? Vivienne told me she saw me by the side of a woman with black and white hair and a red-haired man with emerald eyes. Who does that describe?"

"Me and Eivor." Lifting his head from the door, the prince frowned. "Then why wouldn't you want us to find happiness with each other? I know you said it was about the attention we might receive from the gods, but was it really?"

Arms dropping away, Thorne sighed and stepped back, giving him room to turn around before saying, "I was jealous. I thought I admitted that already."

"But why?"

"Because you're mine and she's mine, but I wanted to be the one to bring you together. I did not know what Calista had planned, and I'm angry... except, it means you're away from the Spire. You're here, safe. Eivor won't let anything happen to you."

Watching Thorne pace away, running a hand through his hair, Rhydwen frowned at the admission. It occurred to him that what the dullaghan was jealous about was the fact he had been with Eivor, with no involvement from him. They had found their own way instead of being pulled together because of Thorne. He had wanted to be in control of everything like he always was. Scoffing in frustration, the prince wished he could do something to Thorne, but it was out of the question. There was no finding relief by dragging the dullaghan to a training yard.

"You're jealous because we fucked without you."

He slanted a look over his shoulder at the prince. "Yes."

"I love you, you fucking idiot!"

Even the shadows seemed to recoil from the anger in his voice, but all Thorne did was chuckle. Claws slipping free of his fingertips, Rhydwen longed for something to tear apart. He took a deep breath, holding it for a count of five, before reining in his temper and his talons. If the dullaghan knew what had transpired, he gave no sign. Instead, he walked across to the window to gaze out of it while fluttering drapes framed him. The shadows stretched across the floor and walls, fingers of longing that wrapped around Thorne.

"What do you want, Thorne?" he demanded, pouring every drop of frustration he could into his voice. "Because you can't fuck with us. It's not fair. We have an opportunity."

"Yes, we do. Eivor is our future, and we cannot ruin it. I nearly killed her."

"But she survived."

"This time. She doesn't trust me." Thorne turned to stare across the room at him. "Wants to fuck me, yes, but even that is tempered with fear. I don't want her to fear me."

Rhydwen crossed to the bed, sitting on the end of it to rest his head in his hands. "Give her time, my love. Stop being so... I don't know, whatever it is you have been. She knows I love you, and she doesn't want to come between us like that."

"Like that?"

"She wants to come between us in bed, and I'm very much looking forward to it. Aren't you? Don't you want her trapped in our arms while she falls apart completely and utterly because of our touch?"

"Yes."

Lifting his head from his hands, the goblin smirked. "I can't wait to watch her ride your face while I suck your cock. There are lots of things I'm anticipating."

"Like what?" Thorne took several steps towards him, and Rhydwen chuckled. "While you were fucking her, my sweet, were you thinking of me?"

"Not constantly, but it's hard to think of anyone else when I'm deep in Eivor's warmth. She's so different from you. You're ice and she's fire."

"I'm sorry I bound you to me without your consent."

He cocked his head, studying the approaching dullaghan. "Why did you? I'm not as well versed in matters of mates as Eivor. You mentioned your sanity earlier."

Perching on the end of the bed next to him, Thorne grasped his hands in front of him and sighed heavily. "Yes. Dullaghans are blessed and cursed with a one-way mate bond. We meet a person and feel a pull, a need to possess, an unavoidable love for them. You're not my first, but the others have been human and elf. Most of the time, that's the case."

"I don't know how I feel about that."

"We were given a higher chance of finding a mate within humans and elves because of their short lifespan. That is the curse. So many loves lost to death, leaving us grieving for something we had no control over in the first place. If we do not claim the name of a mate, we slowly go insane. Only the death of our unclaimed mate will free us."

Eyes wide with horror, Rhydwen placed a hand on Thorne's thigh. "Stars!"

"I never told you what you are to me because I feared what might happen if your mother found out. If she knew what you meant to me, she would have used you. So, I claimed your name without your permission and kept it a secret. All the while, I pretended you were nothing more than a fancy I had taken, and I let her continue doing what she wanted to you."

"Because we're mortal now. Even the might of the dullaghan cannot withstand the might of the goblin nation. My mother would have pitted her army against yours, and while you would have killed so many of them, you would have lost in the end."

Thorne clenched his jaw, nodding in confirmation. Dropping his gaze to the floor, Rhydwen considered what he would have done in the same situation. He knew what his mother was like, the lengths she was willing to go to. There was no doubt in his mind that Thorne had done the right thing. It was Eivor that felt wrong. Eivor that left a bitter taste in his mouth.

"I wish things had been safer for you to tell me before now, and I understand why. But Thorne, how dare you take away Eivor's freedom like that! She's a brilliant woman. If you had sat down and explained your concerns to her, I'm sure she would have consented."

The temperature dropped, a flicker of rage rippling through the dullaghan's magic. "I did what I needed to do! Besides, I had no idea if it would work when I did it. No dullaghan has ever claimed the name of someone who wasn't their mate, let alone two names. When it worked... and then we were liberating Diwan. I've barely had a chance to spend time with her, or win her trust, but I'm here now."

"Keep your distance for a few days. Give her time to sort out her feelings. Give me time to talk to her. I'll plead your case, and then you can start earning her trust."

Rubbing his face, Thorne chuckled bitterly. "I hope I haven't ruined everything before we could start something. The bond created when a dullaghan claims a name can only be broken by death. At least I can trust you to convince her to give me a chance."

He suspected it would not take much to convince Eivor to give the dullaghan a chance. Thoughts churned through his mind, overwhelming, and yet one stood out. It had been days since they had last kissed. A deep-seated craving for Thorne's touch cut through everything else, prompting him to turn to the man beside him. Rhydwen reached for his coat, turning slightly as he pulled Thorne in. Icy hands cradled his face, their lips meeting in a demanding kiss. One filled with a promise of more.

"I missed you, love," Rhydwen murmured, rubbing his nose against Thorne's.

"I know." Pushing the prince onto his back, Thorne studied him sorrowfully. "I feel it across the bond. The deep ache of your longing when I'm not with you. Since I claimed your name, that pain has always been the thing to guide me home to you."

Hands trailed over his chest, fingertips brushing over scars to toy with the smattering of fine hairs that were almost golden red. Thorne held his gaze in the darkness, a faint smile lifting the corners of his lips. He knew he had the advantage, and Rhydwen chuckled.

"What?"

Running a hand over Thorne's coat, he chuckled again. "Would you like me to fetch the lantern, or are you happy in the dark?"

Thorne pulled back, giving him room to get up. "Go fetch. Gives me time to undress."

Sliding from the bed, Rhydwen wrapped the shadows around himself, letting them carry him through to the other room. The lantern flickered pathetically, barely holding on. Locating another one, he carefully lit it from the dying flame of the first. Carrying them both through to the bedroom, he admired the half-naked man perched on the edge of the bed, pulling his boots off. Thorne glanced up at him, arching a brow as he dropped the second boot on the floor. With the shoes gone, the dullaghan was free to stand and let his unbuttoned trousers slide to the ground beside them. Raking his eyes along the line of Thorne's body, the prince hummed in delight. He loved everything about the older man.

There was a hook on the wall beside the bed, safely out of reach. Hanging the lantern there, he heard Thorne settling onto the mattress. Not turning to look at him, Rhydwen slid open the top drawer of the table next to the bed. Reaching in, he located the jar of ointment they needed. When he turned with it in hand, his gaze settled on Thorne's outstretched form, head propped up on his hand. Arousal flooded through him, cock hardening at the sight and the slow delighted curl of the other man's lips.

"You're so fucking beautiful, Thorne," he said, tossing the jar at him before crawling onto the bed. "And I need you to fuck me."

"Is that so?"

Settling on his knees, Rhydwen plucked the jar from where it had landed, unscrewing the cap to stick his fingers in and scoop out some of the oily contents. Reaching for Thorne's cock, he stroked his ointment-covered fingers along the frozen shaft, carefully slathering it over the other man's length. Groaning, the dullaghan grabbed his wrist, shifting to sit up.

"On your back, Precious."

The command tugged at him, and Rhydwen released the hold he had on Thorne's cock. When he lay back, the dullaghan wasted no time retrieving the jar, coating his fingers in the ointment before setting it aside. His hungry gaze kept the prince pinned in place as he nudged his legs apart to kneel between them. Cock twitching in anticipation, Rhydwen bit back a moan when the frozen fingers slid across his skin, seeking his arsehole. They circled it, sliding easily thanks to the ointment before the tip of one pressed into him.

Rhydwen loved and hated the cold spreading from the finger piercing him. A second joined it, twisting and stretching him, spreading the ointment to prepare for the cock that would soon replace them. With his fingers buried in the prince's arse, Thorne wrapped his other hand around the eager shaft bobbing in front of him. Each thrust of his fingers matched the stroke of his hand, coaxing a moan from the goblin. His thumb found the fluid beading at the tip, swirling it across the silken head.

"Please," Rhydwen whimpered, thrusting into Thorne's hand.

Pushing a third finger into him, Thorne tutted disapprovingly. "Patience."

When the hand left his cock, Rhydwen whined in disappointment. Fisting his own penis, Thorne finished rubbing the ointment into it. Satisfied the goblin was stretched enough, he withdrew his fingers and replaced them with the head of his cock. Taking his time to push into Rhydwen, Thorne leaned down to kiss him, cradling his cheek gently while the prince wrapped a leg around his waist.

Thorne broke the kiss, whispering, "I do love you."

Once he was buried completely, the dullaghan wrapped a hand around Rhydwen's cock. Matching the steady stroke of it with his gentle thrusts, he groaned at the dig of fingers in his arse, encouraging him to move. The prince rocked his hips, back arched as pleasure curled through him. Pleas spilled from his lips, desperate words intended to encourage Thorne to thrust harder, faster, but they were ignored.

"You're mine, Precious. Until we die, you belong to me."

Teeth grazed his neck, nipping at his ears, and Rhydwen felt the threads of his orgasm snap. The press of Thorne's mouth to his stole the breath from his lungs, the dullaghan swallowing his whimpers as he continued to stroke his cock. His cum clung to his skin, coating his penis and the hand stroking with the same slow, steady pace it had since the start. Making no attempt to speed up, the dullaghan kept going, silencing each agonised whine with a kiss until Rhydwen thought he was going to shatter.

Buried to the hilt, Thorne stilled as his own peak struck, the ice of him spilling into the goblin. It was a sensation Rhydwen doubted he would ever get used to. The dullaghan were never warm, not even their blood. He knew that from the time Thorne had accidentally cut himself shaving, and he had tended to the injury. Foreheads pressed together while they caught their breath, Rhydwen ran a hand over Thorne's back to bury it in his hair. The silken strands slipped through his fingers, impossibly soft.

"I love you, Thorne."

A smug smile greeted his words. "Love you too."

Unwilling to pull apart yet, Rhydwen wrapped his arms around the other man. "This thing with Eivor won't change how I feel about you."

"I know. But Rhyd, I want you to know I would burn kingdoms down to protect you. No one will ever take you from me, and if they tried, I'd make them suffer."

There was nowhere he felt as safe as he did when he was in Thorne's embrace. "I would do the same for you. Whatever it took to stay with you, I'd do it."

Lifting himself slightly, Thorne cradled his face, gazing at him tenderly. "For the rest of our lives, my sweet prince. I can't promise I won't let you down again, but I can promise I'll try not to. You're mine, but I'm yours. Always."

"Forever," Rhydwen murmured, stretching up to kiss him.

# THIRTEEN

"Those fucking humans!"

"To be fair, Your Majesty, Samphire knows Talaroo is a threat. They don't want to risk Oisin's ire by being seen to side with you."

The newly appointed chancellor swallowed nervously when Eivor's gaze turned in his direction. Her rage was an icy whisper through the chamber, and he glanced at his fellows for support. None of them looked eager to lend him help.

"Has the envoy left yet?"

"Not that I'm aware of. We'll send someone to check."

Eivor smiled slowly, a plan forming that she knew would get her point across to anyone who doubted her intentions towards Oisin. She was thankful Rhydwen and Thorne were busy elsewhere, leaving matters of state to her. The prince would support her actions, but Eivor knew the dullaghan was more likely to argue against it. Easier to avoid the discussion and ensure everyone knew who was in command of Diwan.

"Well, hurry along then." She waved at the door. "You don't want my patience to wear thin. It wouldn't be pretty... and I'd need another chancellor."

A goblin guard sniggered, tapping her claws against the walls as an aide hurried from the chamber. Knowing what they expected her to do to the nervous man if he displeased her further, Eivor cocked her head and considered her options. If Lord Jeffery had slipped out of the palace with his company, it was not the chancellor's fault. She had to accept that she had not thought to issue orders to forbid the humans from leaving. With Thorne's return from the Spire the day before, Eivor knew she did not have time to waste. They needed to prepare for Oisin. The sooner it was over with him, the sooner they could shift focus to King Tigernach and the danann.

Part of her had reservations about plotting war against the greatest army known to Tir. The danann were War's force. His beloved winged warriors. With the increasing number of husk makers joining them, their power grew, and Eivor did not know how they could hope to defeat the Lord of Rainbows and his army. They needed allies who were not afraid of War's champion or risking the gods' ire. Her sensible side argued dealing with Oisin was enough, and they should forget the danann. But her anger over being left to suffer while they fell at Silaine's feet was not something she could easily dismiss.

"Majesty, what will we do if we cannot convince Lord Jeffery to argue in our favour?" The justiciar looked nervous, but Eivor smiled at the woman.

"Do you really think I'm going to give him a choice?"

"You'll manipulate his mind?"

"No."

"Then how?"

Eivor remembered the unsatisfactory night the human diplomat spent in her bed. "I'm going to show him what happens when someone displeases me. And then I'm going to explain, in detail, what I was thinking while he was sticking his pathetic cock in me after accepting a night in my bed as a reward from Cathair for agreeing to support Oisin."

Disgusted mutters came from each person around the room. They all knew what Cathair had done to Eivor. If the look on her face was anything to go by, she was happy to remind them not one person had dared stand up for her. Staring at them from the head of the table, she wondered if she would ever truly trust her court. It would be easy to kill the simpering fools and start over. She could go among the common folk and elevate people who wanted to serve her. People who had been as powerless as she had been while Cathair ran roughshod over her kingdom.

But Eivor recalled those in the room cowering from her glare had been as powerless as the rest. Trying to help her would have cost their lives. It had lost lives in the beginning until all thoughts of doing anything were replaced by memories of corpses strung from the walls outside.

Her power surrounded them, picking up on the questions lurking in their minds. They might have been powerless and terrified, but she had been beaten, tortured, raped, locked in her cage without access to her magic, and Eivor understood why they had doubts. Maybe they were right to wonder if she was still sane. Some days, she was not so sure she was. When those thoughts crossed her mind, Eivor reminded herself it had only been a hundred years, and she was not so weak as to be broken by the likes of Oisin and Cathair.

'You're all looking glum!" Rhydwen sounded cheerful, striding into the chambers as though he owned the place. "Is her majesty keeping you from your lunch?"

"We're attempting to deal with Lord Jeffery, the delegate from Samphire, Your Highness," the chancellor replied.

"Attempting? That doesn't sound good. I doubt he snuck out of the palace in the middle of the night... well, he could have tried. My forces would have had fun with that. General, have there been any attempts to slip away into the darkness?"

Beside him, a dark-haired goblin with three long scars on one side of her face grinned. "No. We would have feasted on them."

"Humans tend to be quite sweet."

"I prefer elf."

Half smiling, Eivor said, "I'm sure we can secure some elves, General Vesta. Oisin took over the elven republic of Jelcobine, so there's bound to be a few in his army."

"We should start discussing those plans," Vesta said, eyeing the council dubiously. "You still haven't appointed a general-in-chief."

"That would require having someone capable of filling the position. Find me a Diwanian soldier I can count on, and I'll make them my general. In the meantime, I have you."

"Oisin won't wait."

"I know. We're doing our best."

Bursting into the chamber, the aide sent to discover if the envoy from Samphire was still in the palace grabbed the arm of a fellow for support. They were breathless from running and held up a hand to plead for a moment to gather their words.

"Lord Jeffery is packing."

Chuckling, Eivor met Rhydwen's gaze. "Excellent. Have him brought to Cathair's cell. I think it's time I reacquainted them."

Her command had the goblins exchanging curious looks. Striding the length of the room to her seat, Rhydwen arched a brow and leaned in so he could whisper in her ear without being overheard by everyone.

"What are you planning, my clever Songbird?"

"A small helping of revenge."

Kissing her cheek before straightening, the prince turned to Vesta. "Have Lord Jeffery escorted as her majesty commands. You'll enjoy this."

Snorting, the ancient warrior signalled to an aide to go. "We'll see about that."

Eivor watched Rhydwen from the corner of her eye. He kept a jovial smile plastered to his face, but she noticed the twitch of his fingers where they rested on her shoulder. Desire to cover his hand with hers coursed through the queen. From the looks directed their way, the council members did not like the familiarity Rhydwen displayed towards her. They were daoine. It should not have been an issue, and she knew if he had been one of them, it would not have. Or even a human. But the prince was a goblin. It was why she had refused to write it into the treaty that any children from their union could not inherit Diwan.

Brushing her cheek against his hand on her shoulder, Eivor murmured, "Escort me?"

"Whatever my queen wants."

What she wanted was to find a quiet corner away from prying eyes where she could shove him against a wall and bury her hands in his silky red hair. They had not shared a bed the night before, Rhydwen choosing to return to his quarters alone to deal with Thorne's revelations. Eivor had missed the warmth of him pressed to her back more than she expected after a few days. It was easy to dismiss it as desperation to return to something of her life before the invasion, when someone had always been curled up next to her at night.

Dismissing the direction her thoughts were going, Eivor accepted the hand offered and rose. "You're such a darling prince, aren't you, Rhydwen?"

Lifting her hand to his lips, he smiled. "I do try."

Her new advisers exchanged nervous looks. None of them wanted to be the one to risk her ire by asking if she expected them to follow. A trip to the dungeons to visit Cathair was an experience they wanted to avoid. They sensed the stares of the goblins dotted around the chamber. Hard looks that seemed to know how fragile their loyalty towards Eivor was. Guiding her to the doorway, Rhydwen nodded at Vesta. Swivelling on her heel, the general slipped in behind the royal duo.

"How do you plan to convince Lord Jeffery to bring Samphire to our side?"

The wicked curl of Eivor's lips had Rhydwen cocking his head. "I believe her majesty intends to show the human what will happen to his people if they side with Oisin."

"Tell me, General, did you ever meet my father?" Eivor spoke quietly, but something about her tone made Vesta's eyes narrow. "Because he taught me well."

"Aye, lass. I remember him bathed in the blood of his competition after he tore their innards apart."

"Sounds like him."

"I also remember Death pressing a knife into his hand and directing him towards toys he wanted broken but couldn't be bothered with himself."

"My father was taught by the best."

Vesta clicked her tongue in amusement. "He was. But I'll hold judgement on your ability to learn until I've seen you in action."

When the doors leading down into the dungeon appeared, Eivor did not respond fast enough to hide her hesitation. The last time she had been through them, she had been dragged by her hair, kicking and screaming, while Cathair laughed at her attempts to break free. Sensing her reluctance, Rhydwen remembered the scars Jola could not heal. He knew what she had been through and understood the sickening twist her gut would be in at the prospect of confronting those memories.

"I'm here, Songbird," he murmured. "Remember, you're in command."

"It gets easier, but you must take that first step through," Vesta said.

Glancing back at her, the gentleness in the general's tone surprised Eivor. "I thought you'd mock me for it."

"Mock you for surviving torture at the hands of two men trained by Annawyn? Never. I know how well her methods work, and I remember how nasty Oisin is."

"Perhaps they didn't torture me as badly as they could have."

"No, I doubt that. Jola informed me how deep your scars run, and we've compiled enough reports of what he did publicly to know Cathair did not go easy on you."

Aware of the watching eyes of the goblin soldiers, Eivor nodded. Pushing herself to move, she walked through the doors and into the darker corridors. Lanterns flickered at regular intervals, illuminating the path they needed to take through the labyrinth. They had designed every twist and turn to disorientate those unfamiliar with the route. Eivor knew her father had played a part in creating it. Craven had enjoyed puzzles and designed the mazes in the gardens for fun. It was among those tall walls of green she had learnt to hunt.

One goblin scraped her claws along the walls, the noise harsh in the almost silence. Eivor imagined how terrifying it would be in total darkness with no way of knowing where they were. The goblins could meld into shadows, slinking along unseen, until they were ready to sink their claws into the tender flesh of their prey. Listening to Rhydwen tapping his against the stone, Eivor could not help the pang of desire making her stomach flutter. Despite knowing the risk, she enjoyed it when he turned them on her in bed. He smiled at her knowingly, bringing his clawed hand to cover hers where it rested on his arm.

"Dinner tonight?"

She nodded, biting her bottom lip. "I'd welcome your company."

"Last night... Thorne came to me after I left you."

"Good. I hope you've sorted everything out between you."

Snorting, Rhydwen shook his head. "Mostly, I think. But we're almost at our destination, so don't fret about Thorne and me."

Her power had picked up on the occupants of the cells they passed, their emotions easy to read even though each chamber was laden with wards. Those wards dampened magic, but the ones entwined in the restraints blocked it completely. Once she was inside with Cathair, her abilities would weaken, but she had the advantage since the manacles cut him off. Not that she cared about what was inside his mind as much as she wanted to cut his skin into strips and feed it to Rhydwen in front of him.

"Your Majesty, Your Highness, General Vesta."

The guards outside Cathair's door greeted them, curious gazes taking in the crowd of soldiers and the few unlucky aides sent by advisers hoping to avoid the situation. Eivor did not care they had not come themselves; the reports from the others would serve well enough. They would recount in precise detail what happened inside the cell. If they did not, she would. Shaking off Rhydwen's grasp, the queen stepped forward to push open the heavy door. It was unlocked, and when she saw the state Cathair was in, she knew why.

Secured to the wall by four chains, his arms and legs were stretched tight, with no room for movement. At least, no action that would not strain his shoulders to the point of dislocation. A twinge of remembered pain made Eivor long to march over to him and pop his joints out of alignment. He had done it to her many times, leaving her dangling there in agony. Behind her, Rhydwen and Vesta waited to see how things would unfold. She did not approach, not yet, not until she had drunk her fill with the sight of him as helpless as she had been. It quickened her heartbeat with pleasure and the thrill of revenge. Lifting his head, Cathair stared, and Eivor watched a mixture of curiosity and anger flicker through his eyes.

"So, the beasts have kept you alive, Pet," he said, voice hoarse.

Ignoring Rhydwen's growl, she smiled slowly. "I must admit, the sight of you like this gives me more pleasure than anything else ever has."

"Oisin will come to avenge me."

"I'm counting on it."

Eivor sauntered over to him, dancing fingertips across the mottled bruises left by Rhydwen's boot. She remembered the display of violence and wondered what he would do to Cathair if given permission. When she finished with him, she would share the remainders with the prince. Mustering a sneer, he met Eivor's gaze. The cold delight present in her icy blue eyes should have sent terror slithering down his spine, but Cathair was confident the fear he had instilled in her would keep her from harming him. Tapping a finger to her chin, Eivor caught the flicker of his eyes to where the manacles blocking her magic had once sat on her wrists.

"It's surprising the goblins had someone capable of releasing you."

"Is it, though? Do you remember who caught you?"

Visions of the headless figure slaughtering his guards played out in Cathair's mind. "I should have killed the dullaghan when he arrived in my office."

"Killing him wouldn't have prevented this." Grabbing his chin, Eivor dug her nails into Cathair's jaw. "Well, it might have saved you from what I'm going to do to you."

"You don't have the mettle, Pet."

"Don't I? You and I are going to have so much fun, Master. Annawyn taught you some of her tricks, but Gebael trained my father, and he trained me."

Laughing in her face, Cathair shifted his focus to the goblins. "You'll let your prisoners torture each other, will you? Is that what Queen Calista has come to?"

"Oh, you're quite mistaken, scum. Only one of you is the prisoner here," Rhydwen replied, a haughty expression appearing on his face to mask his anger. "My mother has entered an alliance with Queen Eivor. Isn't that right, General Vesta?"

Vesta smirked, placing an armoured hand on Rhydwen's shoulder. "That's correct. The young prince is a gift to Queen Eivor and a promise of future relations."

Quickly working out what the general was not saying, Cathair paled. He had not realised the towering red-haired man was Calista's son, but knowing how goblin society worked, it did not come as a surprise to hear him referred to as a gift. It was plain what the Blood Queen wanted from Eivor, and it was more than a festering vendetta against Oisin. The calculation in Vesta's stare when she glanced between the queen and prince confirmed his suspicions. It was more than an alliance; it was a union between two powerful bloodlines.

"Stars above, Eivor, what have you done?" he whispered.

Leaning in close enough that their noses almost touched, Eivor chuckled. "I'm doing what I must for survival. Mine. Diwan's. My father's legacy. When I'm done, they're all going to regret turning their backs on me. Not that you'll care because you'll be long dead."

"The gods will strike you down if you threaten Tir."

"I'd like to see them try."

Her power latched onto the shard of fear cutting through his confidence. It filled her with delight, and Eivor relished the feeling of his mind in her hands. Cathair could not block her out without his magic, and she spared no time barrelling through his thoughts. She twisted and wove, seeking anything resembling pain to drag the sensations to the forefront. There were memories of a glorious golden-haired woman with eyes the colour of a perfect summer sky, and the pain she inflicted on him provided Eivor with precisely what she needed. Lost in the illusion, Cathair forgot she was there, but he was very aware of the hand wrapped around his throat, slowly cutting off his ability to breathe or scream.

"So, that's Annawyn," Eivor murmured. "Her technique is magnificent."

Enjoying the sight of Cathair writhing against the wall with Eivor's hand on his throat, Rhydwen said, "Having fun, Songbird?"

"My father might have taught me all he knew, but he was a warrior. Having access to memories of Annawyn torturing someone is an educational experience for me."

"Your father couldn't teach you the best ways to use your power for this." Nodding, Vesta understood where Eivor was coming from. "Careful not to break his mind. You want to plunder those memories as much as possible."

Releasing him, the queen stepped back and observed. From the way Cathair struggled, it surprised her he had not dislocated both of his shoulders yet. She doubted it would be long before he did. Knowing he was suffering because of her, Eivor smiled. It was a joyous smile, and when she swivelled around to face the new arrivals at the door, it widened.

Lord Jeffery took in Cathair's naked form chained to the wall and cowered between a pair of goblin guards. The blood drained from his face when a telltale noise signalled Cathair had finally popped his arms from their sockets.

"Ah, there you are, Lord Jeffery. It's a pleasure to see you again," Eivor said.

The dangerous purr of her voice had the human stepping back, but he found his way blocked. "Your Majesty, I'm pleased to see you're safe after all the excitement."

"You mean after the generous efforts of the goblin army in liberating Diwan from Oisin? Yes, that was rather exciting. Though I suppose you were too busy crowing about your night in my bed and the agreement you reached with my toy back there."

"I would never!"

"Of course not. I wouldn't dare admit it either, especially when the other party involved was coerced and is now rather angry. You're lucky I don't have a knife on—oh, thank you, General. That will do nicely."

Accepting the knife Vesta handed her, Eivor pricked her finger with the tip. It was sharp and perfect for the threat she wanted to convey. The rapid bob of Jeffery's throat as he swallowed repeatedly made her arch a brow. It annoyed her that she needed to leave him alive to deliver her message to the rulers of Samphire. Otherwise, she would have taken her time and extracted the retribution she wanted. He was not the only one Cathair had given her to, but he was in front of her.

"Your Majesty, I'm deeply sorry for any harm I did to you. But you understand the situation I was... am in. You understand the threat posed to my homeland?"

"I understand the only reason I don't cut your balls off right now is I need you to return to your leaders and tell them Samphire will assist Diwan against Oisin."

He stammered, eyes darting around the cell, hoping to find someone to help him. The predatory smiles on Rhydwen and Vesta's faces were almost as terrifying as Eivor's calm smirk. Daoine pressed themselves to the walls in the corridor outside, terrified of what their queen might do but equally unwilling to draw her ire by leaving. An agonised scream from Cathair accompanied the dislocation of his left knee. Huffing in annoyance, Eivor waved a hand at him and released his mind from the memory of Annawyn's torture.

"Can't have him tearing himself apart before I have my fun. Do you know what he did to me, Jeffery? The way he would slide a special blade under my skin to cut off strips. That's when he wasn't whipping me. Rhydwen, Cathair had a flogger in his possession that had shards of glass knotted into the cords. I'm going to want that." Holding Jeffery's gaze, Eivor shrugged. "Do you want to find out how it felt?"

"You have my word, Queen Eivor. I will convince my leaders to muster the army to help fight the empire. Please don't hurt me."

"Pathetic human." Spitting at him, Vesta scoffed.

"Don't worry, Jeffery. I'll send a delegation to escort you. Once the rulers of Samphire realise what they're dealing with, they'll be all too happy to help."

Eivor crossed to him, pressing the tip of the knife into his chest. Trembling with fear, Jeffery prayed to the gods he would be allowed to leave Diwan alive. He swore he would plant a hundred saplings and dedicate them to the god of life if they protected him.

"And if you fail me, my delegation will oversee a leadership change in Samphire. My father might have tolerated you humans, but I'm currently far less amiable, as are my allies. Perhaps when we're done, I'll send you as a gift to Queen Calista."

Glancing at Rhydwen, Eivor smiled. He smiled back, desire turning his emerald eyes into a simmering fire. She wanted to pin him to the wall to fuck him in front of everyone, and she doubted he would complain or make a move to stop her.

"I have a feeling the Blood Queen will gobble you right up, Lord Jeffery."

# FOURTEEN

The wine glass sat in her grasp, a forgotten presence.

"Eivor," Rhydwen said gently, watching her focus snap to him. "You can tell me if something is wrong. We're supposed to trust and support each other."

Her lips twitched with the hint of a smile at his words. Eivor slumped forward and stared at the plates of food arranged between them, placing the glass on the table. She was starving, but the thought of eating anything made her stomach churn. Memories of the encounter with Cathair continued to replay in her mind, as did the ease with which she tormented Jeffery, layering in threats of what would happen to Samphire if they did not help fight Oisin. Part of Eivor wanted to be concerned about how much she enjoyed it.

"I'm sorry, Rhyd. Unfortunately, I'm not much company tonight."

"Well, you have a couple of options. We can talk about what's on your mind, or I can distract you in other ways. I'm happy to do either."

Chuckling, she knew what he meant by distracting. It was an offer that stirred the lust she felt for the man on the other side of the table. Eivor hoped her desire for him would never fade. Nose twitching, Rhydwen lifted his drink, sipping the wine with a knowing smirk.

"You know, a few times today I thought you were going to take me in front of all those lovely people. For a duine, you're awfully aroused by torture."

"Honestly? I was tempted. You're just too pretty. It's dangerous to my focus to have you standing around looking so ripe for the taking."

He choked in surprise, his mouthful of wine spraying the platters in front of him. "What?"

Eivor fluttered her eyelashes, doing her best to look innocent. "I can't help what I want to do to you. All you need to do is stand there with those gorgeous green eyes, hair like blood, and those deliciously sweet lips. As for your arse?"

"I suppose I should expect little better from a duine."

"That's right. You can't hold me accountable for the lust you stir in me."

Rhydwen crossed his arms, arching a brow in amusement. "What about Thorne?"

"What?" It was her turn to be surprised.

"I know our favourite dullaghan stirs similar feelings in you."

Swallowing, Eivor grabbed her glass and took a swig of wine. The sweetness was cloying, and she longed for something that would burn on the way down. Opposite her, Rhydwen laughed at the furious flush of her cheeks and the annoyed look she gave the glass. As amusing as watching her reaction was, they needed to discuss the dullaghan.

"Thorne can't release us," he said. "And I'm not going to stop loving him."

"I know."

"You know what else? I have so many fantasies involving the two of you. It's insane for such a short amount of time. Maybe it's not surprising, considering we know we're probably stuck with each other for the rest of our lives."

The admission had Eivor reaching for a piece of food. Biting into the parcel of rice and meat wrapped in cabbage, she mulled over what Rhydwen might fantasise about. It was easy to imagine the scenarios. Her people held very few reservations about sex, leaving extraordinarily little unexplored.

"What does Thorne want?"

Snorting, Rhydwen replied, "Thorne wanted to fuck you at the ball."

"Oh, I know. Something about him..."

Toying with his food, the prince nodded slowly. He understood. The first time Thorne had crossed his path, he had been serving one of his mother's favourite ladies. From the moment he set eyes on the dullaghan, Rhydwen had wanted the Master of the Hunt. His distraction had earned him a flogging, but Thorne had appeared in his room that night. It was one of his most treasured memories. Whenever he thought he was worthless, Rhydwen liked to recall how one of the most terrifying people in creation had bathed his wounds and tended to them as though he were something precious. Gazing at Eivor, he suspected she would do the same.

"Thorne would burn kingdoms to protect me."

Mouth twisting, Eivor nodded. "You're right."

"Would you?"

"That's a hard question to answer right now."

"Is it? Seems simple to me."

Stroking her wine glass, she studied him. There were moments when she felt a surge of protectiveness towards the goblin. Moments when Eivor experienced the possessiveness that had gotten her in trouble in the past. She had promised him they would be equals, and their family life would be better than what he had experienced. If they failed to defeat Oisin, the prospect of losing him left an ache in her heart.

"Yes."

His eyes widened. "I didn't expect that."

"I'm already emotionally invested in our relationship, Rhydwen. You are my good thing out of all this. The light in the darkness guiding me back from the brink. Which, I suppose, is a strange thing to say considering the circumstances. Of all the reactions you could have had to the treaty foisted on us, you chose to make me smile."

"You didn't need to offer me equality. My mother would be happy if you kept me in a room to be used at your discretion so long as there were children."

"I'm not a goblin; that's not my way. Besides, we both know how it feels, and I refuse to be locked in a cage again. We are charting our path now. Together."

"And Thorne?"

"I'm not going to say no."

Shoulders slumping with relief, Rhydwen selected a cabbage parcel. "Thank the powers. I was not too fond of the prospect of being torn between you when I'd rather have you between us. We'll make this work, but I must warn you, Thorne is very... demanding."

"Is Thorne always cold? Physically, I mean."

"Yes. Why?"

Curling her toes in her slippers, Eivor shrugged. "Just curious."

"You're avoiding something."

"I don't know what you're talking about."

Resting an elbow on the table, Rhydwen leaned forward. "Yes, you do. Your scent shifts when you attempt to lie by omission."

"Oh." The revelation made her determined to wear stronger perfumes.

"So, tell me, Songbird, why does Thorne's chill bother you?"

"I don't like being cold. When I am, my fingers and toes go numb. And painful. They get a strange colouring. It's not something many people have ever known about me, and I'd appreciate it if you don't discuss it."

"That doesn't sound normal. Have you spoken to a healer about it?" Frowning, Rhydwen thought about the times they had left him exposed to the chill of winter. "Even when wrapped up in layers of warm clothing?"

"Yes, healers have examined me. I dress warmly, have extra blankets, and stay close to fires, so I don't get too cold. Thankfully, it doesn't snow here in winter."

"It doesn't?"

"No, we don't get that cold. Hailstorms, icy winds, but no snow."

"I think when it happens, you should have Jola examine you. In the meantime, be honest with Thorne. The cold is tied to his magic. He might be able to lessen it."

Clenching her thighs together, Eivor remembered the feeling of Thorne's icy fingers sliding into her. "It has some benefits."

"Setting aside the wonderful thoughts of Thorne, how do you feel?"

"I'm fine. There's nothing to be concerned about."

Eyes narrowing, Rhydwen knew she was lying. "What did I say about your scent?"

"Yes, seeing Cathair was confronting. It was also good. I needed to have him at my mercy. Delving into his mind was cathartic because it confirmed my freedom. I think part of me had been putting off seeing him because I didn't fully believe that I was free."

"Makes sense."

Eivor ground her teeth, debating if she should say anything about her other thoughts. She knew Rhydwen would be understanding. Goblin nature held a level of savagery that was uncommon among the daoine. The gods had made them that way on purpose, much like they had made the pixies and danann. Each species had once been an immortal army dedicated to the god they served. Annawyn's viciousness had become ingrained in the goblins, and as a mind mage, Eivor knew how destructive that streak could be.

"I enjoyed causing him pain. Going through his memories to find ones of Annawyn made me feel good, and I want to do it again. I want to take knives to his body, carving him open, bringing him to the brink of death before letting the healers repair the damage." Sipping her wine, Eivor held his stare. "I want to cut strips off him and let you eat them from my fingers. Then I want you to fuck me with his blood on your lips while he watches."

Rubbing his mouth, Rhydwen took a moment to mull over her admission. As much as he appreciated the viciousness enmeshed in Eivor's need to repay the pain Cathair had caused her, it reminded him of his mother. It was one thing to make jokes about it, but the thought of going through with the threat left him queasy. He suspected Thorne would be no help in the redirection of Eivor's desires, so it was up to him to temper her thirst for blood.

"You know, the torture you put him through today seemed rather effective."

Propping her chin on her hand, Eivor studied the swirl of emotions surrounding Rhydwen. "You didn't like my suggestion."

"I've seen my mother and sisters do similar for lesser reasons."

"Oh. I'm sorry." She slumped, guilt marring her face.

Her reaction surprised him, and Rhydwen said, "I understand where you're coming from, Eivor. I don't fault you for it. But maybe there are other ways you can torture him."

"Like?"

"Living."

"I don't understand."

Smiling sadly, he nodded. The idea forming in his mind was tenuous, but Rhydwen hoped she would see its merit. It would be his way of getting revenge on his mother as well. He doubted torture was as much a punishment for Cathair or Calista as it was for others. What would be painful was knowing their treatment had not broken their victims. Watching them grow and thrive would take away any sense of victory they experienced. All Rhydwen needed was for Eivor to see the sensibility of it.

"Keep him alive down there. Torture him when you need to vent some frustrations, but don't kill him. Let Cathair keep his mind intact while being powerless to stop you. Just like you were powerless against him. And while he's chained to the wall, trapped in that cell, let him watch you grow despite everything he did and took from you."

Leaning back in her seat, Eivor chewed on a piece of lamb so tender it fell apart on her tongue with a burst of flavour. She pictured what Rhydwen was talking about and considered the long-term pleasure she could gain. They would not keep Oisin alive, so the only vengeance she could have was on Cathair. Knowing what he had planned to do to her in the future, Eivor imagined forcing him to witness her ruling Diwan with Rhydwen and their children by her side. It made her hope they would be born husk makers just so she could gloat. While he slowly withered away, she could shine.

"What made you think of that?"

Rhydwen glanced away, reaching for the open bottle of wine to top up their glasses. "Because I've been told I'm only good at pleasing my betters and providing them with strong daughters. I want to show everyone how wrong they are. With you, I can hold my head high and build something we can be proud of. One day, my mother will come, and we will face her together. Then she'll understand that no matter what she and the others did to me, I never broke. You can do the same with Cathair."

"I didn't consider the long-term possibilities for gratification." It was easy to admit, and Eivor chewed her lip thoughtfully. "You're right to suggest it."

"Thank you for listening to me, Songbird."

"You're not worthless."

A wistfulness to his smile had Eivor rising from her seat to walk around the table. Cupping Rhydwen's face, she tilted it up so she could kiss him. He tasted of elderberry wine, herbs, and lamb with an undercurrent of freedom. It was strange to think of such a thing as having a flavour, but in her mind, it did, and it was him. Grabbing her hips, Rhydwen pulled Eivor onto his lap, careful not to knock her against the table. Her skin bruised easily, and he did not want to add to the mottling of marks unintentionally. Wrapping his arms around her, he deepened the kiss, sensing its hunger.

"Have you eaten enough, my precious?" she murmured, nuzzling his cheek.

"We can come back for more food." Groaning when she wriggled, Rhydwen muttered, "Though we say that every time."

"And every time we end up feeding each other in bed. I do not see the issue."

Her lips latched onto his ear, sending shivers down Rhydwen's spine. "Fuck, Songbird, at least wait until we leave the table."

"If I didn't want to eat the rest of the food, I'd suggest using the table."

Feeling the prick of his claws through the fabric of her dress, Eivor wriggled free of his lap. Licking her lips, she winked and pivoted, striding out of the room. She exaggerated the sway of her hips for his benefit, and Rhydwen watched eagerly. Giving her a few moments, he collected their wine glasses, knowing they would want something to drink. He did not know what she had planned, but he was confident there would be no physical harm involved. When he entered the room, Rhydwen placed the drinks on a small table beside the bed. Eivor was in the next chamber, taking care of her needs and giving him the time to strip.

Sprawling across the bed, he crossed his legs at the ankle and his arms behind his head. Rhydwen gazed up at the familiar ceiling, his eyes following the swirl of paint. It desperately needed a fresh coat, but he knew the image was Eivor's work. They had cuddled close the first morning, limbs entwined, and she told him the story behind the mural. Whenever he looked at it, he imagined her balancing on a ladder to paint the walls of their children's chambers. The paintings changed each time he thought of them, making Rhydwen wonder what would decide the design.

"You look comfortable," Eivor said, peeling her dress off.

Admiring her arse as she bent over to remove her shoes, Rhydwen chuckled. "Thought I'd save you the effort of getting me naked."

"Much appreciated. I do like it when you think ahead."

Standing at the foot of the bed, Eivor admired his body laid out before her. His scars melded into the shadows dancing across his skin in the fire's flickering light. She was steadily familiarising herself with each one, learning their texture beneath her fingers and lips. They were mostly smooth, unlike the raised ridges of the ones Jola could not heal on her body. Several had damaged the delicate nerves below, leaving Rhydwen sensitive in those spots. Eivor enjoyed testing his reactions when she touched those scars. Each shiver and twitch became something more she had learnt about him. She hoped he would associate them with her touch one day instead of the pain that caused them.

Arching a brow in expectation, Rhydwen waited for her to move. "I'd tell you to paint a picture, but you probably already have a sketch in the works."

"Several."

Laughing, he saw the smug curl of her lips. Climbing onto the bed, Eivor stroked the bottom of his feet. Twitching, Rhydwen yanked his feet away, eyes narrowing. Shuffling forwards, she reached for his legs, her fingers dancing over his shins, dipping beneath to brush across the sensitive spots at the back of his knees. Continuing to move her hands upwards to his hips, Eivor kissed the insides of his thighs, finding the marks left by her teeth last time. Rhydwen groaned when she sucked on one of them. Unfolding his arms from behind his head, he buried his hands beneath the pillows.

"Songbird."

Her tongue sought his cock, licking it lazily. A hint of her smugness remained, a gleam in her icy gaze holding him captive. It was rare for a female goblin to give a man pleasure, and Rhydwen doubted he would tire of Thorne and Eivor doing it. The swirl of her tongue around the head before drawing it into her mouth dragged a moan from him. All Rhydwen could do was remain pinned by her stare while watching her draw his cock in and out of her mouth.

Unable to hold back a loud groan, he bucked into her mouth. "Please, Eivor."

Releasing his cock with a deliberate pop, she smirked. "Can't handle it?"

"As much as I like your mouth, I'd rather be buried in a different wet hole."

Licking the head bobbing by her lips, Eivor chuckled when he squirmed. Crawling forward to kiss Rhydwen, she lifted her legs over his so she could straddle his waist. His hands quickly sought her breasts, tips of his claws scratching lightly across her skin. Wrapping fingers around his shaft, she adjusted her position and rubbed the head between her folds. Slowly sinking onto his cock, Eivor moaned in delight. While she rocked her hips, he pinched her nipples between the tips of his claws and rolled them gently. He knew Eivor liked to take a moment to enjoy the feel of his cock.

Bracing herself with a hand on his shoulder and her weight on her knees, Eivor kept the pace slow. She was not in the mood for something quick, wanting to drag it out until Rhydwen was begging beneath her. The tickle of his claws over her skin after releasing her nipples told her he intended to tease her.

He knew, just like Eivor did, that the ridges of his cock rubbed her in all the right places, making it a struggle to outlast him. But this time, she had an advantage. While she had pleasured him with her mouth, Rhydwen had not had the opportunity to touch her. All he could do was reach for what sensitive spots he could while she slowly rode him.

He slipped his hand between them, seeking her clit. Hissing, Eivor quickened her pace, only to realise it had much the same effect as what he planned. Resuming her slow movement, she let Rhydwen's fingers settle on her sensitive bundle of nerves. It was his choice if he wanted to hasten her peak, even though it made it increasingly difficult to focus. The sharp claws of his other hand continued to trace lines over her skin, searching out the spots Rhydwen knew would make her squirm.

"Bastard," she mumbled, losing her rhythm when he dragged the tips over a spot on her lower back that was extremely sensitive. "I wanted to please you."

"You are, Songbird."

Eivor clenched her muscles around his cock in response. "Why then?"

"Because it pleases me to feel you come undone while I'm buried in you."

To prove his point, Rhydwen picked up the pace of his ministrations to her clit. Head hanging, Eivor tried to keep the rock of her hips consistent, but she felt the threads of pleasure tightening around her spine. He had a method of coaxing her to her peak even when she tried to fight it off, the occasional prick of his claw adding to the sensations drawing her taut.

When the cords snapped, Eivor stilled, throat seizing as a whimper escaped her lips. Rhydwen kept teasing her clit, gently thrusting up into her as best he could while the spasm of her muscles squeezed him tight. It did not take much before he spilled himself inside her twitching warmth.

Collapsing onto his chest, Eivor did not move. "I was planning to torture you."

"You did." Kissing her forehead, Rhydwen adjusted her slightly to be more comfortable. "Consider me thoroughly tortured."

"When my toes stop twitching, I'm starting again."

Laughing, he believed her. It would not be the first time Eivor had gone from one round to the next with barely a break to recover. Resting his cheek on the top of her head, Rhydwen inhaled their combined scents and closed his eyes. He enjoyed these moments of stillness when the world faded, and there was nothing but the racing beat of their hearts and the fading agony of their pleasure. Those times when they were curled against each other in bed, still locked together and vulnerable.

The swirling brush of his fingers along Eivor's spine made her twitch reluctantly. She never told him off for it or tried to escape. A resigned sigh did nothing to stop Rhydwen from touching her body, and he delighted in each little breathy whimper.

"I think I'm in danger of falling in love with this," he murmured.

Kissing his chest, Eivor hummed in agreement. "Me too. Everyone else probably thinks we're insane fools. Maybe they're right. Who are we to know?"

"Would it be so bad?"

"I don't think so."

Resting his hand on her lower back, Rhydwen wondered what Thorne would say. He feared how it would feel if the dullaghan criticised him for thinking he was developing feelings for Eivor. It was strange to think of a reason anyone would argue against it. They depended on each other for survival, and building a positive relationship seemed like the wise thing to do. Emotions would ensure they fought harder to protect whatever they built together in Diwan. Especially once children became a factor.

"Do you think we're fools if we fall for each other?"

"No," Eivor replied. "I think it makes sense. Do you?"

"I agree. I'd rather love you than hate you."

# FIFTEEN

Beneath her hands, the stone felt like the only solid connection Eivor had. Her heart was racing from a mixture of apprehension and excitement. Sprawled out in front of her was the city she had only watched from a distance for years.

It looked much the same as ever: wide streets winding between compact buildings. Splashes of green hung from windows and balconies; tiny gardens tended by the occupants. Eddies of smoke rose from chimneys, thicker where it was a business instead of a home. People strode along the cobblestone roads, continuing with their daily lives, as though another invasion had not occurred.

The last time Eivor had stood atop the parapet overlooking the city, the buildings had been a ramshackle mess of damage, fire, and soldiers making piles of corpses. Oisin had not spared the common folk from his invasion, killing anyone who stood in his way. It was a sharp contrast to the goblins. She never thought she would be thankful for their way of slipping through shadows to kill their targets with a quick claw to the throat. They did not need to destroy innocents; their reputation was enough to keep most in line.

"We should go down there." Nudging her, Rhydwen watched a group of people hurrying into the palace grounds. "Just wander the streets, eat some food in a market square, and I don't know, pretend we're normal people."

Eivor dug her nails into the wall, the twinge of pain a welcome distraction. "I'm not sure we can do that, Rhydwen. Not yet."

"Why not?"

"My parents used to; we all did. But those days aren't these days, and I don't know how my people will react to me strolling through the streets as though nothing has changed. There was a war and a hundred years of occupation during which people were slaughtered, homes destroyed, and lives ruined. Oisin and Cathair were ruthless. For all they know, I was complicit."

Hoisting himself onto the wall, he nodded thoughtfully. "True, and I bet the city was a mess after they invaded. You won't know what those people down there think of you until you face them. Since we arrived, you've been clawing together something resembling what your parents had, and it's admirable. But it would help if you got in touch with your people."

"And what would you know about getting in touch with one's subjects?" Cocking her head, she tried not to feel nervous about his perch on the wall. "Could you hop off there?"

"Hop off... are you worried about me falling, Songbird?"

"Yes. Stop looking at me like that."

Rhydwen slid off the wall and closed the gap between them, giving her a smug smirk. "Like what? Have I offended you, Majesty? Should I get on my knees to beg forgiveness?"

Flustered, Eivor shot a look at the guards, who were quietly observing. His arms slid around her waist, a comforting presence drawing her into his warmth. Kissing her forehead, Rhydwen rubbed his nose against hers and smiled at the tiny giggle that escaped her lips.

"Say yes," he murmured.

"Yes?"

"Good girl."

Brushing her lips against his, Eivor hoped the breeze kept him from smelling the effects of his words. "What did I agree to?"

"Going on an outing with me!"

Rhydwen let go of her waist and grabbed her hand instead. Squeaking when he pulled her along, Eivor realised what he had planned. The guards followed, curiosity written in their expressions. Avoiding the stairs in the gate tower, he selected the narrow steps set on the inside of the wall for soldiers to use for access. Taking them slowly, he tossed a grin over his shoulder, and Eivor could not help returning it. A worried voice at the back of her mind urged caution. It was ignored by her eagerness to please Rhydwen. When they reached the ground, it surprised her to see Thorne waiting in the wall's shadow.

"Having fun?" Pushing away from the stone, he swept his gaze over them.

"We are." Rhydwen pulled Eivor closer, nodding at the open gate. "Join us for a walk in the city? It's time the queen got back in touch with her people."

Falling into step on the other side of her, Thorne snorted in amusement. "I don't think so. It's not safe for either of you to be wandering around the streets with so few guards."

Bristling at his dismissal, Eivor replied, "We'll be fine. I used to go to the city without an escort, as did my parents and sisters. Rhydwen and I aren't exactly defenceless, and with a couple of guards following, no one will dare harm me."

"I know this is his idea, pretty magpie."

"But he's right. I need to re-establish my connection with my people. Especially since we're going to war with Talaroo. My parents weren't absent rulers, and I won't be either."

Emotions flickered across his face, breaking the icy countenance. Eivor flinched, expecting his power to wrap around them as a threat. When it did not come, she glanced at Rhydwen, and he winked. The shadow of the gate came between them and the sky, distracting Eivor for a moment. It was disconcerting to see goblins lurking where daoine soldiers should have been, and it reminded the queen she needed to put more effort into rebuilding her forces. Fearsome as they were, the goblins would not be enough to fight Oisin.

"I sent River with the Samphire delegation," Thorne said suddenly. "I thought it was a good idea to have someone who could slip back here easily with any news."

"River? Do all dullaghan have such interesting names?" Eivor chuckled.

"Some of us kept the names the gods gave us. Others selected new ones after the war ended, and we were no longer obligated to serve as we had. River changed—"

Rhydwen gasped. "We can't buy anything!"

Eivor shared a look with Thorne and saw the glimmer of protectiveness in his gaze as she said, "It won't be a problem. Don't worry, Precious, I'll buy you something pretty."

"The little prince hasn't been let loose in a city like this before." Tutting, Thorne did not hide his smile. "Best be careful, or he'll empty your coffers."

"I'm sure we can indulge him this once."

Glaring, Rhydwen let go of Eivor's hand. "There's no need to tease me."

Touching his shoulder gently, she tilted her head and glanced at the first sprawl of buildings. "Have you truly never been allowed to roam a city?"

"The Spire isn't like this."

"Right. Well then, let's go find you something to eat." Straightening her spine, Eivor strode onwards without waiting for them.

Scrambling after her, Rhydwen pretended not to hear Thorne's amused snort. He grabbed Eivor's hand, placing it on his arm. Following a short distance behind, the dullaghan admired them hungrily. Sunlight gleamed off the intricate braids adorning her hair, the twists of white shining like the stars on the darkest winter night. Next to her, his hair was a cascade of fresh blood spilling down a slate cliff.

They were a beautiful pair, elegance oozing from them like magic. Silk hid their bodies from view, only hinting at the forms beneath the layers. He wanted to threaten anyone who dared look twice and yell that they belonged to him and no one else could have them. Eivor glanced back, and Thorne suspected she was aware of his possessive thoughts.

People stopped what they were doing to stare in amazement at the sight of Eivor. They had known she was alive, but few from outside of the palace had seen her since before the war. The scrutiny had the queen shifting nervously, her eyes darting from person to person as her power registered the mixed emotions. Stories and rumours ran rampant through Diwan over her involvement with Oisin and Cathair's rule. Some claimed she had helped the invasion, while others agreed the whispers of her treatment suggested otherwise. Those who believed the stories of her torture looked on with pity.

"What do you want to see, Rhydwen?" Smiling at him, Eivor scrunched up her nose.

He clicked his tongue thoughtfully. "Didn't you say something about food?"

"I did. There used to be this lovely cafe that served the most delicious sweets. I'm sure they'll have something with raspberries since they're in season."

"I love raspberries... and sweet things."

Thorne chuckled and said, "You'll have to see about having chocolate brought across from the Spire. Maybe they could grow it here."

"Not likely," he replied. "Cocoa trees like humid regions."

Curious, Eivor guided them through the streets towards where she remembered the cafe being. "What is chocolate?"

"It's a sweet delicacy made from the fruit of the cocoa tree. I don't know the process required to produce it, as the keepers carefully guard the information. What little I know about growing the trees comes from a grunt who told me about his work."

"I keep hearing that term, but I don't understand what you mean by it."

Rhydwen cringed, uncomfortable with explaining that aspect of goblin culture to her. "Grunts are undesirable males and serve as a workforce. Those slightly less undesirable fill other roles in our society, and we all live in fear of demotion."

"Oh." Squeezing his arm, Eivor shot a pleading look at Thorne.

Quickening his pace, he settled in on the other side of Rhydwen. "You're here now."

"And I'm not letting you go anywhere."

"Pretty magpie collecting shiny things."

Laughing, Rhydwen shook his head at them. "Actually, the kind of magpie her form takes after doesn't collect shiny things. I researched them as much as I could before we came here."

Eivor leaned forward to give Thorne a wicked grin. "But we are very territorial."

"Have you tried shifting forms yet?" Thorne knew the question would unsettle her.

"No. Jola doesn't think it's a good idea to try until I'm in a better physical condition."

"And you're just going to take her advice?"

"Of course. She's a healer... and she's terrifying."

Their quick exchange gave Rhydwen a chance to study the buildings lining the streets. People watched them, and his nose twitched from all the scents. Life smelt complicated, so many layers intertwined to add to the colours and textures of everything else. Most people missed it, either because they lacked the ability to enjoy it, or were too busy surviving to notice. He pitied both groups.

Eivor turned them down a different path, and the scent of fresh bread was the first thing that struck Rhydwen—closely followed by the sight of dozens of small tables and chairs with people occupying half of them.

She halted, smiling wistfully at the sight. "Bessie's Cafe. This place has existed longer than I have. Mother used to tell me stories about when she was pregnant with me and would send my father to fetch macarons because she craved them like nothing else."

"And the palace couldn't make them?" Rhydwen asked in surprise.

"It's Bessie's secret."

Meeting the gazes of the people seated outside the cafe, they reminded Thorne of his reservations about leaving the palace. He kept his power under control, not wanting to frighten them into doing something regrettable. It was essential to be on his best behaviour if he wanted to convince Eivor to stop looking at him with distrust. Rhydwen had made him promise to try to win her over with charm.

"Well, I'm looking forward to trying them," Thorne said, waving at the tables. "Shall we pick a spot to sit? Any preference? I think that one is well-positioned."

"Have you been to places like this before?"

"They're not unique to Diwan. Tir is an amazing, diverse place. Not everywhere has grown in the same manner, and there are a lot of different ideas. But the Fog stifled development."

Giddy over an unfamiliar experience, Rhydwen dismissed Thorne's choice and went to a different table. "This spot. Thorne, you'll have to tell us about some of those ideas."

"Why?"

"Because we could bring some of them to Diwan?"

Thorne sighed. "No, I mean, why this table?"

"Oh!" He grinned, nodding at Eivor. "So people can approach and speak to their queen. That's the main reason we left the palace, after all. She needs this."

She arched a brow when Thorne pulled a chair away from the table for her. "Thank you."

Inclining his head, the dullaghan waited for her to sit before shifting the chair slightly closer. His fingertips trailed across the back of Eivor's shoulders, following the dip of her dress where it exposed skin. Nose flaring, she tilted her head back to peer at Thorne, magic picking up on his desire to lean down and kiss her.

Rhydwen dropped onto a chair, affording him a view of the street and the rest of the tables at the cafe. He wanted to watch people going about their days. It also placed his back against a wall, making it harder for anyone to slip behind him.

"How do we buy food?" He watched the uniformed daoine flutter from table to table.

Repositioning his chair closer to Eivor, Thorne nodded at a uniformed duine staring at them. "If it's like any other such place I've been, they'll come to tell us what is available, and we tell them what we'd like."

"That's correct," Eivor said, raising a hand to wave to the one watching them.

Approaching slowly, the nervous duine man was careful to avoid their gazes. "Your Majesty, we did not... you weren't... I'm sorry! It is an honour to have you here."

Her throat froze from nerves, words unable to form. Eyes wide, Eivor glanced at Thorne, and he leaned forward, reading the desperation in her gaze. Smiling to appear disarming, he focused on the man.

"Her majesty was telling us about your macarons."

"Oh yes, we have several flavours. Rose, lavender, raspberry, blackberry, honey, and plain. Would you like a mixed plate?"

Recovered from her moment, Eivor replied, "Three mixed plates, please. We'd also like some peppermint tea and candied fruit."

Thorne watched the excitement appear on Rhydwen's face. "Do you have anything with fresh raspberries? If so, we'd like some of those as well."

Stammering, the duine nodded. "Of course. Yes. I will take your order inside. Do you want it brought out all at once or staggered?"

"Staggered, please. Start with the cakes and tea. If we can't eat everything, we can take the macarons back for later." Smiling warmly, Eivor was thankful for Thorne's request and the light in Rhydwen's eyes. "We're happy to sit here for a while."

"Whatever Your Majesty wants! We are here to serve."

His words dulled her smile, so Thorne reached over to place a hand on her leg. Stroking it gently, he hoped it was as reassuring as he wanted it to be. Eivor's lips twisted, and she glanced down, but Rhydwen was too busy looking around in fascination to notice.

"It's strange to hear it," she murmured.

"You've heard it before."

"Only from people Cathair allowed near me. This is different."

"Say the word, and we'll return to the palace the moment it gets too much for you."

A little brightness returned to her smile, and Eivor covered his hand with her own. "Thank you. He's right, though. I need to re-establish the bond I had with my people. Before Oisin invaded, I was the people's princess."

"What are you talking about?" Rhydwen returned his focus to them.

"Our sweet magpie was about to tell me how she was the darling of her people." Smiling, Thorne dropped his gaze to where his hand sat covered by hers.

Noticing it, Rhydwen grinned and put his hand on her other leg. "I'd believe it."

Closing her eyes, Eivor covered his hand as well. Beneath her fingers, she felt the contrasting temperatures of their skin. One incredibly warm, the other as chilly as a winter morning. It was strange to find them equally soothing, but she did. Breathing deeply, Eivor let the scents and emotions wash over her. She heard the confused chatter of the people seated at other tables and the scuff of more people arriving. Word of her presence was rippling out through the city, drawing those curious enough and with time to spare.

"I thought I should bring these to you straight away!"

The voice of the server prompted Eivor to open her eyes. He placed a plate down on the table with three small tarts decorated with fresh raspberries and a dusting of sugar. Bowing as he backed away, he waited for a word of approval.

"Thank you," she said. "They look delicious."

Almost bouncing in his seat from eagerness to try the food, Rhydwen grinned. "I'd say they look scrumptious! Thank you so much. I'm sure we'll enjoy them."

He did not wait for Eivor to select hers before plucking the one with the most raspberries from the plate. Hearing shocked gasps from the watching daoine, Eivor smiled indulgently at Rhydwen while Thorne chuckled. Pausing with his teeth part way into the tart, the goblin stared at them in confusion before noticing the stunned looks directed at him.

"Don't worry, Precious. I'm not offended."

Lowering the tart without finishing his bite, Rhydwen frowned. "I'm sorry."

"It's considered polite to wait until the queen has taken a bite before you shovel food into your mouth," Thorne said in amusement.

"I'm not standing on formality with him." Eivor chose a tart. "Or you. I don't care if Rhyd eats before me in a situation like this."

"But they care."

Sweeping her gaze across the people, Eivor remembered her parents laughing with each other over plates of baked goods. People had always smiled indulgently, pleased to see their king and queen happy, just like they had smiled at the sight of her enjoying herself with her friends. They no longer knew what to think, making Eivor realise that seeing her happy was a double-edged sword.

Raising her voice so people could hear her clearly, Eivor said, "I'm happy to talk to anyone who'd like to speak to me."

The two men raised their brows when she promptly bit into the tart she was holding. Following her lead, Rhydwen finally sunk his teeth the rest of the way into his food. His delighted groan made Thorne smile, as did the flicker of pleasure in Eivor's eyes. He wanted to watch them eat and then chase the crumbs from the corners of their mouths with his tongue. A smear of the raspberry filling taunted him from where it stuck to Rhydwen's cheek.

"So, you're alive then."

They gazed at the woman who had arrived at their table, hands on her hips. White handprints decorated an apron, and a fine-spun net covered her short hair. Bowing her head, Eivor lowered what remained of her tart to the plate, putting it next to Thorne's untouched one. Quickly finishing his, Rhydwen shook his head at the guards, cautioning them to stay back.

"Yes, and I'm overjoyed to see you alive, Bessie." Eivor nodded at Rhydwen first, then Thorne. "These two are responsible for my freedom."

Bessie's eyes narrowed. "You got names?"

"I'm Prince Rhydwen, and he's Thorne," Rhydwen said, giving a charming smile.

"You're a goblin."

"Not by choice, I can assure you."

Snorting, she nodded at him. "You've got tart on your face. Now, girly, is it true?"

"That depends on which rumour you're talking about." Picking up the last bite of her tart, Eivor popped it in her mouth while Bessie studied her.

"The one that has you as a caged little bird, ready to be tortured whenever Cathair felt like it. They said he had you restrained, cut off from your magic."

"Thorne destroyed my restraints and restored my powers to me."

"Is that so?" Bessie shifted her focus to him.

"Indeed. When I came to free your queen, she bore wounds on her back from where Cathair had whipped her days before." Thorne held Bessie's gaze, refusing to flinch.

Pursing her lips, the duine woman nodded slowly. "Thank you, dullaghan."

"She wants to restore your fair kingdom."

"And when Oisin returns for vengeance?"

Eivor smiled slowly. "We're going to defeat him. Never again will we bow to a tyrant like Oisin. Whatever it takes to keep Diwan free."

"Even an alliance with goblins and the dullaghan?" There was a hint of accusation in Bessie's voice.

"Oisin marched into Diwan a hundred years ago. Where were our other allies when he did? Or the gods? The Lord of Rainbows knew what was going on and did nothing to help us. But you know who has come to help free us? Queen Calista."

"At what cost?"

"A unified family."

Grasping the back of the fourth chair at the table, Bessie stared at Rhydwen in shock. "A unified family? Is he the Blood Queen's son? She wants you to marry him?"

"Don't you think I'm pretty enough for your queen?" Rhydwen pouted, and Thorne thought he resembled a kicked dog.

"I've watched my queen grow for thousands of years; I'm less concerned about how pretty you are than I am about your willingness to die to protect her."

Turning his emerald eyes to Eivor, he smiled in adoration. "It might be early days, but I'm willing to burn the world for her. Anyone who dares cause her harm will suffer for it."

Bessie took in the blush creeping across Eivor's cheeks and the determination in Rhydwen's gaze before turning to Thorne. "And you?"

"I would bring down the Veil to protect them," he replied.

"Good to know. Now, you enjoy your food, and I'll make sure people hear the right story. We did what we needed to survive with Cathair in charge, but we remain loyal."

Watching her stride off, Eivor rubbed her mouth in surprise. "Should have done this sooner. I'm glad you suggested we come out here, Rhydwen."

He beamed at her. "You can reward me later."

"Yes, I will." Switching her focus to Thorne, Eivor placed a hand on his wrist and smiled. "Thank you. I know you were saying what she wanted to hear, but I appreciate it."

"It wasn't a lie, pretty magpie. I'd kill anyone who dared harm either of you."

# SIXTEEN

"Did you have a good time in the city today?"

Staring at her reflection while the maid unlaced the back of her gown, Eivor wished it was someone else standing behind her. She did not want to talk about the day she spent with Rhydwen and Thorne. Not yet. Not while the pleasure of it was still thrumming through her. If she discussed it with someone else, Eivor feared the loss of her enjoyment, and she was not ready for that. It had physically hurt to part ways with them when they returned to the palace, but knowing they were joining her for dinner helped.

"It was wonderful. I needed it more than I realised."

The maid smiled, carefully slipping the dress from Eivor's shoulders. "I'm glad it helped. I heard you went to Bessie's. Did your prince enjoy her cakes?"

"They were even more delicious than I remembered. Have you ever heard of chocolate?" Helping to remove her undergarments, Eivor stroked a bite mark on her breast.

"No, I can't say I have. What is it?"

"A sweet food, apparently. The goblins make it from the fruit of the cocoa tree."

"Never heard of it."

Gazing at her naked form in the mirror, Eivor debated if she wanted to wear an evening gown or something more revealing. "I look forward to trying it one day."

Humming in agreement, the maid gathered the discarded clothes. While she took them away, Eivor started unravelling the braids of her hair. Delicate silver pins formed a stack on the dresser, glittering in the dying sunlight shining through the window. The bars of her cage remained in place, casting shadows through the brightness. Having them removed remained low on the list of priorities. Eivor knew it was no small task, but she wanted to rip them from the stone. They had installed them while keeping her strung up on a wall in the dungeons, enduring weeks of torture.

"I thought you might like this to wear tonight."

Looking at the garment the maid was holding, Eivor nodded in approval. "That certainly fits my mood. Thank you. It's just what I wanted."

Giving her a knowing look, the other woman said, "Is there anything else you need?"

"Could you start a bath for me?"

"Already done."

Pleased by the response, Eivor kept unravelling her hair. "Thank you. That's all."

"Enjoy your evening, Majesty."

She finished with the last braid as the maid left the room. The pin joined the pile, another sliver of silver to catch the light. Settling her gaze on the white silk and lace shift and sheer black dressing gown, Eivor let her thoughts drift towards how Rhydwen and Thorne would react. Aware of a bath waiting, she quickly headed to the room where the tub sat full of warm water. Lavender filled the air, lending a scent as soothing as the water would be once she was soaking in it.

Careful as she stepped into the bath, Eivor sunk into the water. The warmth seeped into her muscles, chipping at the edge of the ache left from walking around the city. Her feet were sore, but it was a pleasant discomfort. Slinging her arms over the tub's sides, Eivor settled her head back and closed her eyes, inhaling the steam. She needed to relax as much as possible before Rhydwen and Thorne arrived for dinner, especially when she had a fair idea of what they would expect from her.

Thinking of Thorne following through with the promises he had made during earlier encounters had her pulling her arm from the side. Eivor danced her fingers across her skin, tracing over the bruising left by Rhydwen's teeth. She trailed them lower, imagining they were Thorne's, seeking their way towards the spot between her thighs. The warm water of the bath did not hide how slick she had become at the idea of the dullaghan touching her. Her fingers stroked through it, circling the sensitive bundle of nerves.

"Impatient magpie," he murmured, lips grazing the top of her ear. "Don't stop."

"Thorne..."

Following the line of her jaw, he chuckled at her breathy moan. "I felt your desire calling me. You want me to replace your fingers with mine and keep touching you."

His lips trailed down the side of her neck. Eivor tilted her head sideways, exposing more of it to his attention. Skin prickling at the flick of his tongue, she kept toying with her clit and waiting for Thorne to add his hand to hers. A voice at the back of her mind prevented her from stopping, and Eivor knew it was because he had commanded her.

"Don't think I didn't notice your eyes on me all day." Running a hand through the mess of black and white hair hanging over the end of the bath, Thorne wrapped it around his fingers. "Such a needy queen, my pretty magpie."

Eyes fluttering open at the painful tug on her scalp, Eivor whimpered. "Please—"

Thorne kissed her, cutting off whatever she planned to say. His knees pressed against the tub where he had dropped to the ground. It was not the most comfortable position, but the mild pain was worth it to have Eivor pleasuring herself while he swallowed her moans. Nipping her bottom lip, Thorne tightened his grasp on her hair and chuckled.

"Remove your hand."

Disappointment ripped a whine from Eivor, but she followed his order. "Why?"

"Because our darling prince will be here shortly, and I want you desperate for release, knowing we're the only ones who can give it to you."

Eivor's nose flared, telling him she knew what he would do. "No, please."

Brushing his lips across hers, Thorne smirked. "Save the begging for later. You're only allowed to orgasm if Rhydwen or I let you. No touching yourself, because your pleasure belongs to us now, Eivor."

A thrill coursed through her at his words. She wanted to test the limits of the command, but when she went to return her fingers to her slit, Eivor felt the whisper of his power through her mind. Trying to move her hand was like pushing against a wall.

Releasing her hair, Thorne pushed himself up, using the side of the bath, laughing as he went. He watched the movement in the water and the flex of her fingers hanging over the edge. What surprised him was the lack of frustration on Eivor's face. Instead, she looked excited.

"It's time you got out," he said, picking up the towel left for her by the maid. "We don't want to leave Rhyd waiting. He might break something."

Climbing out of the bath slowly, Eivor avoided looking at Thorne. She needed to focus on anything other than what he had told her she could not do. Desire was an ache that refused to fade, spurred on by the smug curl of his lips when she glanced at him. Reaching for the towel in his hands, Eivor's eyes narrowed when he moved it away.

"Say please."

"What?" she grumbled. "You can't be serious."

"I won't complain if you march into dinner naked and dripping. Neither will our company. He'll be all too willing to put his tongue to good use."

The comment summoned memories of how good Rhydwen was with his tongue, and Eivor bit back a groan. "May I please have the towel?"

Handing it over, Thorne's grin did not fade. "Do you need my help?"

"I can manage."

"Can you, though?"

Snarling, Eivor wiped the water from her skin with quick movements. She did not care if she was perfectly dry, just that she was not dripping wet.

Tutting in amusement, Thorne plucked the damp towel from her grasp and bid her to stand still. The material felt impossibly thin in his hands, each slow stroke across her body adding to the persistent ache between her legs. He knew what he was doing, and the twitch of her muscles beneath the brush of his fingers confirmed the effectiveness of his plan.

"That's better. You're free to move."

Eivor bared her teeth and stalked out of the bathroom. Going straight to her bed, she snatched up the shift, silk sliding through her fingers. Bunching it in her fist, she watched the room's reflection in the mirror from the corner of her eye. Thorne's presence lowered the temperature, despite the crackling fire. It seemed risky to pull on the slip of fabric with him lurking just out of sight. She wondered if he would stop her from dressing as part of whatever game he was playing. Nakedness was not an issue, but Thorne had a way of making her feel vulnerable, and his power over her did not help.

"Are you going to stand there like a deer in a trap?"

"An oddly astute description."

Thorne laughed, circling until he was visible in the mirror. "You can't escape me, pretty magpie. It's hardly a fair hunt, but you can always run."

Her heart raced at the hint of a threat in his voice. The low purr of it carried the promise of what Thorne would do once he caught her. Curling her toes into the fur covering the floor beside her bed, Eivor thought about running. She wanted to dart past him and out of the chambers, leading the dullaghan in a chase through corridors she knew as well as the back of her hand. If she was going to run, she needed to go before Rhydwen arrived. Evading Thorne would be hard enough without adding the predatory goblin prince into the mix.

"Go on, do it."

Holding the shift to her chest, Eivor watched him draw closer. "Why?"

Fingers trailing down her spine, Thorne sensed her desire. "Because you want me to hunt you. The thought of fleeing until you run out of places to hide fills you with more desire than you care to admit. So go on, flee, my pretty magpie. When I decide you've run enough, I'll catch you and make you scream my name."

"You've already said I can't escape you."

"That's what makes it so delightful," he murmured, moving her hair over one shoulder. "For all your running, you know there's nowhere to hide from me. I claimed your name, Eivor. Wherever you go, I can slip through the Veil to be there."

Kissing the nape of her neck, Thorne heard the hitch of her breath. He reached around, snagging the fabric she was clinging to. It slipped from her fingers, and Eivor's hand dropped to her side. Tossing the slip onto the bed, he nuzzled her ear and pressed his palm to her abdomen. She was warm, the scent of lavender clinging to her skin, leaving Thorne with the intense desire to forego dinner so he could consume her instead.

"When there's no way to escape, surrendering saves you from pain."

His hand slid across her skin, shifting enough for his fingers to stroke between her legs. Eivor wanted to widen her stance to allow him easier access, but resisted the desire. Doing what she could to keep her breathing even, she assessed the gap she had to spin out of Thorne's grasp and run for the doorway. It was a futile endeavour and a waste of energy Eivor was willing to indulge in if it reminded the dullaghan she was not his toy.

"The sooner you surrender to me, pretty magpie, the sooner I'll soothe the ache that's keeping you from thinking straight." Catching the slight shift of her feet, Thorne smirked knowingly.

Eivor's pirouette reminded him of watching her dance. She was fluid with grace, feet gliding across the floor without faltering. Letting her go, Thorne heard the click of the distant door and the ripple of Rhydwen's magic. There was no reason to dash after the fleeing queen when the red-haired goblin was walking toward them without a clue of what was going on. When she crashed into his chest, his hands grasped Eivor firmly to keep her from falling to the ground in a heap. Aware she was naked, Rhydwen met Thorne's amused gaze.

"Songbird," he murmured, dropping his lips to her ear. "Are you trying to fly away?"

Tossing her head back, Eivor stared at him. "I..."

"Smell delicious? Yes, you do. I think Thorne's been getting you ready."

"Oh, I can't claim responsibility for all of it. Our queen was too impatient to wait for us, and she decided to see to her needs alone." Crossing his arms, Thorne smirked. "But don't worry, I took care of that problem, and she won't be doing it again."

Cocking his head, Rhydwen wondered what he meant. "I'm not following."

"I'm forbidden from touching myself. He used his power to command me," she whispered, watching the predatory gleam appear in Rhydwen's eyes.

"Really? You can do that, Thorne?"

"If she really wanted to. I'm sure she could fight it off." Taking a step, he sensed Eivor's desire to wrench herself from Rhydwen's grasp and try fleeing again. "But she doesn't want to. Any more than she wants to break free of my command that the only pleasure she'll find is if you or I give it to her."

Instincts kicking in, Rhydwen's claws pricked her skin, and he tightened his hold on her. "It seems our sweet queen wants to run away from us."

Eivor stammered, unwilling to risk the sharp weapons keeping her pressed to Rhydwen's chest. "No, no, of course not. But dinner. I'm hungry. Are you hungry?"

A growl rumbled through him, warning her not to move. He sought her mouth, capturing it in a kiss that had Eivor melting into his embrace. Hand splayed across his chest, she matched the demanding press of Rhydwen's lips. The claws holding her tight stroked her skin, leaving behind thin red lines that faded slowly. Thorne watched them hungrily, drinking in how beautiful Eivor's ephemeral glow was against the deep forest green of Rhydwen's coat. Her power curled around him, soothing the stirring of his blood lust.

"Rhyd, she has a point about dinner," Thorne said, a hint of wickedness in his tone. "We should eat first, and she can ruminate over her decisions."

Reluctantly ending the kiss, Rhydwen glared at him. "What are you on about?"

"Go put on the pretty outfit you chose for dinner, Eivor. The one on the bed."

Drawn from his grasp by the pull of Thorne's power, she met Rhydwen's gaze. His claws retracted, letting her walk to the bed where the thin scraps of fabric waited. Chuckling, the dullaghan marched over to the younger man and grabbed his arm, pushing him into the other room. Without Eivor in his line of sight, Rhydwen picked up the scent of the approaching servants with their meal. Eyes darting to the door to alert Thorne, he lingered between the bedroom door and the way out into the hallway.

"What are you planning to do to her, Thorne?" Keeping his voice low, Rhydwen watched the servants enter with their food.

"I'm not planning to do anything to her."

"Don't lie to me."

Half-smirking, Thorne shrugged. "I'm not lying. We're not going to do anything to her while we eat dinner. That's the point."

Humming thoughtfully, he nodded at the bowing servants. "And in all your little games, my love, did you stop to ask Eivor if she wanted to play?"

"You're underestimating how powerful she is, Rhyd. If she didn't want to play, she'd cast off my commands and stop me. But if you want to hear it from her lips..."

"Thank you, Thorne. She was a prisoner for years. We need to give her the freedom to say no. Without it, she'll never truly trust us."

Closing the gap between them, Thorne cupped Rhydwen's cheek gently and kissed him. Guilt flickered through him at the reminder of what had been done to the pair he desired. He heard Eivor's appreciative moan and pulled back from Rhydwen to eye her sideways. Hands on her hips, she stood a short distance away with the white silk shift clinging to her figure. The black robe hung from her shoulders, folds of translucent fabric creating a shifting curtain around her. Both garments complemented the waves of her hair, the firelight making them shimmer.

"Oh, don't mind me. Keep kissing him," she said, smirking at them.

Rhydwen took in the sight of her and groaned. "Powers, Songbird."

Arching a brow, she dropped her hands and sauntered to the table. They watched, and Thorne's hand remained on Rhydwen's cheek. While the silk covered her, it clung to her breasts and hips, the wrinkles changing with every move. Leaning on the back of a chair, Eivor purposefully positioned herself to taunt them and reached for a small bread roll. Gazing at them, she bit into it and groaned at the burst of flavour. It spurred Rhydwen into motion, but Thorne grabbed his arm, keeping him from rushing over.

"Our precious prince wants to hear you consent to this."

"How thoughtful of him."

Digging his fingers into Thorne's, Rhydwen attempted to peel them from his arm. "I don't want you to feel forced into anything. Especially since someone used his power."

"If I said I didn't want to play this game, would you release me, Thorne?" She held his gaze, and all signs of mirth faded. "Or would you leave me in this state until I was driven to agree to your terms? You said you want me desperate."

"I don't need to force you. If you don't want to play, I'll let you go, and then I'll wait for you to come to me. Because you know you would. You've wanted to since the first time you saw me," he replied confidently, lifting a shoulder nonchalantly.

"True. I won't deny it." Taking another bite of her food, Eivor's gaze shifted to Rhydwen. "I also know it would make you happy, and bless my heart, I want to make you happy. We're legally bound to each other for the sake of our lives and Diwan, and I don't want to be unhappy."

He growled at Thorne, prompting the other man to release his arm so he could dart to the table. Touching Eivor's cheek, Rhydwen wanted to tear the silk from her body. The scent of her desire was maddening, and it told him the conversation was part of the game to her.

"Say it," he whispered.

"You have my—" Eivor kissed him. "Enthusiastic consent for this."

"I want to watch Thorne fuck you right now."

Startled, the man in question walked over to join them. "That's not the plan."

Baring his teeth, Rhydwen let his claws appear the slightest amount. "I don't care what your plan was, love. I want to sit here sipping wine while you sink your cock into her."

Happy to give him what he wanted, Eivor inclined her head to the lounge. "There?"

"Yes. Go on, Thorne, strip and lay down."

Stripping as he walked over to the lounge, Thorne wondered what Rhydwen was thinking. He sensed nothing more than the overwhelming desire they both felt, and it pushed at his limits. He understood then that they could turn his power over them back on him. Perching on the edge of the seat to remove his boots, Thorne watched Rhydwen fondle Eivor's breasts, the silk shimmering with the movement of his fingers. Once he was naked, he sprawled back, arms crossed beneath his head.

Brushing his lips over Eivor's ear, Rhydwen murmured, "Our dullaghan is waiting for you to ride him. Show him how happy you are that he's here."

Eivor grinned, hips swaying as she approached him. Swallowing when she slid the dressing gown from her shoulders, it surprised Thorne that she left the shift on. Bunching it up around her waist before straddling him, she wrapped a hand around his cock, stroking it gently. Watching her position the head before she sank onto it, Rhydwen reached for a bottle of wine and popped the cork.

Biting her lip, Eivor remained still while adjusting to the icy hardness buried inside her. Her arousal had a hold over her, and she doubted it would take much to reach the climax Thorne had denied her in the bath.

Pouring a glass of wine, Rhydwen admired the sight and took a sip. "Don't move."

"What are you doing?" Thorne desperately wanted to grab Eivor's hips to make her move. "As much as I enjoy having her warming my cock, I'd rather—"

"I thought you wanted her desperate?"

Eyes widening, Eivor caught on. "Please, Rhydwen."

Sipping his wine, he smiled. "It's a pity I can't draw like you, Songbird."

"Bastard."

Returning his glass to the table, Rhydwen strode over to them. Kneeling behind Eivor, he cupped her breasts through the silk, claws pinching the nipples firmly. It made her buck against Thorne, clenching his cock tightly enough to draw a groan from him. Not caring if Rhydwen scolded him, he unfolded his arms and grabbed Eivor's hips, encouraging her to move. She did it willingly and tried to rock back against the hardness she felt pressing into her arse. Thorne kept the movement slow, meeting Rhydwen's mischievous green gaze.

Nipping Eivor's ear, he continued to roll her nipples in the tips of his claws. "Look at him, waiting for you to ask permission. He knows how much you need it."

"Please," she whimpered.

"Admit you enjoy his games." Grazing his teeth over her neck, Rhydwen enjoyed her breathy moan. "You're sopping wet from them."

"Yes! Powers, please, Rhydwen."

Arching back into him, Eivor exposed her throat to his mouth. Kissing her neck, he nipped it teasingly but did not leave a mark. Beneath her, Thorne dug his fingers into her hips, encouraging her to move a little faster. As much as he wanted to feel her come undone on his cock, he did not want to deny Rhydwen his enjoyment. Later, when they were entwined in bed, he would be free to take his time teasing them.

"Ask me nicely, Songbird."

"May I please?" Eivor struggled to speak, a coil of pleasure desperate to snap. "Please, Rhydwen, please."

Releasing her breasts, he slid one hand to her clit to toy with it while the other moved upwards to cover her mouth. "Yes, you may."

Feeling Eivor tighten around him as the peak of her pleasure crashed over her, Thorne did not fight the creep of his own. He did not know if it was because of her magic or the delicate thread of connection between them, but his climax followed closely behind hers.

Rhydwen's hand muffled her moans, his fingers continuing to coax her through the waves of pleasure to the point of over-sensitivity. When he was sure they had finished, the prince uncovered her mouth and removed his hand. She flopped forward, pressing her forehead against Thorne's shoulder while Rhydwen ran his hands up and down her back.

Kissing her temple, Thorne purred when she twitched. "Good girl."

# SEVENTEEN

Nightmares woke Eivor, prompting her to slip from the bed she shared with Rhydwen and Thorne. They did not stir as she stood to the side, gazing at them in the moonlight. Cradled in the safe circle of Thorne's arms, Rhydwen slept with his face buried in the older man's chest. A chill slinked down Eivor's spine, dragging fragments of her dreams back to the surface. She needed to get away from them and take care of the itch of her power. Her mind was too busy to go back to sleep, and lying in bed tossing and turning was not an inviting prospect. Neither was sitting in the other room waiting for daybreak.

Grabbing Rhydwen's coat from the floor, she tugged it on as she crept from the room. The last thing Eivor wanted to do was disturb them and face questions about why she was sneaking away. Clasping the garment shut, she fiddled with the buttons to secure it enough to lock in some of her warmth. Hands free to tackle the door, Eivor was careful to open it only as far as she needed. Guards lurked in the hallway outside, surprise crossing their features at her appearance.

"Your Majesty, is something the matter?"

"No, it's all fine. I'm a little restless and would like to go for a walk," she replied, forcing a smile to her lips. "Would you escort me?"

The goblin bowed her head, signalling to the others to remain. "Of course."

Eivor turned in a familiar direction. She did not know why her feet urged her to follow the halls through the palace, descending dimly lit paths until she reached the dungeons. By her side, the guard made no move to stop her or to voice any concerns she felt. It was colder below, her bare feet protesting the chill. Ignoring the ache, Eivor pushed on. Magic whispered around her, picking up on the torment of the prisoners locked away in their cells. A visit to Cathair was not what she wanted. What she needed was someone insignificant. Someone whose death would be meaningless.

"This one."

Stopping in front of an unguarded door, Eivor turned to the goblin following her. The woman frowned, lilac eyes darting between the queen and the cell. She wondered if it had been a mistake to remain silent during their journey, but now they were in the dungeon, it was too late. Whatever she wanted, the guard was in no position to deny her. Her nose twitched, picking up the scents of the two men back in the quarters they had left. They were the only ones with the influence to stop Eivor from doing anything foolish.

Cocking her head, Eivor sighed. "Please don't send for them."

"I have reservations, Majesty."

"I know. The prisoner in this cell isn't a danger to me. You can stand in the corner and watch me work. Just let me vent my frustrations."

Shaking her head, the guard muttered, "I hope I don't regret this."

"Got a knife I could borrow?"

Eyes wide, she stared as Eivor yanked the door open. Inside, a duine woman huddled on the ground, chains keeping her from moving much. The sound of them entering stirred her from her exhausted sleep, bruised face lifting to stare at them. Recognition appeared in her dark gaze, a sneer of contempt curling her lips. Eivor remembered her clearly. She had arrived with the Talaroonan invasion. Her hands had slit the throats of many children as warnings to their parents. People had whispered a name for her behind her back, but Eivor knew she was aware of it and enjoyed the infamy.

"Child Killer."

"Cathair's little pet."

Holding out her hand to the guard, Eivor chuckled. "I'll take that knife now."

"You haven't got the guts to hurt me, bitch."

Curious, the guard pulled a knife from a sheath on her belt. The blade had a curved edge, with several jagged serrations near the base. It was an unusual weapon and one Eivor looked forward to using. Holding it up, she examined it in the light of the single lantern beside the door. Since being granted her freedom, she had welcomed the feel of many weapons in her hand.

"Oh, I wouldn't be too sure about that, Nera. I'm going to kill you, and then I will do something I haven't done in a long time."

Smiling coldly, Eivor placed the knife on the ground in front of Nera. It sat near her feet while she slowly undid the buttons of her borrowed coat. Realising the queen was naked, the guard cleared her throat, but the only response she got was a face full of green fabric when Eivor threw the garment at her. A hook was buried in the wall beside the door, and the guard hung the coat on it so she would remain unencumbered. Knowing the wards reduced her magic, Eivor crouched to pick up the knife.

"When Oisin invaded my home, my parents held a foolish hope that they could negotiate with him. They held back the defences that could have protected Diwan. My mother denied her true power instead of letting it loose on our enemy. My father forbade me from fighting." Pressing the tip of the blade to a finger, Eivor sighed heavily. "I could have protected my city, but my father did not want me to reveal my abilities."

"You're not a husk maker like your pathetic mother was."

The goblin grunted in surprise when Eivor lashed out with the knife, slicing through Nera's exposed calf. It was a shallow cut, but the scent of fresh blood made her hungry. Twirling the blade in her hand, the queen tutted and rose, moving closer to the prisoner pressed against the wall. Snarling, Nera refused to show fear, choosing instead to cling to the memories of Eivor as a bloodied mess after Cathair finished with her.

"No, I'm not. I think I might be the opposite. My father never wanted people to find out what I could do. It frightened him. Thanks to the Master of the Hunt, I now know it's a gift from Death."

Grabbing a handful of Nera's filthy hair, Eivor hauled the woman up. Hands clawed at her, cracked nails barely registering through the haze of hatred she felt for the prisoner. Magic curled around her, shifting the shadows enough to draw the guard away from her spot at the door. Her muscles burned with the effort, but Eivor knocked Nera's head against the wall before letting her drop to the ground. Chains clanked as she scrambled to get away, a pained grunt escaping her lips when they drew her short.

"Oisin and Cathair have been inside your mind." Nera tried to spit at her, but the guards had been keeping her on the cusp of dehydration. "They know all your secrets."

Eivor laughed before stabbing the tip of the knife into Nera's thigh. "They're good, but I know how to safeguard my secrets. It would take the god of thought to break through all my walls, and I doubt he's in a hurry to visit me."

Creeping closer, the goblin licked her lips and watched Eivor cut through Nera's flesh. Blood flowed freely, the scent overwhelming everything else in the cell. Dragging the bloodied tip down the length of her leg, the queen pressed hard when it reached her foot, leaving cuts across the top. She was not worried about taking her time to kill the prisoner; a quick death would have served her purposes perfectly. Except Eivor remembered what Nera had done to innocent people and felt a need to make her suffer. The blood lust of her guard fuelled her desire to inflict pain.

With her body weakened, it was too easy for Eivor to slip between the cracks of Nera's mind. Magically restrained while blood seeped from each of the wounds, she had no strength to resist the claws digging into her thoughts. Ripping memories from the depths of obscurity, Eivor took her time rifling through them for what she needed. Schematics of Talaroo, discussions for defensive measures, Cathair and Oisin's plans, all of it laid out for her taking. She did not care what state she left Nera in, or the agonised screams caused by her rough approach.

"Thank you for your cooperation, Nera." Withdrawing from her broken mind, Eivor smiled. "Now, there's one more thing you can do for me."

Unable to form words, Nera stared blankly. Intrigued, the guard hovered a short distance away. She could tell death was closing in on the duine, leaving her curious about what else Eivor wanted. The screams had attracted the attention of other guards, but they remained outside the cell. When their shifts were over, she suspected many would seek her out to ask what had happened with the Diwanian queen and the prisoner.

"Tell me your name," Eivor said, her voice low and heavy with magic.

"Claire."

"Well, Claire, would you like to dirty your claws?"

Nose flaring, she nodded enthusiastically. "What do you want me to do?"

"You can finish killing her."

"Are you sure?"

"I am. You deserve a treat, Claire. Go on, sink your claws into her. I won't tell anyone if you lick the blood from her skin." Moving back, Eivor gave the guard room to creep closer. "It can be our little secret, and if you're good, it won't be the only time."

Licking her lips, Claire stared at the prone body. "If I'm good?"

"Yes. You wouldn't want to tell everyone what I do to Nera and ruin your chances of more fresh blood. This can stay between us, and there will be more."

A sliver of fear found its way into her heart, making Claire look at Eivor. She shone in the murky shadows, the moonlight of her naked form brighter than the lantern. Dark splotches blurred the glow where blood had splattered her skin, but it did not take away from her beauty. Gazing at the cascade of black and white hair, Claire felt the press of magic at her mind, urging her to agree to anything Eivor asked. Dropping to her knees, she bowed her head and held out her hands with claws fully extended.

"Wise choice, Claire. She's all yours, but leave her head attached to her body. I need her mostly intact... well, intact enough to stand."

Stepping back as the guard launched at Nera, Eivor did not resist the laugh bubbling from her lips. The sound of squelching heralded the shredding of the prisoner's stomach. It was a reminder of what goblins were happy to do. A small smile curled her lips, and Eivor watched in fascination as Claire used her claws to tear strips of flesh from Nera, bringing them carefully to her mouth.

Blood pooled on the stone beneath them, a puddle of darkness that would have been red in a different light. Part of her wanted to join the goblin, and she knew it was the effect of her magic soaking in the emotions rolling from Claire. But the thought of dragging her fingers through the blood and licking them clean was alluring, leaving Eivor struggling to restrain herself.

"That's enough now, Claire," she said, fists clenched at her side. "Leave her."

Growling in frustration, the guard retracted her claws and crept backwards. She did not enjoy leaving her kill, but Claire knew obeying Eivor would get her more. It gave her reason to do whatever the queen asked, because the moment others knew what was on offer, it would become a fight to remain on Eivor's protective duty. The others would want a chance to sink their claws into a fresh victim and eat their flesh while the queen looked on in approval. Crouched on the ground, Claire gazed at her adoringly and waited.

"Did you enjoy that?" Brushing her hands over the guard's hair, Eivor smiled.

"Yes, my queen."

"I'm glad."

Returning her focus to the corpse of a woman she hated, Eivor drew a deep breath through her teeth. It had been too many years since her last time doing what she was about to do, and her father had always been there to hold her up. Sorrow over his absence made her heart clench. Gathering her magic, Eivor pushed through the sluggishness caused by the wards. Even though Nera was dead, her brain remained in place, waiting for something to make it work. In the absence of a heartbeat, Eivor had discovered she could use her power to move signals through the body.

Gasping when Nera's body twitched, Claire shuffled back. Gazing at Eivor, she took in the look of concentration and the furrow of her brows. Magic hung heavily in the air, suffocating in the amount required to manage what she was doing. Unblinking, Eivor pressed her intentions into the empty vessel of the corpse, urging it to stand. A familiar chill crept through her body, but she understood it, thanks to Thorne. It was an uncomfortable contrast to the sweat and strain of pushing her power more than she had in years. The struggle kept her on task, and Eivor knew all she needed to achieve was a standing body under her command.

Resting her hands on the ground, Claire stared open-mouthed in amazement as Nera stood. Head and arms dangling limply, the body did not move. Straining from the effort to maintain her control, Eivor did not notice the temperature of the cell drop until fingers dug into her jaw and hair. Thorne yanked her around to face him, breaking her concentration, and the corpse collapsed. Snarling, Claire darted for the knife Eivor had discarded while pillaging Nera's mind. Her instincts screamed at her to do anything to protect the queen, even though she stood no chance against a dullaghan.

"What have you done?" Thorne growled, pulling her head back. "I felt your magic through the Veil. It should not have been possible."

His eyes darted to the body of the prisoner. Eivor's magic lingered on it, shadowy tendrils of thought urging the limbs to move. Despite his hold on her, she returned her focus to the corpse, finding it easier to exert control. Nera rose again, and Thorne shifted, staring in shock as she lifted her head and stared back with dead eyes. The chains prevented it from moving, but Eivor needed little room to make her point. Grasp slackening, the dullaghan ignored the armed guard crouched on the ground and stepped closer to Nera, pulling Eivor with him. What magic he could see fascinated him.

"How?"

"I don't need someone to be alive to control their mind. When I was better practised, it was easier to move the dead than the living. They don't push back against my influence. My father—" Eivor snapped her mouth shut when Thorne's gaze whipped back to her.

"Your father knew? What about Malena?"

"My parents told each other everything. Mother kept out of my training, fearing it would increase the chance of drawing Gebael's attention."

The jangle of chains drew his focus back to the corpse. It jumped in place, the motions lacking the smoothness of a living person. Thorne wondered if it was only because Eivor was out of practice or if the magic dampening wards affecting the cell were interfering. Releasing her, he approached the jiggling woman, gaze dropping to the evidence of Claire's part in her destruction. Intestines spilled from the gaping hole in Nera's stomach.

"Interesting," Eivor murmured, staring at the back of his head.

Her control over the body faltered, and keeping Nera standing became a challenge. With Thorne present, the numbness in her feet crept further, cooling her body to distraction. Power snapping back to her, Eivor was forced to let the corpse collapse again and doubled over in pain. It hurt to have the magic rebound. Rushing to her side, Claire dropped the bloodied knife and reached for the queen to support her. Looking between the dead woman and the one who had been using her as a meat puppet, Thorne mulled over what he had sensed. Traces of the Veil lingered on Eivor, tugging at an empty spot in his memory.

"It seems like a waste of magic."

Accepting Claire's help to stand upright, Eivor shook her head. "I could control dozens at once before the war. I'm hardly at my best right now."

"Dozens?"

"Yes. My father trained me. I can't use it on someone who has died from a husk maker's power. We tried that. There isn't enough left."

Thorne wondered why Oisin had been allowed to invade Diwan when they had a pair of Ravens and whatever Eivor's ability was. "Do Oisin and Cathair know about this?"

"The three of us in this room are the only living people who know. Everyone else who knew died when the bastard took my kingdom and executed my parents."

"You." He pointed at Claire. "Leave."

Baring her teeth at him, she kept a firm hold on Eivor's arm. "I'm here to protect the queen."

"Claire, it's fine. Wait outside with the others. Remember, not a word," Eivor said.

Without the goblin holding her up, Eivor felt the creep of exhaustion and cold. She wanted to return to her chambers and sink into a warm bath to deal with the blood drying on her skin. Closing the gap between them, Thorne cupped her face, icy fingers making her groan. The press of his lips against hers drew her focus, stirring the desire Eivor felt every time he touched her. Keeping their mouths locked together, the dullaghan walked her backwards until the wall stopped them.

Suddenly aware of his nakedness, Eivor's hands dug into his hips, and she pulled him closer. Chuckling against her lips, Thorne reached down to wrap his hands around her wrists, lifting them above her head. Pinning them with one, he dragged his fingertips along the length of her arm and down her side until he reached her thigh. Using his body to keep Eivor held up, he lifted her leg and encouraged her to wrap it around his waist. She whimpered, feeling the head of his cock so close to where she wanted it.

"You are so fucking perfect," he whispered in her ear, nipping the lobe.

Grasping his cock, Thorne rubbed it between her folds, feeling how slick she was. With her hands pinned to the wall above her head, a leg around his waist and her other foot up on the tips of her toes to keep her balance, Eivor struggled to wriggle against him.

"Please, Thorne."

"Apologise for sneaking out of bed."

Whining, she stared at him with hooded eyes. "I'm sorry I left the room. You and Rhyd looked so content asleep, and I was too restless to stay."

Pressing the head of his cock to her entrance, Thorne let her sink onto it. Eivor moaned with a mix of pleasure and pain. The cold stone wall was rough against her back, and her leg muscles protested the stretch. Switching the hand pinning her wrists, Thorne lifted her other leg to his waist and shifted back slightly. With the change in position, he found it easier to thrust into her, and Eivor whimpered as her back scraped against the wall. Stroking her throat, he enjoyed each sound and how she did her best to match the pace he set.

"I don't want to be gentle with you, my pretty magpie."

Moaning when a hard thrust caused the stone to scratch a bite mark left by Rhydwen, Eivor said, "Please don't be."

Her reply had him thrusting quicker. Covering her exposed throat with his hand, Thorne pressed down just enough to make breathing difficult. He knew how much she enjoyed it and was rewarded with a breathless moan. The command he had given her days before remained, denying her the climax she wanted. It tempted him to refuse her release, but the lingering taste of the Veil in Eivor's power made him want to reward her. He wanted to surround himself with her magic, feeling the connection to his own.

Feeling his peak closing in, Thorne tightened his grasp on her throat and murmured, "Be a good fucking queen, Eivor, and give me your pleasure."

The tugs of his command pulled at the ache of need, finally allowing it to overflow through her. Eivor tried to moan, but his mouth covered hers, and his hand restricted her throat. Lightheaded with pleasure, she felt Thorne bury himself as deeply as he could manage while she tightened around his cock. Shadows danced at the edge of her vision until he removed his hand to rest his arm against the wall. Foreheads touching, they stayed locked together while she caught her breath and waited for her heart to stop hammering.

Kissing the tip of her nose, Thorne groaned. "I'm sorry."

"Why?"

"This was hardly an appropriate place to fuck you against a wall."

Laughing breathlessly, Eivor felt him twitch inside her. "It's a bit late to say that."

"There are guards outside, and they know what we did."

"At least I borrowed Rhyd's coat. I won't be walking back naked."

Thorne growled at the thought of her making her way through the dungeon and palace with nothing more than a layer of linen to hide her body and the evidence of their union. He felt conflicted over it. On the one hand, he relished the prospect of every goblin and daoine with a sensitive nose smelling his claim on Eivor, but on the other, he wanted to sneak her back, so no one saw. At the back of his mind, curiosity tempted Thorne to find out if he could veil walk with her in his arms.

"Eivor, I—"

"Am going to draw you a bath while you walk back to your room? Yes please, I'd love that. I need to wash off the blood."

Snorting, he carefully extracted himself from her and held Eivor up while she found her balance. "I can do that for you."

Kissing him tenderly, Eivor stroked his cheek. "Thank you, Thorne."

# EIGHTEEN

"Now try."

Thorne's icy power flooded her, leaving Eivor feeling trapped in a frozen lake. It was an effort to focus on weaving her power through his, before turning the combination on the corpse at her feet. Her thoughts slid into the still warm brain far easier than previously, allowing her to command it to rise. To the side, Rhydwen stood with Jola, Claire, and Vesta, the goblins watching in rapt fascination as the dead man staggered over to join a line of bodies with vacant stares. Opening her mind to the threads linking them, Eivor let Thorne's power wash down them and strengthen her control.

"That was the easiest one yet," she said thoughtfully. "Your power definitely influences my ability to... I've never really been sure how to describe it."

He wanted to run his hands across her skin in worship, but Thorne knew they needed to stay focused. "Animate."

Rolling her shoulders, Vesta muttered, "I remember the old god of life saying her power animated us. That you can do this to the dead is disconcerting."

"But useful," Jola replied. "You could do it in battle and use the dead to replenish your forces."

Mouth twisting, Eivor looked at the bodies of dead daoine. There were less than her father had trained her to control, so she pushed through the chill of Thorne's power and latched onto the vacant minds. Breathing slowly, she forced each of the twenty bodies to stand and walk over to join the others. Once they settled into the line, thirty animated corpses waited for further instruction. At the back of her thoughts, the part who knew she was capable of more screamed curses at her weakness. Closing his hand around her wrist, Thorne allowed himself to see the shadow cast by the Veil between life and death.

Inhaling sharply, he saw the glittering threads woven through it connecting Eivor and the dead she was animating. It was beautiful, and Thorne wished he could show her and Rhydwen. Other dullaghan lurked on the outskirts of the courtyard, watching from the Veil. He knew the strange sensation of Eivor's power drew them and hoped the god of death would not make an appearance. While he could protect her from most, Thorne was as powerless as the rest of them against a god. Especially the god who held his leash.

Continuing to grasp her wrist, Thorne slipped his other arm around her waist and pressed his hand to Eivor's stomach. "Make them dance."

"What's the point of making them dance?" Vesta arched a brow, glancing at Jola.

Eivor closed her eyes, recalling the steps of her favourite dance. Pressing them into the minds of her puppets, she made them break into fifteen pairs. It was unnecessary to watch the performance; flickers of sight came from those most recently dead. The older the corpse, the harder it was to control, and the moment any rot set in, the task was impossible. She was thankful for the limitations; aware that without some form of restraint, all power was dangerous. Thorne's hand on her stomach was a comforting weight, and the frozen blanket of his power fed her more energy than she was used to.

The question left her lips before she could think twice. "What if I tried to control someone you killed, Thorne?"

His fingers dug into her. "That's an interesting idea."

"We need a prisoner to kill, Vesta," Rhydwen said, watching his lovers closely.

Grunting, the general eyed the dancing corpses uncomfortably. "I'll get one."

Utterly fascinated, Jola circled the impromptu dance floor. Her magic crept across the performers, unsettled by their state. All her instincts screamed they were dead, but her eyes saw differently to her power, leading to a strange conflict in her mind. She also knew once Calista found out what Eivor was capable of, her expectations for children fathered by Rhydwen would increase. The real question was if the power was because Gebael blessed her at birth. If it was a gift from the god of death, it might not be something she could pass to her children.

Rhydwen approached Eivor and Thorne, his hand sliding between their bodies to rest on the small of her back. Watching them, Jola noted the resulting shift in the dancers. Instead of fifteen pairs, they became ten sets of three, moving in a strange performance. She imagined the dance would be one of seduction if they were living daoine adorned in swaths of silk and surrounded by wine and music.

"I don't see how this will help us defeat Oisin," Rhydwen muttered.

Thorne glanced at the dancing bodies. "Besides the obvious factor of exhausting his forces by throwing waves of animated corpses at them?"

Cradled between them, Eivor concentrated on maintaining her connection to the dead. "You're overestimating my stamina, Thorne."

"And if we find you can more easily animate someone who died at the hand of a dullaghan? A body already tied to the Veil might take a sliver of your power. If so, you can follow a group of us as we cut a path through the soldiers."

The thought of Eivor taking part in a battle had Rhydwen growling. "We can't risk her."

"Rhyd."

"No."

"Would you lock her in her tower again in a misguided attempt to protect her?"

Meeting the emerald eyes she was on her way to adoring, Eivor saw his deep-seated fear. His emotions clawed at her magic, causing the dancing corpses to falter in their steps. Shifting in Thorne's grasp, she reached up to thread her fingers through Rhydwen's crimson hair with one hand and cupped his cheek with the other. Going onto her toes, Eivor kissed him tenderly, ignoring the collapse of the dead under her control. All that mattered was soothing his fear and reassuring him nothing would separate them.

"I wouldn't ask you to leave my side," she murmured against his lips. "Where I go, you go. Be it battle or the frozen wastelands of Ellinjaa to face Death's judgement."

"I'm afraid my battle experience is sorely lacking."

Chuckling, Thorne kept an arm slung around both their waists. "I'm sure you'd manage, especially if our pretty magpie were in danger. Which she wouldn't be."

"You expect me to believe she wouldn't be?"

"I expect you to trust I wouldn't let her be. She would be surrounded by dullaghan. And others." His gaze darted to the sky. "We have allies coming."

Curious, Eivor followed his gaze. "What allies?"

"Others who were loyal to Annawyn. Pixies, strigoi, mara. Unfortunately, we are too far away from the ocean for kelpies, sirens, and merfolk. But Calista spread word Diwan would be safe for Unseelie, so now your army will grow."

"So long as they do not harm my people."

Uncomfortable with the prospect of the daoine being feasted on by those with fewer scruples than his kind, Rhydwen scowled. "Our Songbird is right to be concerned. What guarantee do we have that they won't slaughter the innocents of Diwan?"

A strange glow filled Thorne's icy blue eyes. "We make them as afraid of Eivor as they were of Annawyn. As they are of Calista. They respect power. They understand fear, and I have a suspicion you know how to play on those feelings."

"Whatever gives you that idea?" Relaxing against Rhydwen's chest, Eivor blinked at Thorne. "My people loved me before the invasion. I wasn't the one they feared."

"Magpie."

"What?"

Recognising the quirk of Thorne's lips, Rhydwen chuckled. "Careful, Eivor."

"Fine. Yes, I know how to make people fear me. Not only am I a mind mage with ruthless tenancies and a penchant for torture, but they raised me to be a queen, even though we were mostly immortal." Huffing, she rolled her eyes.

"I expect Rhyd to be the brat, not you, Eivor," Thorne grumbled.

Rhydwen cleared his throat, choosing to redirect the conversation. "A question for you, Songbird. Considering daoine don't tend to just die, how did you practice this?"

"Humans." Shrugging, Eivor did not mind telling them. "What else are they good for?"

"Your father would round up humans to kill so you could practice animating them?"

"And torturing them."

The cheerful way she answered had both men startled. Sharing a look, they silently agreed not to push for more information. Thorne kissed Eivor's temple, aware another dullaghan was approaching through the Veil. Stepping back from them, he turned to greet his fellow as they emerged from the shadows. From the corner of his eye, he watched Eivor stiffen, her nose flaring at the sensation of power rippling through the courtyard. Her sensitivity to their magic remained as fascinating as it was the first time Thorne noticed it.

"River."

"Thorne," they replied, gaze darting to the collapsed bodies scattered across the cobblestones. "Dare I ask what has been going on here?"

"If you wait, we'll give you a demonstration. How are the negotiations in Samphire?"

"As well as we expected. They agreed to fight Oisin. It took a little convincing."

Chuckling, Eivor patted Rhydwen's chest and pulled away. "What do you expect from humans? Did you instruct them to move their soldiers towards the border?"

"I did." Inclining their head, River frowned.

"You look troubled, my friend," Thorne murmured. "What is it?"

Gesturing at Eivor, the other dullaghan said, "Your queen is soaked in the Veil. How is that possible?"

"You'll see. Any luck with the other matter?"

"Some. I met with the mara delegation, and they're happy to kill Oisin's slave traders. The pixies will redirect the freed merchandise to Diwan with the promise of vengeance. Word will spread that this land is a sanctuary for those displaced by the armies of Talaroo. We're spreading the word that it is a safe place for those who hate the gods."

Sighing, Eivor slanted an annoyed look at Thorne. "Are you putting the safety of my people further at risk? I won't risk harm to them."

"That is why you must make the Unseelie fear you. We'll keep working on your ability, it'll help your cause. Not to mention you have the dullaghan serving you," Thorne replied, waving at the corpses. "And Calista's approval."

"I'm duine, not Unseelie."

"And the Unseelie collapsed when Annawyn passed over. You'll be our new queen, the beacon to which those who hate the gods are drawn."

Scratching the back of his neck, Rhydwen was uncomfortable with what Thorne proposed. "Is that necessary? We kill Oisin, get revenge as planned, and then return here to live a happy, comfortable life with each other. No need to risk our future... for what?"

Ignoring him, Thorne approached Eivor. She tilted her head back, holding his icy stare with one almost as cold. Dragging a finger across her cheek, he smiled slowly. The swirl of power surrounding them had Rhydwen shivering, and Jola approached cautiously to stand with him. Drawn from the shadows, other dullaghan stepped free of the Veil, surrounding the courtyard to watch the pair in the middle. Cocking their head, River studied the dark threads wrapped around Eivor. At first, they thought the power was coming from Thorne, but quickly realised it belonged to the queen.

"You know what you want, my pretty magpie," Thorne whispered, leaning in to kiss her cheek. "And I believe in what you can do if you embrace your power."

"Rhydwen is right; we would risk our future."

"The god of time knows all potential futures. If we were such a risk to them, they'd make sure we never threatened their cosy lives."

Rage flickered through her at the thought of being denied happiness because it threatened the gods. "The gods don't care about anyone but themselves."

"Exactly," he purred.

"I'm not Annawyn."

"No, you're not. Your so-called family abandoned you to rot here, but you don't need them anymore. Not when you have us. We will be your family now."

Closing her eyes, Eivor felt the power of the dullaghan surrounding her. Each was an icy pillar holding the curtain between life and death taut. She wondered how easy it would be to pull back the Veil to let the chill of death ripple across Tir. Thorne's hands brushed down her arms, and his lips trailed across her cheek as he pulled back. His absence had her eyelids fluttering open, the sunlight shining on them almost too bright to bear. The dullaghan had drawn closer, becoming a shadowy circle, declaring their willingness to protect Eivor.

"Vesta has a gift for you, my queen."

Eivor's gaze found the chained duine held between a pair of goblins while Vesta approached. "I know that man."

"One prisoner, as requested. What do you want to do with him?"

"Bring him to me."

Signalling to the guards, Vesta joined Rhydwen and Jola. "Did I miss anything?"

"Oh, nothing much," Jola replied vaguely. "Just Thorne working on convincing Eivor to replace Annawyn as queen of the Unseelie. You know, trivial things."

"I'd kneel."

Rhydwen scowled. "I don't like it."

Overhearing them, Thorne glanced back with a smile. Staying at Eivor's side, he waited patiently while she examined the prisoner. The man looked miserable, bruises mottling his skin and dampening the glow all daoine possessed. Next to him, the queen was a radiant source of light and power. He refused to look up at her, but she did not care.

Hand outstretched toward the corpses, Eivor forced them to rise with the curl of her fingers. They lumbered into position; hollow bodies filled only with what instructions she planted in them. Screaming in terror, the duine captive tried to run, but his guards kept a firm hold on the chains.

"I remember you." Lips curling in disgust, Eivor contemplated ripping through his mind for helpful information. "You were one of Cathair's lap-dogs."

"Please, I'll tell you anything you need!"

"Yes, you would. Except I doubt you have any useful information."

Leaning in, Thorne said, "Are you sure?"

"When I say he was a lapdog, I mean it. Cathair wouldn't have let him overhear anything important. He was part of the... fucking entertainment."

"Willingly?"

"He came from Talaroo as a member of Cathair's household. Even helped break me in."

Growling, Rhydwen wanted to rip the man apart with his claws. "Let me kill him."

"No."

"Give me his name, my pretty magpie. Then you can make him dance." Bumping her hand with his, Thorne felt her desire for the man's death. "It is fitting he dies to satisfy us."

Tilting her head thoughtfully, Eivor trailed her power across the man's mind. She drank in his terror, the racing of his heart leaving him feeling like it would burst. It hammered a beat in his chest, and she looked forward to when it stopped. Eyes sliding to Thorne, Eivor's lips curled.

"Gallus Featherfoot."

Thorne heard her voice weave through the Veil, the pull of power calling him. He loved the feeling when it happened, but from Eivor's lips, the offering was more intimate than any given to him before. Breathing in the sweet scent of the perfume she always wore, Thorne prepared to welcome the transition into his other state.

"I accept the name you have given me."

Allowing her magic to watch the transformation of the dullaghan into his headless state, Eivor thought it had drawn a shroud over her eyes. Darkness cloaked Thorne, drawing him beyond her ability to see. When the shadows cleared, the black-cloaked figure stood at her side, nothing occupying the space where a head belonged. The other dullaghan moved closer, River watching in curiosity as Eivor placed a hand on Thorne's arm.

"Do it," she commanded quietly.

Reaching out, Thorne stopped the heart of the chained prisoner. Sensing the moment the thudding beat stopped inside Gallus's chest, Eivor split off a thread of her power, weaving it into his vacant mind. It proved their suspicions correct when she slipped her will into the fresh corpse, finding traces of Thorne's power to draw on. Compared to the other dead in her control, commanding Gallus to rise was as easy as breathing. Dropping the chains, the two guards stepped clear as the former prisoner began to dance.

"By the Veil!" River stared in awe at Eivor before dropping to their knees. "Death's grace, you are magnificent, Your Majesty."

"Well, was it easier?" Rhydwen demanded.

Eivor smiled in delight at her dancing corpse. "Much easier."

Satisfied their experiment was a success, Thorne withdrew from the Veil. Transforming back, she straightened the cuffs of her coat while studying the threads of power wrapped around Gallus. It was clear where Eivor's magic had latched on to the traces left by her own. Looking at each eager dullaghan, Thorne knew they could see it. Whatever questions they might have had about her plan to raise Eivor as a replacement for Annawyn were quashed with one dancing corpse. Even River gazed at the queen with devotion in their eyes.

"I think that's enough for today. We'll do more tomorrow. It's worth having a few dullaghan kills for you to try with. Not just one of mine."

"I'm not tired yet," Eivor replied, making Gallus dance faster.

Glancing at Jola, Thorne tutted. "There's nothing to be gained by pushing too hard."

"Listen to reason, Songbird." Rhydwen approached cautiously to put a hand on her shoulder. "Exhausting yourself won't help rebuild your strength."

Releasing the corpses with a sigh, she rubbed her cheek on his hand. "I feel like I could successfully shift into my magpie form. The longing I feel to fly."

A strangled noise from Jola had Vesta laughing. "I think the healer disagrees with your assessment. You've got plenty of time to get around to shape-shifting, so let's focus on the ability that'll help us defeat Oisin and win over other Unseelie factions."

"I'm a duine. Transforming is part of who we are."

"So is having sex with anything willing, but I don't see you trying to seduce me."

Turning to face the goblin general, Eivor made a point of looking her over. "Do you want me to? I'm quite satisfied currently, but I'm sure I can make an exception for you."

Eyes darting from Rhydwen to Thorne, Vesta smirked at the enraged jealousy on both faces. "I'd rather not end up as one of your dancing meat puppets."

"Wise," Thorne grumbled.

"It's a pity we killed him," Eivor said, flicking a hand at the collapsed body that had once been Gallus. "You could have enjoyed him. Slowly. Cathair has particular tastes."

"As do I, Your Majesty," she replied, stroking the three scars on the side of her face.

Rising to their feet, River cleared their throat. "We should move our discussions elsewhere. Perhaps over a light repast. I have just travelled from Samphire."

"An excellent idea. Her majesty must eat after all the magic she has been using." Hustling over, Jola pinched Eivor's chin and examined her. "Yes, you need food."

Hunger had not started clawing its way through her focus yet, and Eivor wanted to keep practising with the dead bodies. Especially the one Thorne had provided her. Glancing at her two lovers, she doubted they would allow her to remain. There was a flicker of concern in Thorne's eyes as she gazed at River. Whatever the other dullaghan needed to discuss was likely something Eivor did not want to miss.

"Fine. Practice can wait until tomorrow. Remember, I can't use them once a body starts to rot. Whatever this ability is, it has limits."

Rhydwen slipped his hand through hers, squeezing firmly. "All magic has limits."

Holding up a hand, River stopped them from walking away. "I am curious about one thing before we leave. Do you mind?"

"River," Thorne said. "Not now."

"It's fine, ask away." Eivor shot a look at Thorne in annoyance.

"Are you pulling their spirit back from the other side?" River suspected the answer but wanted it confirmed rather than have it eat away at their curiosity.

"No. They're dead and gone. I can't explain it very well, but I can make the brain work for a time by imposing my will on it. The longest I've controlled a body is a day before the connection broke. I suppose you could say they're like a temporary extra limb."

"So, we're not far off by calling them meat puppets?" Vesta sounded amused.

"It's a fairly accurate description."

Mulling over her reply, River said, "What happens if someone tries to kill the body again while you are controlling it?"

"My control snaps. It hurts, but not as much as shifting forms."

"You need a second mind mage to help shield you. If we take this into battle, the enemy will quickly work out that they can kill the bodies again."

No longer annoyed by the questioning, Thorne bowed her head to her friend. "Thank you for the suggestion. It didn't occur to me. Eivor's walls are powerful, but it's better to let someone else take the brunt of rebounding magic."

Smiling at River, Eivor nodded. "Thorne's right. The question is, where will I find a mind mage I'd trust with the task?"

"I think I might know someone," Rhydwen murmured, staring at his feet. "But convincing his mistress to release him might not be easy."

"Do you trust him?"

"Yes. He saved my life once."

# NINETEEN

The layers of silk and lace were armour, her crown a shield, and Eivor embraced them fully. Beneath her, the throne was a monument to power. Her maid had pinned raven curls in place to form a cushion for the circle of gold upon her head. Silvery-white braids framed her face, reaching below her shoulders. Worked through them, glittering green and blue stones were a subtle nod to her lovers. Gone were the gaudy colours Cathair had insisted she wear, replaced with shimmering black that clung to her with every movement.

At the foot of her throne knelt two freshly dead humans under her control. To the side stood the pair of dullaghan responsible for their deaths, the whisper of their power filling the room. They were in their headless states, comfortable with the fear they inspired. In part, it was all a show for the audience gathered before the queen, but they accepted her command. If anyone dared threaten her, they would stop their heartbeats before they placed a foot upon the dais.

"Our freedom is not guaranteed." Eivor swept her gaze over the quiet crowd. "If we want to remain free, we must destroy Oisin."

Murmurs spread through the daoine; their wary glances directed at those they previously counted as enemies. Pixies, mara, and strigoi were scattered among them, doing their best not to react to the fear directed their way. They viewed the goblins with less apprehension, most of the court accepting their part in liberating the city. Compared to how Oisin and Cathair had treated them, the goblins had been friendly. They were helpful and advocated for Diwanians to take back their positions.

"For a hundred years, we remained under Oisin's thumb. He invaded other kingdoms, subjecting them to the same cruelties we have endured. Well, no more. It is up to us to bring the fight to him, to liberate those other lands he controls. We will stop the slave trade he delights in and show the gods we do not need the help they have denied us."

Holding out her hand to Rhydwen, Eivor gave him a slight smile. Lacing his fingers through hers, he lifted them to his lips to place a kiss on the back. The consort's throne remained empty, a seat denied to him, but he told himself to be content with standing by her side. There would be plenty of time once Oisin was dead to convince Eivor to give him the position. Glancing across at Thorne, Rhydwen recognised the stony expression she wore.

"Queen Calista of the Spire graciously came to our aid when no one else has. It may have taken years, but they came. Our people were enemies before The Fog, and we fought on opposite sides of the gods' war. That no longer matters. She helped us because she knows how truly awful Oisin is, and that no one deserves to endure him as we have. As a sign of her desire to build a future as our ally, she sent her son to me in an offer to unite our families. My mother, Queen Malena, was no friend to Queen Calista, but we put that behind us."

Frowning, Rhydwen's gaze darted to where Vesta stood with Jola and other high-ranking goblins. They looked as puzzled as he felt. A few people in the crowd cheered, shouting thanks to the goblins for freeing them from Cathair. Pleased by the positive voices, Eivor's lips curled in a slow smile.

"Since the beginning, the gods encouraged segregation between the First People and those of us created second. They fed the fear instead of encouraging unity. If we want a better, stronger future for ourselves, we must put those feelings aside and see each other for what we are. People with equal hearts and minds who have been pawns of the gods."

Someone shouted, "But they have preyed upon us for thousands of years!"

"Because the gods told them to! They don't need to prey on us to survive. We are all dangerous when we choose to be. Or did I not make that clear?" Flicking her free hand at the two puppet corpses, Eivor chuckled. "The first god of death gave me a gift, and I will use it to destroy Oisin. With this power granted by Gebael, I will use Oisin's soldiers against him and do my best to spare the lives of our people in battle."

"Why not give his name to one of the dullaghan?"

"Do you know the names of all those close to Oisin? Who will take over when he falls? Yes, we could task one of the headless with ending his life, but we need to be in place to crush his army."

"And when it's over?" The question came from further back.

Drawing Rhydwen's hand to her lips, Eivor smiled. "We rebuild together. Former enemies united. I will marry Prince Rhydwen as a sign of hope for a better future when all people live in unity, despite our differences. No longer will we be daoine, goblin, dullaghan, human, mara, elf, strigoi, pixie, or whatever. No. We will be Diwanians, and we will be proud of our unity."

Mouth falling open, Rhydwen stared at her in shock. There was no doubt in Eivor's expression, simply the slightest smug curl tugging at the corners of her lips. Her grasp on his hand remained firm, but she made no move to place him on the empty throne. Eyes darting to Thorne, he took in her surprise. It was confirmation no one had known what Eivor had planned. Uncertainty rippled through the crowd, including the goblins. Marriage was an unusual step among them, just as it was with the daoine, but it was clear what the queen intended it to be. By marrying Rhydwen, she would establish a legacy. Their children would have an incontestable right to Diwan's throne.

"That's unnecessary," Vesta said, voice carrying over the crowd. "Queen Calista doesn't expect a marriage between your families. She respects Diwan as a daoine nation."

"I know what she expects, but my parents taught me to lead by example. My marriage to Prince Rhydwen of the Spire will be one of hope for a unified future where everyone is free to be with the ones who make them happy. Besides, if the danann can pluck husk makers from among the daoine with no one raising a concern, why can I not claim a goblin as my husband? At least I chose him willingly, not because of a magical bond that I had no say in."

Shaking off his shock, Rhydwen said, "If that was a proposal, I accept."

A council member cleared his throat. "Perhaps this is something we should discuss in council. Rather than making hasty decisions, Your Majesty."

"Hasty?" Releasing Rhydwen's hand, Eivor rose to step down from the dais. "I assure you, I've thought over my decision. Hasty would be commanding you to prepare for a wedding before we go to war with Talaroo."

"Of course, Majesty." Bowing, he shot a look at one of his fellows.

Black silk pooled around her feet like ink on the creamy marble. Clicking her fingers at the two corpses, Eivor made them rise, their arms dangling at their sides. She swept her gaze across the crowd, power soaking in the mixed emotions of every person gathered there. Lingering on the clusters of Unseelie, she thought back over the meetings with them. Within a day of River returning from Samphire, they had filtered into Diwan, seeking audiences with the queen others had claimed would be welcoming. Each day, their leaders came to the courtyard where Eivor trained with her power and saw what she was capable of. It helped secure their allegiance.

"We are all in this together. Oisin will come to reclaim Diwan, and we will meet him at the border. It is up to you to decide whether you wish to stand tall or kneel with his boot on your throat. I know what I prefer, but I'm just the one you watched Oisin and Cathair torture."

The wave of shame washing across the daoine contingent told Eivor her words had served their purpose. It reminded her court of what she had endured while they sat back and pretended they were not in danger of the same fate. While she suffered, they hid in their chambers and prayed they were not next. Eivor was the queen they had watched grow under the guidance of their previous rulers. They knew she was as ruthless as her father had been and would follow where she led, even if they disagreed with her approach.

Eivor snorted in amusement before spinning around to stride out of the chamber without looking back. The two corpses ambled after her, pulled by commands whispered through their empty minds. Doing his best not to run, Rhydwen shrugged and grasped his hands behind his back as he followed. He was not the only one to chase after the queen, but he was the first to reach her in the corridor leading out of the throne room. Grabbing her arm, he pulled Eivor close and captured her lips in a kiss.

"Did you mean it?" he whispered.

"Every fucking word."

Kissing her again, Rhydwen ignored Thorne's glare. The puppets stood pointlessly, waiting for direction from the one pulling their strings. Jola lingered further away, busy working out how Calista would react to the news of

Eivor's intentions. She wanted to believe it would please the goblin queen to know her grandchildren would one day inherit the throne of Diwan.

"If you intended to flush out anyone opposed to your rule, congratulations, Eivor, you've succeeded. Marriage to a goblin will certainly do that," Thorne said, her voice dripping with anger. "At least you had the sense to say it wouldn't happen until after the war."

Meeting her icy stare, Eivor smiled. "I thought of that."

"You're playing games with him."

"This isn't a game, Thorne. When we win against Oisin and return victorious, I will marry Rhydwen. He will be my consort, the father of my children, and the one sitting on the throne beside me. At least have the decency to be honest about why you're upset."

Each step she took to close the gap between them increased the swirl of frigid air surrounding Thorne. Clinging to Eivor, Rhydwen swallowed nervously.

"Thorne, Eivor, this is unnecessary. Please."

Hands shot out to grip both of their chins, and Thorne sneered. "You belong to me. If you think I'm jealous, then I'd remind you all I must do is command you not to marry."

Smirking, Eivor replied, "Oh, so this is the behaviour of someone who isn't jealous?"

"Correct."

"Forgive me if I call out your lies. Remember what I am, Thorne. I feel your every emotion, and when you think loud enough, I hear your thoughts without delving into your mind. So, tell me again how you're not jealous at the thought of us marrying."

Fearful of Thorne doing something they would all regret, Rhydwen grabbed her wrist. "Thorne, release us."

"Never!" Snarling, she tightened her grasp. "You are mine."

The two corpses launched themselves at the dullaghan at Eivor's command. It was enough of a distraction to cause Thorne to release them. Shoving Rhydwen behind her, the queen stood with her head held high, magic swirling and desperate to be used. Snapping the neck of one body, Thorne rounded on the queen, and the temperature dropped.

"You think you can defy me, my pretty magpie pet?"

Mouth twisting in a determined sneer, Eivor lashed out with her power. "Kneel."

Her knees buckled and the desire to drop to her knees sent a tendril of fear through Thorne. The slight widening of her eyes told Eivor everything she needed to know, and she stepped back, recalling her power.

"I'm sorry I didn't discuss my plans with you, Thorne."

Anger faltering, her eyes darted from Eivor to Rhydwen. "Why didn't you?"

"Because I am the queen here. You claimed our names, his heart, and a place in my bed, but this is more than that. This is politics. I'm taking the arrangement proposed by Calista and twisting it to my terms. No one is going to dictate my happiness to me."

"With the arrangement Calista proposed, you could have claimed a respectable duine husband to make your consort and father to the future rulers of Diwan."

"I will not keep Rhydwen as my lover to visit when my husband bores me. I'm not like that. He deserves better, and I want to give it to him."

Thorne huffed in amazement, observing Rhydwen biting his lip in a way she knew meant he was overwhelmed. "You don't love him."

"It's been a few weeks since you freed me, Thorne. Give me a few more and I'm sure I'd offer you a different answer. Just because I don't love him right now doesn't mean I won't love him tomorrow. We've already admitted we're not opposed to feelings growing between us. I'm not fighting it. I want to love him so much it hurts."

Jola stared in shock before glancing back at Vesta and the others who had joined them. They had the sense to look uncomfortable with seeing the argument between Thorne and Eivor. Rubbing his mouth, Rhydwen refused to look at either of them, his heart torn over how to respond. He loved Thorne and had done so for decades, but Eivor was his chance at a future he had only dreamed of.

"Thorne, you know I love you," Rhydwen said, keeping his voice low. "But I want this. I don't care that Eivor didn't ask me. I would have said yes either way. She can give me the future I want."

"You're a dullaghan, Thorne. You've claimed our names and a part of us that no one else can. We have no way to do the same for you. My marrying Rhydwen will not cast you out. It's a legality to protect us, our children, and their future." Arching a brow, Eivor held out a hand to her.

Breathing deeply, Thorne hated feeling the way she did over the matter. It should not have been an issue. Meeting the concerned emerald eyes of the man she loved, she knew what Eivor had said was true. She did fear them casting her out. They planned to build a family together, but neither had said what her place would be in it. Dullaghan were servants of Death who slipped back and forth through the Veil dividing the living from the dead. They could not have children. There would be no newly born dullaghan for them to dote over.

"Thorne?" Eivor murmured.

Shaking her head, Thorne turned and fled through the Veil, leaving the conversation before she said anything else that could not be taken back. Left speechless, Eivor blinked at the space where she had been before turning to Rhydwen. He was equally stunned, mouth moving silently. Running away was not something he imagined Thorne ever doing. They gazed at each other, dread and regret digging trenches in their hearts.

"What have we done?" he whispered fearfully.

"Nothing we can fix right now. Come on, Precious; we need to head to the council chambers. People want to speak to me, and I'd like you to be there."

Catching her arm, Rhydwen shook his head. "We've hurt Thorne."

"So it seems. However, I'd argue some of it is not our fault. I felt flashes of emotion that had nothing to do with us. Thorne will come back when she's ready. Until then, we have a kingdom to rebuild and a war to prepare for." Stretching up, Eivor kissed him softly. "Focus on what we can deal with in the here and now."

"What if she doesn't?"

"She will."

"How can you be so sure?"

Eivor sighed, lifting a hand to adjust her crown. "Because, for all her protests, Thorne loves you. You are her mate. She fears abandonment, something I understand, as do you. I regret how the conversation happened, but perhaps it was for the best."

"And what if she ends our relationship?" Rhydwen clenched a fist, resisting the urge to release his claws. "I don't want to lose her."

"I know it's hard to avoid thinking about the possibilities, but all you're going to do is spiral into a pit of anxiety. Please, Rhyd."

Picking up his hand, Eivor stroked it until his muscles relaxed enough so she could wriggle her fingers between his. The tightness of his grasp hurt, but she refused to pull away. Closing his eyes, Rhydwen took several deep breaths and tried to focus on the sweet scent of Eivor's perfume. He appreciated her continuing to use the same mix of acai and black raspberry. It was an acknowledgement she knew what he liked and wanted to please him. Slowly opening his eyes, Rhydwen drank in the concern in her gaze and smiled sadly. Whatever happened with Thorne, he had Eivor.

"I'm sorry."

Glancing down, Eivor's mouth twisted with regret. "I'm the one who should apologise. We can talk about it later, but the longer we stay here, the more impatient people will get. At least being politely scolded with a coating of courtier flattery will distract us."

Drawing her hand to his lips, he kissed their linked fingers. "I arranged for my mind mage friend to meet with us later. Jola helped convince his mistress to let him."

"What makes you so sure I can trust him?"

"You'll see."

Leaning on his arm as they walked down the corridor with the others trailing after them, Eivor hoped she was not wrong about Thorne. The Master of the Hunt was the driving force behind what was unfolding around her. Without that support, she knew they did not stand a chance of defeating Oisin. At her side, Rhydwen was a stew of emotions battering the walls of her power. Instead of gently asking him to rein them in, Eivor let them drown out the rest of the world while she focused on the fragile threads of magic holding the remaining human corpse together. She left the other where Thorne had dropped it.

Passing it, Jola scowled and shared a look with Vesta. "Better get rid of that."

"Never thought I'd say this, but we should suggest she stop practising. There's a limit to how many fresh corpses we can provide."

"At least she's using them until she can't anymore."

Vesta snorted. "True."

"Hopefully, with Thorne out of the way for the moment, we can replace dancing corpses with physical training to help rebuild her strength. She's going to need it."

"This plan they're forming..."

"I know."

"Do you think Oisin will enter the battle to confront her?"

Making a noise of doubt, Jola shrugged. "You remember how obsessive he could be? He thought he had Eivor under control and Diwan secured. That he isn't already here battering down the gate is a surprise."

"The pixies said his forces are on the move."

"Then I hope you're ready, old friend. Because he will slaughter all of us if we don't win." The healer nodded at Eivor pointedly. "And what he'll do to her will make anything Calista has ever done look like a picnic in a field of wildflowers."

Waving at the lumbering corpse, Vesta said, "Once he sees that, he'll keep her alive. Do you think the old Death knew what he was giving her with his blessing?"

"The things Gebael knew that no one else did could fill a library."

"I'm still amazed Craven trained Eivor to use it. Though, I suppose I shouldn't be. I remember coming against him in the arena. He had a ruthlessness to rival Oisin. It always surprised me Annawyn didn't claim him."

Troubled by the reminder, Jola swallowed and gazed at Vesta. "What if she did? Would we know? The only reason we know Gebael blessed Eivor at birth is because Thorne told us. She's a damn powerful mind mage, and the Master of the Hunt is determined to crown her the new queen of the Unseelie. What else does Thorne know?"

# TWENTY

"I am over 3000." Blocking a blow intended for her leg, Eivor grit her teeth against the burn of her muscles. "This should be easier."

Snorting, Vesta darted in for another strike at the flagging queen. "And dead. Again. Perhaps this time, you'll take my advice and stay down."

Eivor groaned, bending over to brace herself on her knees. "Fuck you."

"Is that an invitation?"

"Why did I agree to do this?"

"I'm the one who should ask that. It was your idea. I suggested running laps of the gardens. Your stubbornness doesn't make up for lack of muscle."

Leaning against the wall, Rhydwen watched in amusement. "She's right, Songbird. Just because you used to do something doesn't mean you can pick it up again overnight. You're going to feel those cuddles the ground gave you."

"At least we know I remember what I'm doing. Captivity didn't make me forget how to hold a sword." Straightening, Eivor whimpered at the spasms of pain in her back.

Eyes drifting over her dirty shirt and trousers, Rhydwen suspected it would be a long, hot bath sort of night. He did not mind the prospect of tending to Eivor's aching body. Especially when she had been rebuffing his advances for the last two nights with mutterings about her courses coming. It would be an opportunity to prove he could take care of her, while expecting nothing in return. Rhydwen had overheard her discussions with Jola and knew Eivor was used to suffering through them.

"I don't think you're going to want to move tomorrow," Vesta said, chuckling at the other woman's pained expression. "You might need to carry her to bed, princeling. Because I don't think she wants to walk the distance."

Embarrassment stirred the embers of her determination, and Eivor threw the training sword at Vesta. "You know where that belongs."

"Why don't you put it back yourself?"

"Because I'm the queen."

Peeling away from his spot on the wall, Rhydwen walked over to offer his arm to Eivor. If she asked to be carried, he would do it, but until those words left her mouth, he would simply be there. Smiling, he made a point of running his gaze down her body, enjoying the view of Eivor in something different. Her lips curled in a mixture of understanding and annoyance, but the flush of her cheeks told Rhydwen his look had the desired effect. Noting the pained flinch as she moved, he told himself to summon Jola once they were back in her quarters.

"If my opinion means anything, Songbird, you held up well." Kissing her cheek, Rhydwen winked at Vesta. "Considering you're out of practice."

"Just you wait until I'm back in practice. I'll wipe the yard with your arse and make you thank me for the honour," she grumbled.

"If you say so."

Eyebrows rising in surprise, Vesta suspected he was trying to feed Eivor's determination. "I'll pay to watch that happen."

Standing on her toes, Eivor put her face to his. "You've never seen a Raven fight. Or my father. I fight the way my parents taught me."

Her comment had the general chewing her lip in contemplation. Vesta had seen many Ravens fight and envied the smooth transition between forms that allowed them to attack from the ground and above. That Malena had trained Eivor in their methods was not surprising, and once the queen could transform again, she looked forward to sparring with her. Some of her favourite battles in the past had been against Ravens. Though the greatest of them had been against Eivor's sister, the Battle Hawk.

"I'm sure you're a terrifying opponent," Rhydwen said.

"Aye, she is."

Gasping, Eivor spun to stare at the man in the shadowy entrance. He looked worse for wear, but she would recognise him anywhere. Reluctant to let her run over to the stranger, the prince kept a firm grasp on her arm.

She shook him off. "I thought you were dead."

Holding up his left arm, the man revealed a stump where his hand used to be. "Not for lack of trying, lassie. I'm mighty sorry about your parents."

Vesta stared at him, covering her mouth, recognition flaring in her eyes. "Alistair."

"You know this man?" Wishing he could stop Eivor's slow walk towards the stranger, Rhydwen glanced at the general. "Who are you?"

"Well now, never thought I'd see you leave the Spire, old woman. How's your knee?" There was a hint of a smile when he looked at Vesta.

Throwing herself at him, Eivor did not care who saw her hugging the dishevelled man. "Father sent you with the vanguard, and I thought... they all died. How are you here?"

"Sheer fucking luck. Some bastard Talaroonan took my hand, but I killed him. I wanted to make it back but suffered blood loss. Got taken in by a nice farming family, but by the time I was well enough, Oisin was in charge."

"So you hid?"

"Not the only one, my girl. People talk outside the city, keep their heads down, do their work, and avoid attracting attention. Pay taxes on time, and no one looks twice. Word's spread about what's happened here, and now we're coming back."

Scoffing, Vesta shook her head and approached the two daoine. "Forget Oisin's invasion! I thought you died in the arena."

Alistair smirked at her knowingly. "You mean you thought you killed me? Aye, you came damn close, old woman. But I was Craven's closest friend. Do you think he'd let me die to a few measly claw wounds when he had a Raven for a wife?"

"General, you should know Alistair is aware of my abilities," Eivor said. "He even helped my father procure bodies to train with."

"You and I need to talk." Flashing the claws of one hand at him, Vesta smiled.

"Is that a threat?"

"Not today. I've been telling this one she needs a general of her own. If you're here to kneel to her, I'll recommend you for the job."

He laughed. "Will you now? I wouldn't take the position when Craven was alive. Preferred my freedom to roam and make myself a nuisance."

Suspicious of Alistair's presence, Rhydwen kept his distance. "Songbird, we should get you cleaned up. Jola will want to inspect you for injuries."

"Jola?" Alistair sounded surprised. "Didn't think she'd leave Calista's side."

"She did for this. Queen Eivor needed a healer, and Calista wanted it to be the one she trusted implicitly." Retracting her claws, Vesta extended her hand, and he gave Eivor a gentle shove.

"You know, old woman, you made me a promise the last time you left me bleeding in the sand while an audience watched on and cheered."

"Did I?"

"Aye, you did."

Vesta remembered the day they faced each other in the arena. It had been a promise made in jest, knowing what the outcome would likely be. She had walked away from their bout, leaving him barely alive, and sworn she would never fight to entertain the gods again. Grabbing a fistful of his worn tunic, she yanked Alistair to her. The mocking smirk that had always infuriated her was softer than she expected, his kiss possessing a tenderness Vesta doubted she deserved. Retreating from him left her filled with regret.

"It's only a few thousand years late, lion."

"A promise is a promise." Holding up his stump, Alistair chuckled. "Not much of a lion these days. Can't shift with a missing hand, but I can still hold a sword in the other, and I'll serve my queen no matter what."

Clearing her throat, Eivor gazed at them, a bemused smile making her eyes glitter with mischief. "Father always said you were a heartbreaker, Alistair."

"Guilty as charged. This is the one who evaded my charms."

Rhydwen shook his head in disbelief. "Why don't I take you back to your quarters, and we let these two catch up? I'm sure they've got a lot to discuss."

The two old warriors eyed each other thoughtfully, and Alistair nodded in agreement. "I could use a bottle of wine. Or two. Can't say the drinking is as good outside the city."

"I can catch you up on the last few weeks," Vesta said.

Shoulders slumping, Eivor realised she was being dismissed. Part of her wanted to insist on remaining, but inactivity had given the pain a chance to settle. Everything ached, making her regret the training session. It was a suggestion she should never have voiced. The others were right. There were better ways to rebuild her strength without leaving herself in pain. A tendril of a headache was scratching at the base of her skull, the throb urging her to crawl into bed and hide beneath the blankets.

With reluctance, Eivor said, "I should clean up and let Jola make a fuss. Join us for dinner? Both of you. We have so much to talk about."

Nodding grimly, Alistair understood what she meant. "I shouldn't have let Craven send me with the vanguard. Things might have—"

"Ended the same way. No, I'm thankful you survived, and I'm ecstatic to have you return. Especially now we're preparing for Oisin's retaliation. I'm going to kill him."

A shadow of hatred drifted across the duine warrior's face, and Rhydwen frowned. It did not lessen his distrust, but shifted his suspicions slightly.

"If you cannot, I will. We heard what he did to your parents. Craven..." Glancing down at his stump, Alistair growled. "Craven was my closest friend. I would have died for him. Instead, I'll die for his daughter if that's what it takes. I swear by the gods, Eivor, if you do not kill Oisin, I will."

Meeting his gaze, Eivor inclined her head. "I understand."

"Do you?"

"He killed Lorcan in front of me."

"I'm sorry. He was a good man and would have made fine consort for you."

The grief in Eivor's eyes felt like a punch in the gut to Rhydwen. It was the first time he had heard the name of her former lover spoken by her, and it was a reminder her heart had belonged to someone else. Lorcan had died to make her suffer. No one needed to say it aloud, but Rhydwen knew Eivor would not have decided to marry him if the other man had still lived. In the back of his mind, a voice that sounded too much like his mother reminded him he would never be her first choice. He was a political arrangement.

"Perhaps," Eivor replied. "But I think the man I've chosen will be at least as fine. The Eivor who loved Lorcan was a different woman. I don't know if he would have supported who I'm becoming."

Alistair eyed Rhydwen doubtfully. "It's true then?"

"Yes. I'm sure Vesta will tell you everything. Let me make this clear. I agreed to the treaty, but marrying Rhydwen was my idea and my idea alone."

"That might be so, but in lieu of your father, I'll be the judge of his worthiness."

Brow furrowing, Rhydwen blinked at Alistair. "She is your queen."

"Aye, boy, she is, and I'm the closest thing she's got to family. If you ever hurt her..." His chuckle made the prince flinch. "Regretting it will be the least of your worries."

"I'd never intentionally hurt her."

"So you say."

"I mean it. Eivor is... she is everything." Openly staring at her, he smiled sadly.

Snorting, Vesta let her thoughts on the situation show, drawing Alistair's attention. He could tell from her expression there was much she had to say about the queen, the prince, and their arrangement. They might have been on opposite sides of the arena many times, but he trusted Vesta to speak the truth about what was happening in Diwan. Not whatever illusion Eivor would spin.

"Claire!" Vesta summoned the woman from the shadows. "Make sure the queen returns to her quarters safely. No side-tracking through the dungeons."

"Yes, General."

Wriggling her brows at Rhydwen, Claire nodded at the archway out of the training yard. Thankful for the opportunity to get Eivor away, he placed a hand on the small of her back and gave a gentle push. She hissed in annoyance, shooting a look over her shoulder at him.

"Remember, I expect you both for dinner," she said, dragging her feet.

"Would you stop dilly-dallying and go clean up? Perhaps take something for your pain? I can see the winces you think you're hiding." Alistair grinned, tutting as he shared a look with Vesta. "You put her through her paces."

"She asked for it. I told her it was a stupid idea."

"That sounds right. She always was the stubbornest of the three of them. Too much like her father. Once Eivor latches onto an idea, good luck changing her mind."

"Insufferable old man," Eivor muttered affectionately, and stopped resisting Rhydwen's attempts to lead her away. "Dinner. Or else."

Claire fell into step on the other side of Eivor, examining her nails disinterestedly. "So, who is he exactly? Seems a bit too familiar with the general."

"I hope you're not going to welcome him into your court without a little bit of suspicion, Songbird. Surely you can see how questionable the timing is." Rhydwen kept his hand in place, ready to offer more support if she needed it.

"The gods created Alistair and my father in the same cluster. Their first memories are of standing together while the gods named them. They chose them to be warriors in the arenas, fighting many bouts together. If you think he would bring me harm—"

His claws pricked her back, cutting off her words as Rhydwen said, "Yes, I do. He makes my instincts scream to protect you. I'll do anything to keep you safe, Eivor. Anything."

"If you're truly concerned, I'll delve into his mind."

Unsure of what she thought, Claire rolled her shoulders and flashed her claws. "Maybe that's for the best. Before you get too excited by his return, make sure he isn't a threat. If he considers you family, why did he wait until someone else freed you?"

Blue eyes like ice glanced in the goblin woman's direction. "You were born during the Fog, weren't you? You never knew the horrors of the arenas. I was born before they ended, and I remember the carnage. Alistair knows the value of survival."

"And sometimes survival means making a deal with your enemy." Rhydwen rubbed his face. "You would have called me your enemy a year ago, but here we are."

Opening her mouth to argue, Eivor saw frost creeping across the cobblestones. Rhydwen stared in shock at the figure stepping out of twisting shadows, a dusting of snow creating a sheen on the black of her clothes. Delicate icicles clung to her hair, but the mix of fear and determination left the prince speechless. Inhaling sharply, Eivor stepped forward, moving to slap Thorne. Catching her wrist, the dullaghan shook her head in warning, snow falling from the waterfall of black hair.

"Careful, my pretty magpie."

"How dare you walk away like that and make us worry!"

Lips twitching, Thorne yanked Eivor to her. "You were worried about me?"

"Yes!"

"I'm flattered, but you had nothing to be concerned about." Shifting her gaze to Claire, she nodded. "I need you to fetch the general. We have a problem."

Rhydwen looked startled while Claire darted off. "What do you mean?"

"What do you think I mean?"

"I don't know. That's why I'm asking."

Stroking Thorne's cheek, Eivor caught flashes of a forest she knew well. "We're out of time, aren't we? Oisin is coming for us."

"Yes."

"Right. I need to return to my quarters to clean up. You can tell me everything while we walk. Rhydwen, fetch Jola. It will be a long night of meetings, and I need pain relief."

"I'd like to know—"

"And you will." She did not hesitate to silence him. "Thorne will tell you while Jola fusses over me. You know what she's like. It's quicker this way."

Gaze drifting over Eivor's clothes, Thorne took in the state of her. "What were you doing?"

"I was having my arse kicked by Vesta."

"Are you hurt?"

"Mostly my pride, but yes, a little. It's the hurt of a fool who overestimated what she was capable of after years of inaction."

Snorting in agreement, Rhydwen said, "Vesta tried to talk her out of it. Said to start slowly with basic exercises and running, but no, Eivor insisted on a sparring session."

"Sometimes a lesson needs to be learnt the hard way," Thorne murmured, releasing Eivor's wrist. "I'm not sorry for leaving as I did, but I apologise for making you worry."

"I'll go find Jola. Meet you in Eivor's quarters. Don't dawdle. You know she hates to be kept waiting." Spinning, Rhydwen did not hesitate to run.

Stepping back, Eivor's mouth settled in a grim line. "You've been in Ellinjaa, haven't you? It explains the snow when you arrived."

"How do you know there isn't snow on the other side?"

"Because this is the first time you've appeared from the Veil with snow."

Thorne snorted, nodding slowly in agreement. "True. And yes, I was."

"Why?"

Brushing snowflakes from her skin, Thorne did not answer. She did not want to fight with Eivor before discussing what was coming. Oisin's army was nearing the border, leaving them with days to scramble for a defence.

"Because we have more important things to worry about, all I will say is that I went for help. Now, shall we walk and talk? Or do you want to anger Jola?"

"Fine, but we haven't finished this conversation. You made Rhydwen cry."

The comment was a stab in her heart, and Thorne let Eivor walk without her. It had not occurred to her that her actions would cause Rhydwen pain. Glancing back, the duine huffed, but did not stop to let the dullaghan catch up. Scrambling after her, Thorne saw the simmering anger in Eivor's eyes when they slid her way.

"I saw Oisin's army. They'll reach the forest on the border within a few days."

"We knew it was coming."

"Thought we had more time. I half expected him to send people to find out what was happening and threaten you before resorting to this."

Eivor ground her teeth and did not reply. Her mind was a whirlpool of possibilities and memories of meetings where her father discussed defensive strategies. There had been options he refused to consider that would have impacted Oisin's invasion. One thing she was certain of was she would do whatever it took to protect her people. Diwan would not fall back under the control of the bastard from Talaroo. She would sooner raze the kingdom than surrender it to anyone, especially Oisin.

"There might be a way we can stop them," she murmured, eyes sliding in Thorne's direction. "But I have a suspicion my idea won't be well received."

"If you think that, why bother suggesting it?"

"From what you saw, would you say most of Oisin's forces will go through Nelkin Forest? Or are they going to take the time to go around?"

Scowling, Thorne considered what she had seen. "I'd say through. From what I sensed, he has husk makers leading the way."

"We cannot allow them to enter Diwan."

"That's a given. But unless our numbers have drastically increased in the few days I've been gone, we're outnumbered."

Sadness tinged her faint smile. "Yes, we are. But there's one way we can tip the balance in our favour. We just need to make it to the forest first."

What Eivor was thinking of doing crashed into Thorne's mind, and she gasped. "You want to burn the forest with Oisin's army within? How?"

"It'll take coordination, oil, and a handful of dullaghan willing to scare the wits out of the enemy while the flames take hold. Who doesn't fear the hoof beats of a headless rider?"

"And the fire?"

"All we need to do is make sure our side of the forest is lit. The dry season will take care of the rest. I've seen bushfires turn those trees into an inferno in a matter of hours."

Troubled by the straightforward way she suggested burning an army alive, Thorne sighed. "I see why you doubt the others will welcome your idea."

"My father refused to do it the first time. I won't make the same mistake."

"People will call you a murderer."

"All because I burned my enemy alive? Yet, they would hail me as a victorious queen if we met in combat and slaughtered them."

"I don't want to see you lose, so I'll support your idea. But are you prepared to face the consequences of your decision when the fires have died?"

Eivor smiled, and her chuckle reminded Thorne of the god she had briefly served. "If it secures the freedom of my people, I'll endure whatever name they want to call me. Let them make me into the villain if they must. My spine is strong enough."

# TWENTY-ONE

Everything hurt. Her muscles burned from overuse. It had been more hours than Eivor could remember since she saw her reflection, but she suspected some of Vesta's blows had blossomed into bruises. Muscles and joints had seized from sitting for half the night while they discussed options and made plans for fighting Oisin. Jola had kept her supplied with mild pain relief, but the bitter taste of the concoctions had long since faded, leaving her feeling like someone had dragged her down a street and run her over a washboard. Pain dug vicious thorns into her skull. Her lower back ached with an unwelcome familiarity, and she doubted her temper would improve.

Covering her eyes to block out the dancing colours at the edge of her vision, warning her of an impending headache, Eivor tried to focus on what Alistair was saying. He had surprised her with his support of her plan to set a forest on fire while the Talaroonan army was in it. Others had argued against it, but she was determined to destroy as much of their enemy as possible without killing her people or their allies. The pixie leaders had sent warriors to prepare the forest, their ability to veil walk and fly giving them the best chance of getting things done before Oisin's forces entered the trees.

Rhydwen squeezed her leg gently under the table as he leaned closer to murmur, "How are you feeling, Songbird? You don't look good."

She shook her head and lowered her hands. Forcing her eyes open, Eivor flinched at the spike of pain from the light. People were not paying her attention, focused on what Alistair was explaining about the land on their side of the forest. As horrible as she felt, the sight of her people seated side-by-side with those they had once considered enemies filled her with joy. Without the gods encouraging discord, they stood a chance at building something together they could all be proud of. It would not happen overnight, but Eivor looked forward to the day when everyone was welcome.

"They're discussing the minor details now. Surely there's no need for you to stay?"

"I'm the queen," she whispered.

Scowling, Rhydwen sought Thorne's gaze, hoping for support. "You'll use a lot of magic in the upcoming battle. Don't make me summon Jola."

Blinking away the floating patches in her vision, Eivor sighed. "I need her anyway."

Thorne studied her, noting the signs of pain accompanying the flickers over the bond. She understood Eivor's desire to remain in the meeting, but it was pointless if the information would not be retained. Better to put her to bed with a sleeping draught than continue the sham of being an active participant of the war council. People would be less annoyed by her leaving than by repeating the information they thought they had already given her.

"Be reasonable, Eivor. You're clearly in no fit state to continue. Jola has been slipping tonics to you all night. It is not weakness to admit when you need to stop."

"But what—"

"We have made the crucial decisions. You won't miss anything important."

Their furious whispers drew the attention of others, and Alistair fell silent. He frowned at Eivor, familiar enough with her to recognise the signs of pain. Cocking his head, he nodded to Vesta before rising from his seat. It was better for everyone if the meeting ended, and it would allow his queen to depart without feeling embarrassed.

"I think it's time we put this meeting to bed. Quite literally. We must leave tomorrow if we're to be in position before Oisin crosses the border. We can gain nothing more from talking." Alistair swept his gaze across each person in the room. "I recommend we all get some rest. Do you agree, General Vesta?"

"I do. Everyone should make their preparations before retiring for the day. We've spent the night making plans, and the sun will be up again soon. Your Majesty," Vesta said, bowing slightly to Eivor.

Smiling tiredly, she nodded in agreement. "It's a good idea. We all need rest."

Relieved he would not need to argue with her, Rhydwen rose and held his hand for Eivor to take. Accepting the help, she did her best not to wobble where she stood. No one said anything, but their thankfulness was written into the emotions flooding the chamber. There was much to be organised, and the longer they sat in the council chamber discussing minor details, the less time they would have to make their plans. The daoine participants wanted to warn their friends and family and tell them to run in case the defence failed.

"General, Alistair, I trust the two of you can coordinate our departure tomorrow?" Eivor looked from one to the other with a raised brow. "Keep me informed."

She stepped free of her seat and allowed Rhydwen to lead her from the room. Outside was darker, the only light coming from lanterns interspaced along the hallway. Guards and aides watched Eivor walk away and prepared for their orders. Shutting her eyes, she trusted Rhydwen and Thorne to keep her safe and listened to the sounds of the palace. It was eerily quiet, their footsteps echoing. Eivor hoped they could stop Oisin and keep the sounds of bloodshed from replacing the silence.

"Thorne, can you fetch Jola? I'll take Eivor back to her chambers and get her to bed." Rhydwen did not want to wait too long for the healer to attend to Eivor.

Smirking, the dullaghan eyed Eivor sideways. "Perhaps you should carry her."

"Tempting."

"I can walk," Eivor muttered.

"You're hobbling like an elderly human. Save the protests for something worthwhile and let him carry you like the dashing prince he is."

Grinning, Rhydwen wriggled his brows at Thorne. "Dashing, am I?"

"Very. Throw her over your shoulder and ignore anything she says. Tell her you won't give her a massage if she misbehaves."

Vanishing into the Veil, Thorne left them with their escort of guards. Scooping Eivor up in his arms, Rhydwen kissed her forehead. She did not argue, too tired and sore to care. All she wanted was to crawl into her bed. It felt like every part of her body hurt, making her wish Vesta had refused to train with her. In hindsight, Eivor knew the session would never have happened if Thorne had arrived sooner. They would have spent the day in planning sessions instead and prepared to leave a day earlier.

"We'll get you out of this dress and into bed as soon as possible. I'd say you should eat something, but I think sleep will be better for you."

Groaning when a spasm struck her lower back, Eivor pressed her face to his shoulder. "There's some irony to be found in the timing of this."

"True, and we can joke about it after we beat Oisin."

"What if we don't, Rhyd? What if we lose?"

Lips thinning, Rhydwen refused to consider the possibility. "That won't happen, Songbird. We're going to roast his soldiers, and then you're going to accompany Thorne and the other dullaghan straight to him while turning their kills into your puppets to distract the others."

"Rhydwen."

"Then you're going to gut the fucker without hesitation."

"I don't want to be captured by him again," she whispered.

"You won't be."

"Please, Rhydwen."

Snarling, he almost dropped her in anger. They were nearing her quarters, and Rhydwen did not want to fight with her over the chance they might fail. A life in which Oisin imprisoned Eivor again was not one he wanted to consider. Neither was the one in which she was dead. He needed to believe they would win.

"Promise me if it goes bad and we can't escape Oisin, you'll make Thorne kill him."

He exhaled, anger fading slightly. "Of course. All the dullaghan know he is not permitted to leave the battlefield alive."

Rubbing her cheek against his shoulder, Eivor cracked open her eyes slightly. "I wish the rules governing the dullaghan were vague enough that we could tell them to kill anyone in charge of Talaroo. It would be so much easier."

"We'll capture his army commanders and dismantle his rule."

"I could have an empire."

"Would you like one?"

"No. We'll free the other captured nations from Oisin's rule and help restore them. It might incline them to ally with us."

The guards spotted them coming and opened the door. Servants had kept the fires and lanterns going for Eivor's return once the meeting ended. A tray of fruit sat on the table, drawing Rhydwen's attention long enough for his stomach to register his hunger. He wondered if she would want to eat some to help keep her energy up. Spotting the bowl of mixed berries, he decided to return to get it once she was in bed.

"I'm going to set you down next to the bed. If you feel unsteady, hold the post."

Carefully lowering her legs, Rhydwen did not let go until her hands gripped the post at the end of the bed. The laces at the back of her dress became his target, fingers dancing through the silk ribbons holding her bodice tight. Since arriving in Diwan, silk had quickly become his favourite material. His mother owned garments crafted from a different type of silk, but she only wore them for special occasions. One day, he would get his hands on bolts of the precious spider silk to gift Eivor. One of his favourite things to imagine was her draped in the translucent material and glowing in the moonlight.

"You need to let go now so we can get this dress off. Tell me if it's too much."

Her eyes remained closed, pain causing her to bite down hard on her lip. Eivor felt a vulnerability that would have left her anxious with anyone else, but Rhydwen's gentle touch and whispered praise wrapped a sense of safety around her. In his hands, she knew no harm would come to her. By the time he had stripped her clothes from her body, Eivor wanted to collapse onto the bed and pretend there was no world outside. He picked her up again and carried her to the bathroom, where he helped her take care of her needs. There was no teasing, no wandering hands seeking to tempt her, and every touch was careful.

When he laid her down on the bed, Rhydwen pulled a blanket over her and kissed the tip of her nose. "I'll be right back. Is there anything I can get you? I know your courses are upon you, and I want you to know you don't need to feel ashamed of them."

"Thank you, Rhyd," she mumbled, pressing her face into a pillow. "My maid ensured she stocked up my supplies. I'll sort myself out once Jola has been."

Sighing, he returned to the other room to collect the bowl of berries. As he walked, Rhydwen plucked a raspberry from the mix and plopped it in his mouth. It was a little under-ripe, a touch of sourness cutting through the flavour he adored. When he returned to the bedroom, Eivor had stretched out on her stomach, face buried in the pillow. Her exposed back bore faint scars, the remnants of the torture she had endured. They haunted him. Part of his mind raged that he had failed to protect her, even though it had happened before he knew she existed.

"When Jola has been and given you something to help with the pain, I'll treat you to a massage. You know how good they feel."

The pillow muffled her response, and Rhydwen chuckled, perching on the bed beside her. Brushing her hair to the side, he encouraged Eivor to turn her head so he could see her face. Her eyes opened enough to make out his expression, and she watched him eat another berry from the bowl in his lap. Hunger twisted her stomach, but the pain hammering to break free of her skull brought waves of nausea with it.

"I'm sorry."

His brows rose in surprise. "Why?"

"I get terrible headaches. Always have done."

"With your courses?"

"Not just with them."

Rhydwen wanted to stroke her hair and offer comfort but was wary of causing her more pain. "What can I do to help you?"

"You can move out of the way, boy," Jola said from the doorway. "And help her sit up enough to drink what I give her."

"Songbird, I'm going to slide an arm under you."

Brushing his lips against her temple, Rhydwen waited for her to grunt. As gentle as he could, he helped Eivor roll onto her side. She clung to his waist, leaning against him with her eyes clenched shut. Jola clicked her tongue in frustration, fingers dancing over the queen's head and down to her neck and shoulders. Magic wove through her, picking up on the various aches and what her body was going through as part of its natural fertility cycle.

"How long do your headaches normally last?"

"A few days. But if I treat them when I first notice the signs, less."

Grunting, Jola shook her head and looked at Thorne standing in front of the windows. "And you expect her to ride out to battle like this?"

"I'll manage."

"You can barely open your eyes in this low light."

"Blindfold me."

Sniggering, Rhydwen could not resist enjoying the idea. "Tempting."

"I'm not joking," Eivor grumbled. "Blindfold me, and I'll ride with Rhyd. Whatever it takes to get me to the battle so I can stick a knife into Oisin."

Thorne stepped closer to the bed, her power like a cold mist. "You'll ride with me."

"No, I'll ride with Rhyd. Not because I don't want to ride with you, but because if I need to be protected, you're slightly more dangerous than he is. And you'd make me too cold."

Nodding slowly, Rhydwen hoped it would not displease Thorne that he agreed with her. "If you needed to shift, it would take longer to stop to get her off your horse."

"Eivor can tolerate my power."

"No." Jola crossed her arms, glaring at the dullaghan. "Not in this state. I've known plenty of people who suffer from these debilitating headaches and terrible courses. She should stay in bed until the worst passes, and I'll insist on it in the future. But this is war."

"You can sulk all you want, Thorne, but it won't change anything. I'll do whatever is needed to help make it easier for her," Rhydwen said, pressing a kiss to the top of her head.

Squinting at him, Eivor smiled faintly. "Thank you."

Tempted to tell the queen he was only saying it because goblin culture expected males to tend to their women, Thorne dug her nails into her palm. It was unfair of her to ruin the affectionate moment between them because of her jealousy. She knew it was partially because it was something she would never experience. Rhydwen would never bend over backwards to care for her in the same situation. Watching him dote on Eivor was a glaring reminder the dullaghan were not on equal standing with everyone else.

"Keep her up while I fetch a few things. I'll give you something strong for the pain now because once we leave the palace, it won't be safe to give you anything that will make you sleepy. Or anything that might impair your magic."

None of them spoke while Jola hurried from the room. Keeping her face pressed to Rhydwen's chest, Eivor did her best to ignore the warring emotions swirling around her chamber. She wanted to scream at them to stop thinking and feeling, but it would not help. They needed to talk, but her head hurt too much to listen. Somehow, their much-needed conversation about why Thorne fled would have to be fit in before they faced Oisin and his army.

"We need to talk." The fabric of Rhydwen's shirt was soft against her cheek.

Thorne sighed heavily, making sure the curtains covered the window completely. "Yes, but not now. I feel flickers of your pain."

"How long have you been experiencing them?"

"Since the pain started."

Cringing, Rhydwen understood what Thorne was not saying. "You only feel things from us when what we're experiencing is strong."

"Indeed."

She wanted to look at Thorne, but opening her eyes was too much effort, so Eivor settled for simply saying, "I'm sorry."

Walking around the bed to stand next to them, Thorne reached out to stroke their cheeks. "Don't be. When I feel those flickers, I know you're alive."

Rhydwen searched her gaze, questioning how she felt. "Our Songbird is right. We need to talk. You and me most of all. There are things we need to decide."

"I don't want to fight with you."

"Then we won't fight. We'll talk like reasonable people."

"Can we—"

"Her majesty needs rest," Jola said, approaching them with a cup in each hand.

"Yes, she does," Rhydwen replied. "We'll make sure she gets it."

Humming with disbelief, the healer pressed the edge of a cup to Eivor's lips. "Drink this first. It's ginger to help settle your stomach. I don't want you vomiting."

Taking slow sips, Eivor felt her stomach revolt against the drink. Once the nausea settled a little, she pulled back. The scent of ginger faded, replaced with something bitter that made her glad for the first drink. Doing her best to gulp it without bringing it back up, she screwed up her face.

"Ginger again, please," she whispered.

Returning the cup of lukewarm ginger tea to Eivor's mouth, Jola chuckled. "Good thinking. You can use this to chase away the taste of the other."

"One day, someone will devise a way to make medicines taste less unpleasant." Pulling a disgusted face, Rhydwen winked at Thorne. "How long will it take, Jola?"

"Not long. Keep her upright until she falls asleep, then we'll lay her down."

Feeling useless, Thorne asked, "What can I do?"

"I made some blends to help relieve her muscle aches when she wakes. You can put them next to the bath. There are also some salves I want one of you to rub into her stomach and lower back to help ease her cramps."

Pulling back from the cup, Eivor pressed her lips together and fought the urge to vomit. Her stomach protested the liquids combined with the lack of food. Hunger demanded to be satisfied, but she feared the result if she ate anything.

"Not sitting well?" Jola recognised the signs.

"No. I'm hungry, and those drinks did not help."

Rhydwen reached for his abandoned bowl of fruit. "I have some berries. Would you like to try eating those? You can have them one by one and see how you handle it."

Agreeing with him, Thorne nodded. "Better than nothing. You need to keep your strength up."

Confident they could handle Eivor, Jola returned to the other chamber. Plucking a blackberry from the bowl, Rhydwen held it to her lips. Eating slowly, Eivor had to admit it was a clever idea. It was easy to squish the fruit in her mouth and swallow without setting off her nausea. He kept his selections small, placing each on her tongue. Leaving him to deal with feeding Eivor, Thorne backed away to join Jola. She wanted to go through what was needed to help combat the queen's pain.

Noticing the moment Eivor stopped moving, Rhydwen carefully twisted to place the bowl down. He wanted to stretch out in bed with her cradled against his chest. He would have if the dullaghan in the next chamber had not fled them days before. The conversation he needed to have with Thorne could not wait, and it was best to get it over with while Eivor could not become involved. It was important for Rhydwen to sort out his relationship with Thorne. Without peace between them, there would be no peace as a trio.

Laying her out in the middle of the bed, Rhydwen drew one of the thinner blankets over Eivor. He did not want her to overheat when Jola's drugs might keep her from being able to do anything about it. The room was warm enough to be comfortable with daylight approaching outside and the fire crackling away in the corner. Kissing her gently, he slipped from the bed and picked up his bowl before heading to the sitting room. Thorne was alone at the table, staring at an arrangement of items with a distant look on her face. The windows were uncovered, the bars dark lines against a pale sky.

"Did Jola tell you everything we need to know?"

"Yes. She also reminded me we need to rest as well." Thorne glanced at him. "I'm sorry for leaving as I did, but I needed to get away."

Plopping down on the lounge with his food, Rhydwen snorted. "Good thing you did."

"She might not be in as much pain if I hadn't."

"You know I love you."

Turning, Thorne stared across the room at him sadly. "I've known for years."

"I never asked you to say it back."

"Maybe you should have."

Chuckling, Rhydwen swallowed a blackberry. "I didn't need you to say it, Thorne."

"Why not?"

"Because if you didn't feel something for me, why did you stay by my side since the day we met? You've protected me from my mother for years."

"I'm not a cruel person, Rhyd... and you're my mate."

Waving a raspberry at her, he replied, "Eivor wants to love both of us. She's used to a different life than we are. Before Oisin, her life was happy and stable. That's what she wants to rebuild with us by her side. Don't you want that?"

"Dullaghan can't have families," Thorne whispered. "I never thought much about it before we came to Diwan. When Eivor declared she would marry you, it forced me to acknowledge what I wanted."

"We're your family."

"You'll give her children."

The realisation struck Rhydwen, and he sighed. "Dullaghan cannot have children of their own. The gods didn't think of that when they made you."

"Or they did and didn't want us to create more."

Hopping to his feet, the prince crossed to Thorne and cupped her cheeks. The faint shimmer of tears was present, but nothing trickled down her cheeks. Smiling sadly, Rhydwen leaned down to kiss her tenderly, feeling arms slip around his waist.

"I'm sorry, and I know it doesn't help your pain, but our children will be just as much yours. If you decide to stay, you'll be with us through all of it. We want you to be."

"I don't want to be anywhere else, Precious."

# TWENTY-TWO

With one of Jola's concoctions dulling the pain, and the numbing effects of the salves on her lower back and abdomen, Eivor prepared to enter the cell. She knew that outside, people were mounting horses and leaving for a battlefront they were determined to control. As soon as she was done with her visit to the man on the other side of the door, Eivor planned to join them. First, she needed to give her former captor a parting gift.

"Are you sure you want to spend your energy on this?" Rhydwen murmured at her side. "It's going to be a hard ride, and you'll need everything you have when we get to the end."

"I'm not planning to use much. Just a little so he doesn't relax."

Opening the door, Thorne waited for Eivor and Rhydwen to walk past before joining them inside. Huddled on the floor with barely enough slack in his chains to move, Cathair did not lift his head to see who had entered. He was used to being tormented by the goblin guards. Occasionally they allowed members of the court who had suffered to come in and return the favour. But no one had permission to harm him permanently, so Cathair dismissed them.

"What are you going to do to him, pretty magpie?" Thorne studied the man, longing to kill him for everything he had done to Eivor.

At the word magpie, Cathair's head rose. "Well, well, well. Hello, Pet."

Eivor snarled, preparing to lash out, but Rhydwen quickly grabbed her. Held back from attacking him with her hands, the queen drew on her power. When she requested to be brought to the dungeon, she had planned to lock Cathair's mind in a torturous loop. Not enough to break him, but enough to keep him at the edge of madness until she returned with Oisin's head to place at his feet.

She looked forward to the look on his face when he discovered his beloved king was dead because of her.

"Do what you came here for, Songbird. Don't waste time listening to him," Rhydwen murmured, green eyes locked on the smirking prisoner.

"Look at you, Pet, letting a goblin put his hands on you. Your parents would be disgusted by how far you've fallen." Spitting at them, Cathair laughed.

Clenching her fists, Thorne resisted the urge to snap his neck. "Are you sure you want to keep him alive? I'm happy to kill him now."

"No," Eivor replied. "I want him to suffer. Let him waste away in this cell, never setting eyes on the sun again. He can watch us grow stronger together."

Stretching her power into Cathair, she did not allow him the opportunity to speak. Digging her magic through his mind, she fed memories of pain into his thoughts, planting whispers of anguish. Not to trap him in agony, but to chase his every waking moment. They would crawl into his dreams, clawing to the surface until he woke, screaming in horror. She wanted him to jump at shadows, wondering if they were real or a figment of his imagination. For Rhydwen's amusement, Eivor wove in the sensation of claws tapping across his skin like the bites of the venomous ants found in the forest. He would never find a mark, but it would convince his mind it was as real as the hoof beats added as a tribute to Thorne.

"I'm done here. Let's go," she said, spinning around to walk from the cell.

"You think you can beat him, Pet?" Cathair rasped, unable to hide the squirm as her magic settled into his mind. "Oisin is stronger than you."

"I will beat him, and when I'm done, I'll bring his head back as a gift."

"I think he'll be bringing your head back."

Laughing, Thorne kicked him. "You really think the bastard is going to escape his fate? His name has been given, but we're letting our queen have her vengeance."

"It's a pity the god of life didn't destroy all the dullaghan."

Ice filled his veins, and Cathair had a moment to regret his words before Thorne grabbed his throat. Hauling him from the ground, she tightened her grasp until he gasped for breath and clawed at her arms. Sensing Rhydwen next to her, the dullaghan snorted when he touched her shoulder gently.

"We don't answer to the gods, snake. They gave us freedom, so we found a new queen to serve." Glancing at Eivor standing in the doorway, Thorne smirked. "And she is magnificent. You were just too stupid to see it."

Dropping him in a heap at her feet, Thorne watched Rhydwen kick the man for good measure. Eivor cleared her throat, drawing their attention while Cathair coughed and sucked in rasping breaths. Delight lent the prince's eyes a shine as he skipped across the cell to join the woman waiting for them. Before they departed, Thorne wanted one last look at the man.

Cathair blinked, chains jangling. "You would put her on Annawyn's throne?"

"Yes."

"You're a fool. She's no god."

Leaning down, Thorne smiled wickedly. "I've watched her raise the dead to do her bidding. Just because you and Oisin fucked up does not mean I will. She will be the Unseelie Queen, and we'll have more than Annawyn ever gave us."

Watching them leave, Cathair flinched when his cell door slammed shut. Straightening his jacket, Rhydwen smiled at his two lovers and offered them an arm. Eivor accepted it, leaning into his warmth with a troubled expression.

"One day, I'll be able to look at him and not feel..." She sighed, shaking her head.

"I know." Kissing the top of her head, Rhydwen quashed his anger. "There's nothing wrong with feeling that way. At least seeing him will fuel your rage before we fight Oisin."

Thorne grunted, casting a look back down the poorly lit hallway. "I wish you'd let me kill him."

Arching a brow, Eivor said, "No, his death is mine. Besides, didn't we have that little fantasy involving me carving out his heart while you held him down and feeding it to Rhyd?"

"And we will do that. One day. Many years from now." Keeping his voice cheerful, Rhydwen nodded to the guards they passed on their way out of the dungeons. "First, you're going to let him witness your rise to greatness."

"I love that you're always able to make me approach things differently."

Falling into a tense silence, it was not surprise them to find Jola waiting at the dungeon entrance. She squinted at Eivor, grunting in annoyance when her magic picked up something she did not like. Pointing at the queen, she scowled.

"How much magic did you use?"

"Very little."

"Then why are you—"

"I woke up exhausted, Jola. My head hurts, as does the rest of me. I used as little as possible on Cathair, but I needed to do it."

Huffing, Jola crossed her arms and glared at Thorne and Rhydwen. "And you didn't think to stop her from wasting energy like that?"

"Nope," Rhydwen replied with a pop of his lips. "We agreed with her."

"Why?"

Respecting her concern, Thorne said, "Because she needed it."

"At least you ate." Shaking her head, the healer marched in front of them. "Did you talk it out as well? Don't need the three of you fighting."

Choking, Eivor glanced sideways at Thorne. "We talked."

"Good."

Rhydwen pressed his lips together to hide a smirk while Thorne looked unimpressed. Most of the talking had been done by the dullaghan while they listened patiently. Arguing had seemed a pointless endeavour when everything she said made sense. Part of him wondered if Eivor had slipped some of her magic into the conversation to keep things calm and not just because of her headache. Slipping his free hand into his coat pocket, Rhydwen fingered the fabric tucked within. It sat there, waiting for Eivor to admit she was struggling with the sunlight. He had noticed her wince whenever they passed through a patch of bright light, and it was obviously causing her pain.

"I think you should ask Jola to give you something for the pain," he whispered to her. "Before what you've already had wears off, leaving you suffering."

"You just want me in a drowsy state, so I can't tell you off when you get handsy."

"I hadn't thought of that."

Eivor sniggered at his eager grin. "You're supposed to be taking care of me, not taking advantage of my vulnerable state."

"I can do both." The prince winked cheekily.

"Now that I think about it, I should probably ride with Thorne instead."

Catching her name, Thorne peered at them. "What did you do, Rhyd?"

"I didn't do anything!" He quickly added, "Except promise to look after her."

The grand entrance to the palace was a sprawling wall of glass and carved marble arches. Courtiers stood on the terraces, watching the people mounting their horses. Many of those destined for the battle had slipped away in the dawning light. They had orders to see to and no need to take part in the pomp. Shading her eyes, Eivor stared out at the startling number of daoine fluttering around in ill-fitting armour with weapons strapped to their belts. Men and women of the court who would never have joined in a fight wanted to do what they could to keep Oisin from retaking Diwan.

"You look stunned, pretty magpie," Thorne murmured, standing at her shoulder.

"All these people..."

"Aye, and there's more already on their way," Alistair said, approaching them. "This is their land, and they're keen to protect it. Everyone knows the bastard won't be forgiving."

Eyes narrowing, Rhydwen shifted to place himself slightly in front of Eivor. He remained untrusting of the older duine despite everything she had told him. Thorne did not have an opinion, only a shrug when asked what she thought. Alistair chuckled at his move, winking before returning his gaze to Eivor.

"Are you feeling up to this, lass?"

She nodded grimly. "I'm riding with Rhydwen, and Jola will keep me supplied with pain relief, so the headache doesn't cause too much hassle."

"Pity she can't cure it. They've always been a bother for you."

Jola frowned at him curiously. "You know about her headaches?"

"I do. Eivor has suffered from them since she was a few years old. They got worse as she got older, but no healer has been able to stop them. Same as her icy hands and feet. All we've been able to do is give her what she needs to get through it and time to recover."

"It's unusual. Your kind doesn't tend to get sick."

Alistair laughed, but stopped when he saw Eivor flinch. "That's not entirely true. We're less likely to get sick, but it's not impossible. It happens. A plague could rip through the city tomorrow, and we'd be as defenceless against it as a human."

"It's something we're learning to deal with," Jola said. "Mortality remains new."

"Alistair, is everything ready to go?" Redirecting the conversation, Eivor clung to Rhydwen's arm. "The sooner we get there…"

"It's as organised as it's going to be. People started leaving yesterday to head for where we plan to confront Oisin. Once word spread through the city, people were voluntarily arming themselves to defend their home." His gaze held pride, though his smile was grim.

She hated the thought of how many innocents would die in the fight. They had a right to defend their home, and Eivor appreciated their efforts, but she wished there was another way. One that did not involve untrained civilians taking part in a battle to secure their freedom. Brushing aside the stabbing pain behind her eyes, she peered at the sky and noticed the winged forms of transformed daoine. A handful of pixies fluttered among them, iridescent wings glittering in the sunlight.

"There's nothing to be gained by standing here talking. Let's go."

Guiding them to where servants waited with horses, Alistair wrinkled his nose at Thorne. "It's been fascinating so far this morning."

"How so?" She suspected she knew.

"I hadn't watched dullaghan summon their magical dread mounts out of the Veil in a long time."

Head shooting up, Eivor swivelled to peer at Thorne in curiosity. "Wait, your horses aren't living creatures?"

"Not exactly." Wriggling her fingers, Thorne smirked. "Still want to ride with Rhyd?"

"She does," Jola said, voice heavy with disapproval.

Their words faded as Eivor felt the temperature drop. Emerging from nothing, the massive black horse she had seen in the throne room the night the goblins liberated her city appeared behind Thorne. It oozed magic and ice, leaving a swirl of death in its wake. She wanted to run her hands over the beast and discover how it felt to be in command of something so magnificent. Sensitive to the chill of the dullaghan's power, her fingers ached, reminding Eivor why she could not ride with Thorne.

"When the war is over," she murmured, meeting Thorne's gaze. "Then you can take me for a ride."

"I'll hold you to that."

While Thorne's horse kept Eivor distracted, Rhydwen checked the mount provided for them. The broad-chested gelding looked strong, his coppery-brown coat shining healthily. Goblins rarely used horses, preferring to slip through shadows. Most of their army was already making their way to the battlefront in that manner, covering the distance quicker than a horse. They would prepare traps within the forest, digging pits and laying snares to disrupt Oisin's army. Anything and everything they could manage would help keep the invading daoine within the trees long enough for the fire to surround them.

"I'll mount first," Rhydwen said, slipping a foot into the stirrup. "Thorne, help her up."

Hovering close, Jola observed carefully. She trusted Thorne and Rhydwen to keep Eivor safe, but the risk of her headache bringing on a wave of dizziness kept the healer's anxiety high. A short distance away, Alistair observed in silence, his eyes darting from one person to the next thoughtfully. He knew what Vesta had told him about the situation, but refused to let it be the only source of information before he formed judgement. The way Rhydwen looked at Eivor reminded him of Craven and Malena, endearing the goblin prince to Alistair.

"How do you feel?" Resting a hand on her leg, Jola peered at Eivor.

Thankful for Rhydwen's arm around her waist, she wriggled a hand to avoid adding to the pain in her head. "I've been better, but I've also been worse."

Hauling herself into her saddle, Thorne chuckled. "Stop fretting, healer."

Pointing at Rhydwen, Jola scowled. "Do not let go of her. If you think something is wrong, stop and tell me straight away."

"It's a headache, Jola. I'll be fine," Eivor replied gently.

Brushing his lips against her ear, Rhydwen murmured, "This will be a long ride. Between Jola worrying about you and the press of your lovely arse against my cock—"

"I suggest you focus on controlling the horse, or I'll switch company. I'm sure Claire won't mind me riding with her. Her conversation is probably better than yours."

"You wouldn't leave me."

"Do you want to bet on it?"

Chuckling, he adjusted their positions to something slightly more comfortable. Thorne brought her horse over, watching while the handful of guards assigned to protect Eivor sorted themselves out. Satisfied his queen was safe, Alistair sought his mount, moving to join Vesta and the other officers still in the city. Many had been dispatched in shifts the day before to make their way to the forest. As word spread to the countryside, more still would rush to join them. Very few Diwanians wanted to remain under Oisin's rule and would do anything they could to avoid it.

Resting against Rhydwen's chest, Eivor closed her eyes. Sitting in silence and partial darkness was easy while they waited to leave. As soon as the horse started moving, she needed to focus on remaining on its back without being a hindrance to Rhydwen. For the moment, though, Eivor delighted in the warmth of his body against her back and the tickle of his breath against her cheek. She also enjoyed the shift of the horse below her, feeling the muscles adjust as it moved a hoof. The last time she had ridden was before Talaroo invaded.

He wanted to tuck her head beneath his chin. "I'll keep you safe, Songbird. I promise. You don't have to worry about falling, so sleep if you need to."

"Not today," she murmured.

"Tell me when you need the blindfold. It's in my pocket."

"I haven't left the city in years, Rhyd."

Thorne cocked her head, listening to their quiet words. "You want to see as much of your homeland on the way just in case we don't win."

Humming in agreement, Eivor glanced at her. "I'm sorry."

"Don't be. I'm not in denial; I know there is a chance we're all doomed. We may not survive, but even if we don't, we can rest knowing Oisin won't either."

"You haven't told us how you're going to ensure his death if we fall," Rhydwen said.

Lips curling in a smug grin, Thorne winked. "It's a dullaghan secret."

It was a simple loophole in the conditions of a dullaghan accepting a name. Each dullaghan carried a folded piece of paper with Oisin's name written on it, and if Eivor failed, the others would read their slip and accept the offering. No need for someone to speak it, but the name needed to be penned by someone else. A dullaghan could not take advantage and write it themselves. One day she would share the secret with Rhydwen and Eivor, but not yet.

A horn blast heralded the company of riders moving out. Daoine flew above them in a plethora of forms while pixies kept watch. Between the horses slinked other animals where those who could travel in their shifted forms did so. It cut down on mouths to feed and the logistics of tending horses. Many preferred to fight in their animal forms, especially those with the shape of a predator.

"I forgot what it was like to travel with your kind," Thorne said.

Rhydwen peered through a gap in horror. "Is that a snake? It's huge!"

"Daoine."

"I think I saw a giant frill-necked lizard."

Giggling, Eivor understood his amazement. "Yes, you probably did."

"Why are the horses not panicking?"

"Because they're used to it."

Tightening his hold on her, Rhydwen stared at a massive boar hurrying past. "I don't know why anyone would want to fight the daoine. Honestly, if I came face to face with a pig that size, I'd turn and run for my life. And I'm a goblin."

"What about them?" Thorne pointed at a pair of brightly coloured birds, marvelling at the iridescent purple on their wings. "They're not so scary."

"True. And I bet you're adorable in your magpie form, Songbird."

Smirking, Eivor recognised the birds Thorne had pointed at. "I'm sure I'm not."

"I don't believe you. Your feathers are probably the shiniest black and white."

"And my beak is the sharpest. I've skewered many eyeballs in my time. My mother taught me to fight in my bird form from the day I could successfully transform. She did the same with Astoria. Admittedly, I was always jealous of her hawk form."

It was understandable jealousy, and Rhydwen asked, "Sharper talons?"

"Yes, and she could fly higher than me. Sometimes I envied Silaine's wolf form, but not as often. I wouldn't trade my wings for paws."

Curious, Thorne studied her where she remained safely held against Rhydwen's chest. "What about your magic? Would you trade it to be a husk maker?"

"No. I enjoy being a mind mage and my special gift." Eivor glanced at her. "Besides, if I had been a husk maker, things would have worked out differently, and we may never have met. I wouldn't trade the two of you for that ability."

"If you had been a husk maker, you might have defeated Oisin."

"My mother could have, but she didn't use her powers. If I had been born a husk maker, it wouldn't just be Diwan that was different. I'm 3000 years old and remember the faces of the previous gods. I've met the danann. They would have realised sooner the Ravens hadn't ended, and I'd have found myself bonded to a pair of overgrown pigeons."

Eyebrows arching in surprise, Thorne realised she had not considered it. "True."

"I much prefer the two people I've picked for myself."

"Free will?"

She chuckled. "Well, as much free will as one can have in this situation. People have a right to make their own decisions. I'm more appreciative of it than I used to be."

"As am I," Rhydwen said, kissing her head. "I never had it before."

"The optimistic side of me looks forward to ways we can improve those rights for the people of Diwan once this is over. I think they deserve more say in the kingdom's governance."

# TWENTY-THREE

Thorne's hands rested on her waist after she helped Eivor down from the horse. A small smile graced her lips at the trust in the gaze directed her way. The long hours riding had not helped the queen get over her headache, but in her vulnerability, she felt safe with them. It was a strong enough emotion to flicker across the ties binding her to the dullaghan. Eyes lingering on the plump lip caught between teeth, Thorne tuned out the sounds of thousands of people surrounding them. She wanted to kiss Eivor and promise everything would work out.

"I'm steady," she murmured, redness creeping across her cheeks. "You can let go, Thorne."

"What if I don't want to?"

Clearing his throat, Rhydwen cut into Thorne's attention. "We don't have time for you to cosy up to our Songbird. She needs to eat, take something for her pain, and rest while you and Vesta find out how much progress they've made."

"One kiss, pretty magpie."

She half-laughed, the sound breathy with a mix of embarrassment and desire. The slightest nod brought Thorne's mouth crashing against hers, and Eivor clung to her for balance. It was hard and demanding, the tightening of the dullaghan's hands on her hips pulling her closer. When the fight was done, Eivor looked forward to spending days in bed, wrapped tightly in her embrace. Or his, depending on which body Thorne returned to after going into their headless state.

Nipping Eivor's lip, Thorne purred in delight when she whined and considered kissing her again. "Always so eager, my pretty magpie."

"Thorne, that's enough," Rhydwen said in annoyance. "There's a battle coming for us, and Eivor needs rest. She needs pain relief. Now let go of her so I can see to that."

Keeping an arm around her waist, Thorne moved Eivor away from the horse so Rhydwen could dismount. "She'll rest better if we relax her first."

"That wasn't relaxing," Eivor replied.

"It wasn't meant to be. Rhydwen, take our magpie to whatever shelter there is for her and let Jola do whatever she feels is necessary. Make her eat something."

Kissing Eivor gently, Thorne reluctantly withdrew her arm and allowed Rhydwen to take her place. The ride had been hard on the queen, but they had done what they could to lessen the impact. For much of it, she had curled against Rhydwen's chest, a blindfold wrapped around her eyes to block light and a cloak shadowing her face. Jola had kept her dosed with as strong a pain relief as she dared, but they all knew they could not risk giving her anything that might dull her mind. Eivor needed to be clear-headed to fight.

Nuzzling Rhydwen's shoulder, she let him support her while staring at the jumbled lines of people and animals. "I trust you to make the necessary decisions, Thorne."

"I know."

Melting into the crowd, Thorne left to seek Vesta and the others. She knew Rhydwen would not leave Eivor. It was the only reason she felt safe to do so. With the dullaghan gone from their side, they felt the day's warmth. Holding her prince tighter, Eivor did not argue when he guided her away from the chaos of horses and people. There were tents in the opposite direction of the forest, scattered among the gullies and dips of the countryside to make them harder to ambush.

Slinking to their side, Claire pointed to a tent nestled against an outcrop of rock. "That one there. As soon as we got here, I asked around and found out we can use it."

"Thank you, Claire. Have you seen Jola?" Keeping an eye on the ground, Rhydwen guided Eivor across it and avoided the stones.

"She said she'd be there as soon as she had what she needed."

A trickle of water ran through the gullies. Helping Eivor hop over it, Rhydwen inhaled the clean scent. It told him why they had set the camp there. Fresh water was an essential supply for any amount of people and would come in helpful to prevent the fire from spreading to precious farmland. No one wanted to see them consumed by the inferno planned for Oisin's army. Claire held the tent open, watching her fellow guards seek suitable spots from which they could protect the queen from strangers.

"Well, this is cosy," Eivor said, nodding at the empty tent.

"You don't need much since we won't be here for long. We'll be back in your shiny palace in a few days, surrounded by plush cushions and silky blankets."

Turning in his arms, she tilted her face back to gaze at Rhydwen. "Ours."

"What?"

"Not my shiny palace. Ours. I'm going to marry you, Rhyd. You'll be ruling right beside me for the rest of our lives." Glancing away, Eivor chewed her lip anxiously.

"You're bothered by something."

"I wish we could extend the contract to include Thorne."

His eyes widened. "That's... Songbird, you're brilliant! Why can't it be?"

"I'm sure someone could find a legal reason."

"Let them. They will draw up the contracts when we return victorious. When it happens, we tell them what we want. We'll deal with it if they find a reason to stop us. Laws can be changed."

Resting her head on his shoulder, Eivor wondered if she would need to change a law to ensure they could have the future together they dreamed of. "Do we tell Thorne about this idea, or wait to surprise her?"

"I want to tell her, but waiting is safer."

"Good point."

Searching the tent for something to sit on, Rhydwen sighed. "You need to rest."

"Can I remain standing until Jola makes me? It feels good after being stuck on the back of a horse. I can't wait to shift forms again."

"You don't enjoy riding?"

"Flying is better."

"I can't fly. A horse is it for me."

Released from his grasp, Eivor stretched as best she could. Her muscles protested, stiff from enduring days in the saddle. She did not remember it leaving her legs as pained as they were, but before Oisin caged her, riding had been an almost daily activity. It was something else she would need to train for. The list seemed to grow with every passing day.

"Rhyd, I'm sorry. I didn't mean to make you feel inferior."

Humming, Rhydwen did not respond, knowing she had not intended her words to be hurtful. It was not the first time he had heard something like it. Those who could fly always sang praises of the gift. He was not upset, but did not see the harm in making Eivor squirm a little before granting her forgiveness in a kiss. Picking up on the amusement beneath his mildly unhappy expression, she arched a brow and stretched again, pushing just a little more than the time before.

"Oh, Precious, did you think you could fool me?"

Snorting, Rhydwen had to shrug. "I thought I could make you extra apologetic."

"To what purpose?" she said, the taunt carrying a hint of mischief. "Do you think if I feel bad about voicing my preference for flying with my wings, I'd offer you something to assuage my guilt? Are you hoping I'll get on my knees and suck your cock for forgiveness?"

"I... what? No! I didn't think anything like that. Fuck, Eivor, I wouldn't ask you to."

"What wouldn't you ask her to do?" Jola demanded, pushing her way into the tent.

They stared at each other in a mix of embarrassment and amusement. A need to save themselves from a lecture kept their lips pressed tight in silence. Glancing between them, Jola tutted in disapproval before focusing on Eivor. Magic wrapped around the queen, soothing some of her anxiety as it assessed her physical state. The healer planned to do as much as possible to ease her pain before the battle began. Once it did, Jola and the other healers would remain back, resting and preparing for when they would be needed.

"Well, good news, young lady. You're no worse than yesterday."

"I could have told you that and saved you the magic. My head pounds a little less, my muscles don't ache so badly, and the cramps have been tolerable. Your salves helped a lot, and when the day comes that you must return to the Spire, I'm going to politely request you teach my healers how to make them."

Chuckling, Jola held out a flask containing a slightly stronger tonic for pain. "Here, this will help. What you're going to do will need all the energy you can get."

Eivor nodded, accepting the flask, and unstopping it to take a swig. "I know. That is why I'm here instead of meeting with the commanders. Animating as many corpses as I'm likely to do will exhaust me by the end."

"Yes, it will."

"I'll do my best to delay using my gift until necessary. Magic shouldn't be wasted needlessly in battle, and I'll be surrounded by skilful fighters who'll protect me."

"You know, it's strange I have to say this, but thank you for being sensible."

Rhydwen glanced between them in confusion. "I don't understand."

"Many people will rush into a fight and spend their magic early, without considering when they should actually use it. They end up exhausted, vulnerable, and a bigger burden than if they had thought things through. I know the heavy use of my power will worsen my headache. I also know I'm not as powerful as before my imprisonment, so I need to save my energy for when I need it," Eivor said.

"Exactly." Pulling a tub out of her bag, Jola passed it to the prince. "Give her a massage now and again before she goes out there. Everywhere."

"Everywhere?" He grinned cheekily.

Eivor continued to sip the flask, rolling her eyes as she swallowed as big a mouthful as she could tolerate. "Don't worry, Jola. He knows what you mean."

"True, I'm just teasing."

There was affection in her gaze when Jola tutted at him. "Remember your place, boy."

"Gladly. I rather like it these days."

"Rest, Eivor. Eat. I'll check in when I get a chance, but I need to help the other healers prepare. No matter what happens, we have a job to do."

Eyes narrowing, Eivor said, "Remember what I ordered."

"Don't worry, we'll have mind mages with us to assess any of Oisin's forces that come our way. If they're true loyalists, they'll be dealt with."

Realising what they were discussing, Rhydwen stared at the pot in his hands. He wanted to believe healers cared enough about life to treat people indiscriminately, but understood why they had decided otherwise. On a battlefield where they were outnumbered, those with unwavering loyalty to Oisin would be nothing but trouble. Anyone they could convince to change sides would have priority for treatment. Lifting his gaze to Eivor, Rhydwen wondered if she would feel guilty over those deaths.

"Jola, don't forget to get some rest yourself," he murmured. "You'll need it."

"I will." Inclining her head, the healer departed as abruptly as she appeared.

Shaking the tub in his hand, Rhydwen wriggled his brows at Eivor. "We should see to the massage I've been commanded to give you."

Freezing with her lips on the mouth of the flask, she blushed. When he did not look away, Eivor finished her drink and replaced the stopper. There was nothing to lie on, and she had other needs to tend to before stripping down to her undergarments for a massage. She needed it for more reasons than managing her muscle pain. Knowing what would happen, Eivor doubted she could rest without help to relax.

"I need to tend to..."

Following the vague wave of her hand, Rhydwen nodded. "I know. I'll send Claire to fetch our packs, so you have your supplies. We need a bedroll for the ground."

"People are sharing these tents in shifts, aren't they?"

"Most likely. If we can't win, people will flee in droves. They'll run as hard as they can to somewhere beyond Oisin."

Securing the flask to her belt, Eivor tried to avoid the creeping doubts. They howled like a pack of ravenous wolves at the edge of her mind. Watching Rhydwen shoot a tired look at the top of the tent brushing his head, she smiled faintly. He was too tall to stand comfortably, and there was something endearing about how he hunched to avoid the canvas.

"Come on, Songbird. Let's get you sorted out so you can rest."

Moving easier thanks to the medicine, Eivor did not need to lean on him as much for help to navigate the uneven ground, but she welcomed his support. Rhydwen's touch was a comfort, his desire to care for her providing the queen with something to focus her power on. She wanted to wrap those feelings around her like a protective blanket to block out the rising levels of fear rippling through the makeshift army. People sat in clusters eating or tending to weapons and armour, while others discussed plans. Eivor watched people carrying supplies towards the towering forest. They still had time to add to the flammable materials, dig pits, or set traps, and they would work as long as possible.

"This is going to work," she muttered, primarily to herself. "We will not be defeated by the bastard again. Diwan will remain free."

Uncertain if she wanted him to respond, Rhydwen met Claire's concerned gaze. "Can you track down our things and take them to the tent?"

"Do you want me to locate Kallis?"

"Please. We should keep him close."

Claire bounded away, feet carrying her swiftly across the rocky earth. Tracking her path, Eivor hoped Rhydwen's mind mage friend was up to the task. They had met a few times, familiarising themselves with each other's magic, but she held a sliver of doubt Kallis was powerful enough to help protect her while she was controlling corpses. Her walls were strong; they had kept Oisin and Cathair out even while the men stripped her of access to her magic. It was the surface of her mind that was vulnerable, her active thoughts, including those responsible for controlling the dead who danced on her threads. Any disruption would sever those threads, costing her power and time to defend herself and re-establish her hold over the bodies.

"Kallis needs to eat and rest as well," Eivor said, carefully avoiding a cluster of sharp-looking stones. "It's important for him to be at full strength."

"I know. So does he. I'm glad Sophia will be with us during the battle. She's one of my mother's best warriors, and it'll be a relief to have her protecting you."

Swallowing what she had planned to say at the fearful look on his face, Eivor bumped her head against his arm. Rhydwen smiled sadly, kissing the side of her face as they walked. They headed away from the forest and the camp in silence. It was easier than talking when words could not convey the depth of what they felt with the shadow of war dragging icy fingers down their spines. Death awaited many of the surrounding people, and Eivor half expected to feel his presence wandering among them. She hoped the gods kept their meddling far from her war. Their chance to stop it had long since passed.

Claire found them again quickly, a small bundle in her hand. Helping Eivor, she chattered away, making random observations to distract the queen from the tension running rife through the gathered forces. While she located their things, the guard had overheard enough talk to know they were preparing for Oisin's army to enter the forest. It was poor timing. The new arrivals would have little time to rest before the inferno was lit. As soon as they were on their way back to the tent, Claire planned to tell them what she had learned so they could adjust their preparations.

"You're troubled. I hear your mind running in a thousand directions, and it's impossible to chase a single thought before it shatters into a thousand more," Eivor muttered, pulling her coat back on. "How do you function with such a noisy mind?"

She shrugged, unsure what the queen was talking about. "I'm a warrior."

"True."

"But yes, I am troubled. I thought I'd tell you once we were done here."

"Which we are."

Humming, Claire guided Eivor back to where Rhydwen waited. She watched his face light up with delight when he saw the duine she guarded. It was a look she envied. One day she would find someone who gazed at her with such adoration, but first, they needed to survive a war. Surrendering Eivor to the waiting prince, Claire nodded at the lurking shadow in the distance. Their eyes followed her movement, understanding dawning as they stared at the frantic activity along the tree line.

"It's beginning, isn't it?" Rhydwen was the first to look away from the forest.

"Yes. Oisin's forces have entered the other side."

Eivor inhaled sharply, her stomach clenching with fear for her people. If the enemy was in the forest, their time was almost up. It was not so big it would take days for them to cross. Her eyes located the sun, gauging its position, and knew the leading edge of Oisin's forces would be upon them by midnight at the earliest, giving them little time to rest and prepare for the fight. Rhydwen squeezed her hand in assurance, but it did nothing to make her feel any better.

"Thorne will tell us everything as soon as she's finished with the other commanders," he said, hoping it would ease Eivor's worries.

"I know. We should hurry back to the tent. Our time is short, and I need to rest as much as possible before it begins. Because once the fires are lit…"

"There will be no rest for the wicked?"

She smiled faintly at his comment, gaze remaining on the sky. "Considering I've already been told I'm a monster for planning to burn part of Oisin's army alive, I should embrace all the wickedness I possess. My people's survival will depend on it."

"Is it truly wickedness if you're doing it to save countless innocent lives?"

Cocking her head, Claire eyed a cluster of mara watching them. "Is anyone truly innocent? We are all the villain in someone's story."

"True," he replied, nodding thoughtfully. "But there are levels."

"I don't care how terrible I must become to protect the people who depend on me. Whatever I must do, I will do gladly to ensure Diwan is a free land and a sanctuary." Eivor meant every word, her voice heavy with determination.

"Hold your fury tight, Songbird," Rhydwen murmured.

"He's got a point, Majesty. You're going to need it in battle." Baring her teeth when a strange duine approached, Claire lifted a hand to flash her claws. "Keep it buried until you need it, right when you think you've got nothing left, and then use it."

Eivor did not need anyone to tell her how to use her anger. She had decades of it buried deeply. Every moment of agony, all the torture Oisin and Cathair had put her through, and beneath that, the knowledge of what they had done to countless others because she and her parents had failed to protect them. A failure she was determined not to repeat. Gaze dancing from person to person as they passed by, Eivor made them a promise. If they fell in battle, their sacrifice would not be in vain. They would be victorious.

"I have enough rage to feed an army."

Hearing the bitterness in her voice, Rhydwen squeezed her hand. "I know you do."

She halted their progress to wave at the people preparing for battle. "I am furious on behalf of each and every one of them! For those who died in all the lands Oisin has invaded and those who have not. I don't need to see their faces or hear their stories to be angry for them."

People heard her raised voice, drawn like moths to a flame to listen to Eivor's rant. She felt them lending their anger to hers, feeding the simmering fury that drove them all there. It spilled from the daoine into the others who had none of their own, those who had answered Thorne's summons. They needed to share it and know they were not alone in their feelings. Drinking it in, Eivor was happy to don it like a cloak to wear into battle when she would need the collective emotion to fuel her.

"Oisin does not know what he's done," Rhydwen said, his anger over his sister joining the rest. "He thinks he broke you, but he was wrong."

There was ice in her eyes. "He caged a monster, and now it's coming back to bite him."

# TWENTY-FOUR

They gathered along the edge of the forest, fires lit and ready to spread at a signal. Anticipation ran high with the knowledge they would soon face Oisin's army. Dullaghan lurked in the darkness of the trees, scattered throughout where they could observe the markers and report back when the approaching forces passed them. Once they reached the last point, flames would chase along the prepared tinder to consume the forest in a raging inferno. Many hated what they were going to do, but they knew they had to pay a price to keep their freedom and even the odds.

Eivor understood it perfectly. She had prepared for what was coming and accepted the responsibility of giving the order. The deaths would be on her hands. It was her burden, and no one else needed to carry the weight. As she stood at the front of the makeshift army, Eivor felt Rhydwen and Thorne's hands brush her occasionally. They took turns reminding her of their presence, trying to convey comfort without it being obvious. People looked upon the queen as a pillar, and she was. Standing tall, hands clasped behind her back, she was unwavering in the face of the task before them.

Stars glittered as distant witnesses. Lifting her gaze to them, Eivor offered her apologies and begged for forgiveness. Not for the destruction but for the cloud of smoke that would soon block their view. They would decorate the night with a haunting glow; yellows, oranges, and reds consuming the shadows left by the trees. Breathing deeply, she listened to the murmur of conversation behind her. People tried to distract themselves from the wait and the creeping dread accompanying it. Every time another dullaghan appeared out of the darkness, the tension rose.

"It's time," Thorne murmured, gaze resting on the approaching man. "Clove's the last one, Eivor. They're in position, and it's up to you what we do now."

She felt the edge of the blood lust coming through the trees. The enemy knew they were there, and they were coming to claim their lives. Some hungered for it. Eivor felt their desires, just as she sensed the reluctance of others. It was past the point of no return, so she swallowed her emotions and nodded, acknowledging what Thorne had said.

"Do it. Let's light this forest on fire."

"Are you sure?" Rhydwen whispered on the opposite side of her to Thorne.

There were very few things she felt so sure about, but she knew they needed to follow the plan of they wanted to survive. "Yes, I'm sure. We must do this, Rhyd."

"Sometimes you need a last chance to question your decision and know it's right."

Appreciating his point, Eivor smiled and raised a hand, signalling to the nearest soldier tending the fires. Shoving a torch into the flames, the duine held it high for everyone to see. Cheers erupted up and down the lines as others followed suit. They threw them onto the waiting fuel, igniting the oil and other flammable materials placed as a border around the trees. Pixies had doused trees with pitch, the inky substance catching quickly to turn them into towers of flame. It would take little before the entire forest was consumed.

Fear rolled outwards from the soldiers as they faced a wall of fire. The traps set through the forest had claimed a decent number of them, leaving many paranoid about what dangers were waiting in the shadows. Now those shadows were steadily vanishing, replaced with smoke. It was worse than the darkness. Glowing light cast confusion through the haze; each moving shape making it worse. Latching onto the emotions, the mind mages waiting on the outskirts of the forest fed every feeling of panic and terror back into the army. They pushed them through the soldiers, encouraging them to descend into chaos.

"It's working. People are dying," Thorne murmured.

"How do you know?" Glancing at her, Eivor was curious about what the dullaghan sensed that everyone else could not. "Can you tell how fast they're dying?"

"I feel the ripples in the Veil as they die. They're dropping increasingly quickly as the flames spread. It's not just the fire; they're killing each other in their panic."

Tilting her face back, Eivor drank in the heat. A strange wailing sound drifted out of the burning forest, holding the Diwanian side in fascination. It took them a little while to work out what they were hearing, but cheers erupted in parts of the line once they did. Those who felt the strongest about protecting their homes held no regret in celebrating the agonising deaths of their enemy. The wail was the screams of the dying as the fires consumed them.

It was a song that tugged at Eivor's love of music. "It's beautiful."

Rhydwen blinked, swallowing his surprise. "It's the sound of hundreds dying."

"Thousands."

They looked at Thorne, and Eivor smiled. "Wonderful. The more that die in the fire, the fewer there will be to fight when it's over."

Joining them, Vesta and Alistair watched the flames. The Diwanian side of the forest had been prepared, land cleared as a firebreak to prevent it from escaping across the countryside. They knew they were not safe, but waiting farther back was not an option. As soon as the fires died, they would swarm through to confront Oisin's forces. Orders had been issued for everyone to rest while they could, but with the blazing forest, it was challenging to relax.

Listening to the screams, Eivor hummed. She wanted to sing along, her voice rising to match the haunting wails. Deep down in the darkest part of her mind, it felt like the song had found resonance. Keeping her gaze locked on the dancing flames, she surrendered to the urge, allowing her voice to flow freely. Rhydwen stared open-mouthed in shock while Thorne closed her eyes to listen. Neither had heard Eivor sing despite hinting at the desire to do so. She had met their suggestions with deflection; her reluctance to indulge them the result of being forced to perform for Cathair's pleasure.

Her voice rose high and clear above the murmurs of the army, the words pouring forth from the recesses of her mind. Eivor did not know where she had heard the song before, nor did she care. What she knew was the lyrics spun a story of a woman rising in the night to become a queen. Others joined in, lending their voices to the tune, even those who did not recognise it. Some did, and it dragged forth memories of the old Unseelie court surrounding Annawyn. Thorne was one of those who knew it, and the words enticed a smile.

"Do you remember when this was performed after we were freed?" Vesta glanced at Thorne, eyes gleaming in the firelight. "Oh, how it pleased our mad queen."

Chuckling, Thorne inclined her head, gaze remaining on Eivor. "It's a curious thing."

"How does she know it?"

"That's a good question, General. I'm not entirely sure we'll get an answer from her. However, Alistair, I suspect you have the information we seek."

Saluting them with his stump, the duine warrior did not turn away from the fire. They were correct; he knew how Eivor had learnt the song, but Alistair had no intention of sharing the information. Not while she was standing with them. He had promised her father to protect her from her parents' choices. Though he suspected there would soon be no option but to speak of those things. Especially with Thorne tugging the strings behind her throne. Realising Alistair intended to remain silent, Vesta growled, her claws extending slightly.

"You know something."

"Oh, nothing that concerns you, old woman. What I may or may not know is not a thing to be discussed while we watch our enemy burn in a forest fire we lit," Alistair replied.

Carrying her suspicions in silence, Vesta huffed and turned to weave through the lines of soldiers. She needed to check in on her forces while they waited. It was unlikely the flames would die down before sunrise. They would bear witness to the destruction they wrought, then finish whoever remained alive on the other side of the forest. Everyone hoped the numbers would be low.

"I don't trust you," Rhydwen said to Alistair, green eyes glowing in the light. "If harm comes to Eivor because of the secrets you keep, I'll gut you myself."

The song came to its conclusion, but Eivor slipped into another. From the fires, the screams grew distant as the inferno consumed its way towards the centre. Those soldiers trapped within the walls of flame weakened in the swirl of smoke. Many would fall from inhaling the polluted air long before they burned. As the voices of the dying faded, the only music accompanying the singing forces was the crack of collapsing trees. Led by Eivor's sweet voice, the Diwanian defenders continued to weave a story of strength.

"Believe me, young goblin, if I hurt my niece, I'll do it for you."

Thorne chuckled, the sound carrying a hint of ice. "Anyone who harms our queen will wish for the mercy of death, and it will not find them."

Grunting, Alistair glanced from Rhydwen to Thorne. "I admire your fervour."

"You say that like it's a bad thing."

"Not at all."

"And yet..."

"I spoke honestly; I admire it. Craven was much the same for Malena. There was nothing he wouldn't have done for her."

Cocking her head, Thorne wondered if her desire to elevate Eivor resulted from something the former king had done. She had heard rumours of Craven being involved in both sides of the conflict between the old gods. When the battle was over, she knew she needed to seek his spirit on the other side of the Veil to find out the truth. It was something she should have done the moment Eivor's powers were revealed to her. Thorne suspected Craven was not the only one on the other side she should seek. There was a chance Malena had information.

Eivor's voice faded while others continued to sing. Magic crept across her skin, the intensity of emotions experienced by the dying army in the forest coupled with those of her army becoming a flood threatening to wash her away. There were countless feelings; no one person felt things the same way as the next. She enjoyed the nuances of emotion, but so many at once was an unbearable thing to put any mind mage through. Staggering under the weight of them, Eivor accepted Rhydwen's arm around her waist.

"It will be a long night," she murmured, leaning into his embrace. "I should sit."

Eyeing her in concern, Thorne did not move closer. "Do you need Jola?"

"No, I'm fine for the moment. Merely overwhelmed by all the emotions."

Grunting, Alistair nodded. "Cathair kept you isolated. Not such a good thing for a mind mage who thrives on the emotions of those around them."

"Isolated and magically restrained."

"Even worse. I'm sorry, there's not much we can do for you."

Lurking behind them, Kallis grumbled, "Not just her. We're all feeling it."

Helping Eivor sit, Rhydwen offered the other man a faint smile. "Are you holding up?"

"He is," Sophia replied, clicking her tongue at her lover. "I won't tolerate failure."

Eivor wanted to say something about the goblin's tone but held off. It was not her place to interfere in a relationship she had little insight into. They had been together for a long time, according to Rhydwen, and Sophia appeared protective of Kallis. During their handful of meetings leading up to the battle, Eivor had noticed no signs of physical harm on the man, and knowing what she did about goblins, it was likely a good thing.

"I won't let you down, my love. You know I'm capable of what they have asked of me." Kallis touched her arm gently, soothing Sophia's temper.

His long braids of ashen hair took on a silvery glow in the inferno's light, and she wrapped one around her hand, tugging slightly. One thing Eivor had noticed was the higher rank a male goblin was granted, the longer his hair. Rhydwen possessed the longest she had seen, the rich red quickly becoming one of her favourite colours. She caught the end of his single braid, bringing it to her lips. Freezing, he blinked in confusion, allowing Eivor to draw him close enough to kiss.

"Give me something to focus on," she murmured against his lips.

Clearing his throat, Rhydwen remained bent over with his face to hers. "I'm not sure—"

"Honestly, boy, don't you know how to care for a mind mage?" Sophia huffed, nudging Kallis out of the way so she could place a hand on Eivor's shoulder. "Here, use this."

Eyes wide, Rhydwen watched the queen lean into Sophia's touch. When her expression lost some of the pain, morphing into one of relaxation, he felt embarrassed for not realising sooner what Eivor needed. Glancing away, he met Thorne's blank stare and wondered why she had done nothing to ease their lover's discomfort. Moving to stand beside him, Kallis chuckled, but the sound did nothing to quiet the guilt Rhydwen felt.

"You'll get used to our needs. It's only been a short while since you met, and things have hardly been consistent, so, understandably, you didn't know what to do."

"How do I help her?"

Kallis smiled, pressing his fingers to the inside of Rhydwen's wrist. "There's a reason mind mages thrive best with a warrior. Your rage is a gift from the god of war and carries his power for peace as well. It blocks out everything else."

His gaze darted to Thorne, understanding why she had not helped Eivor. "I won't forget next time. Part of me thought she wanted something else. I'm sorry, Eivor, I let you down, and I won't do it again."

"You didn't let me down, Rhyd," she replied, embracing Sophia's rage. "I should have known you weren't aware of how this works. Why would you be?"

"Because you have needs, and it's important I can meet them."

"It's part of the balance. As the gods act to counter each other, so do those who carry threads of their power," Thorne said, mouth twisting in sadness. "Every aspect of magic screams out for completion only offered by those who carry the opposing kind."

Thoughtful, Alistair nodded at the forest. "Peace settles thought, war soothes death, so on, so forth. Combined, they all bring meaning to life. Without life, there is no existence, and it's all one big happy bundle of threads bound up in an infinite knot."

"I've heard a similar phrase used by another."

"Aye, funny that. Diwan wasn't always my home. Remember, I came from the arenas, as did Craven. He won this land through blood, sweat, and tears.

We lost friends to War and Death's lust for bloodshed, and we witnessed what happens when the balance is broken. Even those of you who were born later have seen the results of it."

There was a hint of amusement on Thorne's face. "I bore witness from the start. Unlike you, I saw the good years before things unravelled."

Screwing up his face, Kallis stepped away from Rhydwen and waited for Sophia to return to him. "Is the history lesson necessary?"

Rhydwen dropped to his knees next to Eivor, resting a hand on her leg. "It's helpful, and it's not like we have anything better to do."

Confident the prince understood what Eivor needed from him, Sophia stepped back to stand with Kallis. The fire had consumed the outer edges of the forest where it was first lit, the hotter flames aided by the fuels they had added. Blackened limbs jutted from the smouldering ground, their once leafy crowns nothing but ash in the breeze. It twisted around them with the vague promise of a cool relief that was banished by the fire and drowned by smoke. By the time they crossed the remnants of the forest, they would all wear the burnt remains of trees and people, leaving a stain that would be hard to wash away.

Eivor gazed at the ruins, eyes irritated by the smoke, hoping the wind remained favourable. "When the fires die down, we won't have much time."

"Never fear, pretty magpie; we have eyes on the other side." Stroking her cheek, Thorne met Eivor's stare. "We will know when they move."

"Better to make them cross the embers and come to us."

"The middle will probably be the hottest, considering how we set it up to trap them. We will soon have an estimate of how many avoided the flames and can plan accordingly for how we approach the battle with Oisin."

She knew it was too much to hope for that he had been with the part of his army trapped by the fire. A part of Eivor wanted to pray to the gods that he had been, but she also knew she would never rest unless she saw him die with her own eyes. They would all fear his return for vengeance without solid proof of his death. Thorne tilted the queen's head back, exposing her sooty throat to the tender stroke of her fingers.

"If we cannot find him here, I will accept his name and deliver Oisin's head to your feet, my beloved queen. You have my word."

"You better, or I'll be very displeased with you." Licking her lips, Eivor tasted ash and imagined it was the dullaghan's mouth. "Do you want me to be upset with you, Thorne?"

Bending down, she smirked. "Oh, I know better."

Their lips were a finger's breadth apart, noses touching, and Rhydwen cleared his throat. He hoped it would distract Eivor and Thorne from whatever was building between them. Tugs at his magic summoned the fury of his bloodlust, rippling through his hand on her leg. Watching it become an icy blaze in Eivor's eyes, he could have sworn Thorne drank the rage from her breath. Around them, the temperature dropped despite the inferno.

"I look forward to dancing with you, pretty magpie," Thorne whispered.

"I hate to interrupt whatever this is, but we have a problem."

Pulling apart, Thorne and Eivor stared at River in frustration. The dullaghan shook their head as though banishing the lingering touch of the Veil from their skin. Alistair stepped forward, hand on the hilt of his sword while they waited to hear the news.

"The fire only took about half of Oisin's forces."

"Ah fuck." Alistair's face twisted with rage, magic flickering around him. "I had hoped."

"We all did," Eivor said calmly. "Half is better than none. It evens the odds."

"They still outnumber us! What chance do we stand against superior numbers when many aren't trained soldiers? How are we going to win?"

Thorne slipped her hand into her coat pocket to feel for the slip of paper with Oisin's name on it. "Tell me to go, Eivor, and you know I will."

"No. We follow the plan. Half is less than we hoped for, but better than we expected. Alistair, I want you to ensure people have their masks. It's going to get harder to breathe." Remaining seated, the queen wished she had one of the damp strips of fabric to cover her face. "Thank you, River. Let us know when they move."

"There's a chance Oisin will send troops around the forest even though it'll take them longer. They'll have to cross into Samphire, and the humans are on their way." River shrugged, looking to Thorne for orders.

"If it happens, we'll let them split. He might not realise the humans have been forced into an alliance with us. It might convince them they're doing the right thing if they get to claim some blood." Smiling slowly, Thorne considered another option. "When we enter the fight, I want you to lead a hunt, River."

Their smile was chilling. "With pleasure. A full hunt?"

"Yes."

Alistair chuckled, a wicked gleam in his eyes. "I almost pity the poor fools."

"What's a hunt?" Rhydwen whispered to Eivor.

She knew the stories from her mother. A dullaghan hunt was something Eivor had wished she could witness. Malena had spoken of it as a thing designed to instil terror into those who saw it. When the headless riders hunted, no one was safe from Death's embrace. Giving Rhydwen a faint smile, Eivor touched his cheek.

"It's death on horseback, Precious. The whispers you fear in the shadows and the promise of oblivion you cannot escape."

Holding out a hand to Eivor, Thorne pictured her riding among them to claim the corpses where they fell. They could place her on a white horse, crowned with silver and jewels, and proclaim her their queen. She would lead the hunt, the dead lumbering after them to answer the summons of her magic. If people thought the headless charge was terrifying before, they would know the true meaning of fear with Eivor at the forefront. Slipping her hand into Thorne's, she rose gracefully.

"I can only imagine the terror you would inspire, my queen." Kissing Eivor's hand, Thorne smirked, holding her gaze. "You belong with the hunt."

Her breath hitched at the prospect of riding with the dullaghan. "I wouldn't say no."

"Perhaps it will help turn the tide in our favour."

"Are you sure that's a good idea?" River was startled by what Thorne was suggesting.

Feeling the whisper of death in Eivor's magic, she nodded, confident in her decision. "Eivor is our queen, and she belongs riding alongside us."

# TWENTY-FIVE

They left the horses behind, unwilling to risk harming the beasts. The only hoofprints to be found in the ash came from the glossy black mounts of the dullaghan. Unaffected by the lingering heat and smoke, they crossed the smouldering ground without missing a beat. Faces covered by masks, the soldiers moved cautiously, fearful of the soot-covered trunks left behind by the fire. In some gullies, flames continued to flicker, eating through the built-up fuel left over the years.

"This is as far as we go," Alistair said, stretching an arm out in front of Eivor. "We want them to be at a disadvantage. Remember, the ground is misleading."

Eivor rubbed the back of her neck, feeling the grime coating her skin. "Not my first bushfire, Alistair. I know looks can deceive and to move with caution."

"I wouldn't count on your pretty redhead having previous experience."

Rolling his shoulders, Rhydwen tried not to feel uncomfortable. Sweat trickled down his spine; the layers of armour combined with the warmth from the fire left him wondering if they were being slow-cooked. He could tell he was not the only one suffering. It was more than the heat; his sensitive nose could no longer differentiate between scents. The smoke affected every goblin, putting them at a mild disadvantage. Not enough to make them less deadly, but enough to put them off balance. As uncomfortable as they felt, Rhydwen knew the enemy was suffering far worse.

"Precious?" Eivor nudged him, brows furrowed in concern. "What's bothering you?"

"What?" Blinking, he realised his eyes were watering.

"I asked you a question, but you seemed out of it."

"Nothing to be worried about."

She hummed in disbelief, shooting a look in Thorne's direction. "Are you sure?"

"I'm sure."

Leaning forward in the saddle, Thorne said, "So long as it does not impede your ability to protect our queen during the battle. I'm relying on you, Rhyd."

Growling, Kallis came to the defence of his friend. "We cannot smell clearly."

"You're feeling overwhelmed?" Squeezing his arm, Eivor understood.

"No, just concerned about the fight to come." Covering her hand, Rhydwen smiled faintly. "Don't worry, our inability to smell as well as normal won't stop us from slaughtering our enemy where they stand... but it's hot. We're roasting in our armour. It's a good thing we didn't have to travel far to reach our spot, unlike Oisin's army."

Chuckling, Alistair caught on. "If we're suffering after this short distance, they'll be worse. Good thinking, little princeling. The time to get here will wear them down."

Beaming at the praise, Rhydwen was rewarded with proud looks from Eivor and Thorne. He wanted to prove he was worthy of being the queen's consort. Kallis poked his back, grinning when he glanced over his shoulder. Tendrils of calm crept through him, soothing magic he was familiar with. The other man had helped Rhydwen control his temper many times, and his willingness to ease the anxiety clawing at his gut reminded him of their long-standing friendship.

"Everyone knows to conserve their energy while they can. It won't be long until the enemy reaches us here," Sophia said, a hint of eagerness in her voice. "As soon as they're in sight, it will begin. They won't stop to organise."

Thorne nodded, gaze sweeping over her fellow dullaghan as they waited on their mounts. "They'd be stupid to try when it would leave them vulnerable."

Anticipation was an itch creeping across her skin, chasing away the headache. Eivor knew it would return with a vengeance once the battle was over and everything came crashing down. Even the aches were banished, but a flask of Jola's mild pain tonic hung from her belt next to a knife. Her coat covered them, the heavy black material not as hot as the armour worn by the others. She was thankful not to be wearing anything warmer. Melting would be an unwelcome distraction while controlling the dead in the middle of the fight.

Her biggest hope was that Oisin would find out they were waiting for him and push forward to confront her first. A scenario involving his death before anyone else died kept playing out in the corner of Eivor's mind. If she could kill him quickly, it might save innocent lives. Toying with the hem of her coat and a slightly loose button, she stared at the eddies of smoke wafting from the ground. Brittle trunks leaned precariously, a danger they needed to be careful of once the fight started. All their movement would send ash clouds into the air like a fog, making it harder to see.

"I wish we could lure Oisin out to confront him before it starts," she said, unwilling to look away from where the enemy would appear. "The sooner he and his officers are dead..."

Alistair sighed heavily, tapping the hilt of his sword. "It's going to be hard to draw him into battle. He's likely to hold back until he's confident his forces have taken care of us."

Clicking her tongue, Thorne studied Eivor. "He'll engage once he knows she's here."

"What makes you so sure?"

"Because he's a proud, vicious man who will want to take care of her rebellion and kill or capture Eivor himself. He wouldn't trust anyone else."

"You know a bit about the way he thinks?" Slanting her a look, Alistair questioned everything Vesta had told him about the Master of the Hunt.

Thorne cocked her head, smiling when Rhydwen gave her a concerned look. "I know Oisin well enough to make assumptions about how he'll want to handle things."

"I suppose you get familiar when you served the same god."

"Something you'd understand."

"What is that supposed to mean?"

"That's enough," Eivor murmured, squinting into the murky morning light. "There's something out there. Can't you feel it? Where are the scouts?"

Understanding her nervousness, Rhydwen was thankful for the lines in front of them. They waited in stillness, light filtering through smoke, distorting their appearance. When the Talaroonans arrived, those lines would give them time to prepare. Visibility would be their worst enemy in the fight, though the goblins would fare better than others. Fighting in darkness was their specialty. Fingers twitching, Rhydwen let his claws slip free. He looked forward to sinking them into the enemy and feeling blood turn them slick.

"We're going to be fighting past nightfall. Once the sun sets, your daoine have orders to withdraw and leave the rest to those of us better suited to it," Sophia said.

Suspecting she was trying to ease the tension for Kallis, Eivor nodded. "Without knowing how long it would take for the fires to die down, we had to think of all the plans."

"You're right, there is something out there." Peering upwards, Kallis scratched his arm. "I don't know what, but I feel the brushes of their eagerness."

"The pixies?" Rhydwen waved at the smoke-laden sky.

"They're grounded until the fight starts." Touching his face, Sophia studied Kallis.

Glad she was not the only one who felt it, Eivor resisted the idea of releasing her magic to get a better sense of things. "It's hard to explain. There's something there."

Sharing a look with River, Thorne murmured, "I want you to see what you can find."

"You believe them?"

"I think we'd be remiss not to check. If you ask other mind mages, you'll probably find they sense something. We can't be sure what attention we've attracted."

River tilted their head to eye the sky warily. "You don't think?"

"Checking is the first step to finding out."

Nudging their horse, the black-cloaked rider vanished from sight, leaving a slight chill behind. River's departure had Alistair shift closer to Eivor, his keen gaze dancing over the lines in front. He was not the only one, Rhydwen choosing to extend the claws on one hand fully while the one closest to his future wife remained unchanged. If anything happened, he wanted to be ready to defend without hurting Eivor. They had agreed if things went badly, it was up to him, Sophia, and Claire to get her away while the dullaghan brought them time and protected their retreat.

"Thank you for taking our unease seriously, Thorne." Smiling, Eivor dipped her head. "Hopefully, it's nothing more than cumulative nervous tension."

Clearing his throat, Alistair jokingly said, "Maybe the danann have decided to help."

Suspicion twisted Rhydwen's gut, reminding him of his distrust for the duine. "Surely they'd make themselves known if that was the case."

"It's a hundred years too late. Why would King Tigernach bother now when he did nothing about Oisin's invasion?" Eivor sneered, her hatred written in her expression.

"I meant no harm, Eivor. You're right. Why would they come now? They've had plenty of time to do something about Oisin. They didn't, and now you're doing it instead." Holding his stump up, Alistair tried to grin sheepishly.

Something about his smile added to his doubts, but Rhydwen remained silent. He had made his feelings for Alistair clear. Sometimes he feared her desperation for some resemblance to what she viewed as happier days was clouding her judgement. It made no sense that Oisin and Cathair would have allowed him to slip through their net if he was as close to the former king of Diwan as claimed. Rhydwen just hoped his distrust was unfounded, and Alistair would not break Eivor's heart by betraying her.

Eivor's sneer faded, but a gleam of something unreadable remained. She listened to the silence at the edge of her mind. With their enemy also being daoine, it was too dangerous to communicate using mind speech. Since being freed from the binding cuffs, the noise of her people had been a comforting buzz. No one was projecting their mind voices and alerting the Talaroonans to their presence. They likely knew where to find the forces waiting for them, but there was no point in confirming it or allowing them to listen to conversations that could reveal plans.

A whisper spread back across the lines of soldiers. One of the dullaghan positioned at a critical location appeared in the space left for the riders to come and go. His dark gaze swept across the group to settle on Thorne. He did not need to say a word for them to know why he had come. Oisin's forces had arrived and were crossing the point of no return. If they had hoped to avoid the battle, it was too late. The fight had come, and there was no longer any chance of escaping it. Soon the blood of invaders and defenders alike would soak the ashen remains of the forest, only to be washed away when the rains returned.

"It's begun, Songbird," Rhydwen murmured, gazing at Eivor fearfully.

Eyes wide, she swallowed back the bitter taste summoned by her anxiety. "May their arms be strong, blades sharp, and courage unwavering."

Signalling for the other dullaghan to close ranks, Thorne wished she felt reassured by their presence. She wanted to believe they would succeed in their fight to keep Diwan free. They had a plan, everyone knew their role, and it was essential to hold on to the belief that they would pull it off. Glancing at Eivor standing with Rhydwen on one side and Alistair on the other, with Claire, Sophia, and Kallis at her back, Thorne refused to let the dread seize her throat. Rhydwen and Eivor needed her to remain steadfast.

"Remember to stay within our circle, pretty magpie," she said, straightening in the saddle. "And do not raise the dead unless necessary. We can't have you exhausted early."

"I know."

Meeting Thorne's stare, Rhydwen remembered their many conversations in the quiet of the shadows when Eivor was not paying attention. "I'll make sure she doesn't."

Determined to prove her worth and earn the captaincy of the queen's guard, Claire flexed her claws with a wicked grin. "And we'll make sure anyone you miss doesn't lay a finger on her majesty. I'll enjoy shredding the ones you let through."

Bristling at the suggestion they might miss someone, one of the dullaghan snarled. They shifted their horses closer to Eivor, watching the lines ahead as they sensed the fight start. Each death was a ripple through the Veil, but they could not tell friend from foe. Redirecting her focus to the smoky sky, Thorne wondered where River was. She had not expected them to be gone so long, and she hoped whatever it was would not hinder the fight.

"Kallis, stay close to her majesty no matter what," Sophia said to her lover.

He touched her cheek gently, a sad smile tugging the corners of his mouth. "I will."

"Don't get hurt."

"Never. Besides, you'll be right beside me the whole time."

Biting his lip, Rhydwen watched the adoration in their expressions and wished Thorne was standing with them so he could kiss her. He also wanted to kiss Eivor, but her thin lips and determined glare kept him from making a move. Sensing his desire, her eyes darted in his direction; the icy blue turned stormy by the discoloured sunlight. For a moment, Rhydwen thought she would say something, but shrill horns accompanied River's hurried return, the sound splitting through the sky. The air shifted, turning smoke into swirls that buffeted back onto them, making many people cough as they struggled to draw breath.

"We have a complication!" River was flustered, their normally calm demeanour broken. "You're not going to be impressed by who is above us."

"How many?" Thorne whispered with dread.

Eivor's face fell for a moment before hardening into a blank expression. "We need to keep our focus on Oisin's forces. If we're lucky, the complication will be in our favour."

Holding Thorne's stare, River said, "Thousands. I would be surprised if it weren't the bulk of his army. Most of them are waiting on the edge of the Veil, shrouded in their magic."

"If we'd done the same with the pixies, we would have known sooner." Rubbing her face, Thorne sighed. "Too late now. Lucky for us, Eivor and Kallis sensed something."

Moving closer, River did not want the others to hear. The rest of the dullaghan would sense everything soon enough, but their concern was how Eivor would react when she found out. Thankfully, she was too busy glancing between the sky and the frontline. Head low, the rider leaned in and kept their voice quiet, so only Thorne heard.

"I sensed Ravens... and Eclipse."

"Fuck."

"My sentiments exactly. If Eclipse is here, then Death sent them."

Clenching her jaw, Thorne cursed under her breath. "He sent his precious fucking human captain. I'd like to run him through with that sword."

"You know we can't lift a finger against Merle."

"Is her sister here?"

River shrugged. "I don't know. It's not like I can tell the difference between Ravens."

"But it's likely. Why would the Lord of Rainbows leave her behind? Especially when she's bonded to his brother. Lady Silaine is a powerful husk maker. It would be easy for her to rip through Oisin's lines. My guess is they're here to claim the others."

"That would be my assumption. The danann will attempt to isolate any husk makers among the Talaroonans and take them to the Vale."

The sounds of battle were getting louder, bringing a shift in the air. Shadows passed above them as winged warriors appeared from their position on the edge of the Veil. Eivor's rage surfaced at the sight, rippling across those closest and stirring the blood lust in the warriors accompanying her. They hungered to join the fight. Restraining themselves, they circled closer, waiting for their opportunity. Rhydwen was the only one with something else on his mind. He watched Alistair, observing how the duine gazed up at the waves of danann sweeping down towards the Talaroonan soldiers with weapons in hand.

He had known they were coming; Rhydwen was sure of it. There was nothing to be read from his expression, not even a flicker of surprise when River appeared. It was like he had over-prepared his reaction ahead of time without considering how suspicious he might come across. Whether or not Alistair had known of the danann presence, Rhydwen knew there was no point accusing him. They were soon to join the battle, and the last thing he wanted was to throw Eivor off with suggestions her father's closest friend was working with the people she believed had abandoned her to suffer.

"The fighting is getting closer. We should prepare," Sophia said, nose twitching when she caught a whiff of the blood on the breeze.

In agreement with her observation, the first line of dullaghan moved forward to take their place. They remained with heads in place, unable to transform until they were in combat. Magic whispered in wordless voices, carrying the promise of death. Some of them grinned, the prospect of turning the battle into a hunt making their skin itch with anticipation. River would lead the way in

Thorne's place. A hunt had been promised, and those dullaghan who enjoyed them had every intention of claiming the right to strike fear into the enemy.

Eivor watched the tossing heads and stamping hooves of the heavyset black horses. "I wish I could ride with them. Can you imagine the exhilaration, Rhydwen?"

"It's certainly something," he muttered uneasily.

"I dreamed of this for years."

"And now your chance for vengeance is here." Turning to her, Rhydwen pressed his lips together and shook his head. "Songbird, when you come face to face with Oisin, just kill him."

"That's the plan."

"No, I mean, just kill him. Don't exchange words, don't toy with him, just kill him. Make it quick; get it over with. Delaying it only gives him a chance to kill you instead."

Cupping his face, Eivor stared into the jewel-green eyes she adored. "I will."

"Promise?"

"Yes. I want to go home alive with you and Thorne. To our palace, to lead our people."

Kissing her palm, Rhydwen smiled. "I'll hold you to that promise."

"I wouldn't expect any less."

"Do you think it would be wildly inappropriate to kiss you right now?"

Sliding her hand from his face to the back of his neck, Eivor pulled Rhydwen close. "Absolutely. Do it anyway, and we can call it one for luck."

Giving them a moment to kiss before clearing her throat, Sophia said, "If you're done?"

Thorne was staring at them with longing, so Rhydwen kissed his hand and blew it to her. She wished she could stand with them, but they counted on their reputation as headless riders to help keep the enemy from attacking Eivor. Half-smiling, she pretended to catch the kiss, pressing it to her heart in a gesture intended to convey her feelings for the two of them. The answering grin on Rhydwen's face confirmed the effectiveness of what she had done, but Eivor held her stare, and the wave of emotion across their fragile thread told Thorne everything.

A scream close by caused the group to move. Keeping tight lines around Eivor, the dullaghan summoned weapons from the Veil that seemed to drip with inky blood. It was an illusion intended to add to the fear they inspired. The blades were as real and deadly as the touch of the rider wielding them. Biting her lip, Eivor watched Thorne point her scythe in the enemy's direction, shadows sliding from the edge to vanish back into the Veil. Catching her look, the leader of the dullaghan winked before signalling for them to go.

Claire nudged Eivor, muttering, "Don't leave my side, Majesty."

"You're getting bold for a soldier who got lucky on guard duty." Arching a brow, Rhydwen tried to hide his amusement at her scowl.

"I might have gotten lucky, but I'm going to make sure everyone knows the queen wasn't wrong to trust me. So don't make my job harder, princeling."

Shoving Kallis forward, Sophia directed him between Claire and Eivor. "Hate to break up your moment of self-importance, but he needs to be closer."

"Sorry." Shrugging, he smiled sheepishly, but Eivor chuckled at his undercurrent of smugness. "But she's got a point. I need to stay close enough to touch the queen."

Huffing, Claire begrudgingly allowed him between her and Eivor. "Fine."

"Someone sounds jealous. Should I be worried?" Rhydwen whispered to Eivor.

She shushed him, a faint smile tugging the corner of her lips. "I need to focus, Precious, and so do you. This isn't like taking the palace; this is battle."

"You don't have to remind me. But if I don't make the occasional quip, I will fall apart. So let me joke while I can, so I can fight when I must."

Tracing the profile of his face with her gaze, Eivor understood. Lacing her fingers through his, she squeezed his hand to reassure Rhydwen that she would not let go. Whatever happened in battle, they would face it together, with Thorne by their side and an army of allies determined to keep Diwan free from Oisin's control.

# TWENTY-SIX

The dead littered the smouldering ground where once leaves, moss, and scrub had stood. Her power swept outwards, creeping over the corpses to find those she could use. Eivor knew there was no point in animating them, but it felt good to know where they were. Until Oisin was close, she needed to conserve her energy. Clinging to Kallis with one hand, she watched the dullaghan slide through the Talaroonan forces. Above them, the unexpected addition of danann warriors helped cut down their enemy. No one had broken through the surrounding layers of protection, and Eivor felt the desire to join the fight coming from her goblin companions. They hungered to get their claws bloody.

"They're incredible," Kallis whispered, staring at the winged warriors above them.

Scoffing, Eivor refused to be impressed. Their aerial manoeuvres were nothing more than a mockery in the face of what her people had endured. When the battle was done, and the victory was theirs, she would make her position clear to the Lord of Rainbows. For all their help, they would find no welcome in Diwan. She caught sight of a woman with yellow wings dart past; arrows fletched the same colour released from the bow in her hands. Something about her was familiar, stirring a memory at the back of Eivor's mind of her mother.

"Think what you will, Kallis, but if they didn't have something to gain from helping us, they wouldn't be here. We're nothing to them. They would kill you simply for existing."

"No, they wouldn't."

Eivor cocked her head, frowning at him. "You're a goblin, Kallis. They're danann."

"Yes, but they're only allowed to kill those who break the laws set forth by the gods."

"Do you think they wouldn't find an excuse? The gods would believe anything the mighty King Tigernach told them, and if he claimed you were breaking their laws, they wouldn't question why his warriors had slaughtered you."

His eyes carried a hint of sorrow. "And what about you?"

"I'm going to give him a reason to fear me. Silaine might be weak and easily controlled, but I am not." Jutting her chin, Eivor glared at the danann overhead. "If the Lord of Rainbows thinks he can intimidate me, he's sorely mistaken."

"Do you really believe your sister is weak?"

"She always has been."

Troubled by their conversation, Rhydwen said, "Eivor, she's your sister."

"Not anymore. Silane ceased to be my sister when she abandoned me to Oisin."

Exchanging looks, the two goblins did not know how to respond to the venom in Eivor's voice. Their group moved across the battlefield, careful to avoid the dead. Keeping a reasonably clear path, the headless riders were a terrifying sight that sent many of the enemy running. In complete hunt transformation, skulls rolled between their horses' hooves, icy flames flickering in the empty eye sockets. Laughing manically, the skulls chased after those who ran from them, followed closely by the riders.

"Now, if you want to know what I find beautiful." Humming in approval, Eivor watched a trio of dullaghan cut through a group of Talaroonan soldiers. "They're stunning."

Concerned he might end up arguing with her, Kallis replied, "Each to their own."

"Good call," Rhydwen muttered, eyeing Eivor sideways.

Her attention remained on the dullaghan, gaze darting from one to the next to find Thorne. Somehow, Eivor knew which rider was hers. Whenever she looked at them, it was a tug of recognition she assumed had something to do with having her name claimed. With the danann present, she was reminded not all dullaghan still answered to her lover.

Sensing her stare, Thorne brought their mount closer. The madly grinning skull rolled between massive hooves, icy shadows wisping from its smooth surface. Eivor wanted to pick it up and cradle it in her arms. Memories of the agony touching the space that replaced Thorne's head resurfaced, reminding her of how close she had come to dying. With each step across the blackened earth and the trickle of sweat down her neck, she dreamed. She imagined approaching Oisin with Thorne's skull tucked into the crook of her elbow while the rider remained at her side and the corpses of his soldiers ambled at the other.

A shrill whistle above snapped Eivor's attention away from Thorne. Her gaze found a grime-splattered danann warrior with wings looking like the blood of his enemies had soaked through them. Their eyes locked for a moment before he spun in the air to point his short sword in a different direction from the one they were heading. Suspicion stirred in her gut, and Eivor heard Sophia and Alistair suggesting they follow his recommendation. She recognised him, not just from the reports Cathair had shared with her. He had visited in her childhood, long before her parents banished the danann from their court.

"General Redmond," she whispered, letting go of Kallis's hand. "The prince who stole my sister."

Catching her words, Rhydwen blinked at the warrior. "That's him? Mother tells stories about his brutality in battle and claims his mate is more bloodthirsty than any goblin."

"If the general is suggesting we go that way, we should," Alistair said, his voice more determined than his earlier attempts to convince them. "You don't want to anger him by ignoring his directions. Might be he's guiding us to Oisin."

"He's got a point, Your Majesty. Without a better idea of where the bastard is, we may as well follow his suggestion and go that way. Why else would the danann general be here?" Sophia hoped she was the voice of reason to cut through Eivor's distrust.

Whatever intentions Eivor had of refusing to follow Redmond's pointing were quashed when Thorne's horse shifted in a new direction. The other dullaghan followed the change, forcing the small group to do the same. Snarling, the queen let them see her displeasure. Rhydwen's expression suggested he would not hesitate to pick her up and throw her over his shoulder if she protested. His claws dragged down Eivor's sleeve, snagging the material to distract her long enough for them to establish their alternative path.

"I'll protect you, Songbird," he murmured, leaning in to brush his lips over her cheek.

The danann general remained above them, too far away for his voice to be heard over the sounds of fighting. Eyes locked on his gleaming red wings, Eivor thought about all the things she could use his feathers for. She doubted her ability to forgive Silaine for choosing him. Her sister had put aside the bonds of their family for a man their parents had cast from their lives. Whatever Redmond and Tigernach hoped to achieve by helping, Eivor had no intention of letting them into her kingdom.

"Your Majesty!"

Alistair's breathy call brought her attention back to their situation. Squeezing her eyes shut for a moment to allow her vision to adjust, Eivor ignored the sting from all the smoke and ash. It coated them, and a fresh layer quickly covered any spots cleared by sweat. Even the inside of her nose felt full of it, and smoke was the only thing she had smelt since the inferno began. Ahead of them stood a row of danann, their sleek feathers splattered with blood and the bodies of Oisin's officers at their feet. Redmond had landed in front of them, arms crossed as he regarded the headless riders coldly.

"We have something you want," he said, inclining his head to the space beyond his warriors. "A gift of goodwill from my king to you, Queen Eivor."

No one stopped her from striding toward him. His gaze dropped to her clenched hands, a brow arching as an amused smirk curled his lips. Stopping in front of the general, Eivor let her magic wash out, finding thirty of the most usable corpses within reach. They rose from the ground, sending startled people stumbling to get away. Neither spoke until the puppets dragged themselves through the lines of dullaghan and goblins. Pixies landed among the riders; their glistening wings spread wide and ready to take off again.

Redmond stared at the corpses. "Well now, this is an interesting development."

Sneering, Eivor brushed past, pulling her puppets along after her. No one stood in her way and stunned danann moved to allow her into the ashen clearing where Oisin stood. Exchanging looks, her companions scrambled after her, followed by Thorne and eight other dullaghan. Eyeing the rolling skulls, Redmond snorted and strode into the clearing behind them. His warriors watched on, ready to react if a threat presented itself. The Talaroonan king circled another danann, but the moment Eivor appeared, the warrior peeled away.

"What?" Oisin spun, sword held in preparation to block a blow. "You!"

Eivor halted, her puppets surrounding her. "This is a welcome change of situation."

Eyes widening, he stared at the corpses. As did the danann he had been fighting, the warrior folding back his rainbow wings in surprise. Knowing there was only one with such feathers, Eivor sneered at Tigernach in disgust. His shock faded, replaced by a rapt fascination as he studied the dead under her command. Surrendering to the temptation to toy with him, she sent four lumbering his way. The strain of movement became too much for one with an abdominal wound. Intestines tumbled free, but the body kept moving until it halted in front of Tigernach. Cocking his head, he blinked, eyes drifting up and down the remnants of a soldier.

"Curious, isn't it?" Redmond said, joining him.

"It's rather peculiar."

Smug over their reaction, Eivor faced Oisin confidently. "One hundred years, you fucking bastard! I've waited and dreamed of what I'd do when I finally had you in my grasp."

"Who's controlling those creatures?" Waving at the puppets, Oisin refused to believe she was responsible. "I've been inside your mind. I know what you're capable of."

"Yes, you have, and no, you don't. Some of my walls were too deep for you to notice and built too thick to break. I kept my secrets safe, just like my parents taught me." Flicking a hand, she sent several of the corpses to attack him. "And I learn quickly."

Glancing back at Rhydwen, Eivor winked. He started forward, halting abruptly when she twisted an arm behind her back. Frowning at the motion of her fingers, it took the prince a moment to work out what she was signalling.

While Oisin lashed out at his attackers, Rhydwen slinked along the outskirts, keeping clear of the staring danann warriors. Once he was behind the man they needed to kill, the one who had caused so much pain to the woman he was falling in love with, he waited. Claws extended on both hands, he watched Eivor.

"I should thank you before you die, Oisin." Holding up a hand, she made the puppets stop. "If it weren't for you, we wouldn't be here."

Sensing something at her feet, Eivor looked down to find Thorne's leering skull. Hoofbeats echoed eerily, accompanying the rider joining her to face Oisin. Other dullaghan moved forward, forming a half circle behind the woman they had chosen as their queen. Crouching, Eivor smiled at the skull and scooped it up, careful not to flinch at the biting cold ripping through her. She wanted to scream in agony. Instead, she breathed deeply as she rose, welcoming the icy fingers of the Veil caressing her power.

A hand as breathtakingly frozen as the magic slid onto her shoulder, Thorne's voice a breath against her cheek. "My glorious queen, do you want me to kill him?"

Stroking the smooth dome of the skull, Eivor's smile became a wicked grin. "No, my love, his heartbeat is mine. Rhydwen, make him kneel."

Frozen by a mix of terror and confusion, Oisin lowered his sword. "How?"

"The Unseelie are mine now. They saw what I could become and chose me."

Wrapping a hand around the duine king's throat, Rhydwen grabbed the wrist of his sword hand, forcing him to drop the blade. "And what our queen wants, she gets."

Trickles of blood left crimson lines in the ash coating Oisin's skin. He tried not to struggle, fearful of the claws digging into his throat. Pushed forward to kneel in front of Eivor, the hand on his neck forced him to gaze up at her. Delight danced in the icy depths of her eyes, giving her a wicked appearance vastly different from the cowering and bloody mess he had last seen. Of all the emotions he felt, Oisin decided the indignity of being killed by the woman he thought he had broken was the worst. It would have been better to die on the tip of Tigernach's sword than have Eivor end his life.

Pain wanted to steal her voice, but she pushed on, determined to see her vengeance through. It had almost broken the tethers of magic connecting her to the lumbering corpses in her control, but Eivor felt the frozen power from Thorne's skull seeping across them. She suspected it was the only reason she had not collapsed, screaming in agony. So long as she kept breathing and did not fight the magic of the Veil, she hoped it would not kill her before she was done. The voice at the back of Eivor's mind promised the ice she would give Oisin to it so long as it let her continue. He was her offering.

Shifting Thorne's skull to one hand, Eivor brushed her fingertips over Oisin's cheek. "You took so much from me, Oisin, but in doing so, gave me what I never knew I needed. But just because you're about to die doesn't mean you won't be able to watch us grow. We're going to bind you to your bones."

"No!" It was enough to make him struggle, risking the chance that Rhydwen would tear out his throat. "Are you so pathetic that you can't let me go, even in death?"

Rhydwen snarled, tightening his grasp. "My queen, remember your promise. Kill him."

Her fingers returned to his cheek, and Eivor let the Veil seep through the touch. It went eagerly, happy to claim the bounty she had promised it. Eyes snapping to meet Rhydwen's, she mouthed the command for him to let go. Frozen in place by the consuming grasp of death, Oisin did not notice the withdrawal of the claws that had pierced the skin of his throat. Aware of the bluish whiteness of Eivor's hands, Rhydwen backed away and distracted himself from the twist of her mouth by thinking of the best way to warm her when it was over. Licking the blood from his claws kept him from staring at the joyful fire flickering in her eyes that reminded him of why Thorne knew the Unseelie would embrace Eivor as their queen.

Concerned by what was unfolding in front of them, Redmond fingered the hilt of a blade. "Do you think we should do something, Tigs?"

"I don't know."

Alistair crept over to join them, praying Rhydwen would not notice. "Don't let Silaine near her. I was wrong to assume Eivor would welcome her home...

she... you must understand, Craven thought the deal was the right thing to do. He never thought..."

There was a thud when Oisin's body collapsed, Eivor laughing in delight. Kissing the skull in her hands, she held it out for Thorne to take. Shadows crept from the white bone, encasing her arms as the dullaghan moved slowly. Despite the offering she had given the power, Eivor felt it hungering for more. It wanted her to let it flow freely across the battlefield. Her body was numb, every breath a struggle against frozen lungs, but she refused to surrender. Releasing the skull, she swallowed, wondering when she would feel her fingers again.

"It hurts, doesn't it?" Thorne murmured. "Your heartbeat is too slow."

"Tell the others they're free to hunt at will."

"Pretty magpie, it's killing you."

Cocking her head, Eivor disagreed. "No, because I won't let it."

Gathering the lingering power of the Veil she had taken from Thorne, she spread it across the threads of magic animating the corpses. They had stood without purpose while Oisin held her attention, but now Eivor gave them a reason to move. Wispy smoke replaced their eyes as the dead soldiers moved jerkily towards the lines of danann keeping the area clear. Her power spread further, seeking more viable bodies to claim, ice filling their limbs as they rose to throw themselves at the enemy. Eivor gave them every drop of the Veil she could until the worst of the agonising pain had left her.

"Go hunt, my love," she said, touching a pale hand to Thorne's chest. "Make them pay."

A signal had the other dullaghan departing, but Thorne remained. It was challenging to release the power urging them to join their fellows, but the desire to stay by Eivor's side was strong enough to complete the transformation. The vanishing skull was the first sign of their intention, earning a frown from the woman in front of them. Crinkling her nose, Thorne caught Eivor's hand and brought it to her lips, kissing the back of it. She felt the iciness but sensed none of her power in the queen, allowing her to relax slightly.

"Why didn't you go with them?"

"My place is by your side."

"I wouldn't have minded," Eivor murmured. "Well, maybe a little because I wanted to join you. Visions of riding with the hunt will fill my dreams."

Thorne tucked a strand of dirty hair behind her ear, allowing her the time to refocus before they faced the danann king. It had escaped the thick braid, settling into position framing her face where it had become caught in sweat and stiffened with ash. She was excited by the prospect of getting Eivor back to the palace and into a warm bath where they could banish the remnants of the fire. They would have as many as it took to feel clean.

"One day you can join us. You'll be our wild queen of the hunt."

Feeling Rhydwen's claws dig into her hip gently, Eivor welcomed his chin on her shoulder. "We need to finish this."

"Songbird, look at the king," Rhydwen said, keeping his voice low.

Eivor shifted her attention to Tigernach and Redmond, gaze settling on Alistair. "I see."

"I'm sorry."

"He knew them before. It's probably nothing to be concerned about."

Studying the duine warrior's expression, Thorne replied, "I think Rhyd is right, pretty magpie. He's been right since the start."

Grunting, Eivor shrugged Rhydwen off and moved away from them. To hide the trembling of her hands, she clasped them behind her back as she strode towards Tigernach. Wings outspread, the danann king bowed low, a cocky smile tugging the corners of his lips. He remembered the bold girl she had been before the war between the gods became the convoluted mess it did. As the first child of a Raven, Eivor had drawn a lot of attention from all sides. They had watched her grow, waiting to see what powers she presented.

"It has been a long time, Queen Eivor." Straightening, he examined the ones standing on either side of her. "You look so much like your mother."

Unable to resist lashing out, Eivor slapped him. "You do not get to speak of her."

Chuckling, Redmond flashed a grin. "And there's Malena's fire."

"Careful, you wouldn't want to overestimate your position." Tigernach did not bother to rub his aching cheek and showed his amusement instead.

The threads to her puppets remained connected like a spiderweb. Some had fallen, rendered too damaged for her power to continue animating. They were hers, and Eivor found comfort in knowing no one else could do it. It was tempting to draw them back as a reminder of what she was capable of. She wanted to see Tigernach unsettled and fearful.

"Right, my position. Which position is that? The captive queen who was tortured and raped for a hundred years while no one did a thing to stop it? Or the queen with no intention of grovelling in gratitude for you finally helping after her real allies had already done most of the work?"

"We had orders from the gods to leave things to unfold as they needed to."

Startled by the hatred oozing from her, Redmond knew he was not looking at the gentle but indifferent sister Silaine described. Instinct screamed at him to kill Eivor before she became a danger to the peace the gods were trying to build. There was no gratitude in the gazes of the goblins or the handful of Diwanians accompanying their queen. He had never found himself in a position where their help was unwelcome. It would be difficult to tell Silaine she could not visit her childhood home.

"Ah yes, the gods. Fuck them all. You can take your gods, turn around, and get the fuck out of my kingdom. You and they are not welcome here."

# TWENTY-SEVEN

"Eivor."

The voice was one she would never forget. It fuelled her rage, and she felt her power connect to more corpses, replacing the ones lost in the fight. Eivor stopped caring about how much magic she used. She wanted them to understand her pain. Aware of the outpouring and the puppets cutting through frightened soldiers, Thorne wrapped her fingers around Eivor's wrist. She did not want to use her ability to control the queen, but she did not want her to collapse in the middle of a battlefield.

"My pretty magpie, stop. No more puppets, you're exhausting yourself."

"Listen to her, sister," Silaine said, stepping free of the danann who had brought her. "Please, we need to talk. I can explain everything."

Expression twisting with disgust and unable to resist Thorne's command, Eivor snarled at her sister. "I don't want your explanations! Nothing you say will change anything."

Swivelling in anger, Redmond glared at his mate as she kept close to Silaine. Blood and ash splattered her silvery-grey wings, telling him they had not kept out of the fighting. Their task had been to find the husk makers under Oisin's command so they could subdue them. Before the battle began, they had agreed to keep Silaine away from Eivor, so their reunion did not distract from the reason everyone was there. It had not been his idea. Merle had suggested it.

"Little wolf, don't!" He hurried to put himself between the sisters.

Her blue eyes narrowed, power sparking in their depths as Silaine brushed him off without hesitation. "I can deal with my sister."

Thorne kept a hold on Eivor's wrist, watching the younger woman push one of the most feared warriors on Tir out of her way like he was nothing. She saw the undeniable family resemblance in the lines of Silaine's face, the way she moved, and the determined curl of her lips. It was like seeing a golden version of Malena and had Thorne wondering what Rhydwen and Eivor's children would look like. Fearful of what might happen if the queen tried to attack her sister, she caught Rhydwen's gaze and nodded for him to approach.

"I know what you're doing," Eivor muttered, eyeing Thorne sideways. "Don't get in the way. You've stopped my puppets, but if you push my limits..."

"You promised us a future, pretty magpie. If you attack your sister, the danann will retaliate. Let her say her piece, and then we'll leave. I don't expect you to forgive her, but I'd like to go home with you alive. As would Rhyd."

Staring coldly at Silaine, Eivor wondered if she was paying for their parents' choices. If they had embraced their youngest child, maybe she would not have left her to suffer in captivity. Perhaps Silaine would have fought harder to bring help to free Diwan instead of giving up. There was nothing they could do to change the past. The water had long since passed beneath the bridge, but Eivor swore she would not make the same mistakes with her children.

Halting in front of her, Silaine frowned at the possessive way Thorne held her. "Please, Eivor, can we talk? You and me, like we used to."

"We used to be sisters, Silaine. Now we're not," she replied bitterly. "You and Astoria abandoned me. I watched our parents die while you fled to safety."

"Safety? I ran for months and nearly died seeking help to free you. The only reason I didn't was I didn't want to let you down."

Laughing, Eivor shook her head in disbelief. "And yet you did. Better you had died than to abandon me as you did and then expect me to greet you as a most beloved sister."

"It broke my heart not to come back. I even thought about trying to free you on my own, but Asthore and Red stopped me. They knew I'd end up a captive beside you if I did. Would you have wanted that? For me to be Oisin's captive? He wouldn't have left me in Diwan with you. I'm a husk maker."

Mirroring Thorne and Rhydwen, Asthore and Redmond remained silent, but ready to respond to any perceived threat. None of them knew if the reunion would end in blood or tears. A fearful whisper spread among the danann warriors as Eivor's puppets answered her call to return. They lumbered to a halt, waiting for her to give them instructions. Nothing remained in their minds except her will. Contemplating them, Silaine wondered if they were the reason Craven and Malena had never taught her to use her powers. Eivor was not a husk maker like her, but they were not so different.

"Is Tory special like we are?" Silaine did not hide her bitterness. "Or did our parents only need to hide your powers and belittle mine? Did they tell you how dangerous you are and make you as ashamed of your gifts as they did me?"

"No. Father taught me well, though Mother kept out of my training because she feared Death would notice. They didn't want the gods back in their lives."

"But teaching me to control mine was too big a risk? Would Gebael and Neriwyn have noticed our mother training a new Raven? Your power, though, you're not killing them."

Shrugging, Eivor suspected giving Silaine an explanation was a bad idea. All the faithful danann surrounding them would relay her words to the gods. The eagerness in Asthore's gaze told her everything. Part of her suspected they wanted to fill her court with their people to find out if her power would trigger a similar bond to that between a husk maker and their danann mates. Leaning into Thorne's chill, Eivor refused to let it happen.

"She's controlling them through her mind magic," Alistair said. "I've known the whole time. Craven turned to me for help with training her."

Rhydwen snarled, claws reappearing. "I knew you weren't to be trusted."

"I've protected Eivor's secrets since before she was born. Craven was my brother, and I will do whatever is needed to protect his girls."

Her gaze slid to Tigernach, drinking in the puzzled look he wore, and Thorne knew he was not privy to everything. "Did you know about Gebael's blessing?"

Tigernach straightened in surprise. "No, I didn't. No one mentioned anything. I suppose it makes sense. Malena was his Raven."

Focus returned to Alistair, and he held up his stump. "Gebael wasn't the only one. Long ago, Craven made a deal with Annawyn. She helped him woo Malena, and in return, their firstborn was to be hers to claim."

"My father wouldn't have done that!" Eivor wanted to scream, and her puppets crept closer. "Why would he agree to a deal with Annawyn after everything she did to Mother?"

In agreement with her sister, Silaine said, "Mother married him to get away from the gods and the trauma of what Annawyn did to the Ravens."

Aware of the rage coursing through Eivor, Thorne tightened her hold, and Rhydwen grabbed her other arm. They held her back, preventing the attack on Alistair they knew would come. It did not stop the corpses from closing in on him, icy fire wisping from their eyes. With them came the call of the Veil, confirming to Thorne what Eivor had done with the power that had tried to consume her. These puppets were not the same as those she had animated during training, and the dullaghan feared what it meant.

"Annawyn visited many times, Eivor, but she never tried to take you away. Even after the Fog. She was present the first time you made the dead walk. We believe she did something to Gebael's blessing, twisting it in her way to give you a new power. But you were the only one to receive a gift from him. By the time Astoria was born, the gods had divided. Then you came along, Silaine, a husk maker at last. Oblivion told Malena to offer you to the danann, but Neriwyn rejected you." Alistair hoped they would understand.

Furious over his words, Asthore raised a fist. "Don't you dare suggest Malena would have allowed that bitch god into her life! I knew her! She was my friend, and I know she wouldn't have let Annawyn anywhere near her children."

"You didn't know her as well as you think."

"She tried to destroy the Ravens."

Lips thinning, Alistair stared at Asthore. "Funny which ones survived."

Surprised by the reaction of the three danann, Thorne and Rhydwen yanked Eivor out of the way. Left alone while they joined the corpses surrounding Alistair, Silaine looked to Eivor for help. It reminded her of all the times she had comforted her younger sister, but the flicker of affection vanished under the weight of understanding. Their parents had withdrawn from the gods and their courts, fearing their actions would be uncovered. Even the three of them made sense, and Eivor needed to know if her suspicions were correct.

"Did they make a deal with Neriwyn as well?"

Her question halted the danann, causing them to face the queen. None of them understood why she asked, but Silaine did. Shaking her head, Eivor bid her to remain silent. There was no need for anyone to speak except Alistair.

"Not that I know of. His deal was with Annawyn. Astoria and Silaine's powers have nothing to do with Craven making an agreement with a god."

Eivor hummed thoughtfully. "It makes sense. Astoria inherited the warrior magic from our father. That left Silaine to take after our mother. A husk maker, servant to Death. Perhaps, if Annawyn had not intervened, I might have been one of those. No matter, I'm thankful not to be."

Folding his wings back, Tigernach stared at the corpse closest. "You suspect she changed your magic to make you capable of this? That she turned you into a mind mage who could raise the dead?"

"Honestly, I don't care. Alistair is yours, and this reunion is over. I'm going home to plan my wedding and begin repairing my kingdom."

Bouncing on her feet, Silaine appeared both confused and excited. "A wedding? You're getting married, Eivor? To whom? Lorcan?"

When she saw the pain in her sister's eyes, she covered her mouth in shock. Rhydwen stepped closer to Eivor, kissing her cheek to remind her of his presence. She was thankful for the hands grasping her wrists. They were contrasting temperatures, one warm and the other cold. From them, she drew comfort and strength, knowing they were there for her no matter what. Silaine might have let the gods and the danann convince her to give up on trying to rescue her, but Eivor was confident they would never abandon her.

"Oisin killed Lorcan?"

"Yes, he did. Save me your tears, Silaine. They're meaningless now." Inclining her head, Eivor signalled to Thorne and Rhydwen that she wanted to leave. "Have a good life. Don't bother trying to return. You're no longer welcome in Diwan."

Determined not to let her walk away without gaining something more from their conversation, Silaine said, "I didn't abandon you."

Wresting free of her lovers, Eivor leapt at Silaine and grabbed her coat. Asthore and Redmond moved to aid her, but Tigernach called them back. As much as he did not want the sisters to hurt each other, he knew they needed to resolve their pain.

"How can you say that?" Hissing, Eivor shook her.

"I thought about you every day. Constantly. In the early days, I exhausted myself to the point of being trapped in my wolf form, and the heartbreak over failing you had me considering staying a wolf and vanishing into the forest, never to be seen again. Leaving you a captive was never what I wanted... but I couldn't save you alone."

"So, you mated a pair of danann and proclaimed yourself queen of the Ravens? Yes, that makes perfect sense. I mean, what else would you do while your sister suffers?"

Growling, Silaine bared her teeth. "Build my army! Once I had a big enough flock of Ravens, I planned to come for you. No matter how long it took, I was going to come for you. But the gods knew, and they threatened to move us to one of the eternal valleys where I wouldn't be able to leave without them."

The desire to believe her and the agony of a hundred years of suffering warred with each other in Eivor's mind. "I have no reason to believe you."

"We're sisters, Eivor. You've known me since I was born, and all I ask is if I ever gave you a reason to doubt my love for you. Do you believe I willingly gave up?"

Her power wrapped around Silaine, feeding on the emotions rolling off her. Weaving it through her mind, Eivor tasted the genuine remorse she felt, but carefully avoided her memories. It was a bitter tonic for the hate burning in her heart, but failed to extinguish the flames. None of it changed the fact no one had come for a hundred years. Silaine might have regretted it, but she continued with her life. She had fallen in love, made friends, and built connections.

Eivor shoved her away, releasing the coat to let Silaine stumble backward. "Yes, I do."

"Is that what Oisin and Cathair told you?"

"They didn't need to tell me anything more than what you were doing. I knew you were in the Vale with the danann, going on with your life. Do you deny it?"

Glancing back at Redmond and Asthore, Silaine did not hide her embarrassment quick enough. "No, you're right. I was in the Vale with them and building a life of my own."

Shoulders dropping, Eivor felt the walls around her emotions crumple. Part of her had hoped Silaine would continue to protest. The pain was a raw wound, freshly reopened when she believed she had stitched it tightly with threads spun from stone. Rhydwen darted to her side, quick to prop her up. He saw the glistening tears that stubbornness kept from falling.

"Maybe I abandoned you, Eivor, but what was I supposed to do? Spend my days fretting until I spiralled into someone incapable of doing anything? Why wouldn't I choose to spend them learning, growing, and becoming stronger, so when my chance to help you came, I was not the weak girl who ran?"

A dozen options ran through Eivor's mind. She wanted to cause Silaine the same pain she felt. It was one thing to believe her sister had abandoned her and another to hear her admit it. Throat tightening, she felt like she could not breathe, and her heart was trying to beat its way out of her chest. Rhydwen provided something to cling to, so she did not drown.

"Thank you," she whispered.

Kissing her cheek, he held her tighter. "Anything you need."

"Go home, Silaine. Take your danann and leave."

Crossing her arms, she shook her head. "No. Diwan is my home just as much as the Vale is, and it always will be. You can't keep me away!"

Pulling free of Rhydwen, Eivor drew her knife and had it at Silaine's throat before he could stop her. "Yes, I can. Leave, Silaine, and never come back. Diwan is Unseelie land, and I am its queen. We are not allies."

A whisper caressed her mind, causing both women to turn their heads. "*Feed me your power, little birds. Sing our song in blood as it should be.*"

"What..." Unsettled by the strange voice, Eivor lowered her weapon.

A man strode towards them, mouth twisted in annoyance. His hand clasped the hilt of a sword, familiar tendrils of shadow curling around the blade. Eyes settling on it, Eivor knew she had seen it before. Only two weapons fit the description, and she knew the one approaching was not Oblivion. That blade never left the side of the Executioner. Which meant the sword was Eclipse and its wielder was the human soldier claimed by the new god of death to be his captain.

"Having fun, Merle?" Silaine half-smiled, affection shining in her gaze.

He huffed, swiping a messy lock of hair from his face. "It's over; the Talaroonans have lain down their weapons. I met General Vesta, and she knows what the situation is. Now, why don't you put that knife away, ma'am? Before you do something stupid. My orders are to leave you alive, but if you hurt Laine..."

Thorne appeared at her side, plucking the weapon from her grasp as Eivor continued to stare at Eclipse. "Captain Merle. Your presence is unexpected."

"Right, of course it is. You didn't think you could lead an Unseelie uprising, and they wouldn't send me to investigate? I expected wiser choices from you, Thorne."

*"Touch me, my queen. Your power sings of death so sweetly. We could do so much together. Do you remember what Oblivion offered you? I can offer the same."*

Drawn to the sword, Eivor ignored the group of people flocking to surround her and Silaine. The tendrils of shadowy magic felt as familiar as her own. Hand outstretched, she brushed her fingers against the blade, startling Merle. Yanking it away, he tutted scoldingly as he sheathed the weapon despite its demands for more blood.

"So, you can hear Eclipse. We weren't sure if you'd be able to, even though you could hear Oblivion. That's going to piss off Celi. He'll owe the boss man... actually, let's not go there."

"Why didn't they tell us?" Tigernach's anger stirred his magic, and his wings spread, knocking into Rhydwen. "They know what their predecessors did to her!"

Growling, the prince extended his claws. "Do you mind?"

"And who are you, goblin?"

"Prince Rhydwen."

Realising that beneath the coating of ash, his hair was as crimson as Redmond's wings, Tigernach's brows shot up. Sharing a look with his brother, he inclined his head while the general dropped a hand to the hilt of his sword. At his side, Asthore snorted, reaching out to draw Silaine closer to them. The tension between them rolled out, affecting the others who watched from a safe distance. Alistair remained in place, surrounded by Eivor's puppets, but he hoped that Merle's intervention would guarantee his freedom.

"You're Calista's son?" Redmond kept his tone neutral.

Tossing her head, Eivor replied, "He's my betrothed."

"You're going to marry a goblin!" Silaine was aghast at the idea. "No! You cannot be serious! A goblin? Eivor, have you lost your mind?"

"On the contrary, he helped return it to me. You have your danann, Silaine, and I have my goblin and dullaghan. What either of us does now is none of the other's business."

Running a hand through the mess of his hair, Merle sighed. "Laine, this is how it must be. Have faith in our gods to know what needs to happen. They approve of the union."

"I don't need their approval. You can take it back to them and tell them where to stick it. They aren't welcome in Diwan. We want nothing to do with the gods."

"We know. The god of time has seen the variances."

Thorne sneered, the temperature dropping as magic wrapped around her. "Then why are you here, Captain? Are you simply taking the opportunity to feed Eclipse?"

"Hardly." He scowled. "I'm here because Laine will listen to me... and to ensure you're aware they know everything."

It confirmed to Eivor that the gods deserved her hatred. They had known what was going on in Diwan and every other place Oisin invaded. Every person who suffered had done so while the gods did nothing to stop it. She would make them pay for their inaction. No matter how long it took, they would hold the gods accountable.

"Consider your message delivered. Now, take your army and leave," she said.

"Remember, Eivor, the gods always have a reason."

Turning her back on them, the queen of Diwan signalled for Claire. "Make sure Oisin's body comes with us. I want to reunite Cathair with his king."

Grabbing Thorne, Merle held her gaze. "Protect your queen, Master of the Hunt. That's an order from him. She's more important than you realise."

A strange creaking silenced them before the burnt remains of a massive tree collapsed. Danann scrambled out of the way, the beat of their wings adding to the cloud of ash choking the air. It provided enough distraction for the goblins to collect Oisin's corpse and withdraw to where their fellows waited.

Others had joined them; a mixture of warriors who helped keep Diwan free. Eivor, Thorne, and Rhydwen were the last to retreat, with her lumbering corpse puppets trailing after them.

Halting, Eivor spun around to face Silaine across the clearing. "I'm glad you're happy because you deserve to be. But don't let them break you."

"I'd like to come home for your wedding. It would be better to talk away from here."

"No, I meant what I said. You're no longer welcome in Diwan. Not so long as you serve the gods and bind yourself to the danann. If you see sense, then we can talk."

Silaine stared at her before shooting looks at Redmond and Asthore. "I love them."

"Then you are dead to me, and I never want to see you again."

"Do you mean that?"

Lifting her chin, Eivor met Merle's gaze. "We are enemies, Silaine. Do not seek to come into Diwan and leave alive. Just remember, you chose this path by choosing them."

"Can't I say the same thing about you?"

"No, because while you chose them, Cathair and Oisin raped and tortured me. They traded me for favours and forced me to perform to please them. They blocked my access to my magic, kept me isolated, and locked me in my chambers."

She stepped forward, and the layer of ash covering her face could not hide her anguish. "I am terribly sorry, Eivor. Please, even if it changes nothing, I need you to believe me when I tell you I never wanted to leave you there. Every day I wanted to come for you."

"You're right, Silaine," Eivor said, holding her head high despite the tears threatening to fall. "It changes nothing. Should we see each other again, I hope it's not across a battlefield. Goodbye, and good luck. I fear you'll need it more than I."

# TWENTY-EIGHT

It felt wrong to view the battle as a triumph. A messenger had delivered the news to the city ahead of their return, so the people knew they were safe. Eivor had not expected to find a celebration waiting for them. So many had died, though the dead did not number as high as anticipated, thanks to the danann. Her heart was an open wound threatening to bleed over everything the moment she stopped moving. While they journeyed back to the city, she had focused on that. There had been orders to issue, discussions to hold, and all of it had needed her attention. All of it had made it easy to ignore the pain.

Familiar buildings and walls rose around them, cheers ringing from the rooftops. The echoing voices pierced Eivor's skull like well-aimed arrows. She was tired. A bone-deep weariness had sunk into her after walking away from the battlefield. Despite the desperate ache calling for her to sleep, she knew her people wanted to see a victorious queen. From the sideways looks of concern directed her way, Eivor suspected Rhydwen and Thorne did not believe her words of assurance. Whenever they asked how she was, she swore she was fine.

"I am really looking forward to a warm bath," Claire said, stretching up in her saddle to peer at the palace. "And wine, so much wine. Maybe I'll fill the tub with it."

Lips twitching, Rhydwen bit back a chuckle. "That sounds like a terrible way to get clean. Unless you have something else in mind for your wine bath?"

"Besides getting completely drunk and passing out?"

"Fair enough. There's something to be said for the benefits."

She gave him a knowing smirk. "Not all of us have company to wash our backs."

The comment had him looking at Eivor. She had ridden alone from the battlefield. Rhydwen missed the warmth of her body cradled against his chest and the pride of keeping her safe. Without her in front of him, his arms felt empty.

Jola snorted, amusement chasing the tiredness from her gaze. "Sounds like an effective way to drown. You'll barely notice you're dying when you pass out in the wine."

Trapped in a spiral of thoughts, Eivor did not comment. Beside her, Thorne was a silent pillar of ice. Since retreating from the confrontation with Silaine and the others, she had kept her magic close. As much as she wanted to ask why, Eivor had kept her questions to herself, unwilling to trouble her mind further. Thorne was not the only dullaghan on edge. Most of them seemed to monitor the skies as though they expected the danann to appear. Pixies patrolled the clouds, ready to alert them if needed, but their numbers were not enough to counter the god of war's army.

Breath escaped her lips in the barest of sighs as Eivor watched flower petals rain down from a balcony. They were close enough in colour to remind her of blood. In her dreams, she saw nothing but ash and fire while remembering the screams of the dying Talaroonans trapped in the inferno of her design. She did not regret the decision, but the sound remained lodged in her mind. There was no doubt it would follow her for the rest of her life. So long as Diwan remained free, Eivor was content to endure those nightmares as she did the others.

"I know it doesn't feel like it, but it was a victory," Thorne murmured, brushing a petal from her shoulder. "We killed more of Oisin's forces than the danann did."

"This celebration seems wrong."

"But the people need it. They suffered for a hundred years alongside you, even if sometimes it doesn't appear that way. Knowing the man responsible for it is dead, and the other is captive gives them hope. Don't you feel the same?"

Eivor swallowed, fearful of what Thorne would think if she admitted the truth. "I'm disappointed Tigernach tainted our triumph."

"His involvement meant less of your people died."

"I tell myself that. We are coming home with more people than we thought we would. That's a good thing, and I should be ecstatic."

"What about the danann presence truly bothers you?" Thorne frowned, noticing Rhydwen watching them talk. "Was it because of Silaine?"

"Not exactly. I feel like it's a hollow victory because we're not entirely free, even though Oisin is gone. That man said the gods know. How are we supposed to relax and enjoy our freedom if they're lurking in the shadows, aware of all we do?"

Clicking her tongue, Thorne understood where Eivor was coming from. She remembered Merle's command to protect her queen. He had claimed she was important, which suggested the gods had something planned. Whatever it was, the dullaghan hoped her spies in Death's court could uncover the information. Not all the riders who had remained in the valley of winter were loyal to their god. There were others scattered across the eternal valleys who were willing to trade knowledge for the right price.

"By pretending they're not. We can't live in fear of them watching over our shoulders, pretty magpie. The best thing we can do is carry on with our plans."

"We need to monitor Talaroo. I know Tigernach has sent in forces to help transition it, but we should remain vigilant. The last thing we want is for them to set up a stronghold on our border."

Recalling their departing view of the burnt forest, Thorne doubted anyone from Talaroo would dare cross the blackened land for a long time. The destruction would live on in memory long after the scars on the land had healed. No one would forget it had been Eivor who ordered the inferno that consumed the thousands who became trapped within her net. People would spread the tale across Tir, vilifying her and forgetting the crimes committed against her people by the ones destroyed. Oisin would become the king slain while trying to stop an evil queen from spreading her atrocities to other lands.

She laughed bitterly, understanding why the gods had let things unfold as they had. "To be perceived as good, one must always have an evil to condemn."

"What?" Confused, Eivor arched a brow. "Has smoke inhalation damaged your mind?"

"The gods let all of this happen. Merle passed along orders from Death to protect you because you're important. I haven't been able to stop thinking about it. Why would the gods view you that way unless they planned to use you to make themselves appear better? Now I fear my plan to raise you up as the Unseelie queen in Annawyn's place was one they planted or something they've decided to take advantage of."

"You think they're planning to paint me as the darkness only their light can defeat? Fear, little children, and pray to the gods or else the evil Queen Eivor will come to burn your house down. Obey, or the wicked queen will send her Unseelie horde to eat you."

"I hope not."

Eivor smiled grimly, patting her mount on its neck gently. "We won't know the truth of the matter until it confronts us. I refuse to bow to the gods in worship or fear. Let's gather those who feel the same."

"I'm sorry, pretty magpie."

"There's no point in being sorry, Thorne. Be angry instead. We can use it to build something here in Diwan to protect others like us. Let the gods point fingers and give us labels. While they do, I'll spread my wings and give shelter to the people who need it because I know the truth. Our suffering is their fault."

Determination appeared on her face, and Thorne thought her heart skipped a beat when Eivor looked over the crowd lining the streets. It was a reminder of how she had survived all those years of suffering without breaking. She knew it was not her fault any more than any other victim was to blame. So long as Eivor had anger to cloak herself in, the weight of what happened would not crush her.

"You are incredible," she said, admiration obvious. "No matter what, you don't stop thinking about how you can help others. You have more compassion than anyone could expect when others have treated you so cruelly."

Rhydwen broke his silence, saying, "It's easy to be compassionate when you understand how the others feel. You know their pain and fear intimately; it's not simply an imagined experience where you try to put yourself in their place."

"As a dullaghan, the only understanding I have is of being twisted to a purpose by the gods."

The nonchalant look on Thorne's face reminded Eivor of the insecurities they had learnt simmered beneath her icy exterior. After they settled back into the palace and dealt with the aftermath of the battle, she would dig through the laws with Rhydwen's help to work out the legalities of including her in their marriage. She wanted Thorne to have as much standing in Diwan as Rhydwen. For all their sake. With everything they experienced over the years, Eivor believed power equality was essential for their relationship.

"But you try," she replied. "You're not an unfeeling monster, Thorne."

Snorting, Thorne gave the two of them smug looks. "Only for you."

"That's all that matters." Rhydwen winked at her.

Joyous shouts distracted the queen briefly, her gaze narrowing on a woman with her arms around a young boy. "You believe the gods want to turn me into the monster people fear? Well, look around us. Perception is a funny thing. I'll be the monster if it's needed, but only for the supposedly good people. For those who don't have anyone, I'll be the saviour who'll burn down cities to save them."

Tugging her horse to a halt, Eivor slid from the saddle to approach the woman. Startled, they did not follow, confident she was safe despite the crowd's rambunctious nature. Babbling, the woman dropped to her knees, but Eivor encouraged her to rise again. Clinging to his mother, the boy stared at her in awe.

"Thank you, Your Majesty," she mumbled, overwhelmed at being singled out. "Thank you for making them pay. Talaroo took everything from us."

Crouching in front of the boy, Eivor smiled and drank in the emotions rolling from the pair. "Your mother loves you a great deal. I know how lucky you are."

"Mama is sad a lot, but now she's happy again," he replied.

"When did they kill your partner?"

Shifting her focus to the woman, Eivor felt Rhydwen at her back. The pain in her eyes confirmed her assumption. It was easy to understand why people like her cheered. They had delivered justice to the ones who had caused untold suffering to people like the mother and son. Ruffling the boy's hair, Rhydwen winked and received a timid smile in return.

"During the last lesson."

Inhaling sharply, Rhydwen asked, "What do you mean by lesson?"

Rising, Eivor was glad for his hand pressing against the small of her back. "Cathair would order his soldiers to round up people and kill them to remind us of our place. He made me watch from a window as they dragged them to the courtyard to be slaughtered."

"We all had to watch. The Talaroonan soldiers would go door to door, forcing us to gather in the streets outside the palace where we would bear witness to the executions and what they'd do to the dead afterwards," the woman said, sharing an anguished look with Eivor.

"I'm sorry for your loss. Please, if there is ever anything you need, seek Captain Claire of the royal guard, and ask her to bring you to me." Flicking a hand at the goblin she spoke of, Eivor looked down at her feet. "I know nothing can undo the pain you've suffered, but if we can help make things easier, we'd be glad to."

"Thank you, Majesty."

Tugging her coat, the boy's wide-eyed gaze carried an unexpected seriousness. "Did you get rid of the bad king? Mama said you made sure he was never coming back."

"We did. I killed him myself," Eivor replied.

"Are you going to kill the other bad man? The one who killed my papa?"

He was speaking of Cathair. Frozen by the question, she blinked while her thoughts stumbled over themselves. Hesitant to reveal any plans Eivor had for her tormentor, Rhydwen smiled confidently and nodded at the boy.

"The bad man is paying for what he did."

Vindictiveness twisted the woman's face as she met Eivor's gaze. "I hope he's paying slowly and painfully. He deserves to feel everything we did tenfold."

Reassured by her response, Eivor chuckled. "And he will. Every day for the rest of his miserable life. I'm going to carve our vengeance from his skin and mind."

"Good."

"It doesn't feel like enough because it doesn't make up for what he did."

"Nothing ever will, but knowing he's suffering gives me joy."

A shout from the line of riders distracted Rhydwen from the exchange. Spotting Vesta guiding her mount towards them, he cleared his throat. Claire slumped forward in her saddle, certain she would receive a dressing down over their delay once back in the palace. The general had strict views over what she was supposed to do when guarding the queen. Views Eivor did not seem bothered about, and Claire disagreed they were necessary when Thorne and the dullaghan were circling.

"What's wrong, Your Majesty?" Vesta jerked the horse to a halt, the beast tugging at the bit in protest. "Has something happened? They're waiting for you at the palace."

Fearful they would blame them for holding up the queen, the woman pulled her son close. Catching her response, Eivor directed a scowl at the general. It was not Vesta's fault, but it annoyed her the interruption had caused distress. Touching the woman's arm, she nodded and watched her swallow nervously before returning the nod.

"Remember what I said. Anything at all, you find Claire and ask to see me."

"Thank you, Your Majesty. It means more than you know," she replied, voice wavering.

Ruffling the boy's hair again, Rhydwen smiled at him. "Look after your mother."

Thorne cocked her head, black hair fluttering in the wind, observing the two of them return to their horses. It was not the first time she had noticed how easily they interacted with people. She understood Eivor's confidence, but Rhydwen had not been raised to lead. Each glimpse of the man he could become now he was away from his mother was like seeing the sun peeking out from behind a storm cloud. With Eivor's influence, he had the chance to be a king people would respect.

"Feel better?" she murmured to Eivor as the queen hauled herself into the saddle. "I know the celebration was bothering you."

"Aren't you a little unsettled by it?"

"No. Why would I be?"

Gathering the reins, Eivor sighed. "True. Why would you be? I want Oisin's bones bound as soon as possible. Have you got someone in mind for doing it?"

Wriggling her brows, Thorne replied, "I'm going to do it. Such a thing is simple when you can always see the Veil. Though I'm surprised you don't want to do it."

"I don't know how."

"Would you like me to teach you?"

"No." Shaking her head, she admitted, "I don't want to know."

Respecting Eivor's wishes, Thorne did not press the matter. "Do you want to be there when I do it? Or would you rather wait until it's done?"

The thinning of her lips was a sign of her uncertainty. If Eivor did not know what she wanted, binding Oisin to his bones could wait. Thorne had no intention of denying her the opportunity to see the spirit of the man who killed her parents being ripped from the other side and anchored to his remains. Some places on Tir practised binding regularly, ensuring the knowledge possessed by a dead mage was not lost. Most viewed it for what it was: torture. Binding a spirit to their bones trapped them at the edge of the Veil, unable to move on when they were ready to return to the fabric of existence.

"You don't need to decide now, pretty magpie. We have time."

Her lashes fluttered, and Eivor's gaze slid to Rhydwen. "What do you think?"

"I think you should do what you feel comfortable with. You can trust Thorne to do it properly, and when you're ready, you can summon Oisin's spirit. There's no need to face him unprepared." Shrugging, the prince knew she needed to hear nothing was wrong with not seeing it. "Clean up, rest, and then don your armour before you torture them."

It felt like the column of riders, and shape-shifted daoine had become a river threatening to sweep her away. Drawing a shaky breath through her teeth, Eivor tried to ignore the tightening of her chest. The conversation reminded her the causes of her rage were dead or imprisoned. She had survived, and now the wind behind the sails of her quest for vengeance had died. Returning to the palace alive meant moving forward with a new purpose.

"You're right, Precious. Better I wait until I'm composed."

Satisfied with her response, Rhydwen smiled. "I'm not just a pretty face."

"I'm not sure about that," Thorne muttered.

"Oh, I'm still primarily a pretty face, but I have other uses."

Letting her thoughts drift to what she planned to do to him once they were alone, Eivor hummed in appreciation. "Yes. Yes, you do. Many other uses."

"That's not what I'm talking about!"

Thorne shook her head, smiling faintly. "You didn't specify. So yes, we're going to think about your most pertinent uses. What else are you good for?"

"Lots of things."

The change in conversation helped ease the anxiety tightening its chains around Eivor's lungs. "We know you're good at many things, Rhyd. Especially activities involving your hands and your tongue. You're very skilled with those."

"Why else would we keep him around?" Thorne arched a brow at the befuddled expression Rhydwen wore. "He's got to earn his keep somehow."

"I'm going to assume you're joking and not feel hurt over being reduced to the pleasure my hands and tongue can provide." Rhydwen gave the two women a knowing look.

Eivor drew her bottom lip through her teeth, relishing the low growl of his voice. It was exactly what she needed to drag her thoughts away from a spiral of darkness. Imagining what she would let Rhydwen and Thorne do to her once they locked themselves in her chambers banished the memories of blood and pain. The thought of their touch and the quiet reminders she had the choice to say no filled Eivor with relief. For all the intensity that often overtook them, none of it was forced. She was an equal and willing participant.

Extending her hand to Rhydwen, Eivor smiled apologetically. "We're joking. I promise we would never intentionally reduce you like that."

"When you say it in jest, I don't mind." His fingers entwined hers. "Though it's hard to tell when Thorne is joking. She's so stoic all the time."

"I'm a dullaghan; that's our normal state. We're cold-hearted killers with one purpose," Thorne grumbled, but there was a hint of amusement in her voice.

"Do you believe her, Songbird?"

"Not at all, Precious. Do you?"

"About as much as I'd believe someone trying to tell me the sky is green."

Huffing at them, Thorne ran her fingers through the mane of her horse. "So, we picked on Rhyd, and now it's my turn? I'll remember that later, pretty magpie."

Her eyes narrowed suspiciously. "Is that a threat?"

"Remember who needs to beg who."

"You're going to play dirty."

"Well, once we've all bathed, it should be quite clean."

Sniggering, Rhydwen enjoyed Eivor's indignant scoff. "I'm looking forward to later."

They were a healing balm, but she had no intention of letting them know it. "Just wait, Rhyd. If you're not careful, Thorne will subject you to the same command."

"There's an idea."

Horrified, Rhydwen gazed at Thorne pleadingly. "I'm sorry, love. Please don't."

Tapping her chin, the dullaghan pretended to mull over the idea. "It could be fun."

"I don't beg as sweetly as she does."

"Don't you? Aren't you supposed to be equals?"

Listening to their exchange, Eivor laughed. It felt good to laugh so hard she struggled to breathe. They gazed at her in concern, but she waved away their questions. Calming her mirth, the queen straightened in the saddle and stared at the palace.

"Welcome home, my loves."

# TWENTY-NINE

It felt excessive to take another bath so soon after the last, but as Eivor watched the discoloured water drain away, she doubted she was the only one. She was alone in her quarters for the moment. Rhydwen had returned to the chambers assigned to him to bathe, and Thorne was attending to Oisin's corpse. They had decided it would be better to separate to save time and to banish the ash from the battlefield. Since she was preparing her second bath, Eivor knew they had made the right decision.

Water trickled down her back, sending more shivers across her skin. She had chosen to have a cold bath first, knowing its purpose was to soak off the dirt. It was a decision Eivor was regretting while she ran fresh water to rinse away the layer of grime before waiting for the hot water to fill the tub. The water pipes running through the walls could handle a lot, but the current demand for their services was high, as an unprecedented number of people throughout the palace shed layers of filth. It left her with a flow of water far slower than usual and an impatient bounce in her pacing.

Finally satisfied with the amount in the tub and desperate to warm up, Eivor climbed back into the bath, groaning as the heat made her toes sting. She had not gotten cold enough to turn them numb, but it was close enough. Sinking into the water, her hand sought the wet soap on the rim where she left it. The soap her maid had given her was scratchy, little pieces of something set into the mix to help remove the dirt stuck to her skin. It felt strangely pleasurable, like finally itching at a bothersome spot. By the time Eivor finished, her skin had taken on a rosy hue from being scrubbed too hard. Even her scalp tingled from the number of times she had taken the bar to her hair to get rid of the ash.

She almost did not want to get out of the water, but it was no longer the clear liquid it had been. Though not as filthy as the first round, it was not something Eivor wanted to stay in. Perching on the tub's edge to watch it drain, she contemplated if a third soak was going too far. Eyeing the tap, she decided it was probably better to get a washcloth and sit awkwardly while running the water and doing her best to rinse away anything left. An option she regretted not thinking of at the start. It seemed a better choice than sitting in another tub full of water, only to taint it with any lingering dirt. Settling into position with a cloth in hand, Eivor let the warmth flow over her legs. Her body protested with every twist, but she ignored it.

Each swipe of the warm, wet cloth over her skin and the drizzle of water when she squeezed it was a soothing, repetitive action. They lulled her into a fog of thought Eivor knew she should have avoided. Threads of memory grabbed at her mind, dragging her down while her hands continued to cleanse away the last traces of what had happened. With every movement, part of her needed it to rain and wash the ash from the ground, banishing it like she had drained away what she carried home with her. The fragile shield surrounding Eivor's heart demanded to be allowed to shatter.

Before she could stop herself, she had the tap turned off and scrambled out of the tub. Collapsing on the ground, Eivor balled the sodden mat in her hands, sucking in deep breaths to stave off the sobs clawing their way up her throat. She did not want to break on the bathroom floor. Regaining control over the emotions hammering at her walls, Eivor struggled to her feet, grabbing a towel from the bench to wrap around her damp body. It was not long before her sodden hair soaked the material covering her back. Staggering into the next chamber, she stared at the bed with its welcoming blankets and chose the corner furthest from the door to the sitting room.

Sinking to the floor, Eivor hugged her legs, resting her head on her knees. Wet hair slid from her shoulders, hanging limply on either side where they dripped, forming puddles that soaked into her towel. What warmth she had gained from her bath leeched away, leaving her shivering as she battled the tears trying to break free. She had feared the emotional crash, but had not expected it so soon.

Everything that had happened over the last one hundred years had left scars, and now they burst open.

Rhydwen lingered at the door, wondering how long Thorne would take, when he heard a heart-wrenching sob from the next room. Not hesitating to rush through, it startled him to find Eivor huddled on the ground in a corner. Her hair clung to her arms, face, and shoulders in wet clumps he eased out of the way once he had dropped onto his knees beside her. Tears mingled with the water dripping from her scalp, catching on Rhydwen's fingers as he tilted her face up so he could meet her gaze. Eivor clenched her eyes shut, drops rolling down her cheeks to drip from her chin onto his hand.

"Oh, Songbird, I'm sorry." Shifting his position, Rhydwen rested his forehead against hers. "I should've stayed with you. You needed me, and I wasn't there."

Her mouth opened and closed, no words escaping past the aching of her throat. Whimpering, Eivor jerked her head away from his touch, missing the hurt flickering across his face. It was not intentional. Rhydwen knew she did not want to cause him pain, but her reaction left him feeling inadequate. He was supposed to provide her comfort and be her anchor when the storm of her emotions threatened to blow her away.

"I'm going to pick you up," he murmured.

Eivor did not struggle against the arms slipping around her. Moving carefully, Rhydwen stood slowly, cradling the woman to his chest. As he carried her to the bed, he noticed patches of red blossoming on the towel. He had not smelt the blood in his concern, but it had caught his attention, and he could not shake the scent. Laying Eivor down, he hooked a finger on the edge of the fabric to tug it free. What he saw had Rhydwen inhaling sharply, eyes darting to her face in anguish.

"You scrubbed yourself raw, Eivor."

She buried her face in the pillow. "I'm sorry."

Examining the broken patches of skin, Rhydwen was thankful there were only a few deeper splits. He had seen it before. The last time had been a friend who remained in the Spire. Mulling over why his friend had done it, the prince suspected something similar had triggered Eivor. In the back of his mind, Rhydwen knew she had been handling things too well. What trauma she had buried behind temporary walls out of necessity was returning to claim the emotional toll it deserved.

Gently covering her with the towel again, Rhydwen stretched out beside Eivor, holding her close to curl around her. "When I was a child, my sisters liked to torment me. The only one who didn't was the one Annawyn tortured because of Oisin's defiance. She tried to help me learn how to avoid giving them reasons to lash out. Never blink where they can see you. Right now, no one can see you blink except me, and I'm the one you're safe with."

The warmth of his body seeped into her, and Eivor snuggled in closer, thankful for the security of his arms. "I thought I had more time."

"More time?"

"Before I broke. I held it off as long as I could."

He knew the admission should not surprise him, but it did. Eivor was a skilled mind mage who was more than competent at recognising and manipulating emotions. That she had recognised the signs of her impending breakdown was a testimony to her training. All Rhydwen could do was hold her without question or expectation until she told him what she needed. Everyone had their own ways to cope, but if he knew anything about Eivor, he was confident she would be the composed queen again by the next day. Or sooner if demands were made for her to appear before the court so they could assure themselves of her safety.

Kissing the top of her head, Rhydwen sighed. "Take all the time you need."

"Do you think I'll ever feel clean again?" she whispered. "If I don't keep myself busy, I remember the touch of their whips and the tug of knives through my skin. I remember their teeth biting me in a mockery of lovemaking. Or the caress of hands pretending to be gentle while they told themselves I enjoyed it. For some of them, I pretended as well because if I didn't, I knew what Cathair would do to punish me."

"You'd pull on the mask to protect yourself."

"I fear letting go of the mask because if I do, people will see the broken woman beneath it and doubt my ability to lead them."

It was impossible to miss the waver in her voice. The words were a confession they would keep between them. Rhydwen was determined to spend the rest of their lives providing a safe place for Eivor to lower her mask. If it were safe for someone as strong as her, it would be safe for him to do the same. They could hold each other up while Thorne kept the world from crashing in on their sanctuary. Outside the walls of their haven, the masks would be their shields. Let the world see the wicked queen twisted by magic and cruelty accompanied by her goblin prince and their dullaghan lover. Together, they could face anything.

"You are the most incredible woman I have ever met, Songbird. I saw through your mask the moment I laid eyes on you on the throne in nothing but a robe. Even now, when you feel like your heart is broken beyond repair, there is no one stronger."

"Rhyd..."

"Let your tears fall, Eivor. I'll hold you for as long as you need me to. When you're done, I'll gather those pieces of your shattered heart and stitch them together before kneeling at your feet to remind you of how much I worship and adore you."

Wriggling around in his arms until she faced him, Eivor let Rhydwen see the tears still trickling from her eyes. "And what about you, Precious?"

"What about me?" His mouth twisted in a wry smile. "You have taken me from my tormentors and offered me more than I ever dreamed I could have. The only thing that will break me now is losing you or Thorne. I have broken in the past and had days where I could not see the light beyond the darkness. Sometimes I wished my mother could end me. Then Thorne came, and my life changed. Now I am here. Only death will keep me from you."

"Kiss me."

"I don't think that's a good idea."

Her eyes narrowed, and the hint of annoyance simmering in their icy depths was out of place with the glitter of tears on her cheeks. "Are you arguing with me?"

"Of course. You're hurting, my love, and you need to let the pain out, or it will consume you. Do that first. Kissing can come later."

Eivor did not want to drown in her pain; she wanted to be swept away by the early waves of love she felt for Rhydwen. Swiping the back of her hand over her eyes, she brushed tears from her face. It was enough to acknowledge the damage her past had left her with; she did not deny it existed, just refused to let it keep her from finding happiness. Her hands grabbed his coat, keeping him from escaping as she pressed her lips to his. Rhydwen resisted, keeping his mouth firmly shut until she growled in frustration.

"Rhydwen, please."

He brought his hands to her cheeks, cupping them gently. "Songbird, I would do anything for you... but I am not comfortable with what you're asking when I just found you huddled on the floor, sobbing. The tears are still in your eyes. You want me to kiss you, but then what? Are you going to bury everything behind your walls?"

"No, I'm not burying it. I'm asking for a kiss because I need to feel your affection for me. Replace those painful memories with something real. You talk about what I need and then argue what I'm asking for isn't it?"

"I'm not saying you don't need it; I'm questioning if now is the right time. Why don't you slip on a chemise and come with me? There's something I need to show you, and I think it's something that will help you. You can kiss me after."

Allowing him to draw her from the bed, Eivor did not hide her unsteadiness. His argument had merit, but she could not help feeling the sting of rejection. Rhydwen led her to the wardrobe, finding a simple white chemise and a wool robe to wear over it. He helped her dress, every brush of his hands tender and careful of the spots where Eivor had scrubbed her skin raw. The gentle treatment left her feeling like fragile glass, forcing her to admit Rhydwen was right to refuse her advances.

On his knees, Rhydwen kissed the inside of her calf before lifting her foot to slide a slipper onto it. "You are a survivor, Songbird, and you're not alone anymore."

Rubbing a wool-clad arm against her face, Eivor knew she was still crying. "I know."

Their hands entwined, he guided her from the chambers. Guards watched silently, uncertain of what was going on but unwilling to ask questions. Neither spoke as Rhydwen led them to the surprise he had arranged for Eivor. It did not take long for her to realise their path. She had walked it countless times to visit her parents in their quarters. No courtiers bustled through the halls as they did in her memories, but a few guards were on duty, stopping their patrols to salute the queen and her prince.

"Rhydwen, why are we here?"

He held her hand tight, refusing to let go when Eivor froze in front of the doors to the chambers that had belonged to her parents. "Trust me, Songbird. Please."

Chewing her lip, she nodded and followed Rhydwen in. Eyes widening at the sight of the empty room, Eivor gasped. He took her through each section, watching her reaction as she discovered they had stripped the quarters bare. Nothing remained of the last occupant. The first time he had visited, it had been clear Cathair had taken over every part of the chambers. When Rhydwen asked servants to remove everything, they had been too happy to oblige. Whatever they had done with the items, he did not care and had no plans to ask.

Keeping hold of Eivor's hands, Rhydwen dropped to his knees in front of her. "I am a high-born goblin man, and part of our duty is to provide a comfortable home to the woman who chooses us. These were your parents' quarters, and then Cathair took them over. Now I want to turn them into something for us."

"They're empty…"

"I planned to make them comfortable, then present them to you, but every time I stared at the ceiling in your bedroom, I pictured your touch bringing colour to the walls. So yes, they're empty, but I will go to the ends of the world to get you any materials you need to paint every wall and ceiling the way you want. We will make this our sanctuary."

Fresh tears welled in Eivor's eyes, spilling down her cheeks as she stared at the blank walls. No bars adorned the windows, and sunlight filtered through the glass, illuminating the room. It was strange to recall all the time she had spent with her parents in the now empty space, so she imagined the sound of

Rhydwen's laughter echoing through the rooms. Thorne's smug chuckle went with it, making Eivor ache for the dullaghan's presence at her side. Part of her mind dared to weave in the giggles of children.

"Oh no, please don't cry!" Scrambling to his feet, Rhydwen pulled her into a hug. "I'm sorry, Eivor. I thought you would like this gift."

Pressing her face to his neck, she felt laughter escape. "I do. These are happy tears."

"They are?"

"Your gift is perfect, Rhydwen. Thank you. I don't deserve how good you are to me."

He scoffed, pulling back so he could see her eyes. "I'm going to have to—"

Rising on her toes, Eivor kissed him, silencing whatever he had planned to say. She did not want to argue; all she wanted was to show her appreciation for everything Rhydwen did for her. When he did not retreat, her hands tugged the coat from his shoulders, letting it drape awkwardly until he dropped his arms to let it slide free. Underneath sat an ornately embroidered shirt, almost the same shade of green as his eyes. He did not stop her from pulling it over his head or undoing his belt and tossing it to the side. Every touch of her fingertips on his bare skin sent pleasure straight to his hardening cock.

"Songbird," he murmured, burying a hand in her damp hair to tug her head back. "Are you sure you want to do this here? A bed would be more comfortable."

"I don't care about comfort, Rhyd. Right now, all I want is you."

"Is that all?"

Nipping at his lips when he kissed her, Eivor growled. "No, it's not. I also want you to lie down and let me show you how much I want you."

"Is that an order?"

"Are you going to deny your queen?"

Rhydwen smirked against her mouth. "I wouldn't dream of it."

Stepping back to watch appreciatively as he freed himself of his boots and trousers, Eivor regretted Thorne's absence. Her distraction was brief, replaced with lust at the sight of Rhydwen's naked body sprawled out on top of his coat. Arms crossed beneath his head with his hair fanned out around them, he arched a brow, lips curling in a cocky grin. Shedding her robe and chemise, she dropped to her knees to straddle him. His grin gave way to a groan when Eivor's hand grasped his cock, stroking it gently. Desire curled through her, and she adjusted her position so she could guide the head to where she desperately wanted to feel it.

Unfolding his arms, Rhydwen brought his hands to her hips, steadying Eivor as she sunk onto his cock. He loved being buried inside her and knowing how much pleasure they both received from it. Arching her back, she gripped her legs for balance. It altered the angle, coaxing a strangled moan from Eivor as she found her rhythm. Claws extending the barest amount, Rhydwen danced them across her skin, seeking sensitive spots to make her jolt. Each hitch of her breath and the slight pause in her rocking made him want to crow in triumph. Trailing his fingers over her hips, he avoided her clit on purpose, wanting to drag out every moment of pleasure possible until Eivor begged for release.

"Bastard," she whimpered, catching on to his game.

"You know Thorne's rule."

Disappointment briefly pierced through her haze when Rhydwen's use of the dullaghan's name did not summon the woman to their side. It faded as quickly as it came, chased away by the exquisite agony of too much pleasure. Her need to climax battered at the wall of Thorne's command, unable to break through. Chuckling at the pained twist of her lips and the moan that escaped them, Rhydwen grabbed her hips so he could thrust into her quicker. Once he gave her permission, he knew Eivor's orgasm would strike, and he wanted to share the moment with her. Releasing one hip, he dragged his claws up to circle her nipples before seeking her neck to stroke her exposed throat.

"Tell me what you need, Songbird."

Her voice was a breathy moan full of desperation. "Please, Rhyd. I can't. Please."

"Come for me."

The murmured permission was enough to release her from the binds of Thorne's power. Pleasure burst through her, and Eivor felt the familiar dig of Rhydwen's claws into her hips as he held her in place. She could not move, her limbs unwilling to cooperate as the gentle thrusts of his softening cock inside her coaxed more spasms from the muscles encasing him. They made her whimper from oversensitivity, and he chuckled in delight.

"Such a good fucking girl, aren't you, Songbird?"

"It's too much."

He wanted to roll her over and force her to come again. "No, it's not."

"Please."

Pinching a nipple between the tips of his claws, Rhydwen sought her clit with his other hand. As sensitive as Eivor was, he knew how to push her over the edge of a second orgasm. It rewarded him with a keening moan, and she jolted forward stiffly, head hanging as she held herself with trembling arms.

"Give it to me, Songbird. Come again like a good girl."

It was a burning pleasure that flooded her body. Even her legs felt like they were on fire while her toes curled. Eivor's arms gave out, and she collapsed onto Rhydwen's chest. Kissing the top of her head, he remained buried within her while she lay in his embrace. Running a claw up and down her spine, he enjoyed the involuntary twitches of her body, but did not push for more. Eyeing the discarded robe, he wished it was closer so he could use it to cover her while Eivor came down from the pleasure. As soon as she was ready, Rhydwen planned to dress them both and carry her back to her bed. By then, he hoped Thorne would be done.

"I think I love you, Eivor," he murmured into her hair.

She lifted her head to blink at him. "I think I love you too."

# THIRTY

Her hands hesitated on the door to the cell. "Am I doing the right thing by keeping him alive? What if it's a mistake that will bring nothing but more grief? Not just to me, but to my people."

"The decision is yours alone, my pretty magpie," Thorne replied, brushing icy fingers across her hand. "Keeping Cathair alive might lead to people trying to free him."

"He deserves to suffer for what he did."

"Yes, he does."

Eivor's head hung, frustration rolling off her in waves. She had been happily curled up in Rhydwen's arms when Thorne joined them. Now she regretted her hasty decision to come to Cathair's cell to see the results of the dullaghan's work. On the other side of the door was the man who had caused her years of pain and the remains of the one who had given him the order to do it. Oisin was bound to his bones, unable to move on until time wore his remains to dust or someone with the power to do so released him.

"I was so certain this would bring me satisfaction," she whispered.

"And now?"

"I want to move on with my life. Our years are no longer infinite, Thorne. I don't want to spend the rest of mine trapped in a cage when you and Rhydwen have opened the door to let me fly. Maybe killing Cathair will free me."

Leaning against the wall, Rhydwen studied the line of her face. "Thorne is right, Songbird. You are the only one who can make this decision. All we can do is support you."

Her eyes slid in his direction. "If he dies, I can walk away from this cell and never return. But if he lives, I will feel compelled to return over and over to flaunt my life in front of him. Cathair will gloat because my visits will prove he continues to occupy a place in my thoughts. Keeping him alive will hold open the wounds."

"Yes, it will."

"Thorne?"

Cocking her head, the dullaghan blinked. "Yes, my pretty magpie?"

"When a spirit is bound to their bones, they're trapped watching the living?"

"Indeed. They're stuck in between, unable to move on while forced to witness the world continue without them. Unless summoned, they cannot interact either."

She dropped a hand to her stomach thoughtfully. "I want them to see me happy and grow in power. Would it be terrible if I had their bones set into the walls of the throne room?"

Mouth open in shock, Rhydwen caught Claire's startled look. It was not an idea they had seen coming, but as he mulled it over, he realised how perfect it was. Imprisoning Oisin and Cathair in a throne room wall would ensure they saw not only Eivor grow, but Diwan. It would force them to witness the Unseelie flourish under their new queen, a woman they thought they had broken.

"I don't know what Thorne thinks, but I'd say that's a far better suggestion," Rhydwen said. "We would trap them into watching generations flourish."

Thorne wanted to be careful with her answer, knowing whatever she said would affect Eivor's decision. She felt the stares of her lovers, sensing their impatience. They had their reasons for wanting a swift response. One wanted to end her turmoil, while the other wanted to return to the bed they had left behind. Meeting Eivor's gaze, Thorne wished she better understood the emotional repercussions.

"This is what I think. So long as Cathair is still alive, he will be a reminder of what you went through. He will also be a beacon to any of Oisin's loyalists who have survived. With the risk of the danann setting up in Talaroo, do you want to keep him in a position where he can try undermining your confidence? Every time you visit, Cathair will taunt you. If he can flush out a crack in your armour, he'll wriggle inside and try breaking it."

Toying with her skirts, Eivor nodded. "There is no progress when you keep one foot in the past. It will always hold you back. Cathair needs to die."

Leaning in, Thorne lifted her chin with her fingers and said, "You made us an offer once. Do you remember it, my pretty magpie? Because we haven't forgotten."

"I remember coming to an agreement in which you held him down while I carved his heart out to feed to Rhydwen. Are you asking me to honour it?"

Perking up, the prince looked enthusiastic about the idea. "I could eat."

"You can always eat." Thorne chuckled.

"It's not my fault someone put me through my paces earlier."

The reminder of what they had done on the floor of the empty chambers caused a blush to creep over Eivor's cheeks. Her mind offered images of Rhydwen licking his claws clean of Cathair's blood while Thorne held her in place and made her beg for release. Clenching her thighs together, her face turned bright red when Claire pointedly cleared her throat. Rhydwen stepped closer, brushing his nose through the twists of her hair.

"I don't think I need to ask what you're thinking, Songbird," he murmured.

Swallowing, Eivor decided what she would do. "It's time to put an end to this."

"Are you sure?"

Thankful for her choice, Thorne felt obligated to remind her of the finality it would bring. "Death isn't something you can undo. You need to be confident this is the right path."

Her fingers picked at a fold in her skirt, feeling the smooth fabric twist between the tips. It was easy to withhold a response to give the impression she was considering her options. Eivor knew it was one of those times when she needed to listen to her gut instead of her heart or mind. Those parts held too much vindictiveness and demanded to keep Cathair alive so she could deliver torture whenever she felt like it. Instinct screamed above the other voices, telling Eivor to kill him and move on.

"I'm sure. This needs to end. It isn't healthy. How can Diwan heal while he lives? The answer is we can't. Therefore, Cathair must die. Now, can someone give me a knife?"

Claire drew a blade from her belt, holding it out for the queen to take. "You're not going to let me watch, are you? Not when they're with you."

Wrapping her fingers around the hilt, Eivor shrugged. "It might be an idea to send everyone for a break while we're in there. You know how these things go."

"All too well," she replied, eyes narrowing in Thorne's direction. "I'm sure the two of you will have our queen's safety covered. The rest of us will take a break."

"We'll have her covered," Rhydwen mumbled, hiding his mirth.

Shooting him an unimpressed look, Claire signalled for the other guards to leave. "If anything happens to her, I'll kill you. Hopefully, before General Vesta kills me."

Thorne opened the unlocked cell door, holding it so Eivor and Rhydwen could enter. "Don't worry, no harm will come to our queen. Besides, Cathair is in no physical state to attack anyone, and if he somehow got free of his chains, he'd have to go through us."

"If it were just the prince, I'd be more concerned."

Fidgeting with the knife, Eivor glanced up long enough to catch the flicker of insult cross Rhydwen's face. She wanted to assure him she knew he could protect her, but she also recognised he needed to stand up for himself. They were not in the Spire, where arguing with a woman would lead to punishment. It was up to him to find his confidence in his position, and her intervention would not help.

Standing in the middle of the cell, Eivor focused on the stack of bones in the corner, with the skull sitting neatly on top. "They're clean?"

Humming, Thorne slammed the door shut once Rhydwen was through. "Rotting corpses leave such an unpleasant stench. It wouldn't be fair to make the guards suffer."

"How did you do it?"

"I'm a dullaghan."

"Is that your answer for everything?"

"While it continues to leave you so flustered, yes, it is." Thorne smirked at the annoyed twist of her lips. "I know ways to strip a body down to the bones with magic."

Rhydwen watched Thorne prowl across to Eivor, her hands coming to rest on the queen's waist. There was a possessiveness to it intended for the man chained to the wall. Even though the performance was for Cathair, he enjoyed the way Thorne's lips slowly brushed over the queen's cheek and the willing tilt of Eivor's head, exposing her neck. Crossing to the prisoner, Rhydwen crouched next to him and jerked the chains that kept him in place.

"I am a lucky man, Cathair, and I owe you some thanks for it."

Bruises mottled his face, and one eye had swollen shut, but somehow Cathair managed to look haughty as he raised his head to spit at Rhydwen. "Goblin scum."

"My feelings are hurt, but I have Eivor to kiss them better. She set Oisin's army on fire and sang while they burned. It was beautiful. I'm sorry you missed it."

Glaring at the two women while Thorne grasped Eivor's chin and kissed her, Cathair refused to give the goblin any satisfaction by responding. He had seen his king's corpse dragged in, and acceptance had finally sunk its claws into his mind. They had lost to the people they thought they had conquered. Overconfidence and ambition had left Oisin dead and bound to his bones in the corner of a Diwanian dungeon cell. If the knife in Eivor's hand was a sign of his fate, Cathair suspected his death was upon him.

Extending his claws, Rhydwen grabbed a handful of the man's hair and dug them into his scalp. "I wanted more time with you, but I'm going to enjoy eating your heart."

"Is my pet so weak she can't kill me herself?"

"Hardly. She will cut out your heart and let me eat it from her fingers."

Drawn by their exchange, Eivor shifted to face her tormentor in chains. Her magic remained woven through him, working as intended. Eyes drifting over the cuts and bruises decorating Cathair's body, her lips curled in a delighted smile. Whatever the guards might have allowed to happen to him while they were gone from the palace, she knew most of the injuries were self-inflicted.

Despite his confidence Oisin would win, Cathair had tried to end his life to escape the endless torment plaguing his mind.

"You look wonderful, Master," she said, almost purring. "Don't you think he looks delightful, Thorne? Suffering suits you, Cathair."

Stroking the wrist of the hand holding the knife, Thorne smirked. "You've added some bruises since I saw you earlier. Not that it matters, you'll be nought but bones soon."

Cathair remained determined to deny them the satisfaction of seeing him flinch. "If you're going to kill me, get it over with. Or are you too weak, Pet?"

The ice of Thorne's touch helped Eivor hide the tremble of her hand. "There's something to be said for killing you quickly. You do not know how much is yet to come."

"I have the keys," Thorne murmured, revealing what she had retrieved from a guard earlier. "Rhyd and I will take a side each. Don't want the bastard to make it hard."

Eivor missed the chill as Thorne moved from her side. She kept out of the way, giving her lovers room to move as they unlocked Cathair from his chains. It did not take long for self-preservation to kick in, and he struggled to break free. Blood ran down his arm and chest from Rhydwen's claws. Weakened by his imprisonment, the duine was no match for them, his legs dragging across the stones. They delivered him to Eivor's feet, bloody and torn. Licking the claws of one hand, Rhydwen caught her staring, lips parted as her breath hitched at the sight of his tongue curling around the tip.

Following her gaze, Cathair wanted to land a final blow before they killed him. "You can fuck a goblin all you like, Pet, but they'll kill you in the end."

"Fuck him? Yes, I enjoy that. I'm going to marry Rhydwen, and you'll get to watch with Oisin as our children and grandchildren rule Diwan long after we die."

One nod was all it took for Thorne and Rhydwen to pick him up. They did not care if Cathair was hurt by their rough handling, or if any bones fractured when they slammed him against the wall next to Oisin's bones. Adjusting the knife, Eivor smiled, finding peace in the gleam of the blade. She did not hesitate when she drove it into his chest. The feel of warm blood slicking her fingers as she cut Cathair open filled Eivor with relief. He was dead and could never lay another finger on her.

Standing back with the knife in one hand and a heart in the other, Eivor panted from exertion. Blood dripped from her face where it had sprayed during the process. It covered her, and staring at Cathair, she realised she had done more than carve his heart out. His insides were in a heap at his feet, and his eyes rested on the floor on the other side of the cell where she had flung them. Rhydwen was the first to let go of the body, licking the blood from his lips before approaching Eivor eagerly. Leaving the corpse where it fell to follow slowly, Thorne saw the tears of relief in her eyes.

"My queen," Rhydwen said, dropping to his knees.

Words failed her when his claws retracted so he could grasp her wrist gently. Her fingers held Cathair's heart loosely, and Rhydwen cradled them with surprising tenderness before bringing them to his lips. The stroke of his tongue lapping the blood from her skin had her core clenching with need, and Eivor whimpered. Smirking, he kept going, taking his time so she would be slick with desire before he sunk his teeth into the heart.

"Fuck," Thorne muttered, gazing at Rhydwen over Eivor's shoulder. "I did not expect it to look so appealing. The way his tongue finds every drop, leaving your skin clean."

The knife hit the ground, and Thorne kicked it out of the way. Pressing against Eivor's back, she ran her hands over the bodice of the dark blue dress, feeling the damp spots from the blood. Part of her wanted to tear it off, but she did not want to leave the queen with nothing to wear back to her quarters. As comfortable as the daoine were with being naked, Thorne's possessive nature wanted no one else to see Eivor or Rhydwen undressed. They were hers. Nothing and no one would take them from her. If anyone tried, she would destroy them.

Nuzzling her neck, Thorne licked the blood she found, and Eivor's knees buckled. "I'm going to make you beg while he eats the heart from your hand."

Gathering the skirt of Eivor's dress, she twisted the fabric carefully, tucking it in on itself to keep it out of the way. Arching a brow, Rhydwen paused in his task to watch the hand tracing circles across the queen's stomach. Thorne knew she had blood on her fingers, so she extended them to him to lick clean. When his tongue curled around each one, she understood why it had trapped Eivor in a trance. He smirked knowingly, slowly drawing two of her fingers into his mouth before releasing them with a pop.

A strangled giggle broke through Eivor's daze. "Cheeky boy."

"They needed to be clean for what she's going to do with them."

Humming in agreement, Thorne brought her fingers to Eivor's thigh, trailing them in teasing circles. Without prompting, she shifted her feet to make access easier. One arm curled around her middle, keeping her pinned to the dullaghan's chest. Rhydwen turned his attention to the hand the knife had been in, leaving the heart where it was. The moment he drew her fingers into his mouth, Thorne struck. She found Eivor's clit, using her thumb to toy with it while the others stroked through the slickness of her arousal.

"By the time he's finished, you'll be pleading for release." Nipping Eivor's earlobe, Thorne chuckled at her moan. "And while you come undone on my fingers, our darling prince will eat the heart in your hand before turning his skilled tongue on you."

Squirming, Eivor squeezed Cathair's heart tight and wished she could cling to something for balance. It felt awkward to rely on Thorne to hold her up. Fingers curled into her, sliding in easily to seek the spot that would give her the most pleasure. She did not know how they did it, but somehow Rhydwen matched his licking with the strokes of Thorne's fingers. The occasional nip of his teeth helped tighten the coil of need that could not break until they let it. Not for the first time that day, Eivor felt torn between loving it and hating their power over her.

"Thorne, please... oh fuck, please!"

"She can do better," Rhydwen said, drawing a finger into his mouth to suck on it.

Agreeing with him, Thorne added a third finger. "Ask nicely, my sweet magpie."

"I hate both of you."

"That's not very nice. I'll stop if that's how you feel."

Eivor did not want them to stop. "No!"

"Then ask nicely."

Rhydwen's tongue swirling around the finger in his mouth had her whimpering in desperation. "Please may I come?"

Licking her neck, Thorne murmured, "That's better. You may."

The coil snapped, pleasure bursting through her. Not noticing Rhydwen plucking the heart from her hand to study it, Eivor found her moans captured by Thorne's lips. Kissing her, the dullaghan did not stop the steady stroke of her fingers until she tore her mouth away to beg for mercy, the words a mumbled mess that hitched with each touch.

Rhydwen let the untouched heart fall to the ground. "I don't think I'll ever tire of hearing her like that."

"Not going to eat that?"

"There's a better feast standing in front of me." Licking away the traces of blood on his face, he rubbed it on his shoulder for good measure. "Don't think I'll tire of that either."

She tightened the arm around Eivor's waist, knowing she could barely hold herself up. Watching Rhydwen press his nose between her fingers, Thorne felt the brush of his tongue. It fuelled her desire, and she contemplated telling him to stop so they could change positions. Lifting her gaze to sweep it across the cell, she dismissed the idea for later. They would make Eivor orgasm a second time, completing the fantasy that began the night they liberated Diwan. Rhydwen would feast on their queen with the taste of Cathair's blood on his tongue while Thorne held her in place for him.

Pulling her fingers free to give him space to work, she whispered, "Do you like that, my queen? He's going to devour you while the spirits of the men who hurt you watch from the other side of the Veil where they can never touch you again."

"Yes." Burying the hand he had licked clean in his hair, Eivor kept Rhydwen in place.

"Would you like to drag him back to bed so he can feast again?"

"No." Craning her head around, Eivor kissed Thorne hungrily. "I want to drag you to bed so I can feast. Wouldn't you—oh, fuck, too much."

Bucking against Rhydwen's mouth, she moaned. It was too much. Her body felt raw, and Thorne pressing a finger to her clit did not help. Releasing Eivor from the command she had placed on her, the dullaghan whispered the words she needed to hear. Telling her it was unnecessary to gain permission could wait until later, when they were less occupied. Rhydwen groaned in appreciation at the moans spilling from her lips, hands gripping Eivor's thighs to help keep her steady. Her hand in his hair tightened, a painful tug at his scalp, encouraging him to keep going until Thorne forced her to let go.

Sitting back, Rhydwen licked his lips and grinned. "That was as good as I imagined."

"I hope your tongue isn't tired," Thorne replied. "Because we're returning to the room to wash off the blood and do this again."

"Are you expecting her to walk?"

Adjusting her hold on Eivor, she smirked. "Good thing we've got you to carry her."

"What about all this?"

Glancing around the cell, she shrugged. Binding Cathair to his bones could wait until later. Thorne wanted to enjoy her lovers and rest, curled up in bed with them where the outside world could be forgotten. She needed to feel like everything they had been through and done was worth it. Mumbling something unintelligible, Eivor rubbed her cheek against Thorne's shoulder, and Rhydwen staggered to his feet.

Stretching, he nodded at the queen. "Do you think she'll regret killing him?"

"No, I don't. Never."

# THIRTY-ONE

"Are you nervous?"

The question had Eivor covering her mouth to hide her unsettled laughter. She did not know why her stomach felt tied up in knots, but it was, and it took all her self-control not to pace the room. Recognising the look on her face, Jola snorted in amusement and placed a mug on the table. She inhaled the steam, appreciating the scents of lavender and peppermint. It was a little too warm to drink, but the smell helped.

"You've already negotiated the contracts, Eivor. Today is about putting those final signatures on them in front of witnesses and celebrating your union."

She wanted to run her hands through her hair, but her maids had spent hours carefully arranging the black and white locks into a web of braids with emeralds and sapphires woven through them. Eivor had chosen each gem for Rhydwen and Thorne's eyes. Even her gown was a blend of blue and green. With every move, the layers shifted, and the colours altered slightly, reminding her of a sea she had visited once. Her lovers had not seen it yet, leaving Eivor with the anticipation of their reactions when they watched her enter the throne room.

"I know, Jola."

"Then why do you look like you're going to your execution?"

Eivor pinched the bridge of her nose. "I'm terrified when it's time to sign, they will come to their senses and refuse. People think I don't hear the whispers, but I do."

"Stars above, girl! They're head over heels for you. You have spent the last six months repairing your kingdom, and not once have they questioned staying with you. Every day they have been by your side, and that will not change. To-day is about new beginnings for Diwan. Your parliament, the Unseelie Council, everything the three of you have clawed together out of the ashes. I dread the day Calista demands I return to the Spire because I want to witness the future you build."

"As powerful a mind mage as I am, I cannot banish my feelings of doubt. One day, I'll believe I'm worthy of their love."

Jola huffed, nudging the mug closer. "Drink before they knock on your door."

"Have you seen our chambers?" Picking it up, Eivor sipped the warm tea. "Rhydwen had me barred from them, so I don't know what they look like."

"And you can keep waiting until tonight. I'm not spoiling his surprise."

The maids fussing around the chamber exchanged grins, giggling at the look of scolding Jola directed their way. While waiting for the knock, they kept busy packing the last few things to be moved to the queen's new quarters. It had become a game for the palace staff to keep Eivor in suspense. They knew she would not harm them for refusing to tell her what Rhydwen had done, and they enjoyed being part of the secret.

Draining the cup, Eivor hoped it would help calm her nerves quickly. "He is proud of his work. I told him it wasn't necessary, but my Precious wouldn't accept no."

"I'm glad you let him have this," Jola said, squeezing her shoulder.

"Goblins."

"We're a complicated lot. I can only imagine the cultural shift that will originate from here. Those of us who settle in Diwan will grow in ways those who remain in the Spire cannot. Not just goblins, but the rest as well. You're truly going to build a new Unseelie."

Her fingers grazed across the necklace adorning her throat. Glittering stones had been cut into a variety of shapes, each one symbolising the species that had joined her alliance so far. At the centre of them dangled a feather crafted from diamonds and obsidian. Half shining white, half black, like the feathers of the magpie she shifted into. A skilled strigoi jeweller had created it after he claimed a room deep in the dungeons as a workshop. He had made the trio of crowns they would don that day, melting down items left by the Talaroonan occupiers. Eivor loved the symbolic nature of taking the old to make the new.

"Do you think Annawyn knew?"

Inhaling, Jola's lips thinned. "I think we'll never know. Are you sure you don't want to wear some of those pretty bracelets the maids offered?"

"No!" The sharpness of her answer startled the healer. "I'm sorry. Maybe one day I'll be able to tolerate things on my wrists, but I'm not there yet."

"I'm the one who should apologise. I didn't think."

Before they could continue the conversation, a heavy knock sounded at the door. Nervous excitement had Eivor leaping to her feet, hands smoothing the skirts of her gown. A maid hurried to the door, opening it to reveal Vesta. The general was dressed in new armour, an elegant formal coat draped over the top. She had not done up the clasps, giving her a rakish appearance. Her cocky grin when she eyed Eivor appreciatively left behind a swirl of delight.

"You are too beautiful for that rascal boy," Vesta murmured, lifting Eivor's hand to her lips. "At least the Master of the Hunt is worthy of you."

"Come now, General, today is not the day to tease Rhydwen."

"He doesn't complain. The last few people have arrived and will join everyone in the throne room. It's absolutely packed. You're not short on witnesses."

Thankful for the warning, Eivor breathed deeply and reinforced the walls of magic, protecting her mind from the storm of emotions awaiting her in the throne room. She wanted to avoid being overwhelmed and from adding fuel to any headache that dared dig roots into her mind. Feeling the peaceful calm seeping through her hand from Vesta, Eivor smiled, nose scrunching up in appreciation of what the warrior was doing.

"Thank you for doing this."

Vesta winked at Jola as the healer settled on the other side of the queen to escort her from the room. "I wish your parents could be here, magpie. They'd be proud of you."

"Even my mother?"

"Especially her. Never forget the gods created the Ravens to keep the First People from crossing the line to irredeemable. Malena would be proud of what you want to achieve. She knew, like you do, that none of us asked to be created the way we were."

Clearing her throat, Jola said, "Just try to avoid saying things like those fucking humans during any speeches today. Especially with the delegations attending."

Eivor fluttered her eyes innocently. "I would never!"

"Yes, you would."

Nudging her, Vesta grinned. "You're allowed to think it, though."

It felt good to laugh. Guards watched them pass, envious of their fellows who were not on duty. Eivor glanced over her shoulder, looking for Claire's comforting presence, but her goblin captain was absent. She knew where the woman was, but it did not stop her from missing the cheeky smile that greeted her daily. As the one in charge of Eivor's safety, Claire had insisted on overseeing the guards surrounding the throne room.

"I feel like your father would come up with some grand spiel about it not being too late to change your mind and renegotiate, but I won't be doing that." Her smile faded, replaced by the serious mask Vesta wore most days. "Because it is too late."

Staring at her blankly, Eivor was unsure how she was supposed to respond. "Well, that's a reassuring speech, General. Thank you."

"Oh no, if I thought you were making the wrong decision, we wouldn't be here. It's too late to back out because the doors are right there, and they're waiting for you. Plus, Thorne would hunt you down if you ran away."

Imaging her dullaghan slipping into their hunt state sent a pleasurable thrill down Eivor's spine. She had not seen Thorne shift between forms since the battle and knew the leader of the headless riders had been redirecting kills to the others to avoid leaving the palace. Part of the queen appreciated Thorne's constant companionship, but she missed not knowing what form would greet her each day.

"Tempting," she murmured.

"Oh, good grief. Only you would find it tempting to taunt a dullaghan into hunting her."

Her answering grin had Vesta sighing. Scratching her nose, Jola kept quiet, knowing Eivor would take it as a challenge if they suggested it was a terrible idea. Tempted to secure the clasps of the general's coat, she fussed with her sleeves.

"We should take our places and let the queen make her entrance. There's an impatient crowd waiting to get the formalities over and done with so the feasting can begin." Jola nodded at the servants poised at the door. "We can slip around the back."

Stepping away from Eivor, Vesta gave her one last glance over. "Beautiful."

"Do you think they'll like it?" Eivor blushed, looking down at her dress shyly.

"Tell me if they don't, and I'll smack them around."

They left her chuckling at the image of Rhydwen and Thorne on the other end of a scolding from Vesta. Once they were out of sight, Eivor covered her face and breathed deeply, wishing the butterflies in her stomach would settle. Watching her, the servants did their best to be invisible, not wanting to disturb her moment. A compulsion to turn around and close their eyes had them following the directions whispered through their minds.

"Congratulations."

Lowering her hands, Eivor spun to face the stranger. "Who are you?"

He arched a brow, running fingers through his golden curls. "You know who I am, Eivor. Don't worry, they won't remember I was here, but you will."

"The gods are not welcome in Diwan."

"I know, and we agree to your terms. What you're building here matters. The people of Tir need it. Please believe me when I assure you that we have no intention of painting you as the villain in our story. But I wanted to see you today. Our paths have been entwined since before either of us was born. You are as magnificent as Annawyn hoped you would be."

Glancing away to avoid his stare, Eivor bit back her questions. "Have you been interfering with my life as she did?"

His blue eyes reminded her of the sky, but they darkened with regret. "No. I know how it feels to be on the receiving end of her manipulations. We are the creatures of her making, Eivor, but she is gone now. If you ask, I'll undo what she did to your memories."

"You can do that?"

"I'm the god of thought. The mind is my domain."

Turning her back on him, she smoothed her hands over her skirts. It was a tempting offer, and Eivor suspected she should accept. Knowing what Annawyn had done, what she had taught her, all the things banished from her memories, seemed like the right thing to do. There could be no surprises if she knew, and it would answer their questions. Locking her gaze on the door to the throne room, Eivor thought of the pair waiting within.

"Not today. Not when I'm about to finalise my marriage to the two people I know I can always count on... but you already knew my answer."

"True."

"Before you leave, can you tell me how Astoria is?"

He snorted. "Your sister has your strength. We appreciate her ability to keep Dawn under control."

Confused, Eivor glanced over her shoulder at the god. "I don't understand."

"It's a complicated tale. One day, I'll share it with you. Not today, though."

"When you see my sister, tell her I'm glad she's happy."

"You have my word."

The god vanished as suddenly as he appeared, leaving Eivor baffled. A sense of calm settled on her, chasing away the storm of nerves. She watched the servants resume their positions as though nothing had happened. It should have been disconcerting, but the calm did not budge. Nodding at them, the queen waited while they opened the door for her. They heard the buzz of conversation from within the chamber, a strange sound that seemed without words. Try as she might, Eivor could not pick out familiar voices.

Straightening her shoulders, she held her head high and stepped through. Inside the door, Claire waited to give a signal to the other guards. Holding Eivor's gaze for a moment, she squinted suspiciously before holding up a hand. The command spread through the room, the guards clapping their hands to their chests in a salute that had the crowd falling silent. Digging into the calm the god had given her, Eivor allowed a smile to curl her lips and swept her eyes across the gathering before settling on the two she wanted to see.

Her approach sent the crowd to their knees, heads bowed in respect. All except Thorne and Rhydwen. They stayed standing, with their gazes locked on the queen striding across the floor towards the dais on which her throne sat. Eivor felt the weight of their attention, her smile widening at the appreciative expressions they wore. She barely heard the words of the chancellor addressing the crowd while she settled onto her seat. No one else mattered when they stared at her like she was the sun.

Somehow, Eivor remembered what she needed to say, thanking everyone for their part in the battle with Oisin and for helping rebuild Diwan. The pleasantries were a dance before they reached the real reason for the gathering. Servants brought a small table forward, placing it at the bottom of the dais and revealing the final copies of their negotiations. It was strange to think the sheets of parchment waiting for their signatures held as much significance as they did, but Eivor understood why they were important. She was a queen, and her marriage was no simple matter. There was too much at stake for all of them.

When she stepped forward to sign the documents, her hand trembled, but Thorne was there. Her touch stilled the shaking, allowing Eivor to leave her signature without a mess. Plucking the quill from her fingers, the dullaghan left her mark before passing it to Rhydwen. They dared not speak to each other more than necessary, conscious of the hundreds of people watching their every move. Looming over them, the chancellor ensured everything was in order before commanding the documents to be sealed. The table was whisked away as quickly as they had brought it out, replaced by the three representatives chosen to crown them.

Eivor could barely keep her eyes off Rhydwen and Thorne. It was done. She was the queen of Diwan, the Unseelie Queen, and they were her consorts. Their children would rule after them. Kneeling for their crowns, they each repeated the oath created by the newly established Unseelie Council. The crowd remained silent, understanding the seriousness of what they were witnessing. When it was done, the cheers struck like a storm, breaking through Eivor's daze. All she wanted was to fall into Thorne's and Rhydwen's arms.

The wait was not long. With the formalities over, no one wanted to stay in the throne room longer than necessary. Outside, they had transformed the gardens into a spectacle, and tables laden with food waited for them. As soon as Eivor and her consorts retreated through the door behind the throne, people fled the room to head to the festivities. It gave the trio time to catch their breaths while only a handful of guards watched. Claire knew what they needed, chasing servants away and ordering her fellows to keep at a distance with their backs turned, granting the illusion of privacy.

"My wife," Rhydwen murmured, capturing her lips in a kiss. "You look beautiful."

Thorne chuckled, nudging him out of the way so she could also kiss Eivor. "Our wife. And he's right, you are breathtaking today. My pretty magpie, the Unseelie Queen."

Drinking in their kisses, Eivor grabbed their coats and pulled them in for a hug. "I barely remember anything after I saw you standing there, waiting for me. Whoever convinced you to wear blue instead of black needs a reward, Thorne."

"You can reward him tonight."

Beaming, Rhydwen nodded. "I told her it was our wedding day, and it might be nice if we match you. Though as much as I like that gown, I look forward to removing it."

"He argued I should wear a dress."

Hearing the petulance in Thorne's tone, Eivor sniggered. "I would have loved to see that argument. A pity you didn't let me in on it, Precious."

He nuzzled her shoulder, careful not to wreck the intricate work her maids had done. "Next time. I knew she would disagree, but I had to try. Granted, you looked like you were barely paying attention in there, so it was a good thing Thorne wasn't wearing a dress."

"All I could focus on was you."

"A sentiment we share," Thorne said, kissing her.

"Do we have to join the festivities?"

"Unfortunately, yes. They expect us to take part. I'd like to dance with you under the stars tonight, Songbird, and taste the wine from your lips when no one is looking." Rhydwen looked down the corridor to where Claire stood with her back to them. "An afternoon and evening of teasing each other while we feast with people who are happy for us."

One brow raised, and Thorne snorted. "I doubt all of them are happy for us."

"Who cares? I will not let them ruin my good mood."

Closing her eyes, Eivor leaned into Rhydwen's warmth, pulling Thorne with her. She wanted to tell them about her visitor but kept quiet, knowing it would cause upset. It was their wedding day. There was a feast waiting for them, along with music, dancing, wine, a maze of lanterns among the bushes, and hidden spots in the shadows where they could steal kisses. The feel of Thorne's icy lips on her neck had Eivor purring in delight.

"Don't get comfortable, my queen. We need to eat if we're to keep up with what Rhyd has planned for tonight. I've seen his list."

"He wrote a list?" Curious, Eivor let Thorne draw her from Rhydwen's arms.

Leading her towards Claire, the dullaghan smirked. "We might get through half of it before we pass out from exhaustion."

Catching her hand, Rhydwen entwined their fingers. "I have faith we'll manage all of it, even if you don't, love. Besides, it's not that long."

"We have the rest of our lives, Rhyd."

"Our wedding night deserves something special."

Claire heard his comment and rolled her eyes. "How do you put up with him, Majesty?"

Brushing her fingertips along his jaw, Eivor smiled adoringly. "Easily. I could barely eat this morning, so I think joining the festivities is an excellent idea."

Thorne offered her arm to the queen, and she grasped it happily. Stepping back, Claire eyed them admiringly, though she would never admit it where anyone could hear. In the flickering lantern light, the blues and greens of their outfits took on a shadowy quality that suited the trio. Leading the way through the palace to the terrace overlooking the sprawling gardens, Claire listened to their quiet chatter and envied the affection in their voices.

Breaking free of their hold, Eivor stood in front of the glass doors. She stared out at the transformation the gardens had undergone, a hand pressed to her lips in surprise. People flitted like butterflies between tables laden with food and wine, while performers displayed their abilities to eager audiences. Gauzy material fluttered in the breeze, creating the illusion of privacy for those who stood beneath the fabric arches. Sprays of flowers and vines decorated everything, including the ornate poles from which lanterns hung, waiting to be lit when the setting sun robbed them of light.

Slipping an arm around Thorne's waist, Rhydwen kissed her cheek. "It's a pity it isn't sunset. What a memory it would be of Eivor standing there in her dress with all those pretty colours turning the sky into the perfect background for a painting."

"If we don't ruin our clothes later, we can have a portrait artist paint it another day."

Eivor glanced over her shoulder, lips curled with a hint of smugness. "Precious, did you organise everything?"

"Maybe. It's yet another thing we're expected to be able to do." His eyes darted to where Claire scowled. "I'm a goblin male, Songbird. My duty is to please you."

"It's going to be a long night if you don't smile, Captain."

Straightening, Claire realised she was glaring at Rhydwen. "Apologies. As for the organisation, his highness had plenty of help."

"Yes, I expect he did. One person can't manage these things alone." Eivor held out her hands to her lovers. "Shall we? I hear music calling our names."

They stole her breath with their smiles. She had heard Thorne's suggestion of having a portrait done, and Eivor intended to make sure nothing damaged the gorgeous matching coats they wore. The blue and green fabrics were identical to the ones used in her dress, suggesting Rhydwen had charmed the information from the dressmaker. It was hard to care when the result was perfect. Silver embroidery adorned the coats, and magpies were depicted along the hems. Even the clasps were delicate silver birds with wings spread to hold the fronts closed. Eivor looked forward to undoing every single one of them.

Lifting their hands to her lips, she kissed their knuckles. "I am yours, and you are mine, always and forever. No matter what is thrown in our path."

"Is that a promise?" Thorne murmured.

Rhydwen chuckled, winking at the dullaghan leaning against him. "Sounded more like a threat than a promise. Her Majesty is rather scary when she wants to be."

"Incorrigible brat."

The adoration in his gaze when he smiled at Thorne made Eivor's heart skip a beat. "Yes, I am, but I'm your brat. And hers. Isn't that right, Songbird?"

"Now I'm questioning my decision," she replied.

Tugging her hand, Rhydwen pulled her into their arms. "Don't lie. You love us."

Cupping their faces, Eivor brushed her lips against his before doing the same to Thorne. She did not care if they were being watched through the glass wall. At least half the gathering was of daoine, and her kind had no issues with public displays of affection. What mattered was reminding her spouses that they belonged to her.

"I don't regret a thing that happened because it led us here. The two of you are my heart, and I am never letting you go. We've chosen our path. Our future is ours to make."

# THIRTY-TWO

The wind caressed her naked skin, the sunlight kissing it with warmth. Eivor tilted her head back, eyes closed as she wrapped her power around her like a coat. She did not slip into the change, preferring to let it linger at the edge of her mind, waiting for the moment she felt ready. Having Jola, Rhydwen, Thorne, and Claire watching her intently from a short distance away did not help. Instead, all she could feel was the weight of their expectations, like an itch down her spine. They wanted to see her shift into her magpie form now the healer had declared she had recovered enough to do it.

"She's nervous," Rhydwen said, and the concern in his voice prompted Eivor to open her eyes to turn to him. "I can smell it, Songbird."

"It's been so long."

He approached her, leaving the others where they stood. As his arms slipped around her, the calm of his magic did as well. Resting her head on Rhydwen's shoulder, the queen breathed slowly, letting her power soak in his. It filled her with peace, easing the sting of her anxiety. The tips of his claws traced patterns over her back, matching the soft hum of his voice. Eivor nuzzled his neck, pressing a kiss to the sensitive spot behind his ear.

"Thank you," she murmured, squeezing him tighter.

"You needed me."

Eivor had, but it had not been until he came to her that she had realised it. "I know I can do it, but I'm scared I can't. It's been so long, and I know it has been months since I was freed and my magic restored, but a little voice keeps saying 'what if Jola is wrong?' and it makes me hesitate. And you're all over there, waiting for me to shift."

"If you're not ready, then you're not ready." His lips twisted in a grimace. "Though I should warn you that if you don't shift today, General Vesta will be ruthless."

Horror had her eyes widening, Eivor realising her dignity would be at risk if she did not push through her nerves to shift. The goblin general had no qualms about making her opinions clear, even if it meant embarrassing her. There were some things she drew the line at, but Vesta would not hesitate to voice her thoughts where people would hear them. Tossing a glance back at the other three people watching her, Eivor gave them a nod.

"I can stand on the other side of the door if you want," Claire said, shifting awkwardly, her eyes darting between the queen she served and the door.

Huffing at the guard, Jola crossed her arms. "Stop overthinking it, girl. I don't expect you to fly, just shift into your animal form and back. You need to do this."

Rolling her shoulders as she released Rhydwen, Eivor did not admit she doubted she could fly yet. It had taken her months after her first shift to be able to lift from the ground. Being able to transform into an animal did not grant a duine the knowledge of how to move like one. She had needed to learn how to use every muscle. That knowledge had not been lost during her captivity, but she expected it to hurt when she shifted, and it was possible her magpie body could not fly until she rebuilt the basic skills.

A chill settled through her, Thorne approaching to lift her chin. "My pretty magpie, would you like me to make it a command? It would get around your nervousness."

Opening her mouth to refuse the offer, Eivor snapped it shut again, lips thinning as she contemplated what Thorne had said. If she let her wife order her to shift, the voices in her head would lose the battle. They could not twist her around in circles, only rage against the threads of ice digging shards into her limbs until she did as commanded. When she wanted to, she could deny Thorne's power over her, but in this, it would serve her better not to.

"It would," Eivor murmured, meeting the other woman's concerned gaze.

"I don't enjoy doing it, but if you're too much in your head about this, you could hurt yourself. This is your choice to make, Eivor."

Rhydwen slid an arm around her waist, the weight a comfort. "Thorne is right."

"Just let her do it!" Jola called out, impatience flavouring her tone. "All you're doing is making it worse for yourself, Eivor. You are strong enough to do this. If you weren't, we wouldn't be here. I wouldn't let you try if I thought it would do you harm."

She wanted to sink into the endless blue of Thorne's gaze, to wrap herself in the frozen embrace of the dullaghan's power. If there was one thing her wife was good at, it was making her forget everything that was bothering her. Rhydwen was wonderful to talk through things with, but Thorne could empty her mind of everything except the steady sound of her voice. Biting her lip, Eivor wanted to nod her agreement, except she knew the dullaghan would not follow through without hearing the words of consent.

"Please, Thorne, my love, do it. If I don't shift now, I'm just going to make it worse for myself. I've been waiting for this day, but now it's here..."

Thorne smiled sadly, a gleam of understanding in her eyes. "You know, your mother would be proud of you for waiting until you were healthy enough, and for admitting you're scared. I remember being afraid the first time I was given a name to kill. The shift between forms for us is not the same as yours, but it has its complications."

"I'll be right over here if you need me, Songbird," Rhydwen murmured, pressing a kiss to her naked shoulder before he stepped away to give her space.

Taking a deep breath, Eivor focused on Thorne's eyes. "I'm ready."

It was like a snake of ice slithered through her mind and down her spine, wrapping itself around everything that controlled her body. Thorne's power curled through hers, coaxing the ability to shift to the surface, holding it there while Eivor remembered what it was like to transform. She swallowed, bracing against the onslaught of anxious whispers swarming through her mind that had kept her from shifting on her own.

"I want you to stop thinking about anything other than shifting into your magpie form," Thorne said, her voice low and soft, the weight of the command slamming into Eivor's mind. "There is nothing to fear here. You will welcome the magic you command, and shift."

For a moment, Eivor feared her power would revolt against Thorne's orders, but the transformation slid across her skin. Pain followed it, and the dullaghan released her face, stepping back to give her room to change. It had always been easy for her, though not as painless as it was for Astoria, but as her body contorted, reshaping itself into a bird, Eivor was reminded of how much Silaine had hated shifting into her wolf form. Eivor knew it was her own fault and tried to welcome her magic as claws replaced feet, and her mouth became a beak capable of tearing flesh apart.

"Blood and bone," Claire muttered, sharing a look with Jola. "She's gorgeous."

Ruffling her feathers, Eivor stretched her wings. There was no point trying to mind speak with her companions when none of them were capable of it. Her magpie body ached from the transformation, but taking stock of it, she realised it felt the same as it always had. A hundred years of captivity had taken nothing from her other form. She was still a powerful bird. Her claws and beak were weapons, and her wings could carry her anywhere.

Crouching to bring them eye-level, Thorne smiled proudly. "You are exquisite, my pretty magpie. Well done. May I touch you?"

Snapping her beak at the woman, Eivor flapped her wings before folding them back. Turning her head around to preen, she was pleased by how glossy the black and white feathers were. While her beak slid through them, she eyed the two goblin women approaching, and her red-haired husband standing nervously to the side. Her magic picked up on his eagerness to touch her, and the desperate patience he clung to. Thorne's fingertips trailed over her wing, the barest of touches to admire the silkiness of them.

Eivor straightened and hopped across the rooftop to Rhydwen. He stretched out a hand, letting her hold it with her beak. Aware of how much damage she could do if she wanted to, the queen kept it gentle, taking care not to close too far and risk taking off a finger. A nervous squeak escaped the goblin's control, and Thorne chuckled, earning a dismayed look from him. She knew the size of her form was intimidating, though she was smaller than Astoria. Few daoine with bird forms came close to matching the fierce Battle Hawk.

"I don't know why I expected you to be smaller when I've seen so many daoine in their animal forms. You're you sized." He did not pull his hand free, choosing instead to sink to his knees, settling on the sun-warmed stone. "And you are the most beautiful bird I have ever set eyes on."

Releasing his hand, she shuffled closer to rub her head on his chest. Rhydwen's fingers tentatively touched her feathers, nervousness rolling off him in waves. Fragments of his thoughts entered her mind, the whispers of his fear he might hurt her by touching a feather wrong, the knowledge the bones of a bird were more fragile than those of a person. An understanding that it took far less time for a bird to bleed to death. Whipping her head around, Eivor peered at Thorne, unblinking until the dullaghan stood to join them.

"What are you thinking, Precious?" She sat beside Rhydwen, a hand on his shoulder while the other stroked Eivor's wing gently.

"Why does she seem so much more fragile in this form?"

Jola crossed her arms, standing over them while her magic probed at Eivor, earning the snap of a beak. "She isn't. In this form, she could kill you quicker than in her natural one. The animal forms of the daoine are weapons. It's why they don't shrink down to match the true size of the form they take. A real magpie could hurt you, but not like she can. I don't know if they're still alive, but I remember seeing a duine who could shift into a honeybee. The stinger on them was truly deadly."

Startled by the thought, Eivor recoiled, giving the healer a dirty look. She had seen plenty of daoine who shifted into insect forms, but no honeybees. It sounded more terrifying than a spider shifter. With Thorne and Rhydwen gently stroking her feathers, she felt comfortable in her bird form, the anxiety she had felt long since vanished. Lurking behind Jola, Claire stared at her with a fascinated longing, only two thoughts clear in her mind. The captain of her guard wanted to know how soft and silky her feathers were, and how sharp her talons were. Claire longed to compare them to her own out of a desire to understand.

Lifting a foot, she balled the dark grey toes with their deadly claws, snapping her beak at the goblin woman. Snorting, Jola elbowed Claire, an arched look suggesting she understood what the queen was communicating. Squeaking, the guard made no effort to move closer until the older woman grabbed her arm and shoved her at the group. There was a moment of hesitation as she stumbled forward before Claire's lips pursed and she dropped to her knees in front of Eivor, reaching for the extended claw.

"It's rough," she murmured, rubbing a scaled toe between her fingers. "Why did I think it would be smooth? I've touched chicken feet."

Biting back a laugh, Thorne replied, "Careful, Claire, you don't want to insult your queen by comparing her to a chicken. I assure you; she is not a chicken."

"Well, I know that! I mean the texture of a bird's foot."

Warbling at them, Eivor opened her foot and allowed the woman to examine her claws. She pressed the tip of her thumb against the point of one, gasping when blood welled from her skin. Claire's wide eyes confirmed she had not expected the sharpness to rival that of her own claws. Tilting her head, Eivor warbled again, allowing it to become a full song. Singing in her magpie form was a different sound to that of her natural form, but from the amazed look on Rhydwen's face, she knew it had only confirmed his choice in naming her Songbird. Extracting her foot from Claire's grasp, she hopped away from them, continuing to sing even as she lamented the loss of their touch on her feathers.

"Please don't try to fly, Your Majesty." Jola gave her a scolding look. "If you're not strong enough and hurt yourself, you could be stuck."

She disagreed. There was strength in her body, and she had not forgotten how to do it. Her mother had chosen the rooftop as a place to fly from for a reason. It had more than enough room for each of them to circle around to check their wings before venturing beyond the safety of the low wall. Cocking her head, she stared at the walled edge, thankful they had removed the bars that had formed part of her cage while Cathair kept her prisoner. Eivor had made sure she was there when they tore down the first bar. It had been a moment to remind herself she was free, and there was no more cage.

Remembering the laughter of her sister whenever Astoria had thrown herself off, naked and more than capable of shifting before she hit the ground, Eivor took several running steps towards it. Wings spreading, she flapped them, gaining the lift she needed. The mix of shouts from her companions made her trill in amusement, and she was careful not to fly too high. It felt amazing to have the wind in her feathers, her sharp gaze keeping her within the limits of the roof. One lap of it became two, before a third had her heart soaring with the confidence she could do more and fly higher.

The wind lifted her, its whispers of freedom and endless blue horizons tempting her to leave the palace behind. All daoine with wings knew the dangers the sky promised. It was too easy for them to find peace in the clouds, forgetting themselves in wind currents and the joy of flight. A tug at her mind reminded Eivor that her spouses were waiting for her on the rooftop below, their eyes never leaving her gleaming black and white form. They were her home, and she could not, would not, abandon them.

Tucking her wings in, Eivor dove back down towards the rooftop. With her confidence restored and anxiety banished, it was easy to yank her magic to her, wings extending to slow her descent as the shift swept over her. Landing on her knees instead of her feet, she groaned at the ache in her joints. It served as a warning she was not as fit as she had once been. Before the invasion of Diwan, she would have landed on her feet, easily turning a swoop into a steady walk across the stone.

"I thought I told you not to fly," Jola said, striding over to tut at her. "You're going to need some pain relief, silly girl. When I tell you not to do something, you listen."

Rushing over to her, Rhydwen shot the healer an annoyed look. "That was incredible, Songbird! You are amazing and beautiful."

"It was amazing, but Jola has a point, Eivor. You shouldn't have pushed yourself." Slower in her approach, Thorne clasped her hands behind her back, icy gaze promising the queen she would pay for disregarding the healer's instructions.

Eivor rolled her shoulders, taking stock of her body before flashing a grin at her husband as he helped her stand. "I was fine. Don't fret over me, old woman. If you truly had any doubts, you wouldn't have let me shift."

Movement caught her attention, and the queen watched Claire hurry over to where she had left her dress. The guard gathered it in her arms, her awe surrounding her like a cloud. At Jola's huff, her focus returned to the healer, and Eivor chuckled.

"I said you could shift, but I didn't say you could fly. I certainly didn't say you could plunge to the ground, giving me a heart attack, only to shift back right before you crashed."

"Ah, but I didn't."

"You could have! That was highly irresponsible, Eivor Havard. If your shift had been a fraction slower, you would have broken something."

Sighing, she ran a hand through her loose tresses while Rhydwen's conflicted emotions batted against the wall of her mind. Thorne continued to regard her with concern, gaze flicking to Claire when she came to a halt beside the queen, the bundle of fabric hugged to her chest. Reaching for her dress, Eivor accepted the prince's help to pull it on, the soft cotton pleasant against her skin. An itch was creeping across her body, a reminder of the consequences of using magic that had been neglected for so long. The more she shifted, the less it would bother her, but it all took time.

"I'm sorry, Jola. You're right, it was irresponsible. But when I shifted, I felt confident. It has only been a hundred years, and I'm over 3000."

Sympathy replaced the annoyance, and Jola stretched out a hand to cup her cheek. "I know. You're also right, if I hadn't thought you could, I wouldn't have let you. But after all the work I've put into getting you healthy again, I will not let you ruin it."

The others held their breath, waiting for her to respond, but Eivor simply inclined her head. She respected Jola's concern, appreciated it more than she could ever give voice to. No one had ever dared push her around like the healer did. Not even Thorne, though the Master of the Hunt tried her best. Her attempts primarily involved making Eivor follow Jola's orders, and the queen made a show of begrudgingly going along with it to make Thorne feel like she had achieved something. Because she knew how much the older woman liked to take care of her and Rhydwen, and Eivor loved to make her happy.

Jola gave her a nod in return, turning to click her tongue at Claire. "Come on, let's give them some time alone. I'll prepare a tonic for the queen's pain."

"I'll stay on the other side of the door. The general will have my head if I don't do my job," Claire replied, shrugging at Eivor. "She disagrees with me about them being enough."

Laughing as the two goblin women walked away, Eivor drifted away from Thorne and Rhydwen towards the edge of the roof. They followed her, keeping their distance until she beckoned them closer. Standing together at the low wall, they gazed out across the city. Slipping an arm around their waists, the queen sighed in contentment.

"Thank you for helping me, Thorne." Slanting a look at her, Eivor did not smile. "You were right about the nervousness, and I needed you to do it."

She leaned in, nuzzling the side of Eivor's head. "I will always do my best to give you what you need. Even if it means ordering you to do something you're perfectly capable of doing without my help. There's no shame in admitting you were overwhelmed."

"It shouldn't be an issue again. The voices have been silenced."

"Does it always hurt that much?"

Eyebrows rising, Rhydwen leaned forward to gaze at Thorne. "Pardon?"

"That's a complicated question, my love. It hurt more than it used to, but not as much as it did in the beginning. Shape shifting always hurts. Maybe it hurt a little more because you ordered me to shift. But it will get better now," Eivor said.

"I felt an echo of your pain." Returning her gaze to the city, Thorne sighed. "It was unpleasant and I'm glad we don't feel like that when we transform."

Aware of Rhydwen's distress, Eivor turned to press a kiss to his lips. "Don't be upset, Precious. It was nothing unusual for a duine. If you cannot handle me being in pain doing something as natural as shape shifting, how will you handle me giving birth?"

Aghast, the red-haired goblin choked on whatever he had planned to say. Chuckling at him, Thorne reached around Eivor's back to pat him gently. The action received a growl, Rhydwen baring his teeth at his wives. Pulling her arms free, Eivor turned and perched on the wall, gesturing for them to step in closer. Grabbing their shirts in each hand, she yanked them forward with a mischievous grin that banished Rhydwen's concerns.

"I love you both more than anything," she murmured, leaning in to kiss Thorne first before shifting to Rhydwen. "And I am thankful for all the days I have with you."

Thorne reached out to cup her cheek, the corners of her lips curling. "Wherever you go, my queen, I will always follow. I would burn down cities for both of you."

"Why can't I make things sound as threatening as the two of you can? It's a good thing I love you both as much as I do, or I'd feel inadequate about my threats." Huffing, Rhydwen cupped her other cheek, the tips of his claws leaving red lines on her skin. "Like her, I would burn down cities for you, and I would tear people apart with my hands."

"Eivor, I love you." Turning her icy gaze to Rhydwen, Thorne's smile grew. "And I love you, Rhydwen. Nothing matters as much to me as you do."

Contentment filled her heart, and Eivor decided she never wanted to be anywhere else. They were her family, her future, and her forever. No matter what crossed their path, they would face it together, united by their love for each other. Her years of imprisonment were worth what they had brought to her door. If it had never happened, she would never have met Rhydwen and Thorne, or fallen in love with them. Events had unfolded the way they needed to, providing her with everything she needed in life. She could even bring herself to forgive her sisters for abandoning her, since it had brought Thorne and Rhydwen to her.

"Come on, let's go back to our quarters. I'll drink Jola's tonic, and you can show me how proud you are of the fact I shifted into my magpie form."

Grabbing their hands, she swept forward and pulled them along after her. Their future was whatever they made it. Whatever it became, they would face it together, hand in hand. Not even the gods could tear their love apart. The family they were building made them stronger, and with it, they would change their world for the better.

# Acknowledgements

Oh boy, was this book a ride!

When I wrote To Heal a Wolf, it was supposed to be a one and done situation, but Silaine had to go and have two sisters. So along came this book. Like so many things I write, Thorne and the dullaghan took on a life of their own. To say I love my headless riders is an understatement. There's a reason I've somehow ended up writing them as the love interests in several books. Compared to Silaine's book, Eivor's is a darker journey, but she is my strong queen. The one who will not break easily. While this is her book, Eivor will appear again, not just in Astoria's, but in others. As the gods told Merle to tell Thorne, Eivor is important.

As always, Beau, my amazing husband, you are the light of my life. I love you, always and forever. More than you know what. Thank you for being my rock. Without you, I would not be here.

Freya, my love, I miss you. Not a day goes by that I don't think of you.

Thank you to everyone who has supported me through my journey. Each of you is amazing. Anita, my wonderful alpha reader, I love you, and being able to bounce 'what ifs' off you has certainly landed me in weird plots. To my fantastic beta team, but especially Natasha and Erin, thank you. Also, I'm sorry for those scenes. I toned them down. My bad. As for the Books and Bitches Down Under community, wow, you guys are brilliant! So much has been achieved so far, and I can't wait to see what else we do.

I can't not kneel in adoration of my wonderful artist, Vii. You are so talented, and wonderful, Vii. Please never forget that. My eternal gratitude is yours.

To my friends and family who continue to put up with me. Thank you.

Callai, keep being stubborn. Please. I love you, bitch. You're not allowed to escape.

As for you, Chloe. You know what I'm going to say, and the look I'm going to give you. That is all.

A big thanks to Mel, Jess, and the group for being a safe place to hide.

To everyone else, thank you. Thank you for all you do for me and other authors. We love you for it.

# About the Author

Joyce Gee is based in Mandurah, Western Australia. Growing up among the rainforests of Far North Queensland, she loved to vanish into the other worlds hidden within the trees. When she isn't writing, she enjoys drinking tea with a book to read, pottering in the garden, camping with her husband and their two children, or escaping with her camera to capture the beautiful landscape of Western Australia.